'It really *is* your choice, Becky,' Michael said.

She knew that, and a terrible choice it was, too. On the one hand she desperately wanted her husband by her side, rather than in a dangerous place like the Oil Rivers. On the other, her family had been the cause of denying Michael what he saw as his true destiny once, and she did not see how she could be responsible for doing such a thing a second time.

'Becky?' Michael said questioningly.

'I can't tell you now,' she said, as her agonizing choices pulled her first this way, and then that. 'I...I just can't. You're going to have to give me more time.'

As they turned round and made their way back towards her parents' little house, Becky could feel hot tears pricking her eyes.

Sally Spencer was born and brought up in Marston, Cheshire, but now lives in Spain.

By the same author

Salt of the Earth
Old Father Thames

UP OUR STREET

Sally Spencer

ORION

An Orion paperback
First published in Great Britain by Orion in 1994
This paperback edition published in 1995 by Orion Books Ltd,
Orion House, 5 Upper St Martin's Lane, London WC2H 9EA

Copyright (c) 1994 Sally Spencer

A CIP catalogue record for this book is available from the
British Library.

ISBN: 1 85797 870 6

Printed and bound in Great Britain by
Clays Ltd, St Ives plc

To my parents - Gwen and Eric

Author's Note

Marston is a real village in Cheshire and the house in which Becky Taylor – and I – were brought up is still standing, as are many other of the buildings described in this book. All the characters, however, are purely fictional, and any long-time residents of the village who can find their grandparents portrayed within these pages will simply be using their own imaginations as much as I have used mine.

Sally Spencer

PROLOGUE

The man approaching Marston from the south marched with the measured stride of a professional soldier. He was no stranger to the village, but it had been a long while since he'd last paid it a visit. And though he appeared totally in control of himself, anyone who'd known him from his childhood could have seen that not very far beneath the calm exterior of this six-foot sergeant lurked little George Taylor – as nervous as a kitten about the reception he would get when he finally reached home.

At the bottom of the lane, George stopped and took in the view.

It's been five years, he said softly to himself.

Five long, exciting, dangerous years, years in which he had seen things he could never have imagined and visited places which defied description. And all that time, Marston had been here, unchanged and seemingly unchangeable.

He turned his head to look at Cooke's grocery store. The familiar yellow Lipton's Tea sign gleamed in the afternoon sun, the yard brushes Mr Cooke had hung outside swung gently in the breeze. His eyes followed the course of Ollershaw Lane – flanked on each side by squat terraced houses – from where he was standing to the point at which it disappeared at the top of the hump-backed bridge over the canal. It all seemed so . . . so normal, and yet at the same time he was forced to admit that he would have felt more at ease in a Burmese village with its bamboo huts and Chinese merchant's emporium.

For a moment, George considered going into Cooke's store for a packet of cigarettes and a chat. After all, he really did *need* the cigarettes, he told himself, and talking to Sam

Cooke – whom he'd known all his life, but still wasn't family – might be a way of getting back gradually into village life. But it was not in George's nature – not in the nature of any of the Taylors except perhaps Philip – either to put things off or do them gradually. Squaring his shoulders, George set off again in the direction of his mam and dad's little house.

He did not get far. A train was coming along the mineral line which crossed the village, and the railwayman in the smart blue uniform had already pulled the gates across the lane. This had been a favourite spot of Becky's when she was little, George recalled with a smile. When Mam had sent his sister out on errands, she'd always found a reason to delay so that she would be at the railway gates just as one of the huge Puffing Billies was furiously steaming its way through.

What stories she'd come up with to make sure she was right on time for the trains!

'I can't find me boots, Mam.'

Well, she'd only to look under the table, where she'd kicked them seconds earlier!

'I need to go to the lavvie, Mam.'

And it wouldn't be five minutes since she'd last gone!

Did she ever think she was really fooling Mam? George wondered. Didn't she realize Mam knew quite well that the engine driver would sometimes throw her sticky boiled sweets?

Oh, she was a little devil, our Becky, he said to himself.

And now she was a grown-up woman with a baby daughter he hadn't even seen yet.

The train thundered past, rattling the crossing gates and leaving a smell of burnt cinders behind it. The railwayman began to push the gates back over the track and George was on his way again.

He marched up the lane, passing the alley where he'd once listened breathlessly while Gilbert Bowyer, sitting on his camp stool, had told tales of the Far East.

An old soldier's tales, George thought, hardly realizing that in experience, if not in years, he was now an old soldier himself.

Ahead of him, leaning against her front railings, was a middle-aged woman with a beak-like nose and black hair pulled back into a tight bun. George grinned. He wasn't the least surprised to see 'Not-Stopping' Bracegirdle perched there like a hungry crow – he'd only have been surprised if the village gossip *hadn't* been at her post.

'Good afternoon, Mrs Bracegirdle,' he called out.

Not-Stopping jumped as if he'd startled her.

'George?' she said. 'George Taylor?'

'That's right,' George agreed.

'Well, don't you look smart!' Not-Stopping gushed. 'How's the army treatin' you? Have you heard about your sister's baby? Isn't it terrible about your brother-in-law's works?'

'Yes,' George said, quickening his pace, because he knew from experience that though Mrs Bracegirdle was *never* stopping, she could sometimes detain you for an hour or more. 'Yes, it was a terrible shame about Michael's works.'

'And we had a prince come to the village,' Not-Stopping shouted after him. 'A real prince – come to see Ma Fitton.'

'So I heard,' George called back over his shoulder.

God, but the woman could go on. Put her on the beach at Blackpool for a morning, and no matter how many donkeys there were, she'd talk the hind legs off the lot of them.

He was almost level with the New Inn, where his sister Becky's best friend, Colleen O'Leary, lived. She was a funny little thing, that Colleen, he remembered – as timid as a mouse. Maybe it was that big nose of hers that made her so shy, though he'd never found it particularly unattractive.

His thoughts shifted from the daughter to the father. Paddy O'Leary had promised him free ale when he was home on leave and he'd hold the landlord to his word soon enough. But first he had to go and see his mam and dad.

He glanced at the point halfway up the bridge where a tall brick chimney was belching out smoke, and saw the words 'LG Worrell and Sons', picked out in white letters in the

5

middle of the stack.

Well, that's not true any more, he thought.

Old Len Worrell himself had been dead for nearly two years, and one of those two sons – Michael – had left the company a few days after he'd married Becky. All of which meant that the sole Worrell left at the works was that bastard Richard.

It wasn't the time to dwell on Richard Worrell and what he had done to the Taylor family, George told himself. Finally – after weeks of travel through oppressive tropical heat, after the crowded troopship full of seasick soldiers, after more, almost unendurable, days of cooling his heels in the Aldershot Barracks – he was home. And that was all that really mattered.

He gazed with affection at the house he'd been brought up in, at the front parlour which had a wooden fish suspended over it because now it was Ted Taylor's chip shop. The door was closed for the moment, but come five o'clock, when the miners emerged from the Adelaide Mine and the wallers at Worrell's works left the sticky brine pan behind them, the chip shop would be doing a roaring trade.

George opened the back gate and stepped into the yard. Yes, it was still all there. The wash-house with its single tap stood opposite the back door. And beyond that was the coal-shed and the outside lavvie which was as cold as ice in winter and like an oven during the hot summer days.

He walked up to the back door and caught himself in the act of lifting his big fist to knock. There'd have been hell to pay if he *had* actually knocked, he thought. Nothing could be guaranteed to offend Mam more than having one of her own sons asking permission to come in. Still, it did feel a bit odd, just walking straight into a house he'd been away from for so long.

No point in puttin' it off any longer, George told himself.

Bracing himself as he always did when he was about to see action, he raised the latch and stepped over the threshold.

*

6

Mary Taylor was sitting at the table with her head bent over her sewing. She didn't look up. Instead she merely said, 'I hope you gave that fishmonger a real tellin'-off, Ted. Goodness knows, the customers won't spare us a piece of *their* minds if their fish isn't ready an' waitin' for them when they knock off work.'

She'd always done her own sewing, George remembered. Even when Dad had been a salt miner and life was hard, she'd been too proud to buy second-hand or take the gentry's cast-offs which her daughters, then in service, had brought home to her. And she was still making clothes, despite the fact that Dad was now a 'fried fish merchant' and she could easily afford anything Bratt and Evans had displayed in their window.

'I said, I hope you gave that fishmonger a real tellin'-off,' Mary repeated.

'No, Mam, I didn't,' George said quietly.

Now, Mary did lift her head, though her face was frozen in a look of astonishment.

Had she changed much in the time he'd been away? he wondered. A few grey streaks, perhaps, in what had once been pure ash blonde hair. A few wrinkles around the eyes and a little slack skin on her neck. But she was still the Mam he knew and loved, the Mam who had bullied him into escorting Becky on her first day at school and stuck up for him when he wanted to join the army against his father's wishes.

Mary's face was slowly coming to life again and she seemed to be about to find her voice.

'I haven't . . .' she began. 'We didn't . . . You never told us you were comin' home.'

'There was a chance we'd be posted again before we got any leave,' George told her. 'I didn't want to raise your hopes.'

Or my own, he thought. Or my own.

Mary got up from her chair – perhaps just a little stiffly – and threw her arms around her big, strong son.

'You've always liked surprises,' she said, almost crying. 'All of you kids have. I don't know where you get it from. It certainly doesn't come from me.'

It was wonderful to feel his mother's warm, comforting arms around him once more – but he'd never really worried about how *she* would receive him.

'Dad's out, is he?' George asked.

'Yes,' Mary said, sniffing slightly. 'He's gone to see Stanway's about their deliveries. They've been gettin' a bit slack lately.'

'They won't be slack any more,' said a new voice behind them. 'Not after the talkin'-to I've given them.'

George felt his mother's arms drop and turned around to face his father, who was standing in the doorway. Ted was as stocky and solid as his son remembered him, and his expression was as inscrutable as ever. George had never been able to read Ted's face, never known whether his father was poking fun at him or merely being grumpy. And he couldn't read it now, though he did recall what Ted had said when he'd finally given in and allowed George to take the queen's shilling.

'I'll give you me permission,' he'd told his middle son then, 'but not me blessing.'

And how did he feel now, after years of having the time to think over his decision? George suddenly wished he were somewhere else.

'Well, well,' Ted said. 'Look what the cat's dragged in.'

He inspected his son from head to foot.

'Soldiering's put a bit of weight on you,' he continued, 'but with a frame like yours, you can carry it.'

There were so many things George wanted to say – *'Are you pleased to see me, Dad?' 'Have you forgiven me for joinin' the army when I could have made four pounds a week playing football?' 'Can I spend me leave here, or had I better see if Mr O'Leary can give me a room at the pub?'*

– so many things, but George had never been a quick thinker and he couldn't make up his mind which to say first.

8

'Lost your tongue?' his father demanded.

'Hello, Dad,' George said, telling himself that he should have worked it all out in advance, should have planned it just like he planned a patrol for his men.

Ted closed the back door and advanced into the room until he was standing squarely in front of George.

'So you think you can just waltz in any time you feel like it, do you?' he asked.

None of the men who had served under the cool, disciplined Sergeant George Taylor would have believed it if they could have seen him now. His firm mouth drooped uncertainly, and the eyes which had remained calm even under enemy fire now started to fill with panic.

'I didn't . . . I wasn't sure . . . ' he stuttered.

He looked over his shoulder, hoping against hope for some support from his mother – and saw that she was smiling.

'He never could tell when I was takin' the mick out of him, could he?' Ted asked.

'No,' Mary agreed. 'He never could.'

George turned again and Ted threw his arms around his son.

'It's grand to have you back, lad,' he said with a catch in his voice. 'Really grand.'

PART ONE

1892

Chapter One

George had arrived on Thursday, but even though he was on leave, everybody else still had work to do. So it was not until Sunday that the whole family could arrange to get together to give him a real hero's welcome.

But wherever will they all fit? Mary wondered early on Sunday morning as she looked around the kitchen where she had spent so much of her married life.

The kitchen had three doors: one in the back wall which opened on to the yard, another facing it which let on to steep stairs, and a third, diagonally opposite, which led into the small pantry under the stairs. Between the back door and the stair door was the old oak Welsh dresser which contained all the blue and white willow-patterned crockery as well as the receipts from the fish and chip business.

The kitchen table, where the food was both prepared and eaten, stood in the centre of the room and on the far side of it were the easy chairs, facing the fireplace and the cast-iron oven. The window gave on to the yard and Mary's Singer sewing machine rested under its sill. The sofa had somehow been squeezed in between the table and the wall which backed on to the stairs.

Get more than the two of us in here, and there's not room to swing a cat, Mary thought. However did we use to manage?

It was true that this room had once accommodated the whole family – but they'd all been little kids then. Besides, the size of the family had increased, what with the girls getting married and Eunice and Becky having children of their own.

Mary inspected the room once more and decided they'd

manage to fit in somehow. After all, they *were* all relatives.

But relatives or not, the house would have to be smartened up before they came – and this despite the fact she not only swept and dusted every day but also religiously cleaned the place from top to bottom on Saturdays.

'Waste of energy if you ask me,' Ted grumbled as he watched his wife black-leading the grate.

'Well, nobody did ask you,' Mary pointed out. 'And it's my energy I'm wastin', not yours.'

'We should get a maid to do the heavy work,' Ted said.

The grate having been completed to her satisfaction, Mary took down the brass rod from over the fireplace and began to rub it vigorously.

'A maid!' she scoffed, not slackening her pace for even a second. 'Gettin' ideas above your station, aren't you, Ted Taylor?'

'I don't think so,' her husband replied. 'It's not as if we couldn't afford a few pounds a year.'

'There's more to havin' servants than findin' the cash to pay for 'em,' Mary said.

'Is there?' Ted asked. 'Like what?'

The question seemed to stump Mary, and for a second she even stopped burnishing the brass. Then her arm was back in action again and she turned to her husband and said, 'Where would she live? They all expect to live in, you know.'

'She could sleep in the back bedroom,' Ted suggested. 'We don't need it now there's just the two of us.'

'And where would the children sleep when they deign to visit us?' Mary asked. 'On the chip shop floor?'

Had Mary not turned back to her work, Ted would never have dared risk a grin, but since she had, he indulged himself. Not having a maid was nothing to do with accommodation, he was sure of that. This kitchen had been Mary's domain for thirty years, and she was not about to give it over to some slip of a girl who knew a tenth of what she did, thank you very much.

*

By noon, the house was sparkling clean and the odour of brass cleaner was beginning to mingle with the delicious smell of freshly baking scones. By two, Mary had run the flat iron over the antimacassars so many times that Ted was sure she'd all but worn them away. On the dot of four, Mary finished hanging clean curtains and announced that the house was now ready to receive the children of whom she was so proud.

George, who'd been banished from the house during the cleaning operation, was the first to arrive. He was quickly followed by his sister Jessie and Sid, her husband. Sid was wearing a smart new suit, but somehow he looked half undressed without the khaki apron he always wore behind the counter of the Co-operative Wholesale Society in Winnington. Still, he wouldn't always be a counterman, wouldn't Sid – he was a good reliable worker and was heading for promotion.

'You take a seat at the table, George,' Mary said. 'Sid and Jessie, you sit on the sofa.'

'You sound like you've got it all planned out, Mam,' George said.

'When have you ever known her *not* have it all planned out?' Jessie asked.

Eunice and her Charlie arrived next, bringing with them the Taylors' first grandchild, Thelma. Charlie was sent to sit next to Sid and Jessie, while Eunice took one of the chairs at the table. Thelma made a dutiful round of grandparents, aunt and uncles, kissing each one in turn, even the large stranger who she'd been assured was her Uncle George.

'Do you remember me at all?' George asked, giving his niece a big hug in return for her kiss.

'I think so,' said Thelma unconvincingly.

George laughed. 'Well, here's a penny for bein' so kind and polite to your old uncle,' he told her. 'And unless Mr Cooke's changed his habits, he'll be open on Sunday afternoons just so he can sell sweets to little girls with pennies in their pockets.'

Thelma looked anxiously at Eunice for an approving nod, and when she got it she gave George another quick kiss, then dashed out of the door before her mother could change her mind.

'Watch out for waggons,' Eunice shouted after her, though she need not have bothered because very little traffic came up Ollershaw Lane, especially on a Sunday afternoon. 'And let that be the last penny you give her,' she cautioned her brother. 'I don't want her spoiled.'

Mary permitted herself a secret smile. Eunice always had been a bossy girl. Perhaps that was why they'd made her a monitor at the National School and given her the job of teaching the little children to repeat lessons she'd only learned herself a few years earlier. It was lucky, really, that she was married to easy-going Charlie. As long as he had his garden outside their tied cottage in the grounds of the Big House, Charlie was as happy as a pig in muck, and if Eunice wanted to order him around, well, that was all right with him.

Jack turned up next. Bright, irrepressible Jack, who had run away to sea when he was little more than a boy, who had kept sheep and mined for silver in Australia and bought palm oil from the natives on the River Niger.

'The table for you,' Mary told him.

And last came Becky and Michael, with their new baby, Michelle.

'You sit next to Jack, Becky,' Mary said to her youngest daughter, 'and you, Michael, take the easy chair by the grate, next to Ted.'

'The easy chair!' Michael said, with a smile playing on his lips. 'This is indeed an honour, my dear mother-in-law.'

'Don't talk soft,' Mary said, cuffing his shoulder lightly with the back of her hand.

But really, there was a grain of truth in what he'd said. Though she liked all her sons-in-law, it was Michael that Mary really had a soft spot for. He was handsome, but not in a hard way like his brother Richard. He was educated, and yet there was no side to him.

Mary remembered the conversation she'd had with Eunice on the morning of Becky's wedding, the day Len Worrell had sworn he would cut his son out of his will for daring to marry beneath him.

'It's a rum thing, gettin' married when there's no money comin' in,' Eunice had said.

'You just wait an' see,' Mary had replied. 'Michael'll surprise the lot of you yet.'

And hadn't he just! He'd built a successful business out of almost nothing. He had gone to Africa and rescued Jack from the cannibals who were holding him prisoner. Now his business was in ruins, but no one could have predicted that – no one could have known that the land under his works would suddenly subside as it had.

Yes, Michael was a catch, Mary thought as she watched him fussing over the baby daughter who had been born while he was still looking for Jack in Nigeria. But then Becky was a catch, too. She had her mother's hair, and whilst there was no mistaking the fact that she was Mary's daughter, she was beautiful where Mary had only been very pretty. And she'd got spirit, too. She had supervised the dismantling of Michael's works, saving what she could from destruction, even when she was on the point of giving birth.

'You're very quiet, Mam,' Jack said, cutting into Mary's thoughts. 'What's on your mind?'

'Oh, you know – just things,' his mother replied, moving towards the oven and telling herself how lucky she was.

It was a magnificent tea even by Mary's high standards. There was delicious freshly baked bread and scones. There were three kinds of juicy home-made jam and a cake absolutely bursting with fruit.

While they ate, the family talked, filling in the missing years in a way that letters never could.

'Tell us about Burma,' Mary said.

'It's a grand place,' George replied. 'Warm all the year

round and as green as . . . well, so green I wouldn't have believed it if I hadn't seen it with me own eyes.'

'What do they grow there?' asked Eunice's Charlie, a gardener down to his bootstraps.

'Rice, mostly,' George said. 'Acres and acres of it, as far as the eye can see.'

'Humph,' Ted said thoughtfully. 'They must really like their puddin's.'

'Is there still any trouble out there?' Michael asked.

'A bit,' George admitted. 'But it was much worse just after we got rid of the king.'

'I don't approve of gettin' rid of royalty,' Mary said. 'We wouldn't like it if some foreign army came over here and told us we couldn't have our queen any more.'

'He wasn't like Victoria,' George told her. 'In fact, he was a thoroughly bad lot. He was only twenty when he came to the throne, but one of the first things he did was to have all his brothers and sisters killed.'

'Shockin',' Eunice clucked. 'It shouldn't be allowed.'

'Mind you,' George continued, 'It wasn't really all his doin'. They do say it was his mother-in-law's idea.'

'You have to be very careful when you're dealing with mothers-in-law,' Michael said, looking at Mary with a twinkle in his eye.

'Get off with you!' Mary said, reddening slightly.

'Are you goin' back to Burma when your leave's over, George?' Jack asked.

George shook his head. 'We set sail for Egypt next month,' he said.

'Egypt?' his father repeated. 'That's where that mad bugger Gordon met his end, isn't it?'

'No, Dad,' said George, frowning because Gordon was his big hero, the man who had inspired him to join the army in the first place. 'Gordon was murdered in the Sudan.'

'Well, that's only next to Egypt,' said Ted, as if he was talking about a couple of houses down the lane.

'And what are you going to do, now that your works has

collapsed?' George asked Michael.

'I'm not sure yet,' Michael replied.

Becky looked sharply at her husband. She knew that tone in his voice. It said that he knew perfectly well what he was going to do, but he wasn't prepared to tell anyone else until he'd managed to talk his wife into it.

'No,' Michael continued hurriedly, sensing Becky's eyes on him, 'I haven't made my mind up yet. Thanks to Becky, we managed to save all the parts of the works which could be shifted, and when we've sold that, we should have a bit of capital to play around with.'

What was he up to? Becky wondered. But of one thing, she was sure, whatever scheme he came up with – however madcap – he would justify it by saying it was sound business sense.

'Has anybody heard from our Philip?' George asked.

Immediately a cloud of gloom settled over the table as each member of the family thought back over Philip's chequered career. First there'd been Philip the Snitch, spying on his own work gang and reporting back to Richard Worrell. After that had come Philip the Pornographer, selling smutty postcards on the seafront at Blackpool. Then there'd been Philip the Gaolbird, serving eighteen months in Strangeways. And finally, there'd been Philip the Smuggler, abusing his position at Michael's works to hide stolen jewellery in blocks of salt. And where was he now? God only knew.

'No, nobody's heard from Philip,' Mary said finally, with a look of pain on her face. 'All we can do is pray that he's all right.'

'He could end up doing great things yet,' Ted said, more out of hope than conviction. 'His main trouble is, he's always been a square peg in a round hole.'

His main trouble is, he's always taken the easy way out without considering how it might hurt other people, Becky thought.

Still, he was not *all* bad. Just before his last hurried

departure, he'd visited her and offered what little money he had left if it would help to rebuild the works.

The thought of the devastated works naturally turned her mind back to Michael. Just what *was* he planning? Given the curious nature she had been born with – cursed with, her mother sometimes said – she was well aware that she would never rest until she had solved the mystery.

It was not only Becky who was wondering about Michael's plans. Thoughts of them occupied the minds of the three men who were sitting round a table in the New Inn.

'Mr Worrell won't let us down,' Brian O'Reilly declared stoutly. He took a sip of his pint – a slow and careful one because once that was gone, there was no money for any more. 'He's not like that bastard of a brother of his. He knows what good workers we are.'

'Oh, if he wants workers, he'll take us on,' Tom Jennings agreed. 'But what if he doesn't want any?'

'How do you mean?' Brian O'Reilly asked.

'Suppose he decides to move somewhere else, or go into another line of business,' Tom Jennings said. 'What happens to us then?'

'We won't get taken on by anybody else,' Cedric Rathbone said.

That was true enough. The last time they'd all been out of work – after Richard Worrell had fired them for trying to start a union – they soon discovered they were marked men. And the reason had been obvious enough, too: Richard had sent word to all the other owners not to employ them. It had been a very lean time indeed until Michael had come along and offered them places in his new venture.

'He owes us,' Brian O'Reilly said, 'especially you, Cedric. Why, if it hadn't have been for you, he'd have lost everything in the subsidence.'

'It was more due to Beck . . . to Mrs Worrell than me that things got saved,' Cedric said in fairness. 'Besides, he paid us a good livin' wage as long as we were workin', and as far as

I'm concerned, that's the only obligation any boss is ever under.'

'I suppose you're right,' Tom Jennings said. 'Still, it's a bugger of a life, isn't it?'

The other two men nodded their heads in agreement.

It seemed to Becky that most of the important decisions about her life with Michael had been taken in the open air. It was on Overton Hill, one warm autumn afternoon, that he had proposed to her. It had been standing on Burns Bridge that he'd announced his intention to open a rival salt works to his brother's, and asked her if he could count on her support. And now, as they walked hand in hand up the cartroad towards Marston Old Mine, she was sure that he was about to tell her of the new plan he had come up with.

They climbed the steep embankment which led to the canal towpath. It was a warm spring evening, and the only sounds around them were the gentle slapping of the water against the bank and the twittering of the birds which had already begun nesting in the trees. Michael stopped and looked into the canal, as if his mind were a thousand miles away.

'Tell me about it,' Becky said.

Michael's look of abstraction disappeared and was replaced by a self-conscious grin.

'Am I that obvious?' he asked.

Becky smiled back. 'Only to me, I think,' she replied.

Michael's face grew serious again.

'Even if we can raise enough money, I don't think I want to go back into salt manufacturing,' he said.

'Why not?' Becky asked.

'The price of salt has started to drop in recent years,' her husband explained, 'and I don't think it's reached its bottom yet. Besides, ever since some of the owners got together and formed the Salt Union, conditions have changed.'

'Changed?' Becky said. 'In what way?'

'The Salt Union wants *all* the owners to join it, so it can

21

get a stranglehold over the industry. And if anyone won't join, then they want to see that person goes out of business.'

'And you wouldn't join?' Becky said.

Michael shook his head.

She should have known without having to ask, Becky thought. Michael – her Michael – was the kindest, gentlest man she had ever met, yet he was also the most stubborn and independent, and he wouldn't consider, even for a second, putting himself in a position where men like his brother Richard might have some control over his actions.

'So if you don't make salt, what will you do?' Becky asked.

'You remember what I used to buy your brother Jack back from the cannibals?' Michael asked.

'His own weight in salt,' Becky replied.

'That's right,' Michael agreed. 'Salt's a very valuable commodity out there, but at the same time they have something we really want in return for it – palm oil.'

'So you're saying you want to become a merchant?' Becky said.

'Yes,' Michael said. 'Salt out to Africa, palm oil back to England. It's good business sense.'

Michael was not lying to her – he would never do that – but whenever he used the phrase 'good business sense', she knew he was hiding something. It had been good business sense to pay his men a decent living wage, higher than any other owner in the area. It had been good business sense to go to Africa in the first place, where, just by coincidence, her brother Jack had gone missing. She wondered what lay behind this particular attack of good business sense.

Becky put her hands on her hips in a fair imitation of the way her mother had done when they'd been children and had a guilty secret.

Well?' she said, only half jokingly. 'Are you going to tell me, or do I have to drag it out of you?'

'When I was growing up, I always wanted to be a doctor,' Michael said. 'I never told you that before, did I?'

'No,' Becky admitted. And then, because it was hard to

imagine anything deterring Michael once he had made up his mind, she added, 'What stopped you?'

'My father made me a promise,' Michael said, 'and in return I made a promise to him – that I would go into the family business.'

There was that slight twitch at the corner of his mouth which told Becky he was trying to hide something again.

'And what was the promise he made you?' she asked.

Michael shrugged. 'It's not important now,' he said.

'Tell me!' Becky demanded.

'He promised to pay *your* father some compensation for his accident,' Michael said.

So that was how it happened! How different things would have been but for that promise. Michael would have been a doctor, and the Taylors, with no money to start their chip shop, would have ended up in the Leftwich workhouse.

'So it's our fault you never achieved your ambition?' she said sadly.

'Of course not,' Michael responded. 'I didn't have to agree to join the firm. There were other ways to make my father cough up the money.'

'You did it for me,' Becky said, remembering how he had looked at her when she had been a small girl and he had been little more than a boy.

'I did it because my brother caused your father's accident and it was only just that my father should pay,' Michael replied. 'Forget the past, Becky. It's the future we should be thinking about now.'

Becky nodded in agreement. The future *was* what mattered.

'All this talk about wanting to be a doctor,' she said. 'What's that got to do with Africa? Are you going to take a medical degree as well as becoming a merchant prince?'

Michael laughed. 'Of course not,' he said. 'But even a *little* knowledge of medicine would be very useful in a place where the only help available comes from witch doctors. And there are other ways I can help them to improve their lives, too.

Drainage, irrigation, all sorts of things. Simple changes which would make such a difference.'

'And that's what you really want to do?' Becky asked.

A look of pain flashed briefly across Michael's face.

'Of course it's not what I really want to do!' he said.

He sounded angry, though she was sure the anger was directed at himself and not her.

'Then, why . . . ?' Becky asked tentatively.

'It's not what I want to do,' Michael said earnestly. 'What I want to do is stay here, to feel your arms around me in the night, to watch our baby grow day by day.'

'Well, then?'

'I'm not a religious man,' Michael told her, 'but I feel as if God, or Fate – or something, anyway – arranged for your Jack to fall into the hands of the cannibals.'

'For what possible reason?' Becky asked.

'So that I'd go out to Africa looking for him and see the need out there for myself. It's almost as if I was born for Africa, Becky, as if it's been my mission all along, and I never realized it.'

'I see,' Becky said.

Michael put his strong hands on her shoulders and kissed her lightly on the forehead.

'I won't go if you don't want me to,' he said. 'You know that.'

'I couldn't come with you, could I?' Becky asked.

'No,' Michael said softly. 'In a few years, things might be different, but at the moment it's no place for a white woman and her child.'

Becky looked down the canal. A narrow boat was making its way towards them, the horse pulling stolidly as barge horses always did, the bargee standing at the tiller and smoking a clay pipe. How ordinary it all seemed, how very different to the sort of life Michael was proposing for himself.

'You'd be working with Jack?' she said.

'Yes,' Michael agreed. 'I wouldn't even contemplate it

24

without Jack as my partner.'

'And how often would I see you?'

'Much more often than you see Jack. He'll be making most of the journeys up and down the Oil Rivers. I'll have to come back every few months to handle the business from this end.'

The narrow boat drew level, and the bargee tipped his cap to them.

'Grand day,' he said.

'Yes,' Becky agreed without much enthusiasm. 'It is a grand day.'

The barge floated on past them. The narrow boat man had seemed perfectly happy with his lot, Becky thought. Why couldn't Michael be like him?

'Because if Michael had been like that, I'd never have fallen in love with him,' she told herself.

And it was the very things she loved about him which were now driving him to go and do good in a strange hot land thousands of miles away.

'It really *is* your choice, Becky,' Michael said.

She knew that, and a terrible choice it was, too. On the one hand she desperately wanted her husband by her side, rather than in a dangerous place like the Oil Rivers. On the other, her family had been the cause of denying Michael what he saw as his true destiny once, and she did not see how she could be responsible for doing such a thing a second time.

'Becky?' Michael said questioningly.

'I can't tell you now,' she said, as her agonizing choices pulled her first this way, and then that. 'I . . . I just can't. You're going to have to give me more time.'

As they turned round and made their way back towards her parents' little house, Becky could feel hot tears pricking her eyes.

Chapter Two

When Patrick Declan O'Leary had taken over the tenancy of the New Inn he'd been a young man with an unlined face and a shock of red hair which was uncommon enough in the Northwich area to attract a few curious looks. There had been nothing uncommon about the pub itself, however. Like most boozers in the district, it was furnished with a leather settle running along the sides of the wall and round tables with wooden tops resting on cast-iron legs. Its bar was fairly typical, too – a large oak counter set against the far wall which somehow managed to dominate the whole room. Now, nearly thirty years on, Paddy's hair had turned almost white and ceased to be a novelty, the leather on the settle was a little cracked, and there were a few more scars on the bar. Otherwise, nothing had changed.

And a bloody good thing, too, Ted Taylor thought as he walked into the bar flanked by his two eldest sons. There was enough change going on in the world as it was – too much if the truth be told – without buggering up a perfectly decent pub with fresh wallpaper and that shiny, slippery oilcloth stuff.

'Got the night off from the chip shop, have you Ted?' Paddy O'Leary called from the other side of the bar.

'I have that,' Ted replied. 'The missis and the girls are running the place tonight, so me and my lads can knock back a few pints.'

'That's very good of her,' Paddy said.

'Good of her be buggered,' Ted said cheerfully.

Paddy frowned. 'I'm not sure I'm followin' you,' he said.

'It's like the bank,' Ted explained. 'It'll lend you money easily enough, but it always wants payin' back just at the time that's most inconvenient to you. Well, you watch, I won't get off scot-free for this. My Mary'll want payin' back an' all, and you can bet your last shillin' it'll be at some time that's bloody awkward.'

Paddy smiled. 'Your Mary spoils you to death,' he said.

Ted smiled back. 'Aye, you're right there,' he admitted. 'There's not many women as 'ud put up with an grumpy old sod like me for as long as she has.'

Ted ordered three pints and took them over to George and Jack, who were sitting at a table next to the domino board.

'Get them down you,' he instructed his sons. 'And I'll bet you any money you like that in a few weeks, when you're in the jungle or the desert or wherever you're bloody goin', you'll wish you were back here with a glass of Paddy's ale in your hand.'

His sons grinned. They had got used to their father's suspicion of anything vaguely foreign. It was not until he passed forty, they remembered, that he'd even gone beyond Northwich – and that was only because he was a trumpeter in the Adelaide Mine Band, which had entered a competition in Belle Vue, Manchester.

'You might like Africa if you gave it a try, Dad,' Jack said. 'Bits of it, anyroad.'

Ted Taylor took a long draught from his pint, then smacked his lips with satisfaction.

'The difference between you pair an' me isn't that you're young adventurers while I'm just a stick-in-the-mud,' he told his eldest son. 'The difference between you pair an' me is that *I* know when I'm well off.'

The best room of the New Inn was situated to the left of the bar, and the customers in it were served through a hatch set into the wall. It was an ideal arrangement for Not-Stopping Bracegirdle, because every time she rose from her table to order drinks, it gave her the opportunity to see just what the men were getting up to in the bar.

Now, as she returned from the hatch and placed the drinks

before her cronies – Dottie Curzon and Maggie Cross – she had some new information to impart.

'Ted Taylor's in with them two lads of his,' she said in a whisper which carried better than most people's shouts. 'Drinkin' like troopers they are, an' all.'

Dottie Curzon had been experiencing a growing feeling of resentment towards her old friend ever since she'd found out that Not-Stopping had been telling people that Dottie was not so much her name as a description of her mental condition. Now she felt a spirit of rebellion starting to flare up inside her. Troopers were supposed to swear, not *drink*, and she was just about to tell Not-Stopping so when a better idea came into her head.

'But young George *is* a trooper,' she said innocently.

Not-Stopping gave her a withering look, which would no doubt have been followed by an equally withering comment but for the arrival of a new customer – Ma Fitton, the village midwife.

'Hello, Nellie,' Not-Stopping said ingratiatingly. 'And how are you tonight, girl?'

'Me arthritis is playin' me up,' Ma Fitton complained. 'I think it's about time I gave up delivering babies.'

'Oh, surely not,' said Not-Stopping with a mock concern. 'After all, you were a midwife to royal – ' She stopped suddenly, and looked as if she'd have cheerfully bitten off her own tongue.

Dottie Curzon smiled to herself. For years, Mrs Brace-girdle had ridiculed Ma Fitton when she claimed to have once delivered a prince. But Ma had been telling the truth, hadn't she? They all knew that because the prince had actually come to the village to visit her. It had made Not-Stopping look like a fool – and she'd deserved it.

A good gossip's one thing, but sometimes she goes way beyond the bounds of what's proper, Dottie thought.

Like with that other rumour she spread that Ma Fitton was the mistress of Old Gilbert Bowyer, her now-dead lodger – that hadn't been fair, either. It was time somebody taught Not-Stopping a good lesson, Dottie decided and wondered, if she made up her mind to do it herself, whether Ma Fitton would help her.

The bar was almost full when Cedric Rathbone walked in. He stood for a moment and examined the coppers in his hand, though he already knew exactly how much he had.

'A pint, Cedric?' Paddy O'Leary asked.

'I think I'll just have a half,' Rathbone replied.

And he wouldn't even be having that if he hadn't just chopped up a pile of wood for the vicar.

'Give him a pint,' said a voice from the corner. 'I'll pay for it.'

Rathbone turned and saw Ted Taylor sitting there with his two sons.

'If it's all the same to you, Ted, I'll stick to a half,' he said.

He's a proud man, Ted Taylor thought. He won't accept a drink when he's got no money in his pocket to buy you one back.

He wouldn't accept anything else for free, either. After Philip had got Cedric and his mates Tom Jennings and Brian O'Reilly sacked from Worrell's, Ted had tried to make it up to them by handing out extra large portions when they reached the front of the fish and chip queue. He'd even gone so far as to wrap up a fresh fish and give it to Tom as scraps for his cat. Tom and Brian had been grateful, but not Cedric.

No, Ted told himself. That isn't being fair, Cedric *did* appreciate what I was tryin' to do for him, but he still wasn't havin' any of it.

A proud man indeed – and one who couldn't be doing much more than scraping by, now that he wasn't getting a regular wage from Michael.

Colleen O'Leary opened the parlour door just a crack and peeped into the bar. It was something she did every time she thought George Taylor might be in there, having a pint. Yes, he was there, sitting with his dad and his brother Jack.

How handsome he looked!

How strong and confident!

She'd only been a slip of girl when he'd gone away, but now she was twenty-one – what they called in Marston 'a young woman'.

It was stupid to be spying on him like this, she told herself. She was grown up now. Why, her best friend – George's sister Becky – was the same age and was already married with a baby. But then she was not Becky, beautiful and spirited. She was Colleen, timid and plain.

'Big-nosed Papist' they'd called her at school – until Becky had stopped them. And they'd been right. She did have a big nose, and no amount of twisting around in front of the mirror could ever make it look attractive.

She wished she had the nerve to bump into George – casual-like – when he was on his way to Mr Cooke's shop to buy his newspaper, or while he was taking his morning stroll along the canal. But what would she say to him? And what would *he* say to her? When she looked at him, she saw a hero. When he looked at her, could he really see anything more than a big-nosed Papist?

With a sigh, she quietly closed the door and went back to preparing her dad's supper.

It had been a dry spring until then, but the following morning the skies opened.

'It's good for the farmers,' the wallers at Worrell's Salt Works consoled themselves as they biked to work with rainwater trickling down the backs of their necks.

'Lovely weather for ducks,' women with shopping baskets shouted as they rushed past each other in the lane.

'It's a shame you've got such rotten weather for your leave,' Mary Taylor told her son George as he prowled around the little kitchen and wished he was outside, stretching his legs.

The next day brought no relief, nor the one after it. The water level in Forge Pool rose, Witton Brook was in full spate, and even the canal looked like it might eventually spill over its banks.

'Beware of the Second Great Flood,' shouted an itinerant preacher from the doorway of Hall's the newsagents on Northwich High Street. 'Prepare yourselves for the coming of the Lord.'

But his dire warnings were drowned by the gushing water in the gutters and the swish of folding and unfolding umbrellas.

For Becky, the weather seemed a special trial since it kept Michael in the house and served as a constant reminder that she had still not taken the decision which would affect both their futures.

Yet how can I decide? she asked herself as she watched the drops of rain making their slow, steady progress all the way down the big drawing room windowpane.

She knew that Michael would accept it if she said no, but who could guess what the long-term effect of thwarted ambition might be on him? And if she said yes, she would be condemning herself to months of loneliness at a time, which no one – not even her baby or her family – would be able to ease.

If she was to agree to Michael going, then she needed something to occupy her mind while he was away, she thought. But what? The servants took care of household matters, and if she tried to help, she would only embarrass them. Nor would her father feel comfortable if she offered to give him a hand in the chip shop. She wasn't Becky Taylor, the little dressmaker from Ollershaw Lane, any more. Now she was Mrs Michael Worrell, a lady who had taken tea with the mayor and drove around in a carriage.

She wished that she and Michael were not quite so well off, wished that he needed her to work so that she could . . .

And suddenly, she had an idea – an inspiration, almost – and gazing into the rain-streaked windowpane, she saw a picture of the future as it could be, if only she had the will to make it so. It wasn't an ideal solution, of course – only having

Michael with her all the time could be that – but at least it would make her life bearable while he was away. She felt as excited as Mary had been when she'd first thought of opening a chip shop, but, also like her mother, she resolved to proceed cautiously and to say nothing to her husband until she had the whole thing mapped out.

After four days of continuous rain, the clouds were at last exhausted, and though there was still a dampness in the air, it was at least possible to step outdoors. So it was that shortly after breakfast, George left the Taylor house by the back gate, totally unaware of the fact that he was being watched.

From her bedroom window, Colleen O'Leary's eyes followed George as he marched towards the canal bank. He would be gone for at least two hours, she was sure, which would give her plenty of time to put her plan into action – if only she dared.

She walked over to her wardrobe and, almost reverentially, took out the costume she had braved the weather to buy only the day before.

The costume was in three parts – a mock silk green blouse with a high stand collar, a lilac jacket with leg-of-mutton sleeves, and a long swirling dark skirt which gathered in tightly at the waist. Holding the complete ensemble in front of her, Colleen advanced slowly towards the full-length mirror.

The assistant had told her it suited her.

And while I was in the shop, I believed her, Colleen thought.

But now, examining the costume in the cold light of her own room, Colleen wondered if she'd ever find the courage to wear it. And even if she did manage to pluck up the nerve, wouldn't it be obvious to everyone, once she'd stepped into the lane, exactly what she was doing?

'There goes Big-nosed Colleen O'Leary,' they'd say, 'setting her sights on George Taylor. What a laugh!'

Sighing to herself – she always seemed to be doing that,

these days – she returned the costume to the wardrobe.

There was a dampness to the earth which reminded George of Burma after the rains.

Burma! People in Marston were always asking him about it.

'This jungle they've got out there, is it somethin' like Delamere Forest, or what?'

'Do they have proper shops? I mean, is there a Burmese Co-Operative Wholesale Society?'

He answered their questions as best he could, but he was always aware, when he reached the end of his explanation, that he had failed to give them anything like an accurate picture of the Burma he knew.

Part of his failure, he was sure, lay in himself. He was by no means stupid, but neither was he quick-witted like his older brother Jack, nor as artistic as his younger brother Philip. Instead, he was slow-thinking, slow-speaking George, always the last to notice when his father was being sarcastic or one of his sisters was poking fun.

But that was not the only reason Burma remained as vague to folk after he'd spoken as before he opened his mouth, he told himself. To convey the spirit of Burma would have taxed the talents of Jack, Philip – or even Old Gilbert Bowyer, who'd been a marvellous storyteller and had served in the Far East himself.

How could you describe the market, where rich Burmese noblemen rubbed shoulders with the poorest beggars, where child prostitutes openly plied their trade and spice sellers shooed away stray dogs with furious gestures? How could you really make people understand just how thick – and how sticky – the jungle could be?

And if it was impossible to give a sense of the country, then how much more difficult it was to describe his own life in it and the changes which he had undergone since he first went there. He'd been a boy when he landed, a raw recruit who the old sweats had used as the butt of their jokes.

'Nip down to Hung Fu's shop and get me a pound of gumption, will you, young George?'

'Aye, an' while you're there, see if he's got any whores' treasure chests in yet.'

He'd gone, of course, eager to please and totally unaware that they were making a fool of him. Hell, he hadn't even known what a whore *was* back then. Well, those days were long gone. He was a sergeant now, a man whom both officers and men looked to for advice and guidance. His word alone could send a soldier to the prison stockade for years of hard labour. His decision, carefully arrived at, could mean the difference between life and death for the soldiers serving with him.

How could he explain any of this, even to his sister Becky? How could they understand what it was like to come under fire from the dacoits – as the Burmese bandits were called – and to know that the safety of the platoon was in your hands? How could he tell them what it felt like to drive a sabre into a dacoit's throat? How could he give them an idea of the pity he had for his enemy, even as he was killing him?

He reached Burns Bridge, climbed the steep path to the top, and stopped to light a cigarette. In the distance he could see the smoke curling its way out of Worrell's works' chimney, not twenty yards from his parents' home.

He thought how strange it was that he should phrase it that way. His parents' home – not *his* home.

He didn't belong to Marston any more, he realized, and it no longer belonged to him. Perhaps things would be different if he had a girl – someone to love – but what chance did a soldier like him have of ever meeting someone he could take home to Mother?

He enjoyed his life, he told himself. It could be hard, sometimes even dangerous, but on the whole he did not regret his decision to join the army. Why then, he wondered, did he suddenly feel a deep sense of loss – as if someone he had known very well had unexpectedly died?

*

Colleen tiptoed down the stairs, her ears straining for sounds of movement below. She heard the noise of a brush banging against the leather settle, and nodded her head with satisfaction. It was at this quiet time of day – when all the early customers had gone to work – that her mam took the opportunity of sweeping out the bar. And her dad would be where he always was for part of the morning – in the cellar, tapping barrels and checking stock. Colleen congratulated herself on having planned her escape so perfectly.

She crept up the central passage and almost had her hand on the front door knob when her mother called out from the other side of the bar door, 'Is that you, Collie?'

'Yes, Mam, it's me,' she said resignedly, thinking that though her mam had always had eyes in the back of her head, she now seemed to have developed extra ears, too.

'Is it going out, you are?' asked Cathy O'Leary, who even after thirty years in Cheshire often still spoke as if she'd only just got off the boat in Liverpool.

'Yes, Mam,' Colleen said again. 'I've finished me jobs and I thought I'd go out for a breath of fresh air.'

'Well, make sure you're back by twelve,' Cathy said. 'I shall be needing help behind the bar by then.'

'I'll be back,' Colleen replied, feeling as short of breath as if she'd just run a mile.

'Is anything the matter?' Cathy asked, and even through the frosted glass Colleen could detect a note of suspicion in her mother's voice.

'No, nothin's the matter,' Colleen replied, trying to ignore the fact that her heart was beating at a furious rate.

'Come in here a minute,' Cathy said.

And knowing there was no point in arguing, Colleen pushed open the door and stepped into the bar.

Cathy O'Leary was standing at the far end of the bar with a yardbrush in her hand. She had put an old pinny on over her second-best dress and had a faded kerchief wrapped around her head.

Yet she still looks pretty, Colleen thought.

She looked at her mother's nose. It wasn't small, but it wasn't huge, either. Colleen wondered which member of the family back in Ireland she herself had the misfortune to inherit her conk from.

She was so intent on looking at her mother that she didn't really notice the way Cathy was also examining her. Didn't notice, that is, until Cathy said, 'And where in the name of heaven did you get all that finery?'

Colleen felt herself blushing.

'Bratt and Evans,' she managed to stutter. 'I've been savin' up.'

'You must have been,' Cathy agreed, moving towards her daughter.

Colleen took an instinctive step backwards.

'I've got to go,' she mumbled.

'No, you haven't!' Cathy said. 'Stay exactly where you are.'

Colleen stood frozen to the spot. She was conscious of her mother's eyes examining her, now looking at the leg-of-mutton sleeves, now seeing how the skirt hung at the back.

'Very nice,' Cathy said after what, to Colleen, seemed an age. 'It's good taste, you have.'

'Thank you, Mam,' Colleen said, almost in a whisper.

'But the question I ask meself is why you should be wearing such fine clothes on a weekday?' Cathy continued.

'I just wanted to give them an airing,' Colleen said.

'And where exactly will you be giving them this airing?' Cathy asked.

'I don't know,' Colleen lied. 'I hadn't really thought about it.'

'The canal bank's probably as good a place as any,' Cathy said. 'You could go as far as Burns Bridge. It'd be a nice little outing for you.'

Colleen felt so hot that she would not have been at all surprised if her cheeks had suddenly burst into flame.

'Maybe I will go along the canal,' she said, keeping her voice as steady as she was able.

36

'Well, mind you don't trail your skirt in the mud,' Cathy advised. 'And if you happen to come across Mr George Taylor on your travels, give him me best wishes.'

Colleen had been gazing at the floor ever since the dress inspection had started, but now she looked up into her mother's eyes and saw that Cathy was laughing.

Even though he was not close enough to see her face, George couldn't help noticing the way she walked. She moved with dainty, ladylike steps, so different from the great strides of the women who worked on the land, and the mincing, self-effacing gait of girls like his sister Jessie, who had not long come out of service. But then it was not surprising that this woman moved like a lady, because from the way she was dressed, she plainly was one.

So what exactly was a lady doing, alone on a canal bank in the middle of the morning?

As they drew closer to each other, he began to make out more details. The blouse she was wearing was gathered in over a firm bosom, the woman's waist was tiny, and though her skirt covered them, her legs could not be anything but long. Only her face remained invisible to him. She was wearing a straw hat with a large brim which, it seemed to George, was perhaps pulled a little too far forward. In addition she was looking at the ground, perhaps mindful of the fact that it was very easy to trip up along the towpath. The strange thing was, George thought, that despite the fact that he was sure he did not know such a fine lady, there was something familiar about her.

They were almost level now, and George stood to one side to let her pass. For a moment it seemed as if that was exactly what she would do, still with her eyes pointed to the cobbles. And then she lifted her head and George saw to his surprise that she was none other than his sister Becky's best friend, Colleen O'Leary.

'Good morning, Miss O'Leary,' George said.

He didn't know why he'd done that – calling a girl he'd

known all his life *Miss* anything. Maybe it was her clothes or her hour-glass figure which had thrown him off. Anyway, the words were out now, and he couldn't take them back.

Colleen seemed as surprised by the greeting as he'd been himself, but she rallied and said, 'G . . . good morning, Mr Taylor. What a surprise to meet you here.'

'I usually come for a walk along here if the weather's fine enough for it,' George said.

'Why, so do I,' Colleen replied.

In which case, it was a wonder they hadn't come across each other before now, George thought.

He was expecting Colleen to say something like, 'Well, it's been nice talkin' to you, Mr Taylor, but now I must be going.'

Yet she didn't do that. Instead she just stood there, as if she wanted the conversation to continue. But what could they talk about? He'd had no practice at dealing with women who weren't either his own sisters or female camp followers in Burma – and neither of those experiences seemed to be of much use to him now.

He searched his mind for some example he might model his own behaviour on. Who had he seen with ladies? It came to him in a flash of inspiration. Who else should he copy but the officers he'd served under in the army?

'Would you do me the honour of allowing me to escort you on your constitutional?' he asked in a manner which he was sure his colonel would have approved of.

Colleen's face was suddenly flooded with panic.

'Would I . . . would I what?' she stuttered.

'Would it be all right if I came along on your walk with you?' George replied, feeling like a fool.

Colleen was visibly relieved.

'Oh yes,' she said. 'That would be love . . . I mean, if it's not too much trouble you havin' already had your walk and been just set to go home again when we met an' . . . ' She fell silent, embarrassed by her own babbling.

'It really wouldn't be any trouble,' George assured her.

'The more exercise I get, the better.'

'Well, in that case, it'd be a pleasure to have you come with me on me mornin' consti . . . consti . . . walk,' Colleen said in a rush.

George held out his arm, bent at the elbow and perfectly parallel to the ground, just as he'd seen his officers do it. Colleen had no idea what was happening, and for a moment she simply stared at the arm in horror. Then she realized what was expected of her and took the arm in imitation of the posh ladies she'd seen in Northwich.

The preliminary formalities over, the barmaid and the soldier made their way slowly towards the Bluebell Wood.

Chapter Three

Breakfast was the low point of the day for Richard Worrell, because it was the only time when he was absolutely certain to see his wife Hortense. She could have had breakfast sent up to her room – many ladies, he believed, did just that – but Hortense would not willingly give up the opportunity to snipe at him.

And how many topics there were on which she could attack him! His whoring. His love for Becky, the little dressmaker who had married his brother Michael. And, of course, the fact that before the great subsidence, Michael had made a huge success of his business.

'But look where my brother is now,' he'd countered once, before he could stop himself.

'It's only temporary,' Hortense assured him, her voice thick with malice. 'Michael's got a head on his shoulders. If anyone in your family ends up with a knighthood, I know which one of you it will be.'

Yes, breakfast with Hortense was an ordeal, and one that Richard only endured because he refused to be driven away from his own table.

On one particular morning in early April, however, Hortense seemed to do a complete about-face. She actually smiled at Richard as she entered the room, and, before he had time to recover from his surprise, enquired if he had slept well.

'Very well, thank you,' Richard replied, wondering who this strange woman who so resembled his wife could possibly be.

'We should see more of each other,' Hortense said sweetly.

'I'm very busy at the works,' Richard told her.

'I know that, my dear,' his wife replied. 'You work very hard. But apart from when you are away on business trips, you are usually home by late evening.'

Richard was finding it harder and harder to hide his astonishment. 'Business trips' she had said, without a hint of irony or recrimination – despite the fact that they both knew that his nights away were rarely more than an excuse to go to one of the more expensive brothels in Liverpool or Manchester.

'You never visit me, any more,' Hortense continued, giving him what he was sure she believed to be a pretty pout.

'Visit you?' Richard asked, completely mystified.

'You know,' Hortense said, looking down at the lace tablecloth. 'On Thursday nights.'

Before Hortense had become pregnant with their son, Gerald, Richard had always gone to her room on Thursdays, precisely with the aim of producing an heir. But she had always hated it – he was certain she had – and it was a relief to both of them when Hortense had announced that their loathsome coupling had at last had the required result. And now she was asking him to resume his visits! It didn't make sense.

'You . . . er . . . would like me to . . . er . . . return to your bed?' Richard said cautiously.

'Yes,' Hortense said firmly. 'And perhaps this time it could be for more than one night a week.'

Is this some kind of trick? Richard wondered. If it was, what did she possibly hope to gain from it? There were other ways to humiliate him – ways less personally distasteful to her. He looked into her eyes, searching for clues which would explain her behaviour. There was no love there, but he had never expected that. Yet there was *something*, and though he could not put his finger on precisely what, it seemed to contain at least an element of desperation. Desperation? But what had Hortense to be desperate about?

'We are married,' Hortense said, 'and it's only right that we should live as man and wife.'

41

Despite himself, Richard found he was becoming intrigued. He wanted to discover what had brought about this change in his wife. He wanted to see if, finally, he could raise a spark of passion in the cold bitch he'd married.

'Very well,' he said. 'I will resume my visits to you.'

'You could start tonight,' Hortense suggested.

It had been a dispiriting day for Michael Worrell. Since he'd returned from Africa and found his works in ruins, he'd done his best to find alternative jobs for all his former workers. And he'd succeeded with everyone – except in the cases of Cedric Rathbone, Tom Jennings and Brian O'Reilly.

'They were easily the three best workers I had,' Michael told the manager of Woodward's. 'Why, I even left Cedric Rathbone in charge when I went away on business.'

'They caused trouble when they were working for your brother,' the manager countered. 'Something about the union, wasn't it? Anyway, Richard let us all know we'd be better off without that particular bunch.'

'The trouble was as much my brother's fault as anybody's,' Michael protested. 'And when my works started to sink, Rathbone and his pals risked their lives to save as much of it as they could.'

'I'm sorry,' the manager said. 'I really am. But with so many able-bodied men ready and willing to work, why should I take a chance with them?'

It was the same story everywhere he went. His brother Richard seemed to have managed to poison the minds of all the owners and managers in the area.

So just what am I going to do about them? Michael wondered.

If Becky agreed to his African scheme, he could offer them jobs himself – but he already knew what their answer would be.

'We're sorry, Mr Worrell, but we were born and brought up in Marston, and if it's all the same to you, we'd rather stay here an' be poor than go gallivantin' off all over the world.'

He thought of offering them small pensions – he could just about afford it – but that was no good either. Tom and Brian might accept, but Cedric, the one he really wanted to reward for his service, had never taken anything he'd not earned, and would be unlikely to start doing it now.

It was a problem, and one he would have liked to talk over with Becky, as they talked over most of his problems. But Becky had enough on her mind at the moment just trying to decide whether or not to let him return to the Oil Rivers.

Colleen and George met at the same spot every day, halfway between Burns' Bridge and Marston, and though neither of them ever suggested they make it a formal arrangement, both would have been surprised had the other not turned up.

The time after their meeting up followed a pattern, too. George would offer Colleen his arm – which she now took with practised ease– and they would walk along the canal to the Bluebell Wood, then cut through to Forge Pool. And as they walked, they talked.

Sometimes they would discuss the old days.

'Do you remember an old narrow boat man called Mr Hulse?' Colleen asked one day as they stood by the pool and looked across the water.

'The one whose boat you and our Becky were on when the canal bank gave way?' George asked.

'That's right,' Colleen agreed. 'Well, he used to have a dog called Jip who came down here, duck-egging.'

'A dog? Duck-egging?' George exclaimed. 'Now that is interesting.'

He didn't believe her, but he knew that any gentleman would have considered it rude to say so.

'It's true!' Colleen protested, guessing the true feeling behind his words. 'He used to carry them in his mouth, did old Jip. And he hardly ever cracked one.'

'If you say so,' George said, starting to feel uncomfortable as he always did when he suspected someone of taking the mickey.

'If you don't believe me, just ask your Becky,' Colleen said.

'Our Becky would tell me anythin',' George said, grinning despite himself. 'She's always makin' fun of me.'

Colleen looked up at him, her eyes full of seriousness and sincerity.

'But I wouldn't make fun of you,' she said. 'I promise, I'd never make fun of you.'

Her words seemed to embarrass him, and for what felt to Colleen like hours, they stood in an awkward silence. Then, perhaps just to break the tension, George started to tell her about the polo games he had seen in front of the royal palace in Rangoon.

'The officers treat it like a war,' he said. 'In fact, I think they're more serious about that than they are about fightin' the bandits.'

'And do you play yourself?' Colleen asked.

George shook his head. 'I don't even like riskin' my horse Galahad in battle,' he said. 'I'm buggered if I'll take the chance with – ' He stopped suddenly, and looked confused. 'I'm sorry,' he continued. 'I didn't mean to use bad language in front of you.'

'All men swear now and again,' Colleen assured him. 'My dad does, and so does yours. It's only natural.'

'There's never any excuse for swearin' in front of a lady,' George said firmly. He took his watch out of his waistcoat pocket and consulted it. 'It's time we were gettin' back.'

He offered her his arm as he habitually did, and she took it, trying to act like the lady he obviously thought her to be.

On the way home, Colleen did her best to work out just where their friendship was heading. It had been a mistake on her part to tell him she'd never make fun of him, as she had earlier. Well, really it hadn't been so much what she'd said as the way she'd said it. She'd been – what did you call it? – too earnest, too intense. He might start thinking that she was trying to rush him into something, and she wasn't – honestly.

Of course, she had her hopes. George seemed to like her

company, and showed no interest in any other girls. True, he'd done nothing to encourage these hopes of hers yet, but that wasn't to say he never would. It was perfectly possible, even probable, she thought, that soon George would overlook her big nose and ask her to be his girl.

The mangle-house was not just a place to do your washing. In the shadow of the huge cast-iron cauldron which hissed and bubbled as it heated the water, the women from the neighbouring streets pounded their laundry in wooden tubs and exchanged gossip. Plenty of reputations were put through the wringers along with the sheets, and any number of people's less-than-spotless characters were hung out to dry with the clothes on the line which stretched across Lime Kiln Lane.

'You should just hear them,' said Mary Taylor as she and her daughter Becky ducked under the washing on their way to Fleming Street. 'They were a group of old cats when I used to go there, and I bet they've not changed a bit to this day.'

The two women reached Witton Street and passed Lipton's Grocers.

'Everythin's changing,' Mary said, looking around her. 'Everythin'. Even the shops.'

It was true what her mother was saying, Becky thought. When she'd been a little girl, all the shops had been owned by local people, but now there were chains like Lipton's and Home and Colonial. And not only the shops were changing, but also the way they conducted their business. In the old days, tea had been served loose from a big tea chest, but now it came in little yellow packets with Sir Thomas Lipton's name on them. And the same was true of sugar and butter. 'Standardization' was what Michael called it.

'It's the way of the future,' he'd told her. 'You've only got to read Adam Smith to realize that.'

'And who's Adam Smith when he's at home?' Becky had asked.

45

'He's an economist,' Michael replied. 'He spent a lot of time studying a pin factory. They had a lot of people working there, but instead of all of them making whole pins, like they do in other factories, each one was only doing a small part of the job.'

'How do you mean?' Becky'd asked.

'Well, one worker would draw out the wire, another straighten it and the third cut it,' Michael had explained. 'Then a fourth would sharpen it and a fifth would flatten one end to make the head. And because each man got so used to his job, they worked quicker and produced pins which were more or less identical. Standardization, you see. Do you get the point?'

'I think so,' Becky had said doubtfully.

It seemed a big mental leap from pin factories to a quarter-pound of Lipton's tea, but if Michael said this standardization was the coming thing, then he was probably right – he usually was. And if tea could be standardized, and pins could be standardized, why couldn't other things?

'I asked you what you'd got on your mind,' Mary said, cutting into Becky's thoughts and bringing her back to the High Street on which the two were still standing.

'Just something Michael told me about,' Becky said. 'Nothing, really.'

'When you've got that look on your face, it's never nothin',' her mother said. 'What are you planning, Becky?'

'A way to keep myself busy while Michael's abroad,' Becky admitted.

'You'll never guess who I saw walking along the canal together, arm-in-arm an' all,' Not-Stopping Bracegirdle said to her cronies in the best room of the New Inn.

'Well, if we'll never guess, there's no point in even tryin', is there?' asked Dottie Curzon, whose rebellious spirit was growing stronger every day.

Not-Stopping gave Dottie a hard look. For a moment, she considered punishing her old friend by depriving her of this juicy new piece of gossip. But when all was said and done, that would only be cutting off her own nose to spite her face.

'Colleen O'Leary and George Taylor, that's who I saw,' she said. 'Now what do you think of that?'

'What were you doin' on the towpath anyway?' Maggie Cross asked. 'You don't usually go up that way, do you?'

Not-Stopping looked uncomfortable – but only for a second.

'I happened to notice that Colleen was goin' out at about the same time every morning, dressed up to the nines,' she said, 'so I put two and two together.'

'And made six as usual,' Dottie Curzon said, almost – but not quite – under her breath.

'Anyway, I'm not one for spreadin' baseless gossip', Not-Stopping continued. 'So I said to meself, "Elsie," I said, "you'd better go and see for yourself just who she's meeting." And there they were, as bold as brass.'

'Nothin' wrong with that, is there?' Dottie Curzon asked. 'He's a nice lad, George Taylor. Steady.'

'Steady!' Not-Stopping retorted. 'He's barmy if you ask me.'

Not that anybody did, Dottie thought to herself.

'Twelve pound a week he could have earned playin' football,' Not-Stopping pressed on, 'and instead he ups and joins the army. Well, nobody in their right mind does that, do they? And as for walkin' out with Colleen O'Leary, well, I mean, she's not exactly a prize catch, is she?'

On the other side of the hatch, Paddy O'Leary felt the glass he was holding slip out of his hand and wondered why it was that fathers were always the last to find out.

The towels had been up for some time and the final late-night drinker had made his way reluctantly through the front door. Paddy slid the bolts home and then turned to his daughter.

'You can go to bed now, Colleen,' he said, rather more harshly than he'd intended to.

'Go to bed?' Colleen repeated.

'That's what I said!' Patrick replied.

Colleen looked around the empty bar, assessing the amount of work still to be done. 'But Dad . . .' she began.

'I'll talk to you in the mornin',' Paddy told her firmly. 'After I've had a word with your mother.'

Colleen seemed to be on the point of arguing, then, like the dutiful daughter she was, she bowed her head and disappeared through the door at the back of the bar.

'Now what was that all about?' asked Cathy, who had been standing quietly behind the bar watching the whole scene.

'Did you know your daughter was walkin' out with George Taylor?' Paddy demanded.

'I knew *our* daughter had gone for a few walks with him,' Cathy said mildly, 'but that's hardly the same as "walking out".'

'Well, I don't like it,' Paddy told her.

'Don't like it? Or don't like *him*?' Cathy asked.

The question knocked Paddy off balance, and some of his anger drained away.

'Oh, I didn't mean to imply there's anythin' wrong with George Taylor,' he admitted a little shamefacedly. 'He's a fine young man from a fine family. It's just that . . .'

'It's just that what?' his wife asked.

'You know,' Paddy said awkwardly.

'Maybe I do,' Cathy agreed. 'But tell me anyway.'

'Well, we're Catholic – and young George isn't,' Paddy replied.

'We're Catholic and he isn't,' Cathy repeated, nodding her head as if she hadn't realized that until he'd pointed it out to her. 'And tell me, Patrick Declan O'Leary, when was the last time you went to mass?'

Paddy tried to remember. He knew he hadn't gone at Christmas – well, the pub had been so busy, he'd been too tired to turn out for midnight mass. So it must have been last Easter although, now he came to think of it, he couldn't actually recall going.

'A bit over a year, is it?' Paddy speculated.

'Four years if it's a day,' Cathy told him.

Four years! Was it really as long as that? Dear God, how easy it was to lapse!

'Well, you and Colleen still go,' he said defensively.

'I think we should sit down and talk this out properly,' Cathy said.

'We've got the cleanin' to do,' Paddy replied, beginning to wish he'd never brought the subject up.

'Sit, Patrick!' his wife said firmly, pointing to one of the cast-iron tables in the corner.

Paddy sat, and his wife came round the bar to join him.

'Our Colleen's a wonderful girl,' Cathy said.

'The best daughter a man could wish for,' Paddy agreed. 'A dream of a daughter.'

'But even you, her doting father, would admit she's no great beauty, wouldn't you?' Cathy asked.

'She'll always be beautiful to me,' Paddy said, beginning to feel uncomfortable again.

'That isn't what I asked you – and you know it,' Cathy said sternly.

'Well, she's not what you might call . . . ' Paddy began – then he dried up.

'Not what you might call what?' Cathy asked mercilessly.

'What I mean is,' Paddy said, making another stab at it, 'what I mean is, if you look at Becky Taylor and then you look at our Colleen . . . '

'Exactly,' Cathy agreed. 'And don't you think our Colleen knows that better than anybody?'

'I suppose she must,' Paddy admitted.

'Do you remember what she was like as a baby?' Cathy said.

Paddy did, and the memory of her then brought a glow of pleasure to his troubled face.

'She was such a lively little thing,' he said. 'She had the spirit of the Auld Irish kings in her, that one – afraid of nothing or nobody.'

'And then she went to school,' Cathy said, 'and she

changed. Somehow the other kids knocked the stuffin' out of her and she's been like a little mouse ever since.'

Paddy frowned. 'You might be right,' he conceded.

'Of course I'm right,' Cathy said tartly. 'I'm her mother, aren't I?'

'Indeed you are,' Paddy said, smiling despite himself. 'And what a mother! A lioness couldn't be fiercer when it comes to defendin' her cub.'

Cathy smiled, too. 'That's enough of your blarney, Patrick,' she told her husband, and then, becoming serious again, she continued, 'I've seen a big difference in our Colleen recently. Haven't you noticed it yourself?'

Paddy nodded his head in agreement.

'Now I come to think of it, she has altered a bit in the last few days,' he confessed.

'And if that's not due to spending time with George, what is it due to?' Cathy asked.

'But even so . . .' Paddy protested.

'We left the auld country because we were sick and tired of a man being judged by whether or not he burned incense in his church,' Cathy said passionately. 'Let's not make the same mistake with George as all them bigots across the water did with us – let's not risk our daughter's happiness just because the lad isn't one of us.'

'You're right,' Paddy said. 'There's a lot more to a man than his religion. But do you really think it's going to work out between 'em?'

'I've seen the way he looks at her when she's behind the bar serving somebody else,' Cathy said. 'The way his eyes follow her every move. I *know* it's goin' to work out between 'em.'

The moon cast a pale yellow shadow across the floor. A slight draught caused the flame of the candle in Richard Worrell's hand to flicker. In the distance, an owl hooted.

As he made his way along the corridor to his wife's bedroom, Richard thought back to his previous evening's visit. It had been the first time he'd slept with her since she'd become pregnant with Gerald. He'd hoped the encounter would do something to explain her sudden and unexpected amiability over breakfast, but if anything, it had only confused him more. She'd worn a lacy nightdress with a plunging neckline which gave a tantalizing view of her bosom – her best feature. She'd spoken to him in a way which he was sure she thought was seductive and inviting. And yet at the same time, as he climbed into her bed, he had noticed a look of distaste flicker briefly across her face.

Their love-making had not been as he remembered it, either. She'd appeared to be . . . he didn't know quite how to phrase it . . .

'A different woman from the one I knew,' he muttered to himself.

Yes, that was it. She was a *different woman* from the last time they had been in bed together. Of course, it was perfectly possible he'd simply forgotten what she was like. Over a year had passed since their last evening together, during which time he had bedded a score of other women. So it could be just forgetfulness on his part – but he didn't think so.

He turned the corner and his wife's door loomed up ahead of him. He knocked.

'What do you want?' Hortense called out.

What did he want? Could this be the same Hortense who'd greeted him with such affectionate urgency the previous evening?

'Well?' Hortense demanded. 'What is it you want?'

'I want to come in,' Richard said. 'May I?'

'I suppose so,' Hortense replied, and even through the thick wood he could hear the heaviness and impatience in her voice.

Richard turned the handle, pushed the door open, and stepped inside. Hortense was sitting up in bed, but tonight she was wearing a thick flannel nightdress and her hair was full of curling papers.

It was almost as if he had travelled through time, back to

51

the old Hortense he had known before Gerald was born, Richard thought.

'My dear – ' he began.

'I have a splitting headache,' Hortense interrupted.

'Well, perhaps tomorrow evening . . . ' Richard said, turning back to the door.

'No,' he heard Hortense say behind him. 'No, I don't think so.'

Chapter Four

When George had first returned home on leave, the sticky buds of spring had only just appeared on the branches of the oaks and silver birches which grew around Marston. Weeks had passed since then, and now whichever way Colleen looked from the parapet of Burns' Bridge, she could see splashes of lush green.

Yes, everything in nature was growing as beautifully – and as quickly – as her love for George, she thought fancifully. And she was sure he felt something too. It was true that he continued to be polite – almost formal. But if he wasn't interested in me, he wouldn't keep seein' me, would he? she asked herself.

She looked up at him now. He was leaning on the parapet, smoking a cigarette – he had asked her permission before he lit it – and gazing at the village in the distance. He was handsome and strong. He was a hero who had bravely served his queen and country in foreign lands. She marvelled now that she'd ever had the nerve to approach him that first morning on the canal bank, but she was glad that she had. More than glad!

In her mind, she pictured the life they could have together. George would leave the army and get a job locally, probably a foreman's job because he was already used to bossing other men about. They'd rent a little house in the village, and she'd continue to work for her dad until she started having babies. It would be perfect.

George was still staring intently at the village.

'You're lookin' at it as if you thought you were seein' it for the last time,' Colleen said lightly.

'Well, it'll certainly be a while before I get to see this view again,' George told her.

Though the sun was shining brightly, Colleen felt a cold shiver run through her.

'A while?' she said cautiously.

'My leave's all but over,' George replied.

The shiver would not go away. Colleen felt as if she were completely encased in ice.

'But you'll be back in the village soon, won't you?' she said, trying to keep a tremble out of her voice. 'I mean, it's not as if we'll be saying goodbye to you for ever. You're only goin' to Aldershot.'

'We're goin' to Egypt,' George said. 'It might be seven years before I set foot on English soil again.'

'How long have you known about this?' Colleen demanded.

'My orders came through last week,' George said.

'And you never told me!' Colleen said, almost hysterically. '*Why* didn't you tell me?'

The outburst seemed to puzzle George.

'You never asked,' he said.

Colleen saw all her dreams crumbling before her eyes. George had never cared for her in the slightest, she knew that now. He hadn't even bothered to tell her he was going overseas again.

She felt hot tears forming in her eyes, but she was determined not to cry. If she could do nothing else, she told herself, she would at least preserve her dignity.

'I've got to go,' she said.

George looked up at the sun.

'Bit early to be goin' home, isn't it?' he asked.

'I've got jobs to do back at the pub,' Colleen said.

'All right,' George said, sounding more and more perplexed every second. 'I'll escort you.'

He held out his arm for her to take.

'I don't want *escortin*',' Colleen shouted angrily, knocking the arm to one side. 'I managed without being escorted before you came home and I can manage without being escorted now.'

She turned and almost ran down the steep path to the canal bank. George, left alone on the bridge, scratched his head and wondered what he'd done wrong.

The sun was smiling down benevolently, and what few clouds there were in the sky floated lazily by like fluffy balls of cotton wool. It was a fine afternoon for walking along the canal to Rudheath, but Michael suspected there had been more to his wife's suggestion than the simple desire to get some exercise.

Becky had been very quiet for the last few days. Secretive and preoccupied, too. On a couple of occasions he had actually caught her adding up figures on a piece of paper which she had hurriedly put away when she'd seen him standing there. She was up to something – he was convinced of that – but he couldn't work out what it was.

They reached Broken Cross Bridge, and Becky said, 'Shall we get off the towpath for a while and wander down through Rudheath village?'

Michael looked at her quizzically. She was playing with him. Or rather, she wasn't yet, but she was about to. He felt like a puppet, temporarily at rest, but soon to be jerked this way and that when Becky started pulling his strings.

'Why should we go to Rudheath village?' he asked.

'It'll make a change,' Becky said casually, far too casually.

Michael abandoned the idea of his being a puppet, and started to think of himself as an animal being led by the nose to a waiting trap.

Well, why not? he thought. Whatever else you could say about life with Becky, it was never boring.

'All right,' he said. 'Let's go to Rudheath for a change.'

They walked up the dog-legged path to the top of the bridge. The village – little more than a hamlet with a few small farms – lay before them.

'Well, this really is a change,' Michael said. 'Who would ever have thought you'd bring me anywhere as exciting as this?'

Becky ignored the comment.

'I've decided that if you want to go back to Africa, I won't stand in your way,' she said earnestly.

A flood of conflicting emotions swept over Michael. He'd wanted her to say yes, and yet at the same time he hadn't. He felt the pull of Africa, yet there was an equal pull urging him to stay at home. He cursed his sense of destiny, but to Becky he simply said, 'Thank you.'

They walked on, passing half a dozen small cottages with well-tended vegetable gardens.

'We are partners, aren't we, Michael?' Becky asked.

'Of course we're partners,' Michael told her, still with no idea of exactly what kind of trap Becky had set for him. 'We're man and wife – you can't get any closer than that.'

'I mean, *business* partners,' Becky said.

'That too,' Michael agreed. 'I had your name put on the chimney of the works, didn't I?'

'So if I wanted some capital to start up my own business, would you let me have it?' Becky asked.

'Up to half of what we've got,' Michael said instantly.

'I won't need all that,' Becky told him.

They had left the houses behind and now drew level with an old brick barn which, though still serviceable, had the neglected look of a place which is no longer used.

'What sort of business have you got in mind?' Michael asked. 'A dressmaking emporium?'

Becky stopped walking and looked up into her husband's eyes.

'No, not a dressmaker's,' she said decisively. 'I served my time at that and if I never see a needle and thread again, it'll be too soon.'

'Then what?' Michael asked.

'A bakery,' Becky said.

'A bakery!' Michael replied. 'Surely you can come up with something better than that? Bakeries are nasty, poky little places, as hot as hell and full of dust from the flour. You'd hate it.'

'My bakery won't be like that,' Becky said with conviction.

Michael noted the look of determination on Becky's face and smiled.

'How will your bakery be different?' he asked.

'I've been reading that book by Adam Smith,' Becky said. 'The one about the pin factory.'

Michael raised his eyebrows. He had long ago ceased to underestimate Becky, but even so, she was still capable of surprising him.

'And what did you learn from *The Wealth of Nations*?' he asked.

'They had several people making the pins if you remember,' Becky said, 'each one only doing a little part of the job. And because they did it that way, they produced a lot more pins than they would have done if each man had been making the whole thing.'

'Yes, that's true,' Michael agreed. 'But I still don't see what that's got to do with –'

'My bakery will be like that,' Becky interrupted. 'Instead of each worker making a whole pie or a whole cake, they'll be working on a line.'

Michael thought about it for a second.

'In order to make that work,' he said, 'you'd have to bake thousands of pies and thousands of cakes. You'd never be able to sell them all.'

'Lipton sells all his tea,' Becky countered.

'But that's because people recognize his name,' Michael pointed out. 'And he sells his tea through hundreds of shops.'

'Well, people will recognize my name,' Becky said confidently. 'And my pies will be sold in hundreds of shops.' She stopped speaking for a second, and smiled. 'Well, maybe not hundreds,' she conceded, 'but certainly most of the shops in the area.'

Michael looked doubtful. 'I can't see it,' he admitted. 'And I'm not happy about you running a business entirely on your own.'

'I won't be running it on my own,' Becky said. 'Cedric Rathbone's already agreed to be the foreman. And if you trusted him with your business, why shouldn't I trust him with mine?'

Michael shook his head in frank admiration. 'And I suppose you've already got your eye on a building you could use,' he said.

Becky opened her bag, took out a set of keys, and started to walk towards the door of the disused barn.

'As a matter of fact, I do have a place in mind,' she said over her shoulder.

As closing time approached, the only customers still left in the New Inn were Cedric Rathbone and his mates Brian O'Reilly and Tom Jennings. They'd been celebrating all evening.

'We've found some decent jobs at last, Mrs O'Leary,' Tom told Cathy. 'Mrs Worrell's hirin' us as carmen for her new bakery.'

'And she's very kindly gave us a sub on our first wages so we could wet our whistles,' Brian O'Reilly said. 'Now that's what I call a really thoughtful boss.'

Cathy smiled vaguely at them as she pulled yet another round of drinks. She usually liked to see her customers enjoying themselves, especially when – like those three – they'd been through some hard times. But she could have done without it that particular night! That night, she needed to have a serious word with her daughter, and she couldn't do that until they were alone. As the old clock ticked on the wall and its hands slowly moved round, she couldn't help wishing that Becky had chosen some other day to hand out generous advances.

She glanced anxiously across at Colleen, who was pretending to be busy with the washing-up, though she could have finished what little there was ages ago if she'd put her mind to it. The girl had been avoiding her ever since she came back from her walk with George Taylor. And when Colleen started acting like that, it could only be because she had something to hide.

Paddy looked up at the big clock. The hands were finally where Cathy had willed them to be for hours, and he called 'time'. Cedric and his pals finished their drinks, wished the O'Leary family goodnight, and left.

'Your supper's in the oven,' Cathy told her husband as soon as he had locked the front door. 'Go an' have it now.'

'What?' Paddy replied. 'And leave all the clearin' up to you two? That wouldn't be fair.'

'We can manage,' Cathy said. 'Go an' eat your pie before it dries up.'

'It won't take us long to get the place straight if we all muck in,' Paddy said. 'Me pie can wait for a few minutes.'

Cathy sighed heavily. God, but couldn't men be stupid sometimes!

'You remember a couple of weeks ago, when you told Colleen to leave the clearin' up to us and go to bed?' she asked.

'Yes?' Paddy said, obviously still in the dark.

'Well, I want you to go and have your pie – for exactly the same reason!' Cathy said, as pointedly as she could.

'Oh!' Paddy said, finally getting the message. 'I'll go an' have me supper, then.'

Once her father had gone, Colleen moved as far away from her mother as was possible within the confines of the bar.

'I'll finish the bottlin' up, Mam,' she said, and then she sniffed as though she had a cold.

'Forget the bottlin' up,' Cathy said firmly. 'Sit down at that table, and tell me all about it.'

Colleen meekly did as she'd been told, and her mother sat down opposite her.

'Is it George?' Cathy asked softly, although what else could it be?

'Yes, it's him,' Colleen replied, so quietly that her mother could barely hear her.

Cathy reached across the table and began to stroke her daughter's shoulder.

'Is it something he's said?' she probed.

'No . . . ' Colleen said, as the tears which she had been holding in all day finally began to roll down her cheeks. 'I mean . . . yes . . . sort of. He told me he's going abroad. For seven years!'

'You poor little mite,' Cathy said, almost crying herself now.

'He was just playing with me,' Colleen sobbed.

Cathy's eyes suddenly hardened, and the hand which had been caressing her daughter's shoulder tightened its grip.

'Playin' with you?' she said. 'He's not been . . . you haven't let him take advantage of you, have you?'

Colleen shook her head. 'Nothing like that,' she said. 'He's always been the perfect gentleman. But he let me think he liked me – an' all the time, he didn't really care at all.'

Cathy ran her fingers through her daughter's hair. The poor girl was going through hell, she thought, and there was very little she could do about it. All she could hope was that the confidence which George Taylor had awakened in Colleen would not desert her now he was going away.

'There'll be other boys,' she said consolingly. 'Loads of them.'

'I don't want loads of other boys,' Colleen moaned. 'It's only George I want. I love him, Mam.'

'I know you do, my little darlin',' Cathy said helplessly. 'I know you do.'

It was at breakfast that Hortense Sodbury Worrell chose to make her momentous announcement to her husband.

'I'm pregnant again,' she said flatly.

Richard almost choked on the kidney he was eating.

'But you can't be!' he protested. 'We've only been together once.'

'Well, that was obviously enough, wasn't it?' Hortense replied.

When had it been? Richard asked himself. The 4th of April. Two weeks ago now. And the second time he'd tried to approach her, she'd turned him down flat.

'Are you sure?' he asked.

'I'm sure,' Hortense said.

'But how can you be?' Richard demanded.

Hortense looked at him with loathing, as if he were no more than dirt under her feet.

'A gentleman – a true gentleman – would never ask such an indelicate question,' she said witheringly.

'I'm sorry,' Richard said, hating his wife more than ever.

'I should have thought you'd have been pleased,' Hortense continued. 'Didn't you marry me in order to have children – children with a little decent blood flowing through their veins?'

Yes, that was exactly what he'd done. And in a way, he *was* pleased. Yet he couldn't help but feel uneasy about his wife's behaviour of late. Suddenly, without any explanation, she'd become a temptress. And then just as suddenly, after they had only made love once, she had reverted to the cold bitch he'd married.

A cloud of suspicion floated briefly across his mind, but he quickly brushed it away. He was going to be a father again, he told himself, and he'd achieved it with so very little unpleasant effort.

George's final morning at home had arrived, and Mary made him a special breakfast of three fried eggs and slices of a delicious ham she had gone all the way to Dodge's farm to buy.

'You'll not get grub like that in the army,' Ted said as he watched his son wolf the food down.

'You're tellin' me,' George agreed.

'And you reckon you'll be away for seven years,' Ted said reflectively.

'About that,' George replied.

'It's a long time to be gone,' Ted said. 'And me and your

61

mam aren't gettin' any younger.'

'What are you talkin' about?' George said. 'You're both as fit as fiddles, an' you'll live to be a hundred.'

'Maybe you're right,' Ted agreed. 'I'm too bloody awkward to die. But do you really have to go?'

'Course I do,' George said. 'I have signed up for another tour, you know. And besides . . . '

'Besides what?' his father asked.

'I've got responsibilities,' George said as he mopped up his yolk with a slice of fried bread.

'Responsibilities?' Ted repeated. 'A single lad like you? What kind of responsibilities can you possibly have?'

'To the men in my troop,' George said. 'You see, Dad, there's good sergeants and there's bad sergeants, and I couldn't bear the thought of my lads servin' under a bad sergeant.'

A twinkle came to Ted's eye, as it always did when he was about to tease his middle son.

'So you're a good sergeant, are you?' he asked.

'Yes,' George said, missing the point of his father's humour as usual.

'It's a wonder they haven't given you a medal, then,' Ted said, teasing him further.

George looked down at his plate. 'They have,' he said. 'I've got two of 'em, as a matter of fact.'

Ted's mouth fell open in astonishment. 'You've never told me about that before,' he said.

'You've never asked me about it before,' George told him.

Ted shook his head with wonder. 'You're a rum bugger, you are George,' he told his son. 'But I'm right proud of you.'

It was George's turn to be astonished.

'You've never told me *that* before, either,' he said.

Ted shrugged awkwardly. 'Aye, well, I didn't want you gettin' big-headed,' he said.

Becky came round after breakfast to say goodbye to her brother.

'Would you do me a favour?' George asked her. 'Would you walk to the station with me?'

'If you like,' Becky said, and then – remembering what she had heard about George and Colleen – she added, 'Is there any particular reason you want me along?'

George looked uncomfortable.

'Not really,' he admitted. 'I'd just feel happier if I had a pretty girl with me, even if she is me own sister.'

Becky laughed. 'And to think that the first time you took me to school, you made me walk in front of you,' she said.

'We've all grown up a lot since then,' George replied.

And Becky thought she saw a hint of sadness flicker across his face.

The last time George had gone to join his regiment, the whole village had turned out to wish him well. But that had been a Sunday, not a working day, and this time there was only Not-Stopping Bracegirdle to see him off. Or maybe not. Though she could not swear to it, Becky was *almost* sure she saw the curtains twitch in one of the upstairs windows of the New Inn.

She and her brother walked in silence along the road to Northwich. George seemed twitchy and nervous – so different to his normal placid self – and once or twice Becky caught him glancing back over his shoulder.

George's nerves were no better once they reached the station – if anything, they appeared to be getting worse. Though he was doing his best to appear normal, he could hardly keep still, and his eyes were constantly scanning the rest of the platform.

The train arrived. George climbed aboard and quickly lowered the carriage window.

'You take care of yourself when you're abroad, or you'll have me to answer to,' Becky said with mock severity.

'All right,' George said abstractly, glancing first at the ticket barrier and then at the goods office.

'Is something wrong?' Becky asked.

'I thought Colleen O'Leary might have come to see me off,' George said miserably.

'Did you really?' Becky said, the severity real now, because although George was her brother, Colleen was still her best friend. 'Well, the way you've treated her, I'm not the least surprised she hasn't.'

'The way I treated her?' George said, looking genuinely puzzled. 'How do you mean?'

'You spent so much time with her, you led her to believe you were interested in her,' Becky said.

'I was interested in her,' George protested. 'I like her a lot.'

Further down the platform, the porters had finished loading the goods van, and the station master had already emerged from his office, a flag held firmly in his hand.

'Did you tell her you liked her?' Becky asked.

'Of course not!' George said scornfully.

Becky stamped her foot in impatience.

'Well, why on earth not?' she demanded.

'A gentleman doesn't do that sort of thing,' George explained. 'A gentleman is courteous at all times and makes polite enquiries about the weather, the lady's family and subjects of that nature.'

'Where did you ever get that rubbish from?' Becky asked.

'From Burma,' George said. 'That's the way the officers out there treat the ladies who visit the mess.'

'Well, it's not the way we do things around here, is it?' Becky asked exasperatedly.

'Isn't it?' George asked. 'I wouldn't know. I've never had a girl. I was a boy soldier, remember.'

'Think about it, George,' Becky said. 'When Dad was courting Mam, do you imagine for one minute that all he talked about was "the weather, Mam's family and subjects of that nature".'

A sudden look of realization came to George's face.

'It's not the same at all, is it?' he asked. 'The workin' class go about their business different to how officers do.'

'Yes, George,' Becky said with a heavy sigh. 'We go about it completely differently.'

The station master waved his flag and the train, which had already built up a head of steam, began to chug slowly forward.

'How does Colleen feel about me?' George called out urgently. 'Do you think she likes me?'

'Likes you?' Becky shouted back. 'She's head over heels in love with you, you bloody fool!'

Becky had just a second to see the shock on her brother's face before the train was gone – and with it any hope of seeing George again for years.

Chapter Five

Spring slipped gently into summer. It was once again the time of year when courting couples took evening strolls along the river, just as generations of young lovers had done before them. This year, however, the atmosphere along the river bank was very different to that of all the years which had preceded it. Instead of the usual drowsy peacefulness which seemed to cling to the river like a mild evening mist, the air felt as heavy as a winter fog. And should the couples choose to wave at passing salt barges, they would be greeted with a scowl rather than the friendly smile they would have received in the past. The flatmen who worked the barges had no time for young love in 1892. They were very angry, they were very desperate – and they were talking of starting what everyone knew would be a long and bitter strike.

'I can't see what they're complainin' about,' Ted Taylor grumbled at Jack across the tea table one night in early July.

'They're complainin' about the hours they're forced to work, Dad,' his eldest son told him.

'I know it's hard graft workin' on the river,' Ted conceded, 'but most jobs have their share of graft. Nobody's goin' to pay you for doing nowt, you know.'

Jack's black, gypsy eyes flashed with anger. 'It's more than a bit of hard graft they're havin' to put up with,' Jack said. 'The bosses are insistin' that all watermen stay on their boat from twelve o'clock Sunday night until twelve o'clock the following Saturday. Do you know how many hours that is?'

'They're not workin' all that time, are they?' his father asked, his own belligerence rising to match his son's.

'You've no idea what life's like on the river, Dad,' Jack said scornfully. 'No idea at all.'

'Well, explain it to me, then I will have an idea,' Ted said.

'Let it drop, love,' Mary pleaded, feeling the conversation was getting out of hand.

'No,' Ted replied. 'I won't let it drop. If our Jack feels I'm bein' such an ignorant bugger, then the least he can do is put me right on a few things. Well, Jack?'

Jack sighed heavily. 'There's so much to do on a barge, there's hardly ever any time to rest,' he said. 'Oh, they may grab the odd hour of shut-eye now and again, but that's about it. It's affectin' their health, Dad. Honestly it is. The poor buggers are droppin' like flies.'

Ted shook his head in disbelief. 'Well, I might be bein' thick, but I just can't see it,' he said.

'You don't have to take my word for it,' Jack said passionately. 'Or even the word of any of the lads who work the river. Just listen to what the salt heavers in Birkenhead have to say. They're on the point of refusing to work with the flatmen – an' do you know why?'

'No,' Ted said. 'But I bet you're about to tell me.'

'Because the flatmen are so exhausted, they can't pull their weight,' Jack said. 'One of the salt heavers was quoted in the paper as sayin' he'd rather work with drunks than men who can't keep their eyes open.'

'Well, it still seems a bit far-fetched to me,' Ted said.

'You would have understood when you were workin' down the mine, Dad,' his son told him. 'But now you're a self-employed man, you've got no sympathy with the workers any more.'

'And what about you?' his father demanded hotly. 'Did you run that steamer on the Oil Rivers all by yourself?'

'You know I didn't,' Jack replied.

'No, you had men workin' for you. And once you and Michael are set up, you'll be takin' on more. You talk about me bein' self-employed as if it was some kind of crime. Well, if it is, you're guilty of an even bigger one, because you're not just self-employed, you're a gaffer – one of the bosses!'

'But I was a flatman once,' Jack said, 'and there'll always

be a bit of me which is still a flatman.'

Mary rattled her teaspoon in her saucer, a clear sign to anybody who knew her that she wasn't about to take much more on this particular subject. And Ted, who felt he had scored a point over his son, was quite prepared to let the matter drop, too. Yet something about the way Jack had been talking had disturbed him more than he cared to admit.

He examined his son closely, perhaps for the first time in years. Jack looked little different at thirty from the way he had at twenty. His curly hair was still as black as coal, his dark eyes still as untamed as a wild animal's. But the old Jack – the Jack who had thrown up a good steady job on a sheep farm to go prospecting for silver, and then, even more crazily, had sailed deep into Africa in search of palm oil – would never have talked like this new Jack. When was it, Ted wondered, that Madcap Jack had started to get so serious? And wasn't there a fair chance, with the strike looming, that this seriousness would lead him into even more danger than his old free spirit had?

'I've got one more thing to say on the subject, and then I'll shut up,' Ted said.

'All right,' Mary agreed, nodding her head to indicate that it had better be only *one* thing.

'There might be real trouble once this strike starts,' Ted told his son. 'And if there is, I don't want you getting involved in it.'

'If there's any trouble, it's best left up to them as know how to handle it,' Jack said enigmatically.

Becky threw herself into her new business with an energy which surprised even Michael. There was so much to do! The building she had leased might have been fine as it stood so long as it served as a barn, but to turn it into a bakery was an almost herculean task.

'I want at least a third of the slates taken off the roof and replaced by glass skylights,' she told Cedric Rathbone.

'It'll cost,' her foreman warned her.

'Of course it'll cost,' Becky agreed. 'But I can't have my bakers working in the dark. We'll need large windows knocking in the walls, too. Light! Lots of light!'

'I'll see to it,' Cedric promised, accepting the fact he had about as much chance of changing Mrs Worrell's mind as he'd have had of changing her husband's.

'And I want the inside thoroughly scrubbed out and then plastered,' Becky continued.

'It doesn't strictly need plasterin' as long as it's been properly cleaned,' Cedric said.

'I know it doesn't *strictly* need it,' Becky admitted. 'But it'll look better for plastering.'

'Who cares what it looks like?' Cedric asked.

'The workers will,' Becky told him. 'Make the place pleasanter for them, and they'll work better. It's good business sense.'

Cedric tried to hide his smile – and failed.

'You're startin' to remind me of somebody else, Mrs Worrell,' he said. 'Only I can't quite remember who.'

Becky grinned sheepishly.

'Anyway,' she continued, 'it'll have to look nice if we're going to impress the guided tours.'

'What guided tours?' Cedric asked.

'The schoolkids I'll be inviting to have a look round,' Becky said. 'It'll be a lot more interesting for them to see a bakery at work than learning about it at school.'

'They'll get in the way,' Cedric grumbled.

'Of course they will,' Becky agreed, 'especially when they're eating their high tea.'

'High tea!' Cedric echoed incredulously. 'You'll be givin' all these schoolkids high tea!'

'That's right,' Becky said.

Cedric smiled. 'Oh, I get it,' he said. 'You'll be chargin' 'em through the nose for the bread an' cakes – an' there won't even be any transport costs.'

'The teas will be free,' Becky said. 'Compliments of the management.'

Cedric scratched his head. 'It's a rum way to run a business, givin' your stuff away,' he said. 'It doesn't make much sense to me.'

'It makes a lot of sense,' Becky told him. 'When they've had their tour and their free tea, they'll go back home. And once they are at home, whose bread and cakes do you think they'll nag their mams into buying?'

'By, but you're a crafty bugger!' Cedric said. He realized he'd made a mistake as soon as the words were out of his mouth. 'I'm sorry, Mrs Worrell,' he continued. 'I don't know what came over me.'

Becky laughed. 'It's all right, Cedric,' she told him. 'When you're trying to get a business off the ground like I am, being called a crafty bugger is very reassuring.'

Colleen O'Leary sat at her dressing-table, her mind going over and over the conversation she'd had with Becky the day George had left for Aldershot.

'He might not be able to show it, but he really cares about you,' Becky had said.

'Are you sure?' Colleen had asked doubtfully. 'After the way he talked to me on Burns' Bridge just before he left, I thought he didn't want anythin' more to do with me.'

'You should have seen the expression on his face as that train pulled out,' Becky said. 'He looked positively devastated when he realized the chance he'd missed.'

'And now it's too late,' Colleen said miserably.

'It's not too late,' Becky told her. 'Not if you really are as serious about him as you say you are.'

'But he's goin' to Egypt . . . '

'And he'll be coming back again eventually. So if he's important enough to you . . . '

'Oh, he is. He is.'

'If he's important enough to you, you'll wait. God knows, I'd wait for ever for Michael.'

'And I'd do the same for George,' Colleen protested.

'Then write and tell him,' Becky urged her. 'Write and tell

him before it's too late.'

And Colleen had resolved to do just that. Yet days had passed by, and then weeks, and still the letter hadn't been written. It would have been much easier, Colleen thought, if she could just have said it to him, if she could have stood on Burns' Bridge, looked into his eyes, and said, 'I love you, George. You're the only man for me, and if I can't have you, I don't want anybody.'

Yes, that would have been easier. Not easy – she'd have had to screw her courage up – but not half so intimidating as the blank piece of paper which lay in front of her now.

'Come on, Collie,' she ordered herself. 'Show 'em what you're made of.'

She licked her pencil and formed a capital 'D' on the paper.

Whatever Mary might have wished, it was impossible to have her husband, her son Jack and her son-in-law Michael sitting round the same tea table without the subject of the flatmen's strike coming up.

'It's not much more than a battle of words at the moment,' Michael said. 'The flatmen have asked all the workers in allied trades to do nothing which will break the strike.'

'And the owners have said they're "gradually fillin' the places of the men on strike",' Jack said. 'Well, we all know what that means, don't we? They're goin' to start employin' bloody blacklegs.'

'And what else do you expect them to do?' his father asked him. 'The salt's still being made, isn't it? They're not just goin' to let it just sit there, are they?'

'You're a traitor to your class!' Jack muttered.

'What was that?' his father demanded. 'What did you just call me?'

'What do you think, Michael?' Mary asked hastily.

'I think the owners should give them what they want,' Michael told his mother-in-law.

'And you call yourself a businessman,' Ted snorted in

disgust.

'It's precisely for that reason that I say the owners should give in,' Michael said. 'You don't get the best out of your men by working them until they drop. Why, half the time, the flatmen must be so tired that the owners are paying them for doing nothing.'

'In other words,' Becky said with a smile on her lips, 'cutting their hours is good business sense.'

'Exactly!' Michael agreed, smiling back.

There was a loud, urgent knocking on the back door, and when Mary went to answer it, she found Cedric Rathbone standing there.

'Is it our Becky you want, Mr Rathbone?' she asked.

'No,' Rathbone replied. 'It's your Jack I've come to see.'

Conscious that the eyes of all the family were on him, Jack got up and walked to the door.

'Has it started?' he asked.

'It has that,' Rathbone told him. 'The first boat of scabs should be sailing under Northwich Bridge within the hour.'

Jack reached for his coat.

'Don't go getting involved in things that don't concern you,' Ted cautioned his son.

'It does concern me, Dad,' Jack said, slipping his arm through the sleeve of his jacket. 'I've told you before that however well off I get, there'll always be a bit of the flatman in me.'

He stepped over the threshold and was gone.

Michael rose to his feet. 'I'll follow him and see he doesn't get into any trouble,' he said.

'No,' Mary said. 'That'll only make matters worse.'

Michael looked at her quizzically. 'What do you mean, I'll only make matters worse?' he asked.

'I'm sorry, Michael,' Mary said, 'but it's true what I'm telling you. We know what you're really like, but to most of the people in town you're just another one of the bosses.'

'I'll go,' Becky said.

'Don't talk soft,' her father told her.

'She's not talking soft,' Mary said. 'If anybody can keep one of them sons of ours in line, it's their little sister.'

'Aye,' Ted said. 'Aye, you might have a point at that.'

By the time Becky, Jack and Cedric Rathbone reached the river bank, a large crowd of men, women and children had already gathered and the air was buzzing with anger.

'The coppers are here, as well,' Becky said, pointing to four blue-uniformed men who were standing some distance from the throng.

'A few bobbies will never be able to control this lot,' Jack said. 'Besides, I'm not so sure they even want to. They're as much on the flatmen's side as we are.'

A loud murmuring, which soon swelled into a roar, announced the approach of the blackleg boats – a steamer and a towing barge which was called the *Antelope*.

'What the hell's an antelope when it's at home?' Cedric asked.

'They're African deer,' Jack told him. 'They can run very fast.'

'Well, it's a bloody daft name for a barge,' Cedric said. 'That bugger's got no chance of outrunning us.'

As the boats drew level with them, some of the people in the crowd began to call out to the crew.

'Blacklegs!'

'Why don't you go back to Liverpool, where you belong?'

'You're taking the bread out of the mouths of honest workin' men! That's what you're doin'!'

The scab crew on the steamer made no effort to shout back. Instead, they tried to pretend that nothing out of the ordinary was happening. But it was a poor effort at best. It was plain to everyone from their pale faces – and the fact they refused to look at the bank – that they were very worried men.

'It wouldn't take a lot to send 'em into a real beauty of a panic,' Cedric said to Jack.

'I think you're right,' Jack agreed.

Cedric bent down and picked up a large stone. 'Are you any good at throwin' straight?' he asked.

Jack grinned. 'I used to be a wizard at bowlin',' he said, bending down and picking up a stone of his own.

Becky stood in front of the two men with her arms outspread. 'I'm not going to let you do this,' she said. 'You'll get yourselves into trouble and I'm not having you hurting those men on the boat, even if they are scabs.'

'We don't want to hurt 'em, Mrs Worrell,' Cedric told her. 'We just want to put the wind up 'em. And as for us gettin' into trouble, just take a look at them coppers.'

Becky did. The sergeant was examining his shirt cuffs and the three constables seemed to have found something very interesting to look at on the ground.

'Told you they wouldn't interfere,' Jack said. 'They've still got to live in the town after this is all over.'

Becky dropped her arms. 'All right,' she said, 'put the wind up them if you can. But I'm warning you both, if any of them gets hurt . . .'

'Don't worry, they won't,' Cedric assured her. He ran his eyes over the tug. 'There's none of 'em standin' near the funnel,' he said to Jack. 'Let's see if we can hit that.'

The two men threw simultaneously and both stones hit the funnel with a loud clang. A couple of the scabs standing on the deck jumped like frightened rabbits.

'Your shot wasn't bad, but mine was better,' Cedric said.

'Are you blind or somethin'?' Jack asked without rancour. 'Mine was dead centre. Yours fell to the left.'

'You're like a couple of big kids,' Becky told them.

Other people in the crowd decided that this was a good game, and soon the funnel of the steamer was being pelted by a hail of stones and bricks, as if it were the centre of a coconut shy.

'Let's see how much longer they can stand that,' Cedric said.

The boats moved on up the river and the crowd followed them, jeering and throwing the occasional missile. After about half a mile, the engineer on the steamer steered his craft into the side.

'Right!' he shouted to the people standing on the river bank. 'I've had enough.'

To loud cheers from the crowd, he leapt over the side of the boat and landed in a heap almost at Becky's feet.

Cedric Rathbone stepped forward.

'No trouble, Cedric,' warned Becky, who was all too well aware of the little man's reputation as a fighter.

'There'll be no trouble,' Cedric promised her. 'I never kick a man when he's down, Mrs Worrell.'

And then, with all the grace of a natural-born gentleman, he held out a hand to assist the engineer to his feet.

'T'anks, wack,' the engineer said, though the look in his eyes showed he was obviously more than a little concerned about what was going to happen to him next.

'Think nothin' of it,' Cedric replied easily. 'You're a stranger round here, aren't you?'

'Dat's right,' the man said, now puzzled as well as fearful.

'Then let me show you where the railway station is,' Cedric said. 'I imagine you'll want to be gettin' back home.'

Three days before George's company was due to set sail for Egypt, he received the letter. It was given to him by a cocky new postal clerk, who, before handing it over, made a great show of sniffing it under his nose.

'Smells like it's from a lady friend to me, Sarge,' he said.

George frowned. Some sergeants might encourage such familiarity, but not him. Familiarity sometimes led to taking the mickey, and as his dad had demonstrated to him often enough when he was growing up, George was a bit slow to spot when someone else was having fun at his expense. And having fun poked at him was something George couldn't afford. His word had to be law, his orders had to be obeyed without question, because more than once in Burma, his word – his orders – had been the only things which had saved his men from certain death.

'I said, it smells like it's from a lady friend,' the clerk repeated, unaware of what was going on in George's mind.

'You're new, aren't you?' George said, giving the man one of those hard stares which had been known to have enlisted men – and sometimes even officers – quaking in their boots.

'Y . . . yes, Sarge,' the clerk stuttered, finally getting the message.

'Yes, Sergeant Taylor,' George corrected him.

'Yes, Sergeant Taylor,' the clerk said meekly.

'Ask some of your mates about me,' George told him. 'They'll soon put you right.'

Taking the letter from the clerk's shaking hand, he turned smartly on his heel and marched away.

He crossed the parade ground. A platoon of new recruits were being put through their paces by a corporal. George stood and watched them for a few seconds, made a mental note of some faults which he would point out to the corporal later, then walked on. Not until he had reached the other edge of the square did he so much as glance at the envelope he was holding.

The handwriting – precise copperplate – reminded him of his own, and he did not need to look at the postmark to know the letter was from Marston and the writer was another graduate of Mr Hicks's knuckle-wrapping joined-up writing lessons in the National School over the bridge. It wasn't a man's handwriting though, and neither did it belong to one of his sisters. He wondered who had sent it.

An ordinary trooper might have opened the letter then and there, but George did not allow himself the eagerness or impatience of a man in the ranks, and it was not until he was comfortably seated in the sergeants' mess that he slit the envelope with his thumbnail and extracted the single piece of paper which nestled inside.

He glanced down at the signature first – Colleen.

Colleen!

Though his heart was instantly beating faster and his hands were beginning to tremble, he forced himself to read the letter in the slow, deliberate way he would have read new orders.

Dear George,

This isn't an easy letter for me to write. I thought you were very stiff and formel (is that the way you spell it?) when you were here on leave, but Becky said thats just the way people behave in the army and that really you did like me a lot more than you could show. I hope thats really true because you see I like you a lot too.

She wrote as she would say it, George thought affectionately – in one long, breathless gasp. He could picture her, standing behind the bar and licking the point of her pencil as she searched for the right words.

Ive got this far five or six times, then Ive tried to write next bit and Ive crossed it out and in the end Ive got so annoyed with myself that Ive screwed up the letter and thrown it away. There probably is a clever way to say what I want to say but I dont know what it is so here goes. If you want me to wait for you youve only got to tell me. There Ive said it. I hope you dont think Im too forward.

> Your affectionate
> Colleen

If only he'd known before, George thought. If only there'd been some clue that he might fall in love *before* he'd signed on for another seven years, things might have been different. But he hadn't known and now it was too late.

Yet was it too late? he wondered. She'd said she'd wait for him. All he had to do was ask.

'Penny for your thoughts, young George,' said a friendly voice.

George looked up and saw a grey-haired man – Bill Gittings, the senior sergeant – looking down at him and grinning.

'I'm just thinkin' about this letter, Bill,' George said.

'From your lass, is it?' Gittings asked.

'Yes. Well, in a way,' George said awkwardly. 'She is a girl, but she's not really mine, if you see what I mean.'

Gittings laughed as though he understood *exactly* what George meant.

'Playing the field, are you?' he said. 'That's the way to do it. Have your fun while you're young.'

He turned and walked away, leaving George to grapple with his problem alone.

I wish I could have told him all about it, George thought. I wish I could have asked him for his advice.

But that would have been impossible because when you were the youngest sergeant the regiment had ever had, you could never allow yourself to seem green or foolish. When you were the youngest sergeant the regiment had ever had, there was never a waking moment when you didn't feel obliged to prove yourself as mature as the rest of them.

Colleen says she'll wait for me, he told himself again. For seven whole years!

But anything could happen in those seven years. There was already talk of an expedition to retake the Sudan; how would Colleen feel if the only reward for her patience was to learn he'd been killed in action? And even if an enemy bullet didn't get him, there were plenty of nasty diseases which might finish him off long before his time was up.

George went over to the writing table and picked up a piece of paper.

My Dearest Colleen, he wrote, It was kind of you to tell me that you care for me and I want you to know that I care for you . . .

That'll never do, he thought.

It was bad enough for her that he was rejecting her – to tell her that he loved her would only make matters worse. He drew a neat line through the letter and reached for a fresh sheet of paper.

It took him over an hour to complete the letter, and when he had done so, he spent several more minutes just staring at it.

Did it say what he wanted to say? he asked himself. Of course it didn't! Well, then, did it say what he *had* to say? Yes, in that, at least, he had achieved his aim.

While he still had the resolution, he folded the letter, inserted it into an envelope and marched across to the post office.

One failure was not enough to make the salt owners give in to their flatmen's demands. Three days after the first rout, a new blackleg steamer passed under Northwich Bridge, this time with four policemen aboard. But policemen or not, the bricks and stones still flew, and when the bobbies got off the boat at Winnington Bridge – that being the limit of their jurisdiction – the blacklegs deemed it best to take cover below deck. With no one to control it, the steamer soon ran aground, and the crowd went home with its ears ringing with cheers of victory.

Similar scenes were taking place just down the river, in Winsford. There, the Saltmakers' Committee – as they called the trade union – advised its members that though they should not refuse to start loading craft, they should work so slowly as to make sure that the job was never completed. In frustration, the owners brought in two hundred loaders from Liverpool, but the mob which met them was so large and so angry that, as the *Northwich Guardian* said, 'they fled back to the railway station, leaving their bedding behind them.'

Richard Worrell glanced briefly at each of the men who were sitting around the table in his study at Peak House. There was Harold Clegg who owned a salt works in Wincham, and next to him was Baxter Holland, who had a mine near Witton Flash. A dozen men in total, all of them owners and all of them extremely worried.

'We can't let these working-class scum blackmail us any longer,' Richard said by way of an opening remark.

'I don't see how we can stop them,' Baxter Holland said

gloomily.' There's only twenty policemen in the whole of Northwich, and these mobs number hundreds.'

'Of course the police can't handle the situation,' Richard said. 'That's why we'll have to call in somebody else who can.'

'You're talking about bringing in the army, aren't you?' said Arthur Blaine, who owned one of the pits near Witton Flash.

'Exactly!' Richard agreed.

Several of the men sitting around the table shook their heads unenthusiastically.

'It's always a risky business using the army,' Harold Clegg said. 'Put men with guns into a situation like this, and there's a good chance somebody'll get hurt.'

'Precisely,' Richard said. 'That's just what I'm hoping for.'

'I'm not sure I'm following you,' Clegg told him.

'It'll only take one striker getting himself killed to have the rest of them running back to whoever they work for with their tails between their legs,' Richard said.

'I don't know. It seems a bit of an extreme measure to me,' Clegg said doubtfully.

'Extreme!' Richard retorted. 'I'll tell you what's extreme. It's extreme to have salt piling up because there's no one to shift it. It's extreme to be losing orders because I can't make a delivery on time. I can't afford it – and neither can any of you.'

At least half the men seated around the table nodded their heads in agreement.

'I think we should put it to the vote,' Harold Clegg said.

'That's fine with me,' said Richard, who could tell by the way most of the owners were looking at him that he'd carry the day.

Breakfast was normally a quiet affair in the Taylor household, but it was far from tranquil the next morning when Ted Taylor opened his morning paper and read what was there.

'The buggers have gone and called in the troops!' he said, angrily screwing up the offending paper in his fists.

'Did you ever expect them to do anythin' else?' Jack asked. 'Anyway, why shouldn't they? As you said yourself, they can't have the salt just sitting there, can they?'

Ted glared at his son.

'Don't get cheeky,' he warned Jack, 'because as big as you are and as old as you are, I'll still give you a leatherin' if I have to.'

But Jack – being Jack – only grinned.

'You shouldn't play your dad up,' Mary said.

Ted smoothed out the crumpled newspaper and continued to read the article from the point at which he'd lost his temper.

'Well, there's one good thing,' he said.

'What's that, love?' Mary asked.

'At least it wasn't our George's regiment they called in,' Ted told her. 'I wouldn't have liked it above half to know that he was bein' forced to keep down his own folk.'

'His own folk, Dad?' Jack asked, the smile still on his lips. 'But George is the son of a fried fish merchant.'

'You go too far sometimes, Jack,' Mary told her son.

'He bloody does!' Ted agreed angrily. 'And I'll tell you somethin' else, our Jack – '

But whatever he was about to say was interrupted by a knock on the back door.

'I'll get it, Dad,' Jack said, wondering if perhaps his mother was right, and he hadn't gone a *bit* too far this time.

He opened the door to find Ha-Ha Harry Atherton, his father's old friend from his mining days, standing there.

'Will you come in, Mr Atherton?' he asked.

'No, I w . . . won't disturb you,' Ha-Ha said, displaying the stutter which had earned him his nickname. 'I j . . . just came to pick your dad up.' He looked beyond Jack to where Ted was sitting. 'G . . . grab your trumpet, T . . . Ted. We've g . . . got to be off.'

'Is the Adelaide Band giving a performance today?' Jack asked.

'Well, n . . . not what you could really call a proper performance,' Ha-Ha told him.

'If it's not a proper performance, what exactly is it?' Jack asked, though he already had a pretty good idea.

'We're goin' to play for the strikin' f . . . flatmen,' Harry replied. 'Just to keep their spirits up, like.'

'And against his better judgement, me dad's agreed to play with you, has he?' Jack asked.

'A . . . agreed to it?' Ha-Ha said. 'Why he was the one who – '

'I am their lead trumpeter, you know!' Ted called from the table. 'I couldn't let them down, could I?'

He spoke quickly, as if he were trying to stop the conversation then and there, but Jack was not going to let him get away with that – not when he was having so much fun.

'He was the one who what, Mr Atherton?' he asked.

'Suggested that we played for the strikers in the f . . . first place,' Harry said.

Jack turned round to face his father. Ted was looking distinctly uncomfortable.

'I might have mentioned it in passing,' Ted confessed. 'And you can wipe that smug look off your face right now, my lad. You might have talked me round to your way of thinkin' this time, but most of what you say is bloody rubbish.'

'You're probably right, Dad,' Jack conceded gracefully. 'You're probably right.'

Chapter Six

The conversion from filthy barn to gleaming bakery was completed in record time thanks to the efforts of Cedric Rathbone who, when he was not throwing stones at blackleg barges, spent his time harrying the builders and even pitching in himself. The bakery workers had been engaged, too. The head baker, a Frenchman called Monsieur Henri, had been recruited through an advertisement in the Manchester papers.

He was a comical-looking little man with a roly-poly body, a bald head and a huge waxed moustache. At first, Becky had found it hard to take him seriously. And then she noticed his hands which, though they seemed strong, were also slim and elegant, the hands of an artist.

'I 'ave work everywhere,' he told Becky at his interview. 'Many of the finest 'otels in the 'ole of Europe 'ave been proud to 'ave me as their principal pastry chef.'

'But can you bake bread the way the English will like it?' Becky asked. 'You see, the people round here aren't really very open to fancy new ideas from the Continent.'

'I can make you the sweet cakes of Persia so perfect zat even a native 'imself would swear zey 'ad been made in the ovens of Yazd,' Monsieur Henri said. 'I can produce a Black Forest gateau zat ze big-bellied Germans would sell zeir souls for – '

'I know, but . . .' Becky interrupted.

'And if I can do zis, madame,' the Frenchman pressed on, 'do you zink it is beyond my power to bake ze simple English loaf?'

'I suppose not,' Becky admitted.

'Zen something else is bothering you, per'aps?' Monsieur

Henri said.

'I was just wondering why someone with your experience would want to work in a little bakery like this?' Becky said.

'Ah, zat is because of ze drink,' the Frenchman explained.

'The drink!' Becky said.

'Always I 'ave 'ad this weakness for ze drink,' Monsieur Henri told her. 'After a while in a place, I get very drunk and zen I lose my job. Zat is why I come to England.'

'I beg your pardon?' Becky said.

'As long as I stay away from ze fancy 'otels, it is impossible to find a decent wine in this country,' the Frenchman said. 'And wizout wine, what am I to drink? Your filthy English beer? Of course not! It is a joke! And so, because zair is nothing else to do, I stay sober.'

Becky was finding it hard to contain her laughter.

'All right, Monsieur Henri,' she said, 'you can have the job as long as you don't develop a liking for our beer.'

'You will not regret it,' the Frenchman promised her. 'I will make your bakery famous.'

But the bakery wasn't famous yet, Becky thought as she walked down Witton Street with samples of Monsieur Henri's first batch of bread and cakes in her basket. And making it famous wasn't going to be easy. She wasn't just selling bread, she was selling the *idea* of buying bread which was made in a small factory rather than in the familiar corner bakery. And given the conservatism of some of the local shopkeepers . . .

Her first port of call was Peabody's grocery shop on Leicester Street. It was one of those cramped, old-fashioned stores which still sold loose butter from big barrels and smelt pleasantly of coffee and smoked bacon. Mr Peabody himself was a middle-aged man with wary eyes who had been in the trade all his life.

'The bread tastes very good,' he admitted after he'd cut off a slice and nibbled a corner of it.

'Try one of the cakes,' Becky suggested.

Mr Peabody did, and found that very nice too.

'But I can't see any advantage in buyin' it from you rather than from me usual bakery,' he said.

'Because there'll be a big demand for Worrell's bread and cakes,' Becky said, with more confidence than she actually felt.

'Will there now?' Mr Peabody said, plainly unimpressed. 'And how will you go about creatin' this demand?'

'I'm putting advertisements in all the papers,' Becky told him. 'People will try my cakes out of curiosity, and once they find out how good they are, they'll stick with them.'

'And how will they know they're yours?' Mr Peabody asked. 'What's to stop me selling any old bread I like and tellin' anybody who asks that it's Worrell's?'

Becky held up the loaf and pointed to its side. 'This,' she said.

Baked into the side of the loaf was the name of the bakery.

'Now that is clever,' Mr Peabody admitted. 'However did you manage to do it?'

'I had special moulds made,' Becky said. 'And all my cakes will be on special little paper plates with the name printed on them.'

'And you're absolutely certain this idea will catch on, are you?' Peabody asked doubtfully.

'Absolutely certain,' Becky assured him. 'You'll have people coming in to your shop just for my cakes . . . '

'I'm not really a confectioner . . . '

' . . . though, of course, while they're here they'll notice all the other things you have to offer. So because of the cakes, you'll be selling more of everything else as well. And as for your rivals . . . '

'Rivals? What are me rivals when they're at home?'

'The other shopkeepers – the ones who aren't sharp enough to stock Worrell's cakes – well, it won't be long before they start losing their business to you hand over fist.'

Mr Peabody glanced around his shop, his eyes resting on the pyramid of tinned pineapple, then moving on to the sacks of sugar. He was deciding just where, in this crowded little store, he could fit in the tray of cakes, Becky thought happily.

'I've been in this business for nearly thirty years,' he said when he had finished his inspection, 'and it's always provided me with a pretty good livin' just as it is now. So if it's all the same to you, I think I'll stick with what I know.'

'You'll regret it,' Becky warned him.

'I don't think I will,' Peabody replied. 'An' I'd imagine that most of what you call me "rivals" will feel the same way I do.'

When Becky left Peabody's, she was feeling only a little despondent. After all, what did it matter that one tiny shop, run by an old-fashioned grocer, had turned her down? There were dozens of other stores around Northwich, and most of them were bound to see the advantages of selling Worrell's cakes. But as the day went on, she grew more and more pessimistic, and by the time dusk fell, she felt positively depressed.

'I don't hold out much hope, but I'll take a few cakes just to oblige,' said Mr Harris, who kept a general store on New Street.

'I'll give 'em a week's trial an' see how they go,' promised Mr Breeze, whose place of business was located close to the Bleeding Wolf pub on Market Street.

And that was it! She was exhausted, and yet what did she have to show for efforts – two grocers!

She had a master baker, three assistants, four apprentices and three waggon drivers who all wanted paying – and two grocer's shops were nothing like enough to keep even a quarter of her workforce busy.

Every day Colleen waited anxiously for the postman, and every day he brought nothing but bills or letters from that part of the O'Leary clan who had chosen to remain in Ireland. Then, finally, when it seemed she could stand the waiting no more, a letter did arrive.

'Is this the one you've been waitin' for?' the postman asked cheerily. He glanced at the postmark. 'It's from Aldershot. Got a young man in the army, have you?'

'I . . . I don't know,' Colleen stuttered, taking the letter from him with a shaking hand.

'Don't know if you've got a young man or not?' the postman said. 'Well, that is a rum state of affairs.'

Colleen took the letter up to her room. From the thickness of the envelope, she guessed that there was only a single sheet of paper inside, but that told her nothing. It didn't matter how *much* George had written, it only mattered what he had to say.

'I love you' are only three little words, she thought to herself.

She sat down on her bed. The letter seemed to have grown hot in her hand, yet she was not sure she was brave enough to open it. This was the most important letter she would ever receive in her life, she realized. The message it contained meant the difference between a future full of misery and one brimming over with happiness.

She fumbled with the flap of the envelope. Her fingers, normally so nimble, had suddenly become all thumbs, and it took what felt like hours to extract the letter.

Even now, she considered putting off reading the letter till later. But that was foolish. He *had* to feel for her as she felt for him. After all, hadn't Becky told her about the expression on his face as his train had sped out of Northwich station? Hadn't that single look been enough to convince her best friend that George really did care? Feeling courage and hope surging through her, Colleen held the letter up to the light.

Dear Colleen, she read, *I am afraid that on my last leave, I might have given you the wrong idea.*

The wrong idea? What did he mean? Colleen forced herself to read on.

I am a professional soldier, George continued, *and my duty comes above all other things.*

I don't mind that! she told herself. She could stand him

87

putting the army first, if only he would save a tiny part of himself for her.

Yet the next line crushed even that small hope.

So you see, there is no point in waiting, George concluded. *You have your life and I have mine.*

Yours faithfully, George Taylor

He had his life and she had hers! But what kind of life would she have without George?

Colleen buried her head in her pillow, and cried until she was so exhausted that she fell asleep.

When Becky set out for Mr Breeze's shop, there were definitely butterflies in her stomach. He'd try her cakes for one week, he'd said, and now the trial period was over and she was about to find out just how successful Breeze thought it had been.

As she walked along Market Street, Becky was surprised to see Cedric Rathbone standing outside the Bleeding Wolf, when only an hour earlier she'd sent him off to look for business in the completely opposite direction.

That's not like Cedric, she thought. He was usually so reliable, and though he liked a drink as much as the next man, he normally never touched a drop in the daytime.

He was looking the other way up Market Street, and hadn't seen her. Becky stopped in her tracks and studied him. Just what was he doing there? It didn't look like he intended to go into the pub. Instead, he appeared to be waiting for someone.

Two small, ragged children appeared from up a side street and walked boldly up to him as if they knew him well. Cedric dug into his pocket and produced some coppers, then bent down to talk to the kids. Becky, walking on tiptoe, made her way quietly towards them.

'Now do you remember what you've got to do?' she heard Cedric say as she got closer to him.

The two children nodded.

'We've got to go to Breeze's shop an' ask for a couple of

88

Worrell's cakes,' the bigger of the pair said.

'Worrell's *famous* cakes,' Cedric corrected him.

'Worrell's *famous* cakes,' the urchin agreed.

'Right,' Cedric said, opening his hand. 'Here's the pennies I promised you. Go an' spend 'em. But only on Worrell's cakes, remember!'

The children snatched the money and dashed towards Breeze's as fast as they could.

Becky tapped Cedric lightly on the shoulder. He whirled around as if expecting trouble, and then looked shocked when he saw who was standing there.

'Oh, hello, Mrs Worrell,' he said. 'I didn't expect to see you here.'

'I'll bet you didn't,' Becky replied. 'Now would you mind telling me what that was all about?'

Cedric shrugged uncomfortably. 'Just drummin' up a bit of trade for you,' he said.

Becky was touched. 'That's very kind of you, Cedric,' she said.

'Kindness has got nothin' to do with it,' Rathbone protested. 'You pay my wages, but if you don't sell any cakes, you won't be able to keep doin' it, will you?'

'Let me see if I've got this right,' Becky said, almost laughing now. 'In order to make sure I keep on paying your wages, you're spending most of your wages on buying my cakes. Isn't that just a little bit daft?'

Cedric looked stuck for an answer for a moment, then a smile came to his face.

'It's not daft at all,' he said. 'It's just good business sense.'

Becky entered Mr Breeze's shop just as the two children Cedric had given money to were leaving with cakes in their hands.

'One of the poorest families on the street, them,' Mr Breeze told her, 'yet suddenly they've got money to burn as far as cakes go. Funny thing that, isn't it?'

'Yes,' Becky agreed uneasily. 'Very strange.'

'And it's not only them,' Mr Breeze said. 'Half the nippers in the neighbourhood seem to have found a rich uncle.' He walked over to the door and looked down Market Street. 'Aye, there he is now, standin' outside the Wolf,' he continued. 'Work for you, does he?'

Becky felt herself redden.

'Well, as a matter of fact, he does,' she admitted. 'But I want you to know that I had nothing to do with this.'

'He needn't have wasted his money,' Mr Breeze told her.

'Needn't he?' Becky asked.

'Hasn't your baker told you how much of your stuff I've been shiftin'?' Breeze said.

'No,' Becky answered, because, if truth be told, she'd been too afraid to ask.

'Even without the help of your mate down the road, they've been sellin' like hot cakes.' Mr Breeze beamed. 'Ay up, I think I just made a joke.'

Becky could hardly suppress her relief.

'So you'll be wanting the same order next week, will you?' she said.

'I will not,' Mr Breeze replied. 'I shall want double the order at the very least.'

The soldiers called in by the mine owners managed to guard *some* of the scab labour *some* of the time. But they could not possibly be everywhere at once, and the moment they'd gone an angry mob would move in to make the blacklegs' lives a misery.

Slowly but surely, the strikebreakers began to crack under the pressure, and what started as a trickle of them packing up and going home soon became a flood.

'We don't need de aggravation,' they told anyone who would listen as they queued up by the dozen to catch the first train back to Liverpool.

The dragoons did not have much success with the salt loaders, either. They could force the men to turn up for work – dragging them from their homes if need be – but once they were on the job, it was the loaders who were in control.

'Can't you fill that boat any faster?' the captain in charge of the dragoons would demand.

And the loaders – with wide grins on their faces – would reply, 'We're bein' as quick as we can, General,' and then continue to shovel the salt in at a snail's pace.

By the middle of September, most of the owners were beginning to weaken.

'We're thinking of calling in the Bishop of Chester to arbitrate the dispute,' Harold Clegg told Richard Worrell.

'You can't do that!' Richard protested. 'That's as good as telling the bastards they've won.'

'You said the soldiers would get things moving again,' Clegg pointed out. 'Well, they haven't, so now we're going to try another way.'

If only there'd been one death, Richard thought. That's all it would have taken – one death.

The bishop studied all the papers relating to the strike. The flatmen's union would have to pay the blacklegs five hundred pounds for 'loss of employment', he ruled. On the other hand, all the watermen involved in the dispute should be given back their old jobs with their privileges still intact – but their hours of work greatly reduced.

'It's nothing but a bloody climb-down,' Richard complained bitterly to his wife over breakfast. 'We could have beaten them if we'd just stood firm.'

'Perhaps they had a case,' Hortense suggested with uncharacteristic mildness.

'What was that you said?' Richard asked in astonishment.

'Perhaps they had a case,' Hortense repeated. 'Even working men have rights, you know.'

Richard looked at his wife quizzically.

How long have you cared about the workers' rights? he wondered. How long had she even been aware of the workers' *existence*, except on the rare occasions when a maid was late with her tea or a groom had failed to saddle her horse on time?

This change in her was very strange indeed. Maybe it had something to do with her pregnancy – though she had certainly not acted this way the last time she'd been expecting.

Michael and Becky sat in their back parlour, holding hands and looking out at the garden. They'd both been so busy that they had not even had time to notice the change in the seasons, and only now, on Michael's last day in England, did they really begin to appreciate the fact that the lush summer had slid gracefully into a golden autumn.

'You look tired, Becky,' Michael said.

'I am,' Becky replied.

She was more than just tired – she was exhausted. Since the first day she'd tried to sell her bread and cakes in Northwich, she had covered most of the grocers' shops in mid Cheshire. But now, at last, it was starting to pay off.

'Do you remember that grocer on Leicester Street?' she asked. 'The first one I went to?'

'Peabody, wasn't it?' Michael asked.

'That's right,' Becky agreed. 'Well, he came to see me today. Said his trade had really dropped off since the other shops had started selling my cakes, and practically begged me to let him stock them, too.'

'And did you say yes?' Michael asked.

'Of course I said yes,' Becky told him. 'The more shops selling Worrell's famous products, the happier I'll be.'

But she wasn't *really* happy. How could she be when in a few hours Michael would be sailing away for who knew how long?

She looked around their parlour. It was the smallest in the house, and because of that, her favourite. How cosy it seemed when the two of them were there together – and how big and empty it would be once her husband had gone. And if this room would seem too large without Michael in it, how enormous would the rest of the house feel?

'Will you come with me to Liverpool?' Michael asked.

'If you want me to,' Becky told him.

'But if you had the choice . . . ?'

'I'd rather not,' Becky admitted. 'If I see you off at the door, I can always tell myself you'll be back in time for tea, but there's something so final about watching you disappear on the ocean.'

'There's nothing final about it at all,' Michael protested. 'I'll be back almost before you notice I've gone.'

Vast empty spaces, Becky thought, looking around the room and imagining the ones which lay beyond it. Nothing but vast empty spaces.

And suddenly, she had an idea!

'Michael . . . ?' she said tentatively.

'Yes, my dear?'

'With all the money we're paying out in rent, we could buy a house of our own.'

Michael laughed. 'With so much money sunk into our businesses, we couldn't even think of buying a house like this,' he said.

'I'm not talking about a house like this,' Becky said. 'What I've got in mind is something much more modest.'

A smile played on Michael's lips, as it always did when she was starting to amuse him.

'How much more modest?' he asked.

'There's a house in Marston up for sale,' Becky said quickly.

'In Marston? A two-up, two-down?'

'Do we really need any more at the moment?' Becky asked. 'You'll be away for so much of the time and I'll be busy with the bakery . . .'

'And where will the servants sleep?' Michael asked. 'In the coal-shed? Or perhaps in the wash-house?'

'I don't really need servants, either,' Becky said. 'Of course, I'll help them to get new positions, but the only one I want is Daisy. She can do the housework and look after Michelle when I'm not there.'

Michael stroked his chin thoughtfully.

'Would it make you happy to live in Marston again?' he asked.

'I know it's not what you're used to, what with having been brought up posh and that . . . ' Becky said.

'Would it make you happy?' Michael asked insistently.

'Well . . . yes,' Becky admitted.

She didn't really know *why* it would make her happy. Perhaps the smaller rooms of a little cottage would make Michael's absence less noticeable. Maybe it was because being nearer to her mam would help fill the gap her husband had left. Whatever the reason, she was sure that life alone would be much more bearable if she was back in Ollershaw Lane.

'Then if it's what you want, it's what you must have,' Michael said.

Becky threw her arms around her husband's shoulders and buried her face in his powerful neck.

'You're very good to me,' she said.

'Nonsense,' Michael replied. 'My princess must have her wish, even if that wish is to live like a pauper. Besides, such a move would cut down on our expenses considerably, so really it's just . . . '

'Good business sense?' Becky asked.

'Exactly,' Michael agreed.

And they both burst out laughing.

Two weeks after Michael's departure, Becky moved into her new house, halfway down Ollershaw Lane. The move did not go unnoticed – or uncommented on – by Not-Stopping Bracegirdle.

'Just fancy that,' she told Dottie Curzon as the two women stood at the top of Not-Stopping's alley and watched the carts arriving. 'How are the mighty fallen, eh?'

'Maybe she just wants to be closer to her mam,' Dottie suggested.

'Are you going soft in the head?' Not-Stopping demanded. 'Nobody gives up a palace unless they have to.'

You've got a nasty view of human nature, Elsie Brace-girdle, Dottie Curzon said to herself. And don't think I don't know I'm not the only one you've asked if I'm soft in the head.

She remembered the night when George Taylor had come home on leave, when she'd made a promise to herself that somehow she'd make Not-Stopping feel as uncomfortable as Marston's chief gossip herself had made almost everybody else in the village feel. Well, the chance hadn't come yet, but it would. It would. And when it did, Dottie Curzon intended to grasp it with both hands.

Daisy walked around her mistress's tiny new bedroom, sniffing her disapproval as she went.

'There's not even room to swing a cat in here, madam,' she complained.

'But I don't want to swing a cat,' Becky said mildly.

'An' I bet it's damp in winter,' Daisy continued. 'I bet the damp drips off these walls.'

Becky sighed. 'Sit down, Daisy,' she said.

'Oh, I couldn't, madam!' the maid protested. 'Not with you in the same room.'

'Sit down,' Becky said firmly.

Daisy looked around the room for a chair, but the carmen hadn't brought any up yet, and so she plopped herself down on the bed. Becky sat down beside her and took the maid's hands in hers.

'I know this is a big change for you,' she said.

'A *big* change,' Daisy agreed.

'And I know you'll have to do the sort of menial work here that you never had to do when we had a bigger establishment,' Becky continued. She took a deep breath. 'So if you want to give your notice in . . .'

A look of horror came to Daisy's face.

'Oh, don't say that, madam,' she pleaded.

'I'll be sorry to lose you if you do,' Becky continued, 'but I'll give you an excellent reference and you'll find a new 'situation in no time.'

'But I couldn't leave you and Miss Michelle,' Daisy told her. 'I couldn't. I'd die if I did.'

She was almost in tears.

'Nobody's going to force you to leave,' Becky said gently. 'It's just that if you don't think you can be happy here . . .'

Daisy looked around the room.

'It's not a bad place, madam,' she said. 'Not once you've started gettin' used to it.'

'What about the damp?' Becky asked.

'Oh, a good coal fire'll soon shift that,' Daisy told her.

'I wouldn't say no to a cup of tea,' Becky said.

'I'll ring down for it right away, mad –' Daisy began. Then she stopped and laughed. 'I'll just go down to the kitchen and make you a pot, madam,' she corrected herself.

'That would be nice,' Becky said. 'And while you're at it, you might as well make enough for two.'

Daisy was shocked.

'I couldn't do that, madam,' she said.

'For two,' Becky insisted. 'Life here's going to be very different to the way it was in the other house, and you might as well start getting used to it right now.'

Daisy stood up.

'Yes, madam,' she said.

'And you can stop calling me madam, as well,' Becky said. 'That's far too grand a name to use in a little terraced house in Marston.'

'But madam . . .' Daisy said.

'Call me Becky,' Becky ordered. 'And go and make us that tea. Now!'

'Yes, mad . . . Becky,' Daisy said. 'But it doesn't half feel strange.'

When Daisy had gone downstairs, Becky walked over to the window and looked down on the village. Just along the road, Dottie Curzon and Not-Stopping Bracegirdle were standing gossiping at the top of Not-Stopping's alley. Becky could imagine what Not-Stopping was saying about her coming down in the world – and she didn't care twopence about it. She had never been really at ease with servants, even though Michael had said she handled them very well. And for someone brought up in a family where everyone snuggled round the fire of an evening, it had been hard to take those cavernous rooms in the house they had rented when they got married – even when Michael was there.

Well, now she was back in Marston, the village where she had grown up, the place where she had played with little Colleen and had her future foretold by the gypsy with the strange eyes. Her best friend lived just up the road and her mam was only a few steps further. Everything was familiar and comfortable. Though she could never be really happy while Michael was away, she knew she would be happier here than anywhere else.

She had come home – and she loved it.

PART TWO

1893

Chapter Seven

By February of 1893, Worrell's bakery had become such a feature of mid-Cheshire life that it seemed as if it had always been there. No children's party was complete without a tray of the Famous Cakes, and many a housewife was heard to complain that she'd had to buy 'ordinary' bread because the shops had all run out of Worrell's.

It was in March that the 'accidents' started to happen. Tom Jennings was the first victim. Making a mid-morning delivery to Breeze's store, he found the road blocked by an overturned brewery waggon. He should perhaps have waited until the dray could be righted again, but since he didn't want to fall behind on his other deliveries, he paid a street urchin a penny to watch his waggon for him while he went to see Mr Breeze. When he came out of the shop again, the cart was still there, but the urchin was not – and neither was his horse.

'Did either of you pair see what happened to my horse and the lad who was looking after it?' he shouted across to two young layabouts who were lounging around outside the front door of the Bleeding Wolf.

'Feller came,' one of the young men told him. 'Paid the kid a tanner and took the horse away. Said it wasn't your horse at all. Said it was his, and you'd only borrowed it.'

Tom shook his head in disgust. People could be being murdered in the streets and idlers like these two would do nothing to stop it, he thought.

'Do you know where he was takin' the horse?' he asked.

'Said he was takin' it to that bit of waste land up the railway station,' the loafer replied. 'Said if you wanted to talk to him, that's where you'd find him.'

Tom looked up and down the street. Apart from the people working on the brewery waggon, there was nobody else around for the moment. So, much as he didn't like it, he had no choice but to trust the layabouts.

'Will you watch me cart for a bit?' he asked. 'It'll be worth a bob to you when I get back.'

'We'll watch it, mate,' the second layabout replied. 'You could trust us with your life.'

It was over a mile to the patch of waste ground, but when Tom got there, he found the horse tethered just as the young men had told him. Of the man who had taken the horse, there was no sign – but Tom had never expected there would be. The horse hadn't been stolen, it had simply been removed so that he would fall behind on his rounds.

'It's the first time we've ever been late,' he grumbled to the animal as he led it down Witton Street. 'Nothin's ever stopped us gettin' there on time before, not hail, rain, frost nor snow.'

When he got back to his waggon, he discovered that the layabouts had sold off half his stock at bargain prices and then done a runner.

Brian O'Reilly was the next one to be on the receiving end of the dirty tricks. He was right in the middle of Fleming Street when his cart suddenly started shaking.

What the hell's goin' on? he asked himself.

The shaking grew more violent, and there was the sound of cracking timbers.

'Whoa, lad!' he called urgently to his horse.

The animal obeyed, but no sooner had it done so than Brian felt the front of the waggon collapsing from under him. The force of it threw him forward and the next thing he knew, he was lying in the street, a few inches from his horse's hind legs.

'Are you all right, mate?' a fuzzy voice asked.

'I think so,' Brian said, climbing groggily to his feet.

He looked around him, and was not pleased with what he

saw. The front wheels had completely separated from the waggon and lay in the roadway with half an axle each sticking out from their centres. Cakes and loaves lay scattered over the street, though a number of crafty urchins had already begun to scoop them up.

A couple of workmen were examining the left wheel.

'This were done deliberate,' one of them said.

'What do you mean?' Brian asked, shaking his head to see if it would make the stars go away.

'See that?' the workman said pointing to the axle which was projecting from the wheel, 'that's been partly sawn through, that has.'

The police were informed and a round sergeant with lazy eyes came to visit the bakery.

'It could have been anybody done it, madam,' he said. 'Anybody at all.'

'But it's most likely to have been one of my competitors, isn't it?' Becky asked.

The sergeant laughed indulgently. 'Now, now, madam,' he said, wagging his finger at her, 'we don't want to go accusin' people without any proof, do we?'

'Then why don't you get some proof?' Becky said, growing angrier by the second.

'Not an easy thing to do,' the policeman told her. 'Very difficult in a case of this nature.'

'So what *do* you intend to do?' Becky demanded.

'We shall proceed with our enquiries in the normal manner,' the policeman said pompously. He closed his official notebook, wished Becky good day, and left the building.

'He's bloody useless, that feller,' Cedric Rathbone said as soon as the policeman had gone. 'Why don't you let me have a go at gettin' to the bottom of it, Mrs Worrell?'

The thought of letting Cedric loose on whoever was causing her problems was very tempting, but Becky shook her head.

'No, Cedric,' she said. 'This is a respectable business and we'll deal with any problems we have in a proper, law-abiding way.'

The accidents continued. Late one night someone broke into the bakery and poured red paint over the flour sacks. Early one morning one of Becky's best customers had all his shop windows broken, probably by exactly the same 'someone'.

And then it all went too far – at least for Cedric Rathbone. Two rough-looking men stopped Tom Jennings in the street when he was making a delivery, and told him that if he wanted to stay healthy he'd better consider going into another line of work.

'An' I'm not havin' that,' Cedric told Becky, 'because nobody threatens *my* mates an' gets away with it.'

'All right, Cedric,' Becky said, bowing to the inevitable. 'What can I do to help?'

'Just give me a few days off work an' I'll soon get it all sorted out,' Rathbone told her.

It was Tuesday when Becky gave Cedric the time off, and Friday afternoon before he came into work again.

'It's all fixed, Mrs Worrell,' he announced cheerfully. 'You shouldn't have any trouble from now on.'

Fixed? No more trouble from now on? How could he be so sure?

'What exactly have you been doing the last three days, Cedric?' Becky asked.

'I've been followin' Tom's waggon around,' Rathbone said. 'See, I knew them fellers who had threatened him would come back an' have another go, so all I had to do was wait.'

'And they did come back?'

'Yes, this mornin'.'

'So what did you do?' Becky asked.

The little fighter shrugged his shoulders. 'I had a quiet word with 'em,' he said. 'I asked them to stop causin' you mither.'

'And they agreed?' Becky asked incredulously. 'Right then and there?'

'Well, no,' Cedric admitted. 'Not right then and there. But I expect they will agree by the time their swellin's have gone down.'

Richard Worrell looked down at his second son, William, who was sleeping peacefully in his cradle. It was a strange thing, he thought, but he felt absolutely no love for the child.

He had expected to. Experience had told him he would – when Gerald had been born he'd felt like the king of the world. Yet somehow William had left him cold.

He picked up the baby and held it, experimentally, in his arms. Nothing stirred in his heart as it had when he'd picked up the infant Gerald.

'Why can't I care for you?' he asked the sleeping child. 'Is it because when I look at you, I can see nothing of myself?'

It was true. Gerald was growing up in his image, yet William did not resemble him at all.

William woke up, and looked directly into Richard's eyes. And for a second – a brief fleeting second – he reminded Richard of someone. But who? Not himself, and not Hortense.

'Perhaps you take after your grandfather Worrell,' he told the child. 'Maybe that's why I don't like you.'

He took the baby over to the window, so that he could examine him in better light. The nursery overlooked the stables, and from where he was standing, Richard could see his wife talking earnestly to Jack Wright, one of the grooms.

Hortense seemed to have become obsessed with riding in the last year or so, he thought. Still, he shouldn't complain – at least it kept her out of his way. She was obsessed with the new baby too, in a way she'd never been with Gerald, and every minute not spent in the saddle was devoted to William.

Hortense began to walk back towards the house, and Richard turned his attention back to the baby.

'Is there something wrong with you?' he asked. 'Or is it me?'

Certainly, there was nothing physically wrong with the child. He had been born prematurely – barely seven months after the one occasion Hortense had allowed Richard into her bed – but despite that, he had been a bouncing, lively, eight-pound baby.

'Give him to me!' said an angry voice, and turning, Richard saw Hortense standing in the nursery doorway.

She hadn't even changed out of her riding habit, he noted. She'd been so eager to see the baby that she'd come as she was.

'I said, give him to me,' Hortense repeated with a passion which almost frightened her husband.

Richard handed the baby over, and Hortense took her precious bundle over to the other corner of the room.

'You're a beautiful boy,' she cooed. 'A beautiful, beautiful boy.'

She didn't even know he was still in the room, Richard realized. Once she had the baby in her arms, she was completely oblivious to everything else around her.

'You're Mama's angel,' Hortense continued. 'You're a child of love, that's what you are.'

A child of love? Richard remembered the night the previous April when William had been conceived. There had been no love in their coupling. His main feeling had been one of curiosity about his wife's sudden change of attitude towards him.

And Hortense herself? What had she been feeling? She'd seemed almost fearful – though not of the act itself but something else entirely.

A child of love! If she really thought that, the only person she was fooling was herself!

Dottie Curzon had been to Sam Cooke's shop and was on her way back home when she noticed Ernie Bracegirdle coming down the lane towards her.

He was a funny feller, she thought – funny peculiar, *not* funny ha-ha. Even in his youth, when most lads have at least 'something' about them, he could never have been described as what you might call 'a good catch'.

Still, Dottie reflected, in all fairness you had to say that Elsie Walton – as Not-Stopping was then – hadn't been any oil painting either.

Marriage hadn't improved Ernie much. He'd gone from being a fairly scruffy young man to a downtrodden middle-aged one, a tight-lipped feller who spent half his time trying to keep out of his wife's way and the other half sneaking a crafty pint in the New Inn.

The two walkers drew level with each other just where the mineral railway line crossed the lane.

'Good evenin', Mrs Curzon,' Ernie said. 'An' what a delightful evenin' it is, isn't it?'

'Lovely,' Dottie agreed.

She knew she was staring at him, but she couldn't help herself. He was wearing a clean shirt, and instead of his usual greasy cap, he had on the one that Not-Stopping had bought him to use for weddings and funerals. But even more astonishing than the way he looked was the way he was acting. It was said of Ernie that if they handed out trophies for cheerfulness, his mantelpiece would stay bare, yet here he was as chipper as anything.

'I suppose I'd better get goin',' Ernie said.

'Off to meet Elsie, are you?' Dottie asked.

'No,' Ernie replied. 'She's in Northwich. Gone to a meetin' of the Christian Missionary Society. Well, you know how she likes to help them poor heathen overseas.'

I know how she likes to pick up the latest gossip that's goin' round the missionary circle, Dottie thought.

But aloud she said, 'Yes, she's got a very big heart, has Elsie.'

Ernie was twitching now, as if he was eager to be somewhere else – as if she was keeping him from something.

'I have to go,' he said. 'Be seein' you around, Mrs Curzon.'

'Be seein' you,' Dottie replied.

Ernie stepped through the railway gate and took the path which ran along the side of the track.

Now why would he be going that way? Dottie wondered. The track led to Wincham, and what possible business could he have there? If he wanted a drink, there were three pubs closer than the Wincham Hotel. And she couldn't get over that spring in his step. It was as if he'd got a sudden new interest in life.

Dottie was faced with two choices. The first was to go home and make herself a nice cup of tea. The second was to follow Ernie and find out just what he was up to. Without a second's hesitation, she stepped through the railway gate and set off in pursuit of Not-Stopping's remarkably altered husband.

Ernie ambled along the track, saying hello to people coming from the opposite direction, but never once looking round to see if he was being followed. Well, why should he? He knew where his wife was – and who else would take an interest in him?

Only somebody who's tired of hearing she's dottie by nature as well as by name, Mrs Curzon said to herself. Only somebody who thinks it's time Elsie Bracegirdle was made to take a bit of her own medicine.

Halfway between the two villages, Ernie left the track and cut across a piece of waste ground. Dottie hesitated for a second, then did the same.

If he does stop an' ask me what I'm doin', I can always say I'm takin' a walk, just like him, she argued to herself. After all, it's still a free country, isn't it?

Ernie began to walk quicker, and Dottie found it was all her fat little legs could do to keep up with him. Fortunately, he was not going much further. He drew level with a number of wooden huts – several of them painted black and white – and stopped, as if waiting for someone.

So that's what he's up to! Dottie thought. No wonder he'd waited until his wife was safely out of the way before coming here. Not-Stopping would go mad if she found out what he was doing.

'*When* she finds out,' Dottie corrected herself.

Because, when all was said and done, Elsie was still one of her oldest friends and had a right to be told. Besides, it would take her down a peg or two to know that she'd been made a fool of. Yes, Dottie decided, she'd tell Not-Stopping exactly what Ernie was up to.

And then, suddenly, she had a *much* better idea.

'There's only one reason some of these missionaries go abroad,' Not-Stopping told her cronies in the New Inn the next evening, 'and that's because,' she lowered her voice dramatically, 'because they lust after black women.'

It was too good an opening for Dottie Curzon to miss.

'And there's a lot of lusting goes on right here at home,' she said.

'You're right there,' Not-Stopping agreed. 'That Becky Taylor, for one, should never have got married in white. And there's others I could mention like . . .'

'I think it's when a man gets to a certain age he starts to want to wander,' Dottie said.

Not-Stopping sensed some new gossip in the air and narrowed her eyes. 'How d'you mean, a certain age?' she asked.

'Well, when they get into their forties,' Dottie said. 'You know what vain devils they are, and I reckon that when they realize they're past the first flush of youth, they need to do something to prove they're still attractive to women.'

'Dottie by name and dottie by . . .' Not-Stopping began, then her instinct told her that she might be missing a juicy piece of scandal and she changed tack in midstream. 'Do you have anybody in mind, Dottie?' she asked.

'No,' Dottie admitted. 'But you can spot 'em yourself if yer looking out for 'em. There's always signs.'

'Like what?' Not-Stopping wondered.

'Well, take a feller who usually spends most of his time at

home and then suddenly starts slipping out in the evening . . . ' Dottie began.

'Go on,' Not-Stopping said encouragingly.

'He's not been to the pub or you'd smell it on his breath,' Dottie continued. 'So where is he going? You can bet your last ha'penny he's got himself a lady friend.'

'Ladies! Ladies is the last thing *I'd* call 'em,' Not-Stopping said. 'Floozies! Tarty pieces! That'd be closer to the mark.' She waited for her crony to tell her more.

'So how was the Missionary Society meeting?' Dottie asked. 'Anythin' new happenin' on the dark continent?'

Not-Stopping looked hard at her old friend. Dottie was playing a game with her, she decided. She'd learned that somebody in the village had a fancy woman – a bit on the side – but before she'd tell the Queen of the Gossips who it was, she was going to make her work for it.

It galled Not-Stopping to find herself in this position, but it galled her even more that Dottie knew something she didn't.

'How else can you tell, Dottie?' she asked, swallowing a large chunk of her own pride.

'Loads of ways,' Dottie said. 'Fellers like that suddenly start takin' a new interest in life. They look happy, and that's not natural for a married man. Do you follow what I'm sayin'?'

'Yes,' Not-Stopping said. 'I think I do.'

'And then there's the way they dress,' Dottie continued cheerfully. 'They start wearin' clean shirts in the middle of the week, and put on their best caps even when they're only goin' down the road. Well, when you start to see that kind of behaviour, you know you've got a rover on your hands, don't you?'

She'd done her bit – the rest was up to Ma Fitton. Turning slightly away from Not-Stopping, Dottie gave the village midwife a broad wink.

'Talkin' of fellers lookin' smarter, I saw your Ernie in the street and hardly recognized him,' Ma said. 'He looks younger now than he has for years.'

'Does he, now?' Not-Stopping asked, through clenched teeth.

'Yes, he really does,' Ma repeated. 'You must be feeding him right or somethin'.'

'Or somethin',' Not-Stopping agreed.

She took a thoughtful sip of her milk stout and was uncharacteristically quiet for the rest of the evening.

Chapter Eight

'My staff, zey work well, no?' Monsieur Henri said one bright spring morning.

Becky, who was sitting at the old table where she did her paperwork, raised her head and looked around the big old barn which she had converted into her bakery. At the far end, two of the apprentices were stoking up the ovens, while a couple of bakers vigorously kneaded pastry and two more were putting the finishing touches to a batch of the 'fancy' cakes for which there was an ever-growing demand.

'Your staff work *very* well, Monsieur Henri,' Becky agreed. 'And how are you getting on yourself? Are you still managing to keep off the drink?'

The Frenchman shrugged. 'Once I fall off ze waggon,' he admitted.

'Oh, Monsieur Henri!' Becky said disappointedly.

The little Frenchman raised his hands to calm her. 'Do not worry, madam,' he said. 'It was a disaster total.'

'In what way?' Becky asked.

'Well, I know ze beer is dishwater, and so I say to myself I will try ze cider instead,' Monsieur Henri explained. 'I pour a large glass, 'old my nose and drink it entire. Zen I am sick. Zis cider, it is even worse zan ze ale. I would not even pour it down the sink because I 'ave too much pity for ze drains. So you may be assured, madame, zat as long as I live 'ere, I am cured of my bad 'abits.'

Becky had found the story comical, yet Monsieur Henri had told it with a completely straight face, and she was forced to hide her smile. When you talked to him or saw him on the street, he really did seem a bit of a clown, yet watch him at work and it was a totally different story. When Monsieur Henri was in the bakery he could be like a kindly father, a ruthless tyrant and an unrestrained lunatic, all within the space of a few minutes. But above all he was a perfectionist, an artist – perhaps even a genius – and a great deal of the credit for the success of Worrell's Famous Cakes rested on his podgy shoulders.

'We could do with stepping up the number of cottage loaves we bake, Monsieur Henri,' Becky said. 'I've been getting lots of new orders from all over the . . . '

But the Frenchman was no longer listening to her. Instead, his eyes wide with surprise, he was staring at someone, or something, immediately behind her left shoulder. Becky began to turn round – just at the moment when the hands clasped her.

They were big, strong hands. They covered her eyes and stopped her from moving her head even an inch.

''ow dare you treat my madam like zat?' she heard Monsieur Henri say. 'If you were not so big, I make a mincemeat out of you.'

The hands were removed as quickly as they had appeared. Becky stood up and whirled round to face her attacker. Then she saw who was standing there and smiling at her.

'It is your 'usband,' Monsieur Henri said laughingly. 'But of course! 'oo else would be so brave to treat you in this manner?'

'You're away for nearly seven months and then you turn up out of the blue and frighten the life out of me!' Becky said angrily. 'I could kill you sometimes, Michael. Do you know that?'

And then she fell into her husband's arms.

Becky declared a holiday for herself, and she, Michael and little Michelle took the train to Chester. They walked around the walls and climbed the tower from which King Charles had watched as his army was defeated. They strolled down to the River Dee and fed the swans. Then they lay down in the long grass on the river bank, and Michelle – who was exhausted by the excitement of it all – soon fell asleep.

'Tell me about what you're doing on the Oil Rivers,' Becky said, taking her husband's hands in hers and looking into his eyes.

'Things are going well,' Michael told her. 'We have our warehouse set up now . . .'

'What? A proper warehouse? Like you see around the Liverpool docks?'

Michael laughed. 'No, not like that at all,' he said. 'It's what they call a "hulk" out there on the rivers – an old ship which is long past sailing, but can still just about stay afloat. We've thatched the deck with straw matting, and that's where we store the goods we give to the natives and the palm oil we get in return.'

'It doesn't sound very comfortable,' Becky said dubiously.

'It's tolerable enough,' Michael replied.

'Tell me about the natives,' Becky said.

'They're so strange it's hard to know where to begin,' Michael confessed. 'Let me see. They travel around in great long canoes which need at least forty men to paddle them properly. And there's always a tom-tom drummer on board to help the paddlers to keep time. Then there's the chief. He usually stands at the bow, dressed in a long robe made up entirely of coloured handkerchiefs. And on his arms he wears ivory bracelets two or three inches broad and very, very heavy.'

'And are they very fierce?' Becky asked worriedly.

'Not really,' Michael said reassuringly. 'In a way, they're very civilized. They have their own gods, you know. In Bonny, it's the iguana – a big lizard – which is sacred. In the Brass lands, on the other hand, they worship the boa constrictor, a huge snake which squeezes its victims to death.' He laughed. 'The missionaries think they've stamped out the old forms of worship, but they don't know the half of what goes on.'

'So they're really all still heathens, are they?' Becky said.

Michael shook his head. 'No, not all of them. There are *some* genuine converts,' he said. 'They go to St Clement's

Church in Bonny, and you should see what they put on the collection plate, my darling.'

'What?' Becky asked.

'Well, their chief coin is called a manilla,' Michael explained. 'It's made of copper, shaped like a horseshoe and it's this size.'

He held out his fingers to show her.

'But that must be about four inches,' Becky said in amazement.

'Maybe a bit more,' Michael agreed. 'So you can see that when the congregation's feeling generous, the usher has to be a strong man just to carry the plate.'

'Yes, I can,' Becky said, imagining herself struggling with a collection plate full of brass horseshoes.

'And sometimes, instead of manillas they give heads of tobacco or bolts of cloth,' Michael continued, 'so by the end of the service the church looks as if it's been holding a jumble sale.'

'And have you done any of the work you really wanted to do?' Becky asked. 'Any of the work which isn't necessarily "good business sense"?'

Michael looked a little embarrassed.

'Well, yes,' he admitted. 'I did find a little time to help the natives.'

'And what did you do with this "little time"?'

'I've persuaded some of the villages near the hulk to dig drainage ditches,' Michael said. 'It's a good start, but it's *only* a start. There's still a great deal of work to do before we see even a little change in the lives of those poor, unfortunate people.'

A rowing boat glided past on the water. The young gentleman at the oars was too busy demonstrating his prowess to think of anything else, but the young lady he was trying to impress peered out from under her parasol and waved to the people on the bank. Becky and Michael waved back.

How strange this scene must seem to her husband after his

months in the tropics, Becky thought. How odd a lady with a parasol must look now that he had become accustomed to warriors dressed in robes made up entirely of coloured handkerchiefs.

'When do you have to go back?' she asked.

'In about a week,' Michael said.

Becky sat up, horrified.

'So soon!' she gasped.

'I can't leave the business for long at this stage,' he said regretfully. 'Later, I might be able to hand some of the work over to someone else.'

'Which sort of work will you be able to hand on?' Becky asked. 'The "business sense" work or the other kind?'

'All kinds,' Michael told her. 'Then, finally, I might find more time to spend with my lovely wife and my beautiful child.'

Yes, Becky thought, they'd finally have him back, unless he was struck down by one of the nasty tropical diseases which had killed so many white men before him; unless those warriors who he considered quite civilized decided to turn on him; unless one of the boa constrictors they worshipped as gods wrapped itself around him and squeezed him to death. There were so many things which could go wrong on the Oil Rivers, and while he was away there was not a day when she didn't imagine them all happening to him.

Yet just as she'd not been able to deny him his wish to go to Africa in the first place, so now she knew she'd have to force herself not to beg Michael never to return to it. It was his mission in life to improve the miserable conditions of the natives. And it was hers to stay at home, bring up their child – and worry.

Becky looked around her – at the beautiful blue sky, at the peaceful river, and at Michael. She nuzzled her head against her husband's shoulder. Memories of this happy day were something she would store up to take her through the hard times which lay ahead.

*

It being Saturday, the first thing Ernie Bracegirdle did when he entered the house was to hand over his pay packet to his wife.

'Bit of a slack week,' he said as his wife slit the envelope open.

'You're not kiddin'!' Not-Stopping said as she counted out the money on the kitchen table. 'There should have been a lot more than this, what with all the extra hours you've been puttin' in.'

'It's not the hours we work that matters,' Ernie said. 'It's how much salt we make.'

'But if you're on the pans for longer, surely you must be makin' more salt,' Not-Stopping pointed out.

'It's not as simple as that,' Ernie said evasively.

'Why?' Not-Stopping demanded.

'Why what?' Ernie asked.

'Why isn't it as simple as that?' Not-Stopping asked. 'If I spend twice as long on the washin', I expect to end with twice as many clean clothes.'

'Pannin' salt isn't like doin' the washin',' Ernie protested. 'It's more technical.'

An' if you believe that, Not-Stopping thought, you'll believe anythin'!

The pay packet had been sealed when Ernie had handed it over and the figure written on the pay slip exactly matched the amount she had just counted out. Yet with the sixth sense of a born gossip, Not-Stopping was convinced that her husband was holding something back from her. And after what Ma Fitton had said in the New Inn, she knew exactly what he was holding it back *for*.

She slid some coins across the table.

'Here's your pocket money,' she said.

'Thanks,' Ernie said.

He picked up the coins and slipped them into his pocket. For the first time in their married life, he hadn't bothered to count how much she'd given him, Not-Stopping noted. And what possible explanation could there be for that except that his pocket money was now no more to him than the icing on the cake – a little bit extra to add to money he'd already managed to filch?

After they'd finished their tea, Ernie said, 'I think I'll go for a bit of a walk.'

'Please yourself,' Not-Stopping said, and then she noticed that he was reaching for his best cap and added, 'I think I'll come with you.'

Ernie looked dropped on.

'Come with me?' he said.

'Yes,' Not-Stopping agreed.

'Nay, what do you want with walkin'?' Ernie asked with just a hint of desperation in his voice. 'You've never bothered to come walkin' with me before, have you?'

'Maybe not, but I want to come now,' Not-Stopping said firmly.

Desperate times called for desperate measures. Ernie reached reluctantly into his pocket and pulled out a few of the coppers which made up his spending money.

'Here y'are,' he said, holding them out for his wife. 'Go up to the pub and have a couple of drinks with yer mates.'

Not-Stopping folded her arms across her skinny bosom. 'I'd rather go for a walk with me husband,' she said.

Ernie put the coins back in his pocket and sighed heavily. 'All right, if that's what you really want,' he said.

At the end of their alley, Ernie Bracegirdle stopped and looked longingly down the lane.

'Which way are yer takin' me?' Not-Stopping demanded. 'Along the railway lines to Wincham?'

Ernie gave the bottom of the lane one last, wistful glance and then said, 'No, I think we'll have a wander up to Forge Pool.'

They set off up the cartroad. Ernie's head was bowed and he walked like a man who was carrying the weight of a terrible disappointment on his shoulders. They met several people they knew, walking in the opposite direction, and

Ernie responded gloomily to their cheerful greetings.

'Grand evenin'.'

'It is for some!'

It was when they reached Marston Old Mine that Not-Stopping noticed something else that had changed about her husband recently.

'You're not smokin',' she said. 'Come to think of it, I don't think I've seen you with a fag in your mouth for days.'

'I've given it up,' Ernie said.

'Given it up!' Not-Stopping said. 'Whatever for?'

'I've better things to do with me money than waste it on fags,' Ernie told her.

Yes, Not-Stopping thought grimly. I'll bet you have.

It might have been luck or it might have been fate, but two snippets of information were dropped into Not-Stopping's lap over the next couple of days without her even having to ferret them out.

The first came from Archie Sutton, the big-bellied, beer-swigging boss of Ernie's work gang. Not-Stopping ran into him at Sam Cooke's shop.

'I've just popped in for a packet of fags,' Archie said, feeling – as most of the villagers did – a need to explain what he was doing before Not-Stopping had time to put her own sinister interpretation on the situation.

A packet of fags! Well, he could afford them, couldn't he? Not-Stopping thought. *He* wasn't keepin' a fancy piece on the side!

'Oh, you have been workin' my Ernie hard, Mr Sutton,' she said to him in a wheedling tone of voice she normally reserved for the gentry.

'Workin' him hard?' Archie replied. 'I don't know what you're on about, Mrs Bracegirdle.'

'He seems to be spendin' all his time on the pans these days,' Not-Stopping explained.

Archie scratched his big belly reflectively.

'I think you're gettin' a bit mixed up, missus,' he said.

'There's no demand for salt just now. We're puttin' in less hours the last couple of weeks than we have for months.'

Yet Ernie was getting extra money from somewhere – Not-Stopping was sure of that. So the only question was, who the hell was giving it to him?

The answer to this pressing question was provided by Fred Emmett, the village carpenter, who called at the Bracegirdles' house late on Monday afternoon.

'It was Ernie I was looking for, really,' he said when Not-Stopping answered the back door.

'He's not back from work yet,' Not-Stopping told him. 'Puttin' a lot of overtime, I expect. Can I take a message?'

'You could tell him that old Mrs Holland's taken a turn for the worst,' Fred said.

'Can I, now?' Not-Stopping said. 'An' why should that interest him?'

'Well, they don't think she'll last out the night,' Fred told her, as if that were all the explanation that was needed.

'Isn't it the vicar you should be talkin' to?' Not-Stopping asked.

Fred laughed. 'The vicar's promised to stop makin' coffins as long as I give up deliverin' sermons,' he said.

'I don't think I'm followin' you,' Not-Stopping told him.

'I'll have to make the coffin tonight,' Fred explained patiently, 'and I've so much other work on me hands at the moment that I'm goin' to need your Ernie's help again.'

'Again!' Not-Stopping exploded.

Fred's face registered the fact that he must just have broken one of the cardinal rules of the Men-Keeping-Things-From-Women Club.

'Er . . . Ernie didn't . . . like . . . mention it to you?' he stumbled.

Not-Stopping did some rapid thinking. She wanted to catch Ernie right in the middle of his dirty little game, she told herself, and she couldn't do that if he'd already been forewarned by Fred Emmett. So what was the best way to cover her tracks?

Though it took a great deal of effort, she forced a smile to her vinegary lips. 'No, he didn't tell me, and I think I know why,' she said.

'Do you, Mrs Bracegirdle?' Fred Emmett asked uneasily.

'I've a birthday comin' up, you see,' Not-Stopping improvised, 'an' I've had me eye on this coat in Bratt an' Evans. Only, it's a bit expensive. D'you see what I'm gettin' at?'

'No,' Fred replied.

God, but men were thick sometimes, Not-Stopping thought. Still, this was not the moment to point that out to Fred Emmett.

'My Ernie – bless him – is savin' up for the coat,' she said.

Fred realized that by some miracle he was off the hook, and breathed a loud sigh of relief.

'Yes, that'll be it,' he said.

'So you won't tell him I know about his little secret, will you, Mr Emmett?' Not-Stopping said playfully. 'After all, we don't want to spoil his surprise, do we?'

'No,' Fred agreed. 'You can rely on me, Mrs Bracegirdle. I won't say a word.'

There *would* be a surprise, Not-Stopping promised herself. But it would be Ernie Bracegirdle – the lyin', cheatin' bugger – who was on the receiving end of it!

Richard Worrell stood at the top of a small, tree-covered hillock, a pair of binoculars in his hand. He had chosen his spot carefully. The trees gave him cover and from his elevated position he could overlook much of the surrounding countryside, including the oak tree under which he'd once seduced Becky Taylor. It seemed a hundred years past, that seduction, yet he remembered it as vividly as if it had just happened: the heart he'd carved in the oak, entwining her name with his; the Fortnum and Mason's hamper he'd taken with him and the way Becky had giggled when she'd tried the champagne; the sweet feeling of triumph when he'd finally had what he'd been waiting so long for.

There was a sound of pounding hoofbeats in the distance and, swinging his field glasses round, Richard saw two riders approaching. One was a man and the other a woman. His wife – and one of his grooms! Richard followed their progress with grim satisfaction.

The riders reached the oak tree, and Hortense turned towards Jack Wright and made a circling gesture with her left arm. Yes, that was one of her favourite ways of putting her horse through its paces, Richard remembered.

The first circle was a wide, sweeping one, but the second was tighter. The third time they repeated the manoeuvre, they kept in so close to the trunk of the tree that they could almost have touched it.

After the third turn, they reined in. Hortense dismounted and handed the reins to Wright, who was on his cob.

'On *my* cob,' Richard corrected himself. '*My* cob and *my* wife!'

Hortense sat down on the ground, tucked her legs delicately under herself and rested her back against the trunk of the oak. Wright led the horses a little distance from the tree, then set them free to graze.

Richard studied the groom through his glasses. How old was Wright? he wondered. At least forty. And by no stretch of the imagination could he be called a handsome man.

Richard lowered his glasses and shook his head. He'd misread the signs, he decided. A nod here, a gesture there, and he'd built up a picture of infidelity which was clearly preposterous. Looking at them now, it was inconceivable that anything could have been going on between his high-bred wife and this common working man.

I've made a complete fool of myself, he thought.

But he took some consolation from the fact that at least he was making a fool of himself in private. He raised his binoculars again just to make absolutely sure that his suspicions were unfounded.

Wright walked back to the tree and squatted down next to Hortense. Richard frowned. The groom might not be *having* his wife, but he was still far too familiar with her. Richard resolved to give the man his notice that very afternoon.

Wright moved even closer to Hortense, and Richard focussed his glasses on his wife's face and was shocked by what he saw – Hortense was smiling at the groom!

It was not the smile itself which astounded him, so much as the nature of it. Over the years, Richard had seen all kinds of smiles on her face. The smile of triumph when she got her own way. The tight smile she used to greet her social superiors and the patronizing one she reserved for inferiors who had pleased her. Those and many more. But he had never seen a smile like this. It filled her whole face, almost making her glow. She was not pretty – she never could be pretty – but with that smile, which seemed to come from deep within her, she was almost beautiful.

The groom placed his hand behind Hortense's neck and pulled her head gently towards him. And then he kissed her! It was a full, passionate kiss – a kiss which showed that Hortense's lips were no strangers to Wright's. Richard felt his hands tightening around the field glasses.

The couple separated, and Richard swung his binoculars on to the face of the man who had had the gall to take what was rightly his – and then a sudden realization hit him like a bolt from the blue.

His hands went slack and his field glasses fell to the ground. How could he have been so blind? he asked himself. How could it have taken him so long to see just who it was that his son William reminded him of?

Chapter Nine

When Ernie Bracegirdle arrived home from work on Tuesday, there were two surprises waiting for him. The first surprise was that his food was already on the table. The second was that the meal consisted of sandwiches, even though they always had bubble and squeak on Tuesdays.

'I've not had the time to make you a proper tea,' Not-Stopping explained. 'I've been kept busy doin' good works for the United Missionary Society all day.'

'A man's entitled to a proper hot meal after a hard day's work on the salt pans,' Ernie complained, though not so loudly that his wife could actually hear him.

'Rushed off me feet, I've been,' Not-Stopping continued. 'An' if that's not enough, they want me back there tonight.'

'In Northwich?' Ernie asked, suddenly more cheerful, though careful not to show it.

'Of course in Northwich,' Not-Stopping replied. 'That's where we always meet.'

'An' what time can I expect you back?' Ernie asked.

'I can't honestly say,' Not-Stopping told him. 'But I do know it won't be until late on.'

'It's a bit of a bugger when you can't even get company from your own wife,' Ernie said, disguising his ever increasing cheerfulness with a characteristic grumble.

'I expect you'll find something to keep you occupied,' Not-Stopping said, reaching for her hat and coat. 'You might even go and pay a call on your old mate Fred Emmett if you can't think of anything else to do.'

Fred Emmett! Ernie felt a shiver run through him. If Elsie had found out he'd been doin' odd jobs for Fred . . . But no, she couldn't have done, because if she had, she'd have tackled him about it the minute he set foot through the door.

Ernie waited for fifteen minutes after his wife had left, then put on his best cap and set off himself.

It's a stroke of luck her havin' to go out like that, he told himself as he walked jauntily down the lane. A real stroke of luck.

From her hiding place behind the postbox, Not-Stopping watched her husband step through the railway gate and take the track which led to Wincham.

'So I was right!' she muttered.

It had been a gamble laying her ambush here, but not much of one, not after the way Ernie had chosen to go in exactly the opposite direction on that miserable walk of theirs.

As she started to follow her husband along the track, it would never have occurred to her that she could have anything in common with wealthy Richard Worrell. But she had. Both had laid a trap for their spouses – both had given those spouses enough rope to hang themselves with.

Ernie followed the same route as he had when Dottie Curzon had been behind him. And just as Dottie had done before her, Not-Stopping realized what her husband was really up to the moment she saw him entering the black and white shed.

The bugger! she said to herself. The bloody cheatin', lyin', dirty rotten old bugger!

She was already halfway to the shed when she forced herself to stop. Barge in now, and he might still be able to talk his way out of it. Better – far better – to wait and catch him in the act, so no matter what excuse he came up with, it simply wouldn't wash.

She gave him five minutes then strode across to the shed, her umbrella swinging forcefully in her hand. The door was not locked and when Not-Stopping gave it a furious push, it swung open and smashed against the wall. Ernie, who was at the other end of the shed with his back to the door, whirled round.

'What the bloody hell do you think you're . . . ?' he began. And then he saw who was standing there and his mouth fell open in horror. 'Elsie,' he continued weakly. 'I . . . I can explain.'

But there was only one *possible* explanation, now that she'd caught him in the very act of fondling that . . . that thing!

Not-Stopping advanced towards her quaking husband.

'I've given you the best years of me life, an' this is how you treat me,' she shouted.

'Now be c . . . careful, Elsie . . . ' Ernie stuttered as he held up his hands to protect himself. 'You don't want to do anthin' hasty, d . . . do you?'

Not-Stopping swung her brolly with a speed and ferocity which would have terrified a medieval knight. It landed exactly where she had intended it to – right across the top of Ernie's best cap.

'I want her dead!' Richard Worrell thundered as he paced his study in Peak House. 'I want both of them dead!'

The man he was speaking to was sitting at the oak table around which, the year before, the owners had discussed ways to break the flatmen's strike. He was bald-headed and had bad teeth which he continually probed with a dirty toothpick. His breath stank, too, and Richard found it an effort even to be in the same room as him. Yet it was an effort worth making, because Horace Crimp was both the cleverest and most unscrupulous lawyer in the area. It had been Crimp who had shown Richard virtually how to steal the salt works from his brother Michael, and it was Crimp to whom Richard turned for help with the new problem.

'Didn't you hear what I said?' Richard asked his attorney. 'I want them both dead.'

Crimp examined the edge of his toothpick with evident satisfaction. 'If you really do want them dead, it could probably be arranged,' he said, 'but it would be very expensive as well as extremely risky. And are you really sure you want to be a murderer, even from a distance?'

Richard slowly shook his head. 'No, of course not,' he admitted. 'As much as I despise my wife, I would not like to have her blood on my hands. But I *do* want to see them both punished for what they've done to me.'

'That's understandable,' Crimp agreed, 'and certainly it will be very easy to arrange in the case of the groom since he is of no consequence. Your wife, however, raises more difficulties. She is, after all, the daughter of an aristocrat, and so we must tread carefully. Perhaps public exposure of her infidelity would be sufficient revenge for you.'

Richard tugged at his hair with a mixture of rage and desperation.

'Are you mad?' he demanded. 'How can I expose her without appearing a fool myself? Do you think I want my friends sniggering about me behind my back? Do you imagine I'd enjoy being the laughing stock of the county?'

Crimp scratched his bald head.

'Yes, that might be a problem,' he admitted. 'And yet it's hard to work out how you could take any kind of action without the whole matter becoming public knowledge. Perhaps your best course would be to turn a blind eye to the whole business.'

Richard paced the room again.

Could I do that? he asked himself. Could he pretend that he knew nothing of his wife's sordid little affair? Could he sit across from her at the breakfast table, knowing that later in the day she would be in the arms of a common working man?

No! It was impossible!

Besides, to pretend ignorance was to leave Hortense unpunished and still run the risk that word of what was going on would leak out – the worst of both worlds.

'That won't work!' Richard said desperately. 'For God's sake, Crimp, can't you think of something else?'

Crimp probed his rotting teeth again.

'Perhaps the Commissioners could provide us with a solution,' he said. 'Yes, if we can persuade the Commissioners, we might very well have found a way out.'

'Commissioners?' Richard said. 'What Commissioners?'

'Of course, we would have to be careful which doctors we selected,' Crimp went on calmly. 'But I have a friend who will fit the bill, and I am sure he can put us in touch with someone else equally suitable.'

'Commissioners!' Richard exploded. 'Doctors! What the hell are you talking about?'

Crimp explained his scheme slowly and carefully. And as he did so the tension melted away from Richard's eyes and a broad smile came to his face.

'Pigeons!' Not-Stopping Bracegirdle said indignantly. 'He's been keepin' racing pigeons behind me back. Mind you, I'm not surprised he hid it from me. If I'd known he had any spare money in his pocket, I'd have made him buy some new oilcloth for the front room instead of spendin' it on something daft like that.'

It was all Dottie Curzon could do to stop herself from nudging Ma Fitton in the ribs.'

'Fancy your Ernie keeping pigeons,' she said innocently. 'Whoever would have thought that?'

'Well, I had no idea,' Not-Stopping confessed. 'If I hadn't followed him, I'd still have known nothin' about it.'

She was digging herself a pit, Dottie thought happily, a pit so deep that once she fell into it even someone with Not-Stopping's quick tongue and mind would find it difficult to climb out again. Still, it would be a shame to spring the trap too soon because it was so much fun just thinking about it.

'I'll get some more drinks in,' Dottie said, postponing the moment when Not-Stopping would finally realize what a mess she'd landed herself in.

'But it's not your round,' Not-Stopping told her.

'Doesn't matter,' replied Dottie, who was in such a good mood that she'd cheerfully have bought drinks for the whole pub.

Paddy O'Leary served Dottie with her three milk stouts and she returned to her seat.

'I'll swear he's waterin' these down,' said Not-Stopping, holding her bottle up to the light.

'Mine tastes all right to me,' Ma Fitton said, taking a small sip of her drink.

'Well, it would, wouldn't it?' Not-Stopping said tartly. 'Anythin' will taste all right to them as don't know any better.'

Nevertheless, she filled her own glass and took a substantial swig.

'You were tellin' us about your Ernie's pigeons,' Dottie prompted.

'Forget the pigeons,' Not-Stopping told her. 'I'm sick to death of bloody pigeons.' She leaned forward confidentially. 'They say Liz Burgess is expectin' again,' she whispered, 'an' it must be nearly a year since her husband joined the navy. If you ask me – '

'There's one thing I don't understand,' Dottie interrupted.

Not-Stopping gave her a look that would have frozen blood. 'There's quite a lot of things you don't understand, Dottie Curzon,' she said cuttingly. 'Which particular one have you got in mind at the moment?'

'Well, you said you had no idea your Ernie was keepin' pigeons,' Dottie said slowly.

'That's right,' Not-Stopping agreed. 'I'm glad to see you're not deaf as well as daft.'

'So why did you follow him?' Dottie asked.

Only now did Not-Stopping begin to sense that she was standing tottering on the edge of a very deep pit.

'I beg your pardon?' she said, trying to buy time while she regained her balance.

'You didn't think he was keepin' pigeons,' Dottie explained, 'but you must have thought he was doin' somethin' wrong, or you'd never have followed him, would you?'

Not-Stopping's mouth flapped open.

'Yes,' she said. 'I mean, no.'

'You mean, you did think he was up to somethin'?' Dottie

pressed.

Not-Stopping nodded, her face registering the fact that she now clearly appreciated the depth of the trap into which she had fallen, but was still hoping against hope that someone would throw her a line.

'What?' Dottie asked, dashing her last hope.

'I don't follow yer,' Not-Stopping said feebly.

'What did you think he was up to?' Dottie asked patiently.

'Well, you know the kinds of things men get up to, don't you?' Not-Stopping said.

'No,' Dottie replied with a completely straight face.

'She thought her Ernie was seein' another woman,' Ma Fitton cackled, as if the idea had just occurred to her. 'Isn't that it, Elsie?'

'Course it isn't!' Dottie scoffed. 'I mean – let's be honest – who'd have Ernie?'

Not-Stopping gazed around her, helplessly. She had two choices, she realized. The first was to make herself look a fool by admitting that she'd suspected her husband of playing around. The second – no more palatable – was to humiliate herself by agreeing that she was married to a man no one else would want.

'I bet you thought he'd got himself a fightin' dog,' Dottie said, finally throwing the other woman the rope she had been praying for.

'That's right,' Not-Stopping said, almost gasping with relief. 'Fightin' dogs! That's exactly what I thought.' She took a deep breath and pulled herself together a little. 'Now, I was tellin' you about Liz Burgess and that sailor husband of hers . . . ' she continued.

Dottie sat back and let the words wash over her. She had saved Not-Stopping from a tricky situation, and they both knew it. From now on, whenever Not-Stopping got too far out of line, the word 'pigeons' should be enough to pull her back again.

Jack Wright was bedding down the horses for the night when

he noticed the two men standing in the shadow of the stable doorway. He moved closer to get a better view. They were not part of the Peak House establishment – in fact he didn't think he had ever seen either of them before – but there was something about them which frightened him.

'You've no right to be here,' he said, trying to keep the quaver out of his voice. 'This is private property, this is.'

One of the two men, who had a broken nose, smiled unpleasantly to reveal that he had several teeth missing, too.

'We've every right to be here. We got the permission of the owner, Mr Worrell,' he said. He pointed a stubby finger at Jack Wright. 'And that's more than you can say,' he added.

'I don't need permission,' Wright protested, wondering where the other grooms had got to. 'I work here.'

'You *worked* here,' the first tough corrected him. 'Do you know what this is?'

He held out a piece of paper in his hand and Wright, despite his fear, felt compelled to look at it.

'It's a railway ticket to London,' he said.

'One way,' the tough said. 'And you'll be using it as soon as we've finished with you.'

'But why should I want to do that?' Wright asked. 'I was born an' brought up round here. I don't know a single soul in London.'

'Maybe that's why Mr Worrell's sending you there,' the second tough suggested.

Wright gasped. 'You mean he's found out about . . . about . . . ?' he said.

The first tough raised a finger in a gesture that was as intimidating as a sledgehammer.

'It'd be better for you if yer kept quiet about what yer think he's found out,' he advised.

'Mr Worrell said that if yer did talk about it, we was to make it even harder on yer,' the second tough added.

'Harder on me?' Wright asked. 'How do you mean?'

'I mean,' said the first tough, slowly and deliberately stripping off his jacket, 'that before we put yer on that train to London, we're going to give yer the thrashing of yer life.'

'Would you step into my study for a moment, my dear,' Richard Worrell asked his wife after they had finished their supper.

'For what reason?' asked Hortense, suspicious of his tone of voice, which seemed to her to be a strange mixture of humour, anger and triumph.

'There are some people I'd like you to meet,' Richard told her.

'I'm feeling very tired tonight,' Hortense protested.

'That's understandable after the amount of physical exercise you must have had today,' Richard said, with the edge still in his voice. 'Nevertheless, I think you will find our visitors interesting.'

Hortense shrugged her shoulders in resignation.

'All right,' she agreed. 'Provided you don't expect me to stay long.'

Richard smiled. 'Oh, I think I can guarantee you won't be staying long,' he assured her.

He led her along the corridor to his study, then opened the door so she could enter before him. There were two men sitting behind Richard's big oak table. One was a neat, fussy-looking man with a pince-nez, and the other was much larger with a shock of wild hair. In front of the table, someone had placed a single chair.

It looks as if it's set up for some kind of interview, Hortense thought. But who could they be interviewing at this time of night – and for what purpose?

'This is Dr Platt,' said Richard, indicating the man with the pince-nez. 'He's come to examine you.'

'He's not my doctor,' Hortense said.

'No, but he is *mine*,' Richard replied.

'Since when?' Hortense asked.

'Since Horace Crimp recommended him to me yesterday afternoon,' said Richard, who sounded like he was really starting to enjoy himself.

'And what about the other man?' Hortense asked, feeling – though she couldn't explain exactly why – an ever increasing sense of dread.

'Ah, he is Dr Addisson. He's an alienist from London.'

'An alienist!' Hortense exclaimed worriedly. 'But that's the sort of doctor they call in for . . . for . . .'

'For lunatics,' Richard said.

Hortense turned towards the door, but Richard blocked her way.

'Would you take the chair in front of the desk, my dear, devoted wife?' he asked, though it was more of an order than a request.

'No!' Hortense said. 'I won't! And you can't make me!'

'Don't be foolish, Hortense,' Richard said harshly. 'If you won't sit of your own free will, then I'll get the servants to tie you in.'

Hortense looked at the two doctors for help. Platt was examining the notes in front of him. Addisson, on the other hand, was gazing at her with eyes so fiery that they suggested if you were looking for one lunatic in the room, you wouldn't have to go further than him.

No help could be expected from that quarter then. Hortense turned her attention back to Richard. He'd do it, she decided, he'd actually order the servants to tie her down. More, he'd enjoy doing it. Determined to deny him that satisfaction, Hortense walked slowly over to the chair and sat down.

'I'll leave the three of you alone now,' Richard said. 'I expect you have a great deal to talk about.'

And with that, he stepped into the corridor, locking the door behind him.

'Are you aware of the work of the famous Dr Forbes Winslow?' the man with the shock of hair and mad eyes asked Hortense once Richard's footsteps had ceased to echo in the corridor.

'I know nothing about medicine,' Hortense said sullenly.

'Dr Forbes Winslow considers that five-sixths of cases of

133

mental instability in women are brought about by unrighteous sex,' the alienist said.

'What are you saying!' Hortense exploded. 'Are you saying
that I'm mad?'

Addisson turned to his colleague. 'Irrational outbursts,'
he said. 'A sure sign.'

'Do you deny that you have been conducting a sexual
relationship with at least one of your servants?' Dr Platt
asked mildly.

Hortense jumped to her feet.

'With at least *one* of my servants!' she screamed. 'Are you
suggesting that I have been to bed with more than one of
them? How dare you imply that I have granted my favours to
anyone who desired them.'

'Then you don't deny that *one* such sexual relationship
does exist?' the doctor said, unperturbed.

Hortense glanced from the two men to the door and then
back again.

'Come, come, madam,' Addisson said impatiently,
'answer our questions. For, rest assured, you will not leave
this room until you have.'

Hortense stuck her chin out defiantly.

'It is more than a mere sexual relationship,' she said with
pride. 'I am in love with Jack Wright.'

Dr Platt made a note on the sheet of paper which lay in
front of him on the oak table.

'You must agree that it is a little strange for a woman of
your class – especially a woman married to such a handsome
young man – to be attracted to a middle-aged groom,' he
said.

'A classic case,' Dr Addisson muttered, almost to himself.

'My husband is a swine,' Hortense said. 'And I've received
more kindness and consideration from Jack Wright than I've
ever known in my life before. Do you think I planned to fall
in love with a man so far below me? Do you imagine that even
for a moment I wanted it to happen? No! But there are some
things we can't fight, however hard we try.'

'Is he the father of your youngest child?' Dr Platt asked.

'Examine the child for yourself,' Hortense told him. 'If you can find cunning and viciousness in his eyes, then he's my husband's son. If not, then you must draw your own conclusions.'

'Did this groom make unnatural sexual demands on you?' said Dr Addisson, licking his lips. 'Did he, for example, ask you to behave as if you were one of the farmyard animals?'

Hortense gave the alienist a look of pure loathing.

'For all your education, you are the scum of the earth,' she told him, 'and I have no intention of saying another word to you.'

'Withdrawal,' Addisson said complacently. 'Another classic sign.'

'There is really no need for the lady to say more anyway,' Platt said. 'I for one have heard quite enough.'

'Enough for what?' Hortense demanded.

'Enough to persuade me that I would be negligent in my duties if I did not sign the papers.'

'Which papers?' Hortense asked.

'The papers which will allow your husband to have you locked up in a place where you will no longer be able to harm yourself,' Addisson told her.

'You mean – a lunatic asylum!' Hortense gasped.

'Yes,' Platt agreed, doing his best to appear genuinely sorry. 'That is precisely what I mean.'

Hortense felt the room start to spin and groped at her chair for support. They were going to lock her up! There would be no more rides with Jack, no more sweet moments under the oak tree.

A sudden realization came into her mind – a realization so terrible that it banished all thoughts of Jack Wright and of her own happiness.

She was going to be separated from her children!

She always felt guilty about Gerald, because her loathing for his father had prevented her from giving him all the love she knew he was entitled to. But she had meant to make it up to him soon – she really had. And now it was too late!

And what about William? How would Richard treat little William now he knew that the boy wasn't his natural son?

'Please don't have me locked up!' she begged. 'My children need me. Who'll look after them if I'm gone?'

'Their father is a rich man,' Platt said coldly. 'He can employ any number of nurses and governesses.'

But it wouldn't be the same! It wouldn't!

There had to be something she could give them which would save her, Hortense thought desperately. She considered money, but she had very little of her own, and however much she offered, Richard would be able to top it.

She looked across at Dr Addisson, who was staring at her with his hot eyes and seemed at that moment to be the most revolting piece of human slime she had ever met.

'If you refuse to sign the papers,' she told the alienist, 'then I will allow you to take me to bed and do to me all those disgusting things you imagine I did with Jack.'

Addisson's eyes bulged and his hands grasped feverishly at the edge of the oak table.

'I . . . I . . . ' he gasped.

'All of them,' Hortense said, doing her best to fight down the bile which she could feel rising in her throat. 'Anything you can think of.'

Platt looked sharply at his colleague. 'Have you forgotten who we're dealing with here?' he hissed. 'Don't you realize what would be likely to happen if you crossed a man like Richard Worrell?'

The alienist nodded his head weakly. 'I . . . we . . . must go ahead,' he said, almost as if he were choking. 'We have to . . . commit you.'

There was a small brass bell sitting on the table and Platt picked it up and rang it. Almost immediately, there were footsteps in the corridor, then the sound of a key being turned in the lock. The door opened and Richard entered the study. He looked questioningly at Platt. The doctor gave a slight nod, and Richard looked satisfied.

Hortense threw herself at his feet.

'Richard, for the love of God, don't do this!' she pleaded.

'You don't cheat me and get away with it,' Richard said. 'Nobody does.' He turned his head towards the corridor. 'You can take her away now,' he called to the invisible presences who were lurking there.

Chapter Ten

If Clara Gibbons hadn't given notice to her landlord the same day Spudder Johnson first appeared in the village, Mary Taylor might have been content to let life go on just as it had before. But Clara *did* give notice, and Spudder *did* appear – so anyone who knew Mary well could pretty much have worked out what was bound to happen next.

It was on one of those wet, windy May days that Clara chose to break her momentous news. Mary was alone in the chip shop when her next-door neighbour entered and shook herself like a dog to free her coat of the raindrops she'd picked up on her short journey from next door.

'Ted not here?' Clara asked, looking around the shop and seeing no sign of Mary's husband.

'He's gone off to Manchester to play with the band in some sort of knock-out competition,' Mary said. She reached for her scoop. 'Your usual two penn'orth, is it?'

'Yes, please,' Clara replied. 'I might as well take advantage of livin' next to a chip shop while I still can.'

'What d'you mean?' Mary asked. 'While you still can?'

'Me and my Albert are movin',' Clara said. 'Well, there's nothin' really to keep us here now the kids have grown up. And I don't think there'll be any chip shops where we're goin'.'

'No fish and chip shops!' Mary said. 'Just exactly where *are* you goin'? The North Pole?'

'Close enough,' Clara said with a grin. 'We're emigratin' to Canada. Albert's brother's already there. Doin' very well, he is, too. He owns his own house, and how many people can you say that about?'

Not many, Mary realized, as she scooped the chips into a

rolled-up cone of newspaper and then reached across for one of the fried fish. In fact, apart from Becky with her little cottage down the lane, she didn't know anybody who owned the house they lived in. She and Ted had been paying rent on their own home for over thirty years. You never really thought about it – that was just the way things were in Marston.

'So when do you think you'll be settin' out for Canada?' Mary asked her soon-to-be ex-neighbour.

'As soon as we can book our passage,' Clara said. 'Probably some time in the next month or so.'

'Well, I wish you all the luck in the world,' Mary said, handing the package of fish and chips over to Clara.

She meant it sincerely. She *did* hope Clara made a success of her new life. Still, from a personal point of view, the announcement had come as a bit of a shock.

'I'll miss you,' Clara said, as if she'd read Mary's mind.

'And I'll miss you,' Mary told her. 'You can't beat havin' good neighbours, an' you an' Albert have been marvellous ones.' She thought back over some of the trials and tribulations they'd shared with Gibbonses over the years. 'D'you remember the day our Becky was born?' she asked.

Clara laughed. 'Could I ever forget it?' she said. 'You were bangin' on the wall so hard with your poker of yours that it sounded just like you were tryin' to knock it down.'

'I was desperate,' Mary said. 'Really desperate. I thought I was dyin'. I probably would have died if you hadn't come rushin' round.'

'Get off with you,' Clara said awkwardly. 'I only did what anybody would have done in my place.'

She reached into her purse and rummaged through the coppers to pay Mary with.

'Forget it,' Mary said.

'Oh, I couldn't do that,' Clara replied. 'You've got a livin' to make, same as everybody else.'

'I think I can stand losin' twopence on a day like this, when you've got so much to celebrate,' Mary told her.

'Well, that's very good of you,' said Clara. 'I'll see you around.'

But not for much longer, Mary thought.

Mary watched her neighbour as she walked back down the path. Clara had been a slip of a girl that day Becky was born, so slight she'd looked as if a stiff breeze would blow her away. And look at her now – well over forty and with hips you could carry a sack of coal on.

Mary's mind was still on Clara when a young man walked into the chip shop, so it was only when he coughed embarrassedly that she even realized he was there. The first thing she noticed about him – the first thing everybody noticed about him – was that his skin seemed to shine as if he'd just got out of a very hot bath after giving himself a thorough scrubbing. The second thing she noticed was his eyes. They were pale blue and they told her immediately that while he was obviously a very kind lad, he would never have won any prizes at school.

'What can I do for you, love?' she asked.

'I'd like a bag o' chips, please,' the young man said deferentially.

'Don't you want a bit of fish, as well?' Mary asked.

The youth took a handful of copper out of his pocket and counted it – very slowly.

'No, I'll just have the chips, thanks,' he said finally.

Mary scooped the chips into a rolled-up piece of newspaper, then, as an afterthought, put a piece of fish on top of it.

'I couldn't . . .' the young man said.

'It's left over from the last batch,' Mary lied. 'If you don't have it, I'll only have to throw it out.'

He looked on the point of refusing again, then the smell of the fish wafted towards his nostrils, and he nodded his thanks.

The weather had been holding off for a while, but now the skies suddenly opened and rain came pouring down. The boy looked out of the door at the deluge – and Mary looked at his thin jacket.

'You can eat it in here if you want to,' Mary said.

The young man glanced out of the door again, and then back at Mary.

'If you're sure . . . ' he said hesitantly. 'I don't want to be no trouble to you.'

As if he could be, Mary thought. He might look a big strapping feller, but deep inside she knew he was nowt but a poor little mite.

'Tuck in before they go cold,' she encouraged him.

The young man closed his eyes, and from the way his lips were moving she could tell he was saying his prayers.

'You're not a local, are you?' she asked, when, his devotions over, he began to attack his chips.

The young man hastily swallowed a chip before answering.

Now, here was a lad who'd been taught not to speak with his mouth full, Mary thought.

'I've only just moved here,' he said. 'I've got a job workin' at Dodge's farm just this afternoon.'

'And where are you livin'?'

'Nowhere yet,' the lad admitted. 'But I'm lookin' for lodgings.'

'That won't be easy in this village,' Mary told him.

'Oh, I can pay,' he replied. Balancing his chips in one hand, he fumbled in his pocket with the other, and pulled out a crumpled piece of paper. 'This nice lady in Manchester worked it all out for me,' he continued.

'Did she, now?' Mary said.

'Yes,' the lad told her. He smoothed the paper out on the counter and squinted at the educated writing. 'If I earn fif . . . teen bob a week, I can pay ten bob a week for rent as long as I get most of me meals thrown in. An' I'm to put money a . . . aside each week. So much for clothes, so much for new boots, and so much for a rainy day.' He looked out of the door at the downpour, the expression on his face suggesting that he had no idea how money would be any use on a day such as this.

'What's your name?' Mary asked.

'Spudder Johnson.'

'That's a bit unusual,' Mary said.

'Oh, it's not me real name,' Spudder told her.

'You don't say,' Mary replied, doing her best to hide her amusement.

'No, me real name's Clarence, but at the first farm I worked on, the gaffer said I was the fastest 'tater picker he'd ever seen, and folk have been callin' me Spudder ever since.'

'And where are you goin' to sleep tonight, Spudder?' Mary asked.

The boy shrugged. 'As I told you, I'm lookin' for lodgings.'

'It's a bit late in the day to start lookin' now,' Mary said. 'Why couldn't you spend the night at the farm?'

Spudder reddened. 'The gaffer's got three young daughters,' he mumbled. 'An' he said . . . he said . . .'

Mary laughed. 'Don't worry, lad,' she told him. 'I can well imagine what he said. But that doesn't solve your problem, does it?'

'If I can't find a room for the night, I'll sleep under a hedge. I've done it before.'

'Well, you'll do no such thing tonight,' Mary told him, almost before she realized what she was saying. 'You can kip down in our spare room. But it won't be free, mind,' she added sternly.

Spudder examined his coins again.

'I've got twopence farthin',' he said. 'If that's not enough, I'll pay you the rest when the gaffer gives me me first wages.'

Mary smiled. 'I don't want your money, lad,' she said. 'But I've got a job I could use some help with.'

'Will it be difficult?' Spudder asked worriedly. 'Only sometimes, when things are difficult, I make a bit of a mess of 'em.'

'Is peelin' 'taters difficult?' Mary asked.

Spudder grinned with relief. 'No, I think I could manage

142

that,' he said.

'Right,' Mary said. 'There's half a hundredweight of potatoes in the back that need peelin' before the evenin' rush starts.'

'Just show me where they are,' Spudder said.

By the time Ted Taylor returned from Manchester, Spudder had peeled the potatoes, swept up the back yard and cleaned the wash-house windows.

'He's a grand little worker,' Ted admitted, watching him through the kitchen window. 'But who exactly is he?'

'How did the competition go?' Mary asked.

Ted looked at his wife sharply. 'Why do you ask that?' he said.

'I'm interested, that's all,' Mary replied, though actually what she really wanted to know was just how good a mood her husband was in.

'The competition went champion,' Ted said. 'We made all the other bands look like beginners. But stop tryin' to change the subject an' tell me about this lad.'

'He hadn't got anywhere to stay for the night,' Mary said. 'I told him if he did a bit of work, we'd put him up.'

'Did you, now?' Ted said.

'He's ever such a nice lad,' his wife replied. 'And you can see he's completely harmless. I just couldn't bear the thought of him sleepin' rough on a night like this.'

Ted looked out of the window again. Spudder had found some whitewash from somewhere, and was giving the coal-house a coating.

'I suppose there's no harm in him stayin' the one night,' he conceded. 'But only the one, mind.'

'That's all I'm askin',' Mary said, glad that the Adelaide Band had played so well on this particular occasion.

They had meat and potato pie for supper. Spudder tucked into it as if he hadn't eaten for days, but the second the meal was over he was on his feet and collecting up the plates.

143

'Sit down for a minute or two,' Mary told him. 'Give your supper time to digest.'

'I can have the plates washed in a jiffy,' Spudder said.

'Sit!' Mary ordered, and with a slightly self-conscious grin, Spudder sank back into his chair.

'Tell us a bit about yourself, lad,' Ted said as he slowly filled his pipe with black shag.

Spudder looked at him blankly, as if, having told them his name, he could think of nothing more to add.

'Where are you from?' Mary prompted.

'I move around a lot,' Spudder said. 'I went hop pickin' in Kent once.' He grinned. 'That's easier work than pickin' 'taters, that is.'

'But where were you born?' Mary asked. 'Where were you brought up?'

A look of pain came to Spudder's face.

'I don't like to think about that,' he said. 'It gives me 'eadaches.'

'But you like farmin', don't you?' Mary asked, rapidly steering Spudder away from what was obviously a painful subject.

Spudder was instantly more relaxed.

'Oh, I like farmin' all right,' he told her enthusiastically. 'It's a grand job. You're out in the fresh air all the time, close to nature, like. But the thing I like best is the birthin' season. I love watchin' all them little animals comin' into the world and . . . ' He stopped, as if suddenly remembering something he had once been taught. 'I'm sorry,' he said, 'I know it's not the sort of thing you should say in front of a lady.'

Mary laughed. 'I've had eight children, Spudder,' she said. 'You're not going to offend *me* by talking about givin' birth.'

And yet, thinking about it, she realized that she might well feel uncomfortable having this discussion with most people. But Spudder was somehow different to most people. There was an almost childlike innocence about him, though he seemed completely to lack the cruel side of most children's nature.

Spudder rose to his feet.

'If you'll excuse me, I'll do the dishes, then turn in,' he said. 'I won't wake you up in the mornin' when I leave.'

'We'll already be up,' Ted told him. 'We rise at six in this house.'

Spudder grinned. 'I'll have been workin' for an hour by then,' he said.

'But it won't even be light,' Ted said.

'I don't mind the dark,' Spudder told him. 'And I can get me best work done before other folk turn up.'

'Mike Dodge won't pay you overtime, you know,' Ted cautioned him. 'Not that tight old bugger.'

'Oh, I don't want payin' overtime,' Spudder said. 'I just want enough money for me food and board an' – he reached into his pocket for his piece of paper – 'an' a little bit left over for boots an' a rainy day.'

Mary gave Spudder a candle and showed him up to the back bedroom.

'It's nice,' Spudder said, looking round. 'Homely.'

Mary pulled back the blankets and took out the bedpan.

'I've aired it for you,' she said.

'I could have done that,' Spudder told her.

Mary laughed. 'Don't you ever stop?' she asked.

'I like to keep busy,' Spudder said. 'It stops you thinkin' too much when you're busy.'

'I'll leave you to it, then,' Mary said, although her maternal instincts were telling her that what she should really do was stay and make sure he was snugly tucked in.

'You've been very kind to me,' Spudder said.

'Think nothing of it, love,' Mary told him, and before she could stop herself, she stood on tiptoe and kissed him lightly on the cheek.

Ted's pipe was blazing merrily by the time Mary got downstairs.

'He's a bundle of energy, that Spudder,' Ted said.

'He is,' Mary agreed.

'A nice lad an' all. Honest and trustworthy. I suppose some folk might call him a bit slow – '

'That's not his fault,' Mary interrupted.

' – but then nobody's ever accused me of bein' a great scholar,' Ted continued.

'I'm glad you like him,' Mary said. 'Did you know the Gibbonses are emigrating to Canada?'

'Aye, somebody mentioned it to me on the train back from Manchester,' Ted said.

'That'll mean their house'll be left empty,' Mary continued in a voice so completely free of guile that Ted instantly suspected that she was up to something.

'I should imagine it will,' he said slowly, 'unless they're meaning to take it with them.'

Mary laughed so heartily at his joke that his earlier suspicion became a certainty.

'This house used to be full of children,' Mary said, 'but now there's only the two of us. Our Becky's got her bakery . . .'

'Yes, how's that goin'?' Ted asked mischievously.

'You know how it's goin',' Mary replied, annoyed that her husband was steering her away from the subject she really wanted to talk about. 'She's sellin' to half the shops in Northwich and she's started doin' some outside caterin' as well.'

'It's all due to that Monsoor Henri,' Ted said. 'He's a genius, that French feller.'

'It's due to Becky's hard work an' all,' his wife replied crossly. 'But as I was sayin' to you, our Becky's doin' all right, and the other kids are all set up as well . . .'

'Is this leadin' anywhere?' Ted asked. 'I mean, should I go for a walk and come back when you've got to the point?'

Mary took a deep breath. 'Do you remember that first holiday we had together in Blackpool?' she asked.

'How could I ever forget it?' Ted replied. 'The trumpeter

146

in the Municipal Band got taken ill on our second day, and I stepped into his place.' He sneaked a glance at his wife, shifting restless in her seat, and couldn't resist teasing her further. 'It was a good band, that an' all,' he continued. 'Why I bet if they'd entered competitions they could have . . .'

Mary shook her head in exasperation.

'I'm not talking about that,' she said. 'I'm talkin' about the fact we discussed openin' a little seaside boardin' house.'

Boarding houses and Gibbonses moving! It was starting to make sense to Ted. More than that – Mary's idea had given Ted one of his own. There'd been something he'd been trying to get his wife to do for years, and this just might be the chance he'd been waiting for.

'A boardin' house,' he said reflectively. 'Yes, now you remind me, I think we did talk it over once.'

'We did more than that,' Mary told him. 'We had it all planned out. But it was nothin' but a dream really. If we work till we're a hundred, we'll still not be able to afford it.'

'You're probably right, there,' Ted agreed.

'But that's no reason we couldn't set up a little boarding house somewhere else,' Mary said.

Ted found it hard to fight back his smile.

'Have you anywhere particular in mind?' he asked.

'We could rent the Gibbonses' house,' Mary said, as if the idea had just occurred to her.

'I suppose we could,' Ted said. 'But are you sure that if you did, you'd get any lodgers?'

'Oh, there must be dozens of young lads lookin' for decent, clean accommodation,' Mary said.

'Like that lad upstairs?' Ted asked with a twinkle in his eye.

'D'you know, I hadn't thought about him,' Mary said. 'But now you mention it, I suppose Spudder might be interested. So what do you think? Shall we give it a try?'

Ted looked doubtful, though he was laughing inside.

'I don't know,' he said gravely. 'We couldn't run both the chip shop and the boarding house on our own.'

'Oh, I realize that,' Mary said.

'Well, then?'

'We'd have to employ a maid,' Mary said briskly.

Ted pretended to turn the matter over in his mind, then finally nodded his head.

'Aye, if we took on a full-time maid, we might just be able to manage it,' he conceded.

'I'll put an advert in the paper first thing in the morning,' Mary told him.

'You do that,' Ted said.

He had been trying to persuade his wife to take on a maid for years, and now he had finally succeeded in slipping one in through the back door. It was not often he managed to outmanoeuvre Mary, and just for the moment he was relishing his victory.

Chapter Eleven

In the middle of June, the Gibbons family made their tearful farewells and set off for a new life in Canada, leaving Mary Taylor with happy memories and the rent book to Number 49, Ollershaw Lane.

So it was actually going to happen, Mary told herself, feeling the stiff cardboard of the rent book cover between her fingers. What had started out as a vague idea the day she had first seen Spudder was really coming to pass, and in a few short days she would be a boarding house landlady.

She already had her tenants lined up. There was Spudder, of course – it would never have done to exclude him. Then there was Mr Spratt, a big-boned, fleshy man who worked at one of the boat yards in Northwich and, as he put it himself, 'would want a big, home-cooked tea,' when he got back from a hard day's graft.

The last – but no means the least – of the lodgers was a middle-aged man with short black hair which came to a widow's peak at the crown of his head. He had a small moustache and a pointed black beard. His name, he told Mary, was Mr Marvello – although he much preferred to be called the Great Marvello – and he was a prestidigitator.

'A what?' Mary had asked him when he'd told her.

'An entertainer, madam. A very superior kind of magician, and one who, without wishing to sound vain, can still express the hope that one day he will play before royalty.'

Mary wondered aloud why a presti-whatsits should want a room in her little boarding house.

'Because, very occasionally, I am without bookings,' Marvello said, a little embarrassed. 'And when such a rare thing occurs, I need a place to retire to. Besides, I have a few little treasures which it is not convenient to carry around with me, and I would like to leave them with a person I can trust. You are such a person, Mrs Taylor. I can tell.'

Mary was pleased and flattered.

'Oh, I'm honest all right,' she said. 'You can ask anybody in the lane.'

And the Great Marvello – who had, in fact, made a few discreet enquiries – just smiled.

'Spudder can have the front bedroom,' Mary said as she proudly took her husband on a guided tour of Number 49, which was a mirror-image of their own house. 'He'll like that, havin' a view of the street. An' I'll put Mr Spratt in the back bedroom, because workin' in that noisy boat yard all day, he'll appreciate a bit of quiet when he gets home.'

'Got their lives all planned out for 'em, haven't you?' said Ted, but Mary, full of enthusiasm for her new venture, didn't even notice that he was poking fun at her.

'An' Mr Marvello can have the parlour,' she continued. 'It's right next door to the chip shop, but that shouldn't bother him too much, because he won't be here very often.'

The grand tour completed, Ted and Mary returned to their own little kitchen in Number 47.

'I'll do the cookin' in here and take it round to the lodgers on trays,' Mary explained.

'In that case, you might as well convert the kitchen next door into another bedroom, mightn't you?'

'Certainly not!' Mary said, shocked by the very idea. 'The food'll go round on trays, but I'm not havin' *my* lodgers eatin' off 'em. They'll sit down at the table like respectable people, and when they finished their supper, they can use the room as their smokin' lounge.'

'Bloody hell!' Ted said, 'they'll be living better than we are.'

His wife gave him a hard look.

'And so they should,' she said practically. 'They'll be paying guests and I'm not having anybody saying I'm serving them short.'

'As if anybody'd dare,' Ted said, almost under his breath.

There was a knock on the door, and Spudder walked in.

'I've just met that feller I'll be livin' with when I was in town,' he said excitedly.

'Which one?' Ted asked.

'The presti . . .' Spudder began. 'The presti-doody . . . presti-dooley . . .'

'It's all right, Spudder, love,' Mary said. 'We know which one you mean, now.'

'He found this gold coin behind me ear,' Spudder continued. 'Goodness knows how long it's been there.'

'And did he give it to you, since it was your ear it was hiding behind?' Ted asked, grinning.

'Course he didn't,' Spudder said with dignity. 'Finders keepers. Anyway, he says when he's in a show in Northwich or Warrington, I can help him with his act.'

'That'll be nice for you,' Mary said. 'Did you just come to tell us about that, or was there somethin' else you wanted?'

'I've come to move in,' Spudder said.

'You can't move in yet, Spudder, love,' Mary told him. 'We've only just got our hands on the rent book.'

'But if you have got the rent book, the house must be yours, mustn't it?' Spudder said, obviously mystified.

'Well, yes,' Mary admitted. 'But it's not been decorated, you see, and we can't start havin' lodgers until it's been decorated.'

'Let me do it,' Spudder said.

'The decoratin', you mean?' Mary asked.

'Yes,' Spudder said. 'I did a good job of whitewashin' the coal-house, didn't I, Mr Taylor?'

'You did,' Ted agreed. 'An' you did a good job on the wash-house and the lavatory as well.'

'When did he do the wash-house?' Mary asked.

'While you were fussin' about next door in your new boardin' house,' her husband told her.

'But I was only gone a bit over an hour,' Mary said.

'I know,' Ted replied. 'Quick as well as good, isn't he?'

'Can I do it?' Spudder asked. 'Please?'

'But it's such a big job,' Mary said doubtfully. 'Whenever will you find the time? I mean, you're out in the fields before any of the other men, and you stay there long after the rest have gone home.'

'I like to keep busy,' Spudder said. 'Besides, it'll be my way of sayin' thank you for bein' so kind to me.' He looked at her with his big, sad eyes which reminded her so much of an injured puppy's. 'Let me do it,' he pleaded.

It was impossible to resist him.

'All right, Spudder,' Mary said. 'But if you find it too much for you, you must promise to tell me.'

'I won't find it too much,' Spudder said cheerfully. 'You'll see, I'll have this place lookin' like a little palace in no time.'

Spudder was as good as his word. Almost before Mary would have believed it possible, he had stripped off the old wallpaper and replaced it with new, painted all the wood-work and laid new oilcloth throughout.

'You've done a marvellous job,' Mary told him.

Spudder grinned with pride. 'It's me first real home,' he said.

'But you must have had a real home when you were small,' Mary said, then wished she could have bitten her tongue as she saw Spudder's happy face suddenly cloud over.

'I'm gettin' one of me headaches,' the young man told her. 'I think I'll go and lie down.'

'He's made a grand job of the decorating, I will say that,' Mary said to Ted that night after they closed up the chip shop and were having a last cup of tea in their kitchen.

'When are your other lodgers moving in?' Ted asked.

'Mr Spratt's comin' the day after tomorrow, and Mr Marvello'll bring his stuff as soon he gets back from Wigan,' Mary replied.

'It's about time you started thinkin' about taking on a

maid, then, isn't it?' Ted said.

Mary seemed suddenly absorbed in the pattern on the tablecloth.

'Are you with me, lass?' Ted asked. 'I said it's about time you started thinkin' about a maid.'

Mary began to trace the pattern on the cloth with her finger.

'There's no hurry,' she said quietly.

'No hurry!' Ted retorted. 'By the end of next week, you'll have three extra men to cook and clean for, and you say there's no hurry.'

'Maybe we don't really need any help,' Mary said. 'After all, I did bring up six kids on me own.'

'You were younger then and we weren't running a chip shop,' Ted pointed out. 'You can't manage without a maid, and that's that – so there's no point in arguin' about it.'

Mary opened her mouth as if she *were* about to argue, then rapidly closed it again.

'What's the matter, lass?' Ted asked. 'Are you worried that we can't afford it?'

Mary shook her head. 'No,' she said. 'With all the rent we'll be gettin', we can easily pay the wages.'

'Well, then, what's the problem?'

Mary raised her hands from the tablecloth and waved them helplessly in the air. 'I've never had anybody workin' for me before,' she said. 'I don't know how to go about it. I don't even know where to . . . what do you call it . . . interview them.'

'Why not do it here?' Ted asked, indicating the kitchen.

'Oh, I couldn't do that!' Mary protested.

'And why not?' Ted asked.

Mary made another helpless gesture. 'Well, I mean, the girls will be used to big houses, with rooms full of fancy furniture and this isn't really –'

'It's where the girl'll be workin' once you've hired her, isn't it?' Ted interrupted.

'Well, yes,' Mary admitted. 'But even so . . .'

Ted laughed. 'So what you're sayin' is that not only do we hire a maid, but we also have to rent a bigger house for her to work in,' he said.

Mary's cheeks reddened.

'It's not a joke, Ted,' she said.

He saw that it wasn't – at least to her – and became more serious.

'How about if we rented a room in the *Crown* for the interviewin'?' Ted asked. 'Would that make you feel better?'

'Oh, could we, Ted?' Mary asked, obviously relieved. 'And will you come with me, in case I get stuck for somethin' to say?'

Ted sighed theatrically. 'This boardin' house is causing me so much trouble I'm beginnin' to regret I ever came up with the idea in the first place,' he said.

'But you didn't come up with it,' Mary told him. 'It was all my idea.'

'I know,' Ted said, winking at his blushing wife. 'That's me point.'

The advertisement was placed in the newspaper and the room was booked in the *Crown*.

'Are you sure we need a . . .?' Mary asked.

'Yes,' Ted said. 'We *do* need a maid.'

On the morning of the interviews, Mary's first panic was over what she should wear.

'Me best dress'll make me look like I'm puttin' on airs,' she explained to her husband. 'But if I wear one of me old ones, they'll probably think I'm too scruffy.'

Ted knew it would be a mistake to laugh, and instead put his hand comfortingly on her shoulder.

'Let's get one thing straight, love,' he said gently. 'You're the employer and they're the workers. It's them that's got to impress you, not the other way around.'

'Oh, I know that,' Mary said. 'But you will give your boots another going over with the brush before we set out, won't you?'

*

To get to the small private dining room they had booked for the interviews, it was first necessary to pass through the bar parlour, and Mary was shocked to see seven young women sitting there, obviously dolled up in their Sunday best.

'Have they all come for the job?' Mary whispered to the manager as he showed them the way.

'Indeed they have,' the manager replied.

'Fancy!' Mary said nervously. 'An' all from one little advert in the newspaper.'

The hotel's staff had prepared the private room for the interview by removing all the furniture except for one table and three chairs.

'I trust this is satisfactory, madam,' the manager said.

'Oh yes,' Mary mumbled. 'Most satisfactory.'

'Well, you can start whenever you're ready,' the manager said, and took his leave.

Mary sat down awkwardly on one of the two chairs which had been placed on the left side of the table and gazed worriedly at the single chair on the other side.

'Shouldn't we have brought some paper with us?' she asked.

'Whatever for?' Ted said, taking his seat beside her.

'To write things down on,' Mary said. 'Details an' that. I mean, it stands to reason if we weren't expected to write anythin', they'd never have given us a table.'

'For goodness sake, love, calm down,' Ted told her.

'I think I'm a bit edgy because there's seven of 'em,' Mary confessed. 'I never expected seven of 'em to turn up.'

'Well, look on the bright side of things, it gives you plenty to choose from,' Ted said.

'I'd almost rather there was only one of 'em,' Mary said. 'Then I'd *have* to give her the job.'

'An' if she turned out to be no good, you'd only end up sacking her within the week. Then we'd have to go through the whole thing all over again,' Ted pointed out.

'You're probably right,' Mary admitted, fingering the collar of her dress. 'Well, I suppose you'd better ask the first one to come in.'

The first one turned out to be a pretty girl of nineteen who announced herself to be Rebecca Thomas.

'My daugher's called Becky, too,' Mary said with relief.

The girl looked offended.

'Ay'm Rebecca, not Becky,' she said in one of those 'naice' voices that servants sometimes pick up from their employers.

Oh dear, I've offended her! Mary thought in a panic.

And though she had prepared lots of questions to ask – had even practised them in the mirror – she froze, unable to think, unable to speak, able only to sit there with a fixed smile on her face.

'Er . . . tell us where you've worked before, love,' Ted said when it was obvious he could expect nothing more from his wife.

'Ay used to work for a family in Altrincham,' the girl told him.

'And were you the only servant, like?' Ted asked.

'Oh no!' said the girl, as if shocked by the idea. 'Mr Watkins, the master, held a very good position on the Manchester Cotton Exchange, you see.'

'So who else was there?' Ted asked.

'Well there was Cook, of course,' the girl said. 'And then the scullery maid, the boots and the gardener. Ay was employed mainly to help the mistress with her wardrobe, although Ay did occasionally do a little laiht dusting.'

'I don't think you're quite what we're looking for,' said Mary, finally coming out of her trance.

The girl seemed surprised.

'Ay come highly recommended,' she said.

'I'm sure you do, love,' Mary told her kindly. 'But to be honest, I don't think you'd really be happy workin' for us. It'd be somethin' of a step down for you.'

'Ay see,' the girl said, rising to her feet.

'On your way out, could you ask the next one to come in, please?' Ted said with resignation in his voice.

*

Not all of the girls who followed her had had such 'laiht' duties as Rebecca Thomas, but Mary still found it impossible to imagine any of them polishing the brass rod over her grate or donkey-stoning the front doorstep.

'Well, that's the last one, love,' Ted said after the seventh had departed, 'and we're still no closer to gettin' a servant than we were when we started out.'

'I'm sorry, Ted,' Mary said, taking her husband's hand. 'You've been so good and understandin' and all I've done is mess you about. It's just that I wouldn't have felt comfortable havin' any of them girls workin' in my house.'

There was a heavy knock on the door.

'That'll be the manager, I expect,' Ted said. 'Come in.'

It wasn't the manager. Instead it was a middle-aged woman who could have been described as large, though that would have been rather like saying Blackpool Tower was quite tall. She was a mountain of a woman, with forearms as thick as a navvy's, and flaming hennaed hair. Ted had to blink twice to make sure she was really there.

'I'm Aggie Brock,' the apparition said. 'I saw the advert in the paper, and I've come about the job.'

Ted looked at his wife for guidance, and when she nodded he said, 'Sit down, Mrs Brock.'

Aggie lowered herself into the chair, which almost seemed to groan under her weight.

'Have you worked as a servant before?' Mary asked.

'No,' the formidable lady replied. 'Before me marriage I was a bag-stitcher at salt works.'

'So you don't have any experience of domestic work?' Mary said.

'How many kids have you got, Mrs Taylor?' Aggie asked.

'Six,' Mary said, surprised.

'I've brought up eleven,' Aggie said. 'There's not much you can tell me about domestic work.'

'How would your husband feel about you workin' for us?' Ted asked.

'Him!' Aggie said with contempt. 'Even if he was still

around, he wouldn't have anything to say about it – the drunken good-for-nothing.'

'Has he passed on?' Ted asked, before Mary could stop him.

'Passed on!' Aggie said. 'All he ever did was pass *out*, and one night I got so sick of it that I picked him up and threw him out of the kitchen window. I haven't seen hide nor hair of him since.'

'We were really lookin' for a live-in servant,' Ted said. 'You wouldn't be willin' to live in, now would you?' he continued, praying that Aggie Brock would say no.

'I've got me own house,' Aggie said. 'The landlord'd like nothin' better than to get me out . . .'

Ted felt his stomach sink at the thought of this woman living in his back bedroom.

'. . . but I'm not movin' out for him or nobody else,' Aggie continued. 'It's my home, and when they do take me out of it, it'll be in a box.'

An' a bloody big box at that, Ted thought, wondering how he could end the interview without running the risk of suffering the same fate as Aggie Brock's husband.

'Do you think you could work for me, Mrs Brock?' Mary asked suddenly.

'Do you mean, will I take orders?' Aggie asked.

'Yes,' Mary replied, quietly but firmly. 'That's exactly what I mean, Mrs Brock.'

'I won't call you ma'am,' Aggie replied. 'I wouldn't call nobody ma'am. But while I'm in your house, you're the boss, just the same as I'd be the boss while you were in mine.'

'We'll let you know as soon as we've both had time to think it over properly, Mrs . . .' Ted said.

'Can you start on Monday, Aggie?' Mary interrupted.

'It's as good a day as any,' Aggie Brock replied.

They presented a perfect picture together – the man on the horse and the little boy who sat between him and the pommel.

'Faster, Papa!' Gerald Worrell screamed.

Richard urged his mount into a gentle canter. What a wonderful son he'd been blessed with, he thought. Gerald was still not much more than a baby, but he already felt at home on a horse, as long as he was sure his father's strong arms were clasped tightly about him.

'Faster!' Gerald shouted again.

'This is quite fast enough for a little boy,' Richard told him sternly.

'Isn't!' Gerald protested. 'Want to go much faster. Please, Papa!'

And because he could deny his son nothing, Richard increased the pace until they were travelling at a slow gallop.

'Are you happy now?' he asked his son.

'Yes,' Gerald said.

And Richard felt a warm glow inside him which had little to do with the bottle and a half of wine he'd knocked back at lunch.

The old oak tree loomed up ahead. Richard reined in his horse, dismounted and lifted Gerald out of the saddle.

'Papa's tired,' he said. 'We'll rest here for a while.'

'Want to play,' Gerald replied.

Richard laughed indulgently. What energy the boy had!

'What shall we play?' he asked.

'Tigers!' Gerald said emphatically.

Of course it would be tigers! It had been the boy's favourite game ever since they'd seen the magnificent beasts at the circus in Manchester.

Richard thought about the prospect of crawling round on his hands and knees while Gerald cracked his imaginary whip – and even the idea was enough to make him feel giddy. He really must make an effort to cut down on his lunchtime drinking, he told himself.

'I'm too tired for tigers,' he said. 'Couldn't we play something a little quieter?'

Gerald looked disappointed for a second, then brightened and said, 'Just me play.'

Yes, that was probably for the best, Richard thought, because he really did need to sit down and clear his head a little.

'All right, you play it on your own,' he agreed, 'but don't go far away. I want to be able to see you all the time.'

The child immediately rushed off towards the edge of the woods, as if worried that if he stayed any longer his father would change his mind. Richard lowered himself to the ground, rested his back against the old oak tree and took a sip of brandy from his hip flask.

What was it about this place which seemed to draw him to it? Richard wondered. It held nothing but unhappy memories for him. First there had been his seduction of Becky, which could have been a *happy* memory but for what followed it. And then there was the discovery that his wife was deceiving him with a common groom. He should have hated this tree – in fact, he often thought he did – yet he found himself coming back again and again.

He turned his attention to his son, who was taming an invisible tiger with an invisible whip.

What a wonderful child you are! he thought for about the thirtieth time that day.

Gerald had learned to walk and talk at a much earlier age than any of the children of Richard's friends. And he was growing up to look very like his father. In a few years his babyish chubbiness would melt away and he would have the same long straight nose, the same chiselled features. Then he would break a few hearts!

Richard took another slug of brandy and wondered if one of the hearts he broke would be his cousin Michelle's.

'Papa?' said Gerald, who had returned while Richard had been deep in thought.

'Yes,' Richard replied, almost dreamily.

'I want Mama.'

Damn! He'd hoped the child would have all but forgotten about Hortense by now.

'Why are you worried about your Mama?' Richard asked.

'Aren't we happy together – just the two of us?'

'Yes,' Gerald said doubtfully. 'But I want Mama.'

Why does he want Hortense? Richard thought angrily. She had never paid Gerald half the attention he had – never lavished a quarter of the love on the boy that his father had drenched him in.

'Want Mama!' Gerald persisted.

'Shut up!' Richard snapped.

Gerald began to cry, his tiny body heaving with great sobs. Richard took the boy in his arms, full of guilt over being so rough with him.

'Mama's very sick,' he said soothingly. 'She's much better off in the hospital.'

He pictured the 'hospital' in his mind. The walls around the institution were high and forbidding. The grim-faced attendants who ran it were known as 'keepers'. And the title fitted them, Richard thought. They kept the inmates in their care under tight control, because if one of them escaped, it was the keepers who were held responsible, and the keepers who had to bear the cost of search and recapture.

He pictured Hortense, too, as he had seen her on his one and only visit to the asylum. She'd been walking round in a daze, doped up to the eyeballs with morphia or bromide. She hadn't even recognized him, and he'd been glad enough about that. Yes, the hospital was the best place for her, because as long as she was kept behind its walls, her shameful secret could not escape either.

'Where's William?' Gerald asked, calmed down a little by his father's loving touch. 'Is he with Mama?'

'No,' Richard said, thinking of the slatternly woman he'd paid to take the baby away – and was still paying, every week, to raise him. 'No, he's not with Mama. He's gone to live with his own kind.'

'Don't understand,' Gerald said.

'He's gone to live with the working class scum,' Richard replied, and though he had never intended it, there was a harshness in his voice which started Gerald crying again.

Chapter Twelve

It was Saturday afternoon, the time of the week when Becky sat down at the front room table with all her bills and reminded herself that even though there was quite a lot of money coming into the bakery, a great deal of it quickly went out again. She was halfway through totting up what seemed like an outrageous bill for flour when there was a knock on the door and Daisy entered.

'The post's here, missus,' the maid said.

Becky smiled. Daisy knew she wasn't allowed to call her mistress 'madam' any more, yet she found it almost impossible to make her tongue say 'Becky'. So finally she'd settled on 'missus', which was what most agricultural labourers called the farmer's wife.

In some ways, Daisy had adapted well to the change in circumstances that life in the new house had brought. She never complained that she had to do the menial work herself. She didn't seem to mind the fact that she no longer had a cook to prepare her meals, nor that there were no kitchen maids to wait on her.

On the one thing, however, she was adamant. Though Becky told her it looked silly in a two-up, two-down, she refused to abandon her starched maid's uniform in favour of ordinary clothes.

'I'll leave the platter on the edge of the table, then, shall I, missus?' Daisy asked.

'Yes, thank you, Daisy,' Becky replied abstractly as she re-checked the cost of the flour delivery.

That was another habit Daisy had retained from the old days – bringing in the mail on a platter.

'We can't let our standards slip just because we're poor

now,' she'd told her mistress sternly when Becky had dared to suggest that it might be easier just to carry the letters in her hand.

The silver had all been sold long ago – to help finance the business – but Daisy still insisted on a platter, even if it was only made of humble pottery.

As soon as Daisy had gone, Becky looked through her letters. Most had local postmarks and were probably either bills or orders, but the one at the bottom of the pile had been posted in London, and written in a hand that she recognized immediately.

'Oh no!' she groaned.

The letter spelt trouble, she was certain of that. For a moment, she was tempted to throw it away, or at least put off opening it until later. But it had never been her way to run from difficulties, and she supposed it was too late to start now. Sighing softly, she slit the envelope and took out a single piece of paper.

Dear Becky,
  I would like to see you on an important matter, but for obvious reasons, I dare not show my face in Cheshire. So you will have to come to me. Please be outside Osmond's Hotel on the Strand at 3 p.m. next Thursday.
                    Your loving brother,
                              Philip
P.S. Tell nobody you have received this message.

'Typical!' Becky said to the wall. 'Absolutely bloody typical.'

Philip had not written for years, and now, when he had finally deigned to put pen to paper, it was only because he wanted something.

'There's not a word in the letter about Mam and Dad,' Becky told the wall. 'For all he knows, they could both be dead. And now he expects me to drop everything and rush down to London. Well, I won't do it! I won't!'

*

Although Becky had visited Liverpool and Manchester a number of times, she had never been to London before, and she was finding the whole experience bewildering. Everything about the capital seemed bigger, faster or more confusing than anything she had come across before. How many people there'd been on Euston station – soldiers, sailors, men in top hats, women with lap dogs, a whole theatrical company which was about to set off on a tour of the provinces!

How many hansom cabs there appeared to be waiting outside, and what horrifying speeds they travelled at!

Or maybe it's just that I'm a little country mouse who feels lost in the big city, she thought with a smile as she handed over the fare to her cabby, who had weaved his way in and out of the traffic between Euston and the Strand in a truly lunatic fashion.

She checked her pocket watch. Ten minutes to three. Despite the fact there'd been points on the journey when she'd had her doubts that she'd make it at all, she was in plenty of time for her meeting with Philip.

Becky glanced up the Strand. Next to the Osmond's Hotel was a place which advertised itself as a shaving and hair-cutting establishment, and seemed – from the size of the lettering – to be particularly proud of the fact that it had a 'Ladies' Room'.

Becky wondered what it would be like to have her hair done in a shop instead of relying on her mam – as she had done before her marriage – or Daisy, who'd taken charge after she'd become Michael's wife. Try as she might, she couldn't really imagine letting a stranger mess around with her hair.

She looked at her watch again. Five minutes past three. Philip was late – but then she'd have been surprised if he hadn't been.

The street was choked with traffic, mainly horse-drawn omnibuses plastered with advertisements for Fry's Cocoa, Nestlé's Milk and Reid's Stout.

There were a fair number of pedestrians about, too. A toffee-maker pushed his handcart along the road. A chimney sweep walked by, keeping close to the kerb so as to avoid staining the smart frock coats of the city gentlemen with his own sooty jacket. A shoeblack, dressed in the smart red uniform of his trade society, walked hopefully up the street in search of businessmen who might spare a couple of minutes in their busy day to have a shine.

Becky checked her watch for a third time. Philip was already half an hour late.

I'll give him another ten minutes, and then, whether he's coming or not, I'm off, she told herself.

A man with a bushy nautical beard approached Becky, eyed her speculatively, and stopped.

'I wonder if you could help me, ma'am?' he said.

'What is it you want?' Becky asked.

'I'm a sailor, you see,' the man said. 'I works on the ships what go over to America. Well, we 'ad this one passenger on the last trip, foreign bloke he was, wot got took poorly . . .'

'I don't really see why you're telling me . . .' Becky began.

'. . . got took poorly,' the man persisted, 'and my mate sez, "Let's look after 'im special, and there might be somethin' in it for us." So we did – and look what he give us.'

The sailor opened his hand to reveal four large gold coins.

'That's very interesting,' Becky said, 'but I don't see what it's got to do with –'

'They're not American,' the sailor continued. 'They're Greek or Spanish or summat. The bloke who give them to us said they was valuable, only the thing is, I don't know where to go to sell 'em.'

'I can't be much help to you, there,' Becky said. 'I'm a stranger myself.'

'They're no use to me,' said the sailor, looking her straight in the eye. 'I'd give 'em to anybody in exchange for a good old English pound.'

'Be off before I set the law on you!' said a voice from over Becky's shoulder.

The man with the coins glanced at the new arrival, then walked rapidly away.

Becky turned round and saw Philip standing there. He was wearing a double-breasted frock coat with covered buttons and he looked every inch the London gentleman.

'That was no more a sailor than I am,' he said with a grin, 'and the coins he was trying to sell you won't be worth threepence.'

But Becky had already forgotten about the bogus sailor. There was room in her thoughts only for Philip, who, however much of a scoundrel he might be, was still her dear brother. She crossed the pace or two which separated them, and flung her arms round him.

'You should have written sooner,' she said as she hugged her brother to her.

'I was going to,' Philip replied, 'but . . . you know . . .'

Yes, she knew.

They disentangled, and for several seconds just stood looking at one another.

'You get more beautiful every year, Becky,' Philip said, with a look of frank admiration in his eyes.

'And you,' said Becky, 'are as unreliable as ever. Half an hour, you kept me waiting.'

'I'm sorry about that,' Philip said. 'I wasn't late. I was watching you from across the street.'

'But why?' Becky asked.

'To make sure you weren't being followed,' Philip said.

Becky laughed. 'Who'd follow me?' she wondered aloud.

'It was when I saw that con man trying it on with you that I knew it was safe,' Philip said, ignoring her question. 'He wouldn't have come anywhere near you if there'd been even the slightest whiff of danger. They can smell trouble a mile off, can fellers like him.'

'Trouble?' Becky said. 'Philip, what exactly are you on about?'

'I'll tell you all about it later,' Philip promised, 'but first, I'm going to treat you to a slap-up tea at one of the most expensive hotels in the whole of London.'

The doorman of the Carlton tipped his hat with added deference when he saw it was Philip who was approaching, and the *maître d'* in the Palm Court was most concerned that the table he had selected for them was to his young guest's liking.

Becky sat down on one of the elaborately carved chairs and took in the scene. The room was filled with what looked like big ferns, though, given the name of the place, she thought they were probably really palm trees. Every few yards there was an enormous Chinese vase, and at the far end of the Palm Court a small orchestra was playing soothing teatime music.

'Are you impressed?' Philip asked.

'I am, a bit,' Becky confessed. 'You seem to be very well known. Are you a regular, or something?'

'Yes, I do come here quite often,' Philip said airily. 'I consider it one of the more stylish establishments in London.'

The tea Philip ordered was enough to feed an army, but he did not show much interest in the scones and cream cakes himself. Instead of filling his plate, he reached into his coat pocket and took out what appeared to be a magazine.

'Look at this,' he said enthusiastically.

He was holding out a ha'penny comic called *Funny Cuts*. He thrust it into his sister's hand. Becky glanced at the front page. A headline at the top announced a thrilling competition inside, which guaranteed the winner a pound a week for a year.

'Fifty-two pounds,' Becky said, laying the comic down on the crowded table. 'A lot of money. That's over twice as much as Mam and Dad opened the chip shop on.'

It must have been something in her voice which made Philip say, 'How are Mam and Dad, by the way?'

'I was wondering when you'd ask,' Becky said tartly. 'They're very well, as a matter of fact. And to save you the trouble of making any more enquiries, the rest of the family's 'doing all right, too.'

'That's good,' Philip said abstractly, the implied rebuke going completely over his head.

He picked up the comic Becky had discarded so readily, and opened it in the middle. Next he placed it in front of his sister, though he was careful to keep his hand on the top of the page, so the title was hidden.

'Well, aren't you going to look at it?' he said.

'What for?' Becky asked. 'Is it you that's won the prize or something?'

'Just look at the page,' Philip urged her.

'I didn't come all the way down to London just to waste my time reading a comic,' Becky told him.

'Please,' Philip said, with that coaxing way he had about him.

'Oh, all right,' Becky replied, sighing theatrically.

The page was divided into six panels. The central character in each one was a woman with a nose like a crow's beak and black hair tied in a tight bun. In one of the pictures she was sitting in a pub, talking earnestly to two other women. In another, she was standing by her front gate and shouting out gossip to people who were passing by. Underneath each picture was part of the story.

In spite of herself, Becky found she was getting interested. It was not the story which had grabbed her attention, but the character. She looked very familiar, almost like someone Becky had known all her life.

'Don't you see it?' Philip asked. 'Haven't you understood yet?'

'Understand what?' Becky said.

'You can be stupid sometimes,' Philip said exasperatedly. 'All right, if you can't get it any other way, just read the title.'

He removed his hand with a flourish the Great Marvello would have been proud of.

'The Amazing Adventures of Not-Stopping Goodbody,' Becky read.

Not-Stopping Goodbody? Of course, that was who it was!

The artist had got Mrs Bracegirdle down to a tee. But how could anybody living in London possibly have known about . . .

'You wrote this!' Becky said.

'Yes,' Philip said, trying to look modest – and failing.

'I never knew you had it in you,' Becky said admiringly.

'Oh, that's only a minor sideline,' Philip said. 'You don't get to have tea at the Carlton very often on a writer's pay.'

'So what else do you do?' asked Becky, fearing the worst.

Philip turned the comic over and pointed to a line at the bottom of the back page. Publisher: Philip Crawford.

'That's the name I go under these days,' he said.

Becky gave her brother a look which was a mixture of pride and relief.

'Imagine that, you a publisher,' she said. 'And since you can afford to give away a pound a week for a year, it seems like you're a *successful* publisher as well.'

'I'm not selling as many copies of *Funny Cuts* as Alf Harmsworth sells of his *Comic Cuts*,' Philip said, 'but I'm doing all right.'

Becky's relief did not last for long. Even if Philip was a successful publisher, he must have done *something* wrong, or he would never have written her the letter he had – wouldn't have waited for over half an hour before he dared approach her on the Strand. The expensive tea he'd bought her in this posh hotel was only his way of trying to butter her up before he asked for her help.

She looked at him now, staring into his teacup and searching for the courage to say what was in his mind. She tried to feel angry and found she couldn't summon up even mild annoyance. You just had to take Philip as he was: selfish most of the time, but occasionally capable of great kindness. Besides, he was her brother – her baby brother, even though he was older than her – and she couldn't help being fond of him.

'Becky?' Philip said after some time had passed.

'Yes, Philip?' his sister replied.

'I need a big favour, Becky,' Philip told her.

'I know you do,' Becky said, smiling despite herself. 'What have you done wrong this time?'

'Nothing!' Philip protested. 'I swear it. I'm a respectable publisher now. As honest as the day is long.'

They must have some pretty short days in London, Becky thought, but all she said was, 'Well, then?'

'It's from before,' Philip said. 'Unfinished business. Do you remember that chap from Manchester I was working for? Caspar Leech?'

'I don't remember him because I've never met him,' Becky said. 'Was he the feller you were smuggling jewels for when you were supposed to be workin' for Michael and me?'

'That's him,' Philip said.

He looked ashamed of himself, and maybe he was. But you could never tell with Philip. He might simply be *acting* ashamed because he thought that was what Becky would expect of him.

'So what about Caspar Leech?' Becky said.

'He told me when I started workin' for him that if I lost any of the jewels, he'd kill me,' Philip said.

'And you did, didn't you?' Becky said. 'When our works collapsed into that hole, the jewels went with them.'

'That's right,' Philip agreed.

'But that was years ago,' Becky said.

'Time doesn't matter to Leech,' Philip told her. 'He's got a memory like an elephant.'

'You should be safe enough as long as you don't go anywhere near Manchester,' Becky said.

Philip shook his head. His earlier confidence had evaporated, and now he looked like a frightened little boy.

'You don't know how the underworld works,' he said. 'It's like a club. Leech has all kinds of contacts in London, fellers who'd kill as a favour to him and think no more about it.'

'I think you're getting worried over nothing,' Becky said. 'You've started imagining things.'

'I haven't,' Philip protested. 'Listen, I'd only been in

London for a couple of months when a mate of mine told me that Leech had put a reward on my head. Ten guineas! That's a fortune to a lot of people. I know men who'd sell their own grandmothers for ten guineas.'

Becky laughed. 'If there really was a price on your head, why hasn't one of these men who'd sell their own grannies turned you in to Leech long ago?' she asked.

'Because they can't find me,' Philip told her. 'As soon as I learned about the reward, I moved my lodgings and changed my name to Crawford.'

'Well, then, stop worrying,' Becky urged her brother. 'You must be safe by now.'

'That's what I thought,' Philip said. 'Two years without a word about Leech, I was convinced I was in the clear. Then last week I went into this chop house I use now and again, and . . . and . . .'

He was really frightened now. His face was as pale as a corpse's and his hands were trembling.

'Tell me the rest,' Becky said encouragingly.

'I went into the chop house and the owner told me that some nasty characters had been round to ask him if he knew anybody called Philip Taylor. Well, he didn't like the look of them, so he said no. But then they roughed him up a bit and made him admit that somebody called Philip, who looked like the feller they were after, did drop in sometimes for a bite to eat.'

'Don't go there again,' Becky said.

'I won't,' Philip replied. 'But don't you see? If they track me down to a place I don't go to very often, how long will it be before they find out where I live?'

'You've got a point there,' Becky admitted. 'So what do you want me to do about it?'

'Go and see Caspar Leech and persuade him to leave me alone,' Philip begged her.

'Let me get this straight,' Becky said. 'You want me, your little sister, to go and see this big criminal in Manchester – a man who's probably had more people killed than you've had hot dinners – and persuade him to leave you alone?'

'That's right,' Philip said.

'How?' Becky asked him.

'How what? Philip said.

'How am I going to persuade him?' Becky said.

For a second, Philip looked almost on the point of tears. Then, suddenly, he brightened.

'You'll think of something,' he said optimistically.

Becky shook her head in wonder. 'You know, Philip,' she said, 'when I first got your letter, I thought you were going to ask me to do something difficult. But you haven't, have you?'

'Haven't I?' Philip asked.

'No,' Becky replied. 'You've asked me to do somethin' which is bloody near impossible.'

Chapter Thirteen

Mary Taylor soon learned that there was more to running a boarding house than seeing that the rooms were clean and there was food on the table. She had 'staff' now – and staff caused problems.

The first complaint came from Ned Spratt, the big burly lodger who worked in the boat yard.

'I'm not happy,' he announced as he stood in Mary's kitchen, shifting his weight uncomfortably from one foot to the other.

'Whatever's the matter, Mr Spratt?' Mary asked. 'Is it the food that's botherin' you?'

Spratt shook his head. 'The grub's wonderful, Mrs Taylor,' he said, licking his lips at the memory of it. 'That hot-pot you gave us the other night was the best I've ever tasted. Them pork chops we had on Sunday melted in me mouth. An' as for your stewed beef and barley –'

'Are you havin' trouble with any of the other guests?' Mary interrupted, because while it was flattering to hear her cooking praised so lavishly, she really did want to know what the problem was.

'Mr Marvello's pigeons used to keep me awake a bit with their cooin',' Spratt confessed.

'His *what* kept you awake?' Mary said.

'His pigeons,' Spratt repeated. 'The ones he uses in his act. They sleep in his room. But I've got used to them. And they're very clean, really. They have to be. I mean, when they're on stage in front of all them people, he can't have them shi . . . they have to behave themselves, don't they?'

The Great Marvello was away on tour, but Mary made a mental note to point out to him next time she saw him that she was keeping a boarding house, not a zoo. That done, she turned her attention back to Mr Spratt.

'So if it's not the food and it's not the other lodgers, just what is your problem?' she asked.

'It's that maid of yours,' Spratt confessed. 'That Aggie.'

Aggie? But Aggie always seemed to be such a hard worker.

'Isn't she doing her job properly?' Mary demanded. 'Is she leavin' the house dirty?'

Spratt shook his head. 'You can't fault her on her cleanin',' he said. 'You could eat your dinner off that floor when she's finished with it.'

'Well, then?' Mary asked.

'It's a bit embarrassin',' Spratt admitted.

'If you don't tell me what it is, I can't do anythin' about it, can I?' Mary said.

Spratt looked down at the floor.

'She will insist on making me bed,' he said.

'That's what she's paid to do,' Mary told him. 'Is there somethin' wrong with the *way* she makes it?'

'She does it while I'm still in it!' Spratt blurted out.

'She does what?' Mary asked, scarcely able to believe her own ears.

'She says she's got enough to do without waitin' on likes of a lazy devil like me to get up,' Spratt said, 'so she makes the bed while I'm still lyin' there.'

Mary saw it all in her mind's eye – big Aggie lifting the mattress while Ned Spratt, no lightweight himself, was being tossed up and down – and she couldn't help laughing.

'It's no joke, Mrs Taylor,' Spratt protested. 'I like to ease me way into the mornin', and by the time she's finished with me, I feel like I've been trampled by a bunch of wild horses.'

'I'm sorry, Mr Spratt,' Mary said, doing her best to suppress her giggles. 'I'll have a word with her and tell her not to do your room until *after* you've left the house.'

'I'd appreciate it, Mrs Taylor,' Spratt said. 'Honestly I would.'

*

It was no easy task telling off a woman built like a carthorse, but Mary persisted and in the end Aggie admitted that perhaps it wouldn't do any harm to leave Ned Spratt's room till the last.

'But I've got a complaint of me own,' the huge cleaner said.

'About what?' Mary asked.

'That Spudder!' Aggie told her.

'Spudder?' Mary said. 'But he's a lovely lad. What could he have possibly done to upset you?'

'You'd be surprised,' Aggie said, placing hands the size of potato pies on her broad hips. 'Do you know what I caught him doing this morning?'

Mary felt herself start to blush. Though no one ever talked about it, she was well aware that single young men had certain . . . well, needs – felt certain desires. And she had no doubt that if Aggie had caught him doing something to relieve these needs, the big, blunt maid would not hesitate to tell her about it, and in fairly colourful language, too. Still, there was no way out of it – she had to ask the question.

'What was he doin'?' she said.

'Blackleadin' the grate!' Aggie said. 'And if he's not doin' that, he's polishin' the oilcloth. You should see his room. I'm not kiddin', it's sparklin'. There's not a thing out of place.'

'I don't really see what you're so upset about,' Mary admitted.

'I don't go up to the farm and pick all his 'taters for him, do I?' Aggie said hotly.

'No,' Mary agreed. 'I suppose not.'

'Right!' Aggie said. 'Then you tell him to keep his big nose out of *my* work.'

'I'll have a word with him next time I see him,' Mary promised with a heavy sigh.

Seeing Spudder was not usually a problem. The lad was in and out of Mary's kitchen all the time, either asking her if there were any jobs she wanted doing or just sitting and watching her work. That day, however, he didn't come anywhere near, and after she had prepared her lodgers' evening meal, Mary decided that if he wasn't going to come to her, she'd better go to him.

Slipping on her hat, she made the short journey round to Number 49 and knocked on the back door.

'Come in,' said a voice she recognized as Ned Spratt's.

Spratt was sitting at the table, tucking into the food she'd prepared for his supper.

'It's grand, this pigeon pie of yours,' he said. Then a sudden thought occurred to him. 'It's not one of the Great Marvello's pigeons, is it?' he asked worriedly.

Mary laughed. 'No,' she said, 'it isn't. I did look in his room for one, but he seems to have taken 'em all with him on tour.'

'Thank heavens for that,' Spratt said, attacking the pie with renewed pleasure.

Mary wondered why her other lodger wasn't at the table, too.

'You haven't seen young Spudder by any chance, have you?' she asked Spratt.

'He's up in his room,' the boat builder replied. 'When Aggie brought the trays round I did knock on his door and tell him his supper was ready, but he said he wasn't hungry.'

Spudder, not hungry? The lad had one of the healthiest appetites Mary had ever seen, and it just wasn't like him to miss a meal.

'He's not ill, is he?' she asked worriedly.

'I asked him that,' Spratt between mouthfuls of pie, 'and he said no, he wasn't, he just didn't feel like eatin'. So I thought, well, that's all the more for me.'

Mary climbed the steep narrow stairs and knocked on Spudder's bedroom door.

'Go away, Ned!' Spudder called out. 'Leave me alone!'

'It's not Mr Spratt,' Mary said. 'It's me.'

'The door's not locked,' Spudder said miserably.

Mary didn't make a habit of going into men's bedrooms,

but in this – as in so many other things – Spudder was someone to whom normal rules didn't seem to apply. She turned the handle, pushed the door open, and stepped into the room.

Spudder was sitting on his bed with his head in his hands.

'Are you all right?' Mary asked.

Spudder looked up. His eyes were red, as if he'd been crying, and his whole face was pale and drawn.

'Are you feeling poorly?' Mary said.

'No,' Spudder replied. 'I'm just a bit upset, that's all.'

She'd come round to tell him that if he could mess his room up a bit more, Aggie would be much happier. But that could wait till later.

'What exactly is it that's been upsetting you, love?' she asked kindly.

'I like it, livin' here in this house,' Spudder said. 'I don't want to have to move on again.'

'Nobody's askin' you to move,' Mary told him.

'If he sends somebody after me again, I'll have to move,' Spudder said. 'I'll have to.'

'If *who* sends someone after you?' Mary asked.

'They nearly caught me in Northampton,' Spudder said, though he was talking to himself rather than Mary. 'If I hadn't been quick, they'd have had me there.'

'These men who nearly caught you,' Mary said. 'Were they bobbies? Did they have uniforms on?'

'No, they weren't wearin' uniforms,' Spudder said, 'but I think they were them other kind of policemen.'

'Detectives,' Mary said.

'That's right,' Spudder agreed. 'Detectives.'

Mary took a long, reflective look at the poor suffering boy.

'Spudder, have you done something wrong?' she asked, though it was difficult to think of the lad ever breaking the law.

Spudder bowed his head.

'Yes,' he said. 'But I didn't mean to.'

'I'm sure you didn't, love,' Mary said. 'Is it somethin' you could go to prison for?'

'I don't know,' Spudder mumbled. 'But I'd rather go to prison than let him get his hands on me again.'

'Who is *he*, Spudder?' Mary asked.

'I don't want to talk any more,' Spudder said. 'I'm gettin' another one of me headaches.'

Even in the safety of her own little village, Becky had been frightened at the thought of meeting a dangerous criminal like Caspar Leech, but once in the run-down neighbourhood of Manchester where Leech operated, she felt her fear growing stronger by the minute. Poverty was nothing new to her, she'd been brought up surrounded by it, yet the street along which she was walking almost took her breath away.

Ragged children were playing jacks on the grimy pavement and only glancing up to beg from any passer-by who might have a copper in his pocket. Men with clay pipes – but no tobacco to put in them – were sitting on broken doorsteps and looking as if they wished they were dead. Women, old beyond their years, were pegging out their washing to dry in the filthy air which filled the narrow street.

'Stick close by me, Mrs Worrell,' Cedric Rathbone said.

'Don't worry, I will,' Becky replied, shivering slightly.

They reached the building they'd been heading for, a street-corner pub called the Green Man. It was a disgusting place, in an even worse condition than the hovels which surrounded it. Yet the man who owned the pub wasn't poor. Far from it – he probably had more money than most of the swells who rode around in big, expensive carriages.

'Are you sure you want to go on with this, Mrs Worrell?' Cedric Rathbone asked.

'I've got to,' Becky said, clenching her teeth to give herself courage.

'Then let's get it over with,' Cedric said.

Two men in pork pie hats suddenly appeared in the pub doorway. One of them was a tall man with a razor scar running all the way across his left cheek. The other was shorter, but had broad shoulders and a bull-like neck. They were both nasty pieces of work, and between them they managed to block completely the doorway which – a few seconds earlier – had seemed very wide indeed.

'I think yer've come to the wrong place, lady,' the tall bruiser said, looking Becky up and down, from her wide-brimmed hat to the hem of her green silk dress.

'It's the right place,' Becky said, wishing her heart was not beating quite so fast. 'I've come to see a Mr Caspar Leech.'

'On the game, are yer?' the second bruiser jeered. 'Cos if yer are, yer wastin' yer time. Mr Leech likes 'em a bit rougher than you.'

Beside her, Becky felt Cedric Rathbone tense.

'Easy, Cedric,' she said urgently, taking a tight, nervous grip on his arm.

'I wouldn't mind a go with yer, though,' the second bruiser continued. 'What'll it cost me? A couple of bob?'

'I'm here to see Mr Leech on business,' Becky said.

'Mr Leech don't do business with folk like you,' the tall bruiser said, 'so you'd better sling your hooks before you get hurt.'

'We're going inside,' Cedric Rathbone said, 'and if you try to stop us, *you'll* be the ones that get hurt.'

The tall bruiser laughed unpleasantly. 'Are you threatening me?' he asked. 'A squirt like you? You couldn't even reach me face to land a punch.'

'True,' Cedric conceded. 'But you've got a big enough gut and I reckon I could reach that.'

'Yer what?' the bruiser said.

'You've got a big gut,' Cedric said, almost conversationally. 'I reckon I'll keep pounding at that until you fall over.'

The tall bruiser was beginning to sense something about Cedric Rathbone many other men had found out before him – that despite his size he was hard as nails, and getting hurt didn't bother him a bit as long as he could give as good as he got.

'I'll tell yer what,' the tall bruiser said uneasily. 'I'll go an' ask Mr Leech if he wants to see yer. And if he says he does, I'll come down again and let yer in. Fair enough?'

'Fair enough,' Becky agreed shakily.

'An' what shall I tell him it's about?' the tall bruiser asked.

'Tell him it's about Philip Taylor,' Becky said.

Leaving his friend to stand guard, the tall bruiser disappeared into the pub.

If I'm this scared now, how am I going to feel if I actually get inside? Becky wondered to herself.

A minute later, the tall bruiser was back again. 'Mr Leech says he'll see yer,' he said.

The two bruisers stepped aside so that one was standing at each edge of the door and there was room for Becky and Cedric to enter.

'If it's all the same to you, I'd like you to go first and we'll follow you,' Cedric said mildly.

The tall bruiser looked as if he was about to argue, then he shrugged his shoulders. 'This way,' he said, heading for the bar.

You've done it now, Becky told herself as she stepped over the threshold. You've gone so far there's no turning back.

Little light had managed to penetrate through the filthy windows of the Green Man and the inside of the pub was as dark and gloomy as a cave. It smelled too – of dirty sawdust, bad gin and vomit. As she followed the tall bruiser to the rickety stairs, Becky held her nose and tried not to look at the villainous drinkers who surrounded her.

The bruiser knocked on the door at the top of the stairs, and a voice like grinding machinery shouted that they could come in. The bruiser entered the room, and Becky and Cedric followed.

Caspar Leech's lair was in a different world to the pub below it. The fern green wallpaper was new and expensive, the *chaise-longue* in the corner would not have disgraced even the finest house, and the inlaid mahogany table at which Leech was working would have been the envy of many a man of business.

Leech himself was a large man with a broken nose and little piggy eyes. He turned those eyes on Becky now, and slowly examined her from head to foot.

'So this is the girl, is it?' he asked the tall bruiser.

'Yes,' the bruiser said. 'D'you want me to stay, Mr Leech?'

'No,' Leech told him. 'But don't go too far away. I just might need yer later.'

As soon as the bruiser had left, Leech reached in his pocket, took out some gold coins, and thumped them down on the table.

'I'm a busy man,' he said, 'so why don't you tell me where Philip Taylor's hidin', then I'll give yer the ten guinea reward, and yer can get the hell out of here.'

'I've not come to claim any reward from you,' Becky replied, keeping her voice as steady as she could. 'I'm Philip's sister.'

'His sister, are yer?' Leech said. 'So you'll know what that little bastard did to me, will yer?'

'Yes,' Becky said. 'I know.'

'When I give a man some hot jewels and tell him to see they get to a feller I know in London, I expect 'em to get there,' Leech told her.

'He was hiding the jewels at my husband's salt works,' Becky explained. 'The ground gave way and they were lost. It was an accident. It could have happened to anybody.'

'But it didn't happen to *anybody*, did it now?' Leech asked. 'It happened to your bloody useless little brother. I warned him if he lost the goods I'd take it out on his hide, and when I finally find him, that's exactly what I'm going to do.'

'Philip would like to make restitution to you,' Becky said.

Leech screwed up his piggy eyes.

'Restiwhat?' he asked, as if he suspected some kind of trick.

'Restitution,' Becky repeated. 'He's asked me to pay you what the jewels were worth, and add something on top for interest.'

Leech shook his head. 'The money doesn't matter,' he told her. 'It's the principle.'

'The principle!' Becky said. 'What principle?'

'I don't take excuses from nobody, and everybody round here knows it,' Leech said. 'That's why I'm cock o' the walk. That's why the lads who work for me are careful not to make any mistakes. Even if I wanted to let yer brother off – which I bloody don't – I couldn't do it, not without hurtin' me reputation.'

'Be reasonable, Mr Leech,' Becky pleaded. 'If you take the money, at least you'll have something to show for the lost jewels. Otherwise you've got nothing at all.'

'But I *will* have somethin',' Leech said, 'because sooner or later, I'll find your Philip, and when I do, he'll end up hanging from a gas light by his useless bloody neck, just to remind everybody that you don't bugger about with Caspar Leech.'

'Yes, they could do a lot of damage, could half a dozen good men,' Cedric Rathbone said, almost as if he were speaking to himself.

'What was that, Shortarse?' Leech demanded.

'I was just thinkin' that half a dozen strong Cheshire lads could wreck this place before you had time to blink,' Cedric explained.

'Are you threatenin' me?' Leech asked Cedric, just as his bruiser had done earlier.

'It's a funny thing about being cock o' the walk,' Rathbone continued as if he hadn't heard. 'A lot of it's up here,' he tapped his forehead, 'in other people's minds. You get respect from them because they've never seen you bettered. But once they have, that reputation of yours that you're so worried about would be gone for ever.'

Leech smiled, revealing several broken teeth. 'Yer sayin' that if you smashed up my pub, I'd be a laughing stock,' he said.

'Somethin' like that,' Cedric agreed.

'Yer a fool,' Leech said, still grinning hideously. 'And do

yer know why yer a fool?'

'No,' Cedric said evenly, 'but I'll bet any money that you're just about to tell me.'

'Yer let me know yer plans in advance, that's why,' Leech said. 'Within the hour, I can have twenty men guarding this pub.' He reached into his drawer, took out a large cut-throat razor, opened it and held it up so that Becky and Cedric could see the blade. 'Then again,' he continued, 'it might be easier just to have yer throats slit and drop yer in the Mersey.'

Becky gulped.

'Would you look out of the window, please, Mr Leech,' she asked, praying that the plan she'd mapped out with Cedric was going to work.

'Look out of the window?' Leech said, still brandishing his razor menacingly. 'Why should I bother to do that?'

'Because you might miss something very interesting if you don't,' Becky told him.

Still keeping a tight grip on his razor, Leech swivelled round in his chair so he was gazing on to the street.

'That big bugger you can see on the corner is Tom Jennings,' Cedric said, 'and standin' next to him is Brian O'Reilly who likes a fight whenever and wherever he can find one. The redhead's Nobby Clark. I once saw him lay out three coppers when he was so drunk he could hardly stand up himself. Now the feller with that big scar on his cheek is a real case –'

'That's enough!' Leech said, anger blazing brightly in his small eyes.

'But I haven't even told you about Chalky White yet,' said Cedric, who was really beginning to enjoy himself.

Leech turned his attention back to Becky.

'Yer brother's willing to pay what I would have got for the jewels plus interest?' he asked.

'Yes,' Becky replied.

'All right,' Leech said. 'Yer've got a deal. But don't think it's because I'm scared of them sods outside.'

'Of course not, Mr Leech,' Becky said, swallowing back a

gasp of relief. 'You're agreeing because you're a reasonable man. I could tell that from the minute I first set eyes on you.'

On the train back to Northwich everyone was as high-spirited as if they'd been on a day trip to Blackpool.

'You should have seen the look on that bugger Leech's face when he saw you all standin' there in the street,' Cedric said.

The others roared.

'Cedric really laid it on with a trowel,' Becky said. 'He told Leech that Brian was always looking for a fight and that Nobby once laid out three policemen when he was drunk as a lord.'

'And me a teetotaller all me life,' Nobby chuckled.

'Thank you, Cedric,' Becky said, suddenly more serious. 'It was very good of you to help, especially after what Philip did to you when you were working with him.'

'I did it for you and your husband,' Cedric said, 'not for that brother of yours. An' I'll tell you this for nothin', Mrs Worrell. If Philip doesn't make an effort to mend his ways, he's goin' to end up in such deep hot water that *nobody'll* be able to fish him out – not even you.'

'Maybe he won't get into hot water any more,' Becky said. 'After all, he is a successful publisher now.'

Yet even as she spoke she knew she was probably doing no more than kidding herself.

Chapter Fourteen

Seagulls glided across a grey sky, then swooped down on the choppy water which lapped against the quay wall. Squat tugs on the river hooted a noisy warning of their arrival or departure. Both to the left and the right, skeletal cranes twisted and turned, each one suspending an impossibly heavy load from a painfully thin arm. And across the whole scene blew the sea wind, its icy fury knifing its way through even the thickest coat.

Still, you have to expect a bit of cold in the middle of December, Becky thought cheerfully.

It would have taken more than a spot of bad weather to get her down on that particular day, because the only reason she was at the docks at all was to meet Michael, who was coming home from Africa to spend Christmas with his family.

There he was! She could see him walking down the gangplank with a small grip in his hand and a wide smile on his face. Becky dashed to her husband and threw her arms around his neck.

'I've missed you,' she said, almost crying with happiness.

'And I've missed you,' Michael told her. 'Stand back and let me get a proper look at you.'

Becky stood back and Michael's mouth dropped open in surprise.

'What's the matter?' Becky asked. 'Have I grown old and ugly while you were away?'

'No,' Michael replied, still looking dazed.

'Well, then?'

'I thought about you a great deal on the rivers,' Michael told her. 'I'd close my eyes, and I could see you so clearly it was almost as if you were there. But I was deceiving myself, because I never imagined you as beautiful as you look at this moment.'

'Get away with you!' Becky replied, embarrassed. She examined her husband as he had examined her. He was still as handsome as he'd ever been, but . . . 'You look thinner,' she said worriedly. 'And very, very tired.'

'I'm exhausted,' Michael confessed. 'It's the climate on the Oil Rivers. It really takes it out of a man.' He grinned. 'So I hope we haven't got far to walk to the cab.'

'It's just over there,' Becky said, pointing to the landau she had hired at Lime Street station.

'Then for goodness' sake, let's go,' Michael said. 'I can't wait to see that daughter of ours.'

'I would have brought her with me,' Becky said as they walked to the waiting cab, 'but I was worried she'd get a cold, and then she'd be in bed for Christmas and her daddy wouldn't have any excuse for playing with her Christmas presents.'

Michael laughed. 'If I'd really wanted to play with my child's toys, I'd have made sure we had a boy,' he said.

'Oh, you could have done that, could you?' Becky asked.

'Of course,' Michael said, as he opened the cab door for her.

As the landau rattled its way through the streets of Liverpool, Becky began to worry about Michael again. He really *did* look worn out, and she was sure that a few months' rest at home would do him the world of good.

'Do you have to go back to the Oil Rivers *very* soon?' she asked, nuzzling her head into his shoulder.

'I'm not going back there at all,' Michael said. 'I'm putting a manager in charge of the hulk and going further south, myself.'

'How much further south?' Becky asked.

'The other side of the equator,' Michael replied.

'And is there palm oil there, too?' Becky said.

'No,' Michael told her, 'but the people down there want

salt as much as the ones on the Oil Rivers, and they'll be prepared to give us rubber in exchange for it.'

'What's made you so interested in dealing in rubber all of a sudden?' Becky asked.

'It's the coming thing,' Michael said. 'Look at how many bicycles there are now, all of them needing rubber tyres. And once horseless carriages – or motor cars as they've started calling them – become popular, demand will go up in leaps and bounds.'

It sounded plausible, and anyone else would have accepted what Michael said on face value. But not Becky. She had been married to him long enough to know that Michael first decided what he wanted to do, and then searched around for a good commercial reason for doing it.

'What about the other work you were involved in?' she asked. 'The drainage ditches and such like. Don't the people on the Oil Rivers still need you for that?'

'I've taught them enough so they can continue to make improvements themselves,' Michael said. 'Besides, it's a question of priorities. I have to go where I can do most good.'

'So what's really behind the "good business sense" this time?' Becky asked her husband.

'You'll only laugh if I tell you,' Michael said.

'I won't,' Becky told him. 'I promise I won't.'

'Well,' Michael said, 'I'm going to try and put a stop to the slave trade down there.'

Becky didn't laugh, but she couldn't prevent herself from smiling. Put a stop to the slave trade! On his own? What a lunatic, big, wonderful, heroic husband she had.

'You've already planned out exactly how you're going to do it, I suppose,' she said.

'Of course,' Michael agreed.

'Well, tell me about it, then.'

'Everyone needs salt, but the natives who live where I'm going can't produce it themselves,' Michael explained. 'So what they have to do is buy it from the coastal tribes, who make it by evaporating seawater.'

'I don't see what any of this has got to do with stopping slavery,' Becky said.

'Patience, my darling,' Michael said. 'The salt makers on the coast will only take payment for their sea salt in slaves. A girl in her teens is worth about a hundred pounds, a lad of the same age will go for considerably less – say fifty or sixty pounds.'

'And . . .?'

'And if I can persuade the people of the interior they can avoid the long, hazardous journey to the coast by simply tapping rubber and exchanging it for my salt, they won't need to deal in slaves any more, will they? And without the need, the practice itself will soon die out.'

'You're always trying to take the problems of the whole world on your shoulders,' Becky said fondly.

'Not the whole world,' Michael corrected her. 'Just a small corner of it in darkest Africa.'

Becky kissed him softly on the cheek.

'I love you, Michael,' she said.

'And I love you,' Michael replied, 'much more than I can ever begin to tell you.'

On Christmas Eve, Mary Taylor paid her final instalment into the goose club and in return was given a plump white bird which would have graced the table of even the grandest household.

And it was a good job the bird *was* so big, she thought as she walked up the lane with the goose under her arm, because she had a lot of people to feed. Becky, Michael and Michelle were coming to Christmas dinner, then in the afternoon Jessie, Eunice and their families would be round, and no doubt they would like to eat a bit of the goose cold.

At least she wouldn't have to cook for two of her lodgers over Christmas. Mr Spratt was off to visit some relatives.

'But I'll tell you straight, Mrs Taylor, I'd rather stay here,' he'd said when he'd made the announcement. 'My cousin Maggie can't cook for toffee.'

The Great Marvello, on the other hand, would be absent because he had secured a booking at a theatre in Preston.

'A most prestigious engagement,' he told Mary. 'Another step on the ladder of opportunity which must one day inevitably lead to my appearing before royalty.'

Spudder was staying, though, and he seemed to have recovered his composure – and his appetite – since the night Mary had found him sitting in his room and worrying about the mysterious man who kept sending people to look for him.

Mary checked down her mental list to see if she had remembered everything. The pictorial Christmas greetings had been sent – she'd posted early for Christmas, just like the Postmaster-General had asked her to. The fir tree was taken care of, she'd bought that from the man who'd come round with a waggonload of them. She'd ordered a box of oranges and Ted had been sent off to the woods to collect some holly and mistletoe. She'd have to buy some new balloons from Sam Cooke's shop, but the Chinese lanterns they'd used the year before would do perfectly well again.

The clouds had hung heavy in the sky all morning, making the village look grey and miserable. Mary wished it would snow, because somehow Christmas just didn't feel like Christmas without snow.

As she reached her back door, Mary felt a single cold spot of something fall on to her nose, and looking up, she saw thousands of fluffy flakes floating slowly towards the ground.

'That's better!' she said happily.

By morning the village would be covered with a blanket of gleaming snow, and the children would be torn between playing with their new toys and rushing out to build snowmen.

It was going to be a lovely Christmas, she thought as she opened the back door. And it would have been a really wonderful one if only her three sons could have been there.

Not-Stopping Bracegirdle gave a short knock on Dottie Curzon's back door and then, without waiting for an invitation, opened the door and stepped inside.

Dottie was sitting down at the kitchen table, reading what looked like a comic.

'You'll wear your eyes out with all that readin',' Mrs Bracegirdle told her friend. 'Anyway, I'm not stoppin', but I just had to tell you about Michael Worrell. I saw him down by the post office, and he looked that thin you'd think he hadn't eaten for a week. An' I wonder how he likes his new home. Bit of a step down from what he's used to, isn't it?'

She paused for breath.

'D'you fancy a cup of tea, Elsie?' Dottie Curzon said.

'Well, as I said, I'm not really stoppin',' her friend replied, 'but I suppose I could spare a few minutes for a cuppa.'

Mrs Curzon stood up and, with the comic in her hand, walked over to the fireplace.

'Let's have a look at that comic while the tea's brewin', then,' her friend said.

'Oh, you wouldn't be interested in it,' Dottie said. 'It'll only wear out your eyes.'

'My eyes are younger than yours,' Mrs Bracegirdle said tartly.

'Only six months,' Dottie muttered.

'Stop bein' awkward an' hand it over,' her friend told her.

With some reluctance, Dottie passed the comic to Not-Stopping, then slid the kettle hob over the fire and went to get the tea caddy.

'*Funny Cuts*,' Mrs Bracegirdle read out aloud. 'What do you want to go wastin' your money on this for?'

'It's written by somebody from the village,' Dottie said.

'Oh, I knew that,' her friend replied quickly – and unconvincingly. 'Remind me who.'

'Philip Taylor,' Dottie said.

'That's right,' Mrs Bracegirdle agreed. 'I always said that lad would get on in the world.'

Standing by the grate and waiting for the kettle to boil, Dottie kept her back to the table. But she could not help hearing the sound of pages turning, and when she finally risked a quick glance over her shoulder, she saw that her friend had reached the middle pages. Now the fat would really be in the fire.

'"*The Adventures of Not-Stoppin' Goodbody*",' Mrs Bracegirdle said. 'Now what kind of a name is Not-Stoppin'? I've never heard of anybody called Not-Stoppin'. Have you?'

'No,' Dottie said, hardly able to contain herself. 'No, I can't honestly say as I have.'

'Why couldn't he have called her Mable or Brenda or somethin' normal like that?'

Or Elsie, Dottie mouthed silently.

The kettle boiled and Dottie poured the steaming water into the teapot. Next she went to the pantry to get the milk. By the time she had returned to the table, her friend had finished reading the comic strip.

Dottie knew it would be prudent to let the subject of the comic drop, but the temptation to say something was too strong and she soon gave in to the inevitable.

'What did you think of "*The Adventures of Not-Stoppin' Goodbody*", Elsie?' she asked.

'I suppose it's quite funny in a way,' Mrs Bracegirdle admitted. 'But it's a bit exaggerated, isn't it? I mean, nobody acts like that in real life, now do they?'

'That's true,' Dottie said, doing her best to hold in her laughter.

'Anyway,' her friend continued, 'I'm not stoppin' long, but I just had to tell you all about Michael Worrell . . .'

On Christmas Day, Mary forced herself to leave her warm bed just before dawn because – despite what most men seemed to think – Christmas dinners didn't just happen on their own, and she wanted to make an early start.

She was halfway down the stairs when she heard the noise of someone moving frantically around in the kitchen.

'Who's down there?' she called out.

'It's me,' Spudder replied. 'Merry Christmas!'

Mary shook her head in amazement. Didn't the lad ever

sleep?

She opened the door which led into the kitchen and almost fainted at the sight which confronted her. Next to the table stood Spudder, with so many feathers clinging to his clothes that he might have been attempting flight. And all around him was a chaos of holly, mistletoe, Chinese lanterns, Christmas tree decorations and balloons.'

'I plucked an' cleaned the goose an' peeled the 'taters,' Spudder said, blowing off a feather which had settled on his lip, 'an' I lit the fire so the oven would be nice an' warm when you wanted to put the goose in. Then I thought I might as well have a go at movin' the decorations around.' He stopped babbling and began to look worried. 'You're not mad with me, are you?' he asked.

'No, I'm not mad with you,' Mary said. 'But you have to admit, the place does look a bit of a mess.'

'I'll have it all straight again in a few minutes,' Spudder said enthusiastically. 'See, I'm goin' to move the Christmas tree over by the sideboard, and hang them lanterns on both sides of it, then I'm goin' to take the balloons an' . . . an' . . .'

Mary laughed. 'For heaven's sake, calm down a little bit, Spudder,' Mary said.

'I can't,' Spudder told her. 'I'm that excited. I've never had a Christmas like this before.'

A frown came to Mary's face. She knew better now than to ask, but she couldn't help wondering just what Spudder's previous Christmases *had* been like.

At twelve on the dot, Becky and her family arrived from their little house down the road. Michelle looked lovely, Mary thought. She had her mother's hair – and her nana's, of course – and you could tell, even now, that when she grew up she would be as beautiful as Becky. Michael looked a bit thin though, and Mary sometimes worried that her favourite son-in-law was trying to do too much.

'The decorations look lovely, Mam,' Becky said.

'Spudder arranged them,' Mary told her.

And so he had – and rearranged several times until they were almost back where they started!

'Very nice, Spudder,' Becky said, and the young man postively glowed with pleasure.

'Santa brought me this lovely dolly, Nana,' little Michelle said, holding up the toy with considerable pride.

'Only the one?' Mary asked.

'Yes,' Michelle confessed. 'But she *is* very pretty.'

'But you've been such a good girl this year that I was sure he'd have left you more than one,' her grandmother said. 'I'll tell you what you can do. Why don't you go over to the tree and see if Santa's left another one here for you?'

'Do you think he has?' Michelle asked excitedly.

'You never know your luck,' Mary told her.

Michelle rushed over to the tree.

'There is one!' she squealed. 'There is one!'

'Well, open it then,' her grandmother said.

As Michelle began to tear at the wrapping paper, Becky turned to look at her husband. His eyes were fixed on his daughter, and it was plain that though he saw so little of her, he loved her very much.

What an effort it's going to be to wrench himself away from her and go back to Africa, Becky thought. And what determination it must take to make him do what he felt he ought to do – rather than he wanted.

Michelle finished opening the parcel and triumphantly pulled out a golden-haired doll which was even more splendid than the one her parents had given her.

'She's beautiful,' the little girl said. 'I think I'll call her Emily.'

'Why Emily?' Mary asked.

'Because!' Michelle said with determination.

'Because what?' Becky asked.

'Just because,' Michelle said.

'And that should be a good enough reason for anybody,' Ted said, remembering back to the day when he had plucked the name Rebecca out of thin air and bestowed it on his youngest daughter.

It was the juiciest goose any of them remembered eating, a goose that Ned Spratt would have given his right arm to have just a taste of. But in the end even Spudder had had enough, and the family leant back in their chairs, stretched out their legs, and revelled in a feeling of well-being.

'By, but we've had some good Christmases, haven't we, love?' Ted said contentedly to his wife. 'Do you remember the one the year after our Becky was born?'

'We couldn't afford goose in them days,' Mary reminded him.

'Nor fancy toys, either,' Ted said. 'The first doll you had, our Becky, I made meself, out of old scraps of wood.'

'I know,' Becky told him. 'I've still got it.'

Ted grinned. 'You never have, have you?' he said. 'Well, fancy that!'

Spudder was being left out the conversation, Becky thought, and that wasn't right because it was his Christmas, too.

'Are you havin' a good time, Spudder?' she asked.

'I am. I'm havin' a grand time,' the young man replied.

'Still, Christmas is never *quite* the same when we get older, is it?' Becky asked. 'Remember what it was like when you were a kid?'

Spudder froze – and Mary cursed herself for not warning her daughter beforehand that there were certain things you just never discussed with her favourite lodger.

'Is something wrong, Spudder?' Becky asked.

'A room,' Spudder said in a flat, fearful tone. 'A little room with no windows. That's what I remember.'

'And now you can forget about it again!' Mary said, forcing herself to sound more cheerful than she felt. 'After all, you don't want to get one of your headaches, do you?'

'No,' Spudder said. 'I don't want to get one of me headaches.'

Though she wasn't really sure what she'd done wrong, Becky felt awful. 'It's a pity the lads aren't here, isn't it?' she said, doing her best to take everybody's mind – especially Spudder's – off what she'd said earlier. 'You've never met any of my brothers, have you Spudder?'

'No, but your mam's told me all about 'em,' said Spudder.

'Nothin' good, I'll bet,' Becky said.

Mary said, 'Oh, get away with you, Becky!'

And all the others laughed – except for Ted. Mention of his sons seemed to have put *him* in a bad mood.

'Our Jack and our George couldn't be here,' he said to Becky. 'One's got a business to run, and the other's servin' his country. But I would have thought your brother Philip could have made the effort to come up from London. After all, apart from you, none of us have seen him for years.'

As if it had been planned, there was a knock on the door at that very moment, and when Mary opened it, there was a man from Hitchen's Carriers standing at the door.

'Special delivery, missis,' he said, and handed her a letter.

Mary opened it.

'It's from our Philip,' she told the rest of the family. 'He says that he's sorry business has detained him in London, but he hopes we'll all like the presents.'

Ted looked at the empty-handed carter.

'Presents?' he said. 'What presents?'

'They're out on the waggon,' the carter said. 'I'd appreciate it if you'd give me a bit of a hand.'

When they went out into the lane, they could see what the carter meant. The whole waggon was piled high with gifts.

'By bloody hell!' Ted gasped, gazing at the mound of parcels with a glassy look in his eyes.

'Shall we get it all inside before we freeze to death?' Michael suggested.

'Aye, we'd better,' Ted said, coming out of his trance. 'But by bloody hell, just look at how much of it there is.'

They took the parcels into the kitchen, piled the ones for Eunice, Jessie and their families on the sofa, and then began to open the packages which were intended for them.

There was a new dress for Mary and a vanity case for Becky.

'Lovely!' Mary said, and Becky had to agree that her brother did have good taste.

Philip had sent Michael the most up-to-date maps of Africa.

'And he's written in the corner, "These are in case you get lost!",' Michael said.

'Cheeky young sod!' Ted snorted.

Michelle's present was an enormous doll's house.

'Now my dollies will have somewhere to live,' she said happily.

For Ted, Philip had chosen the very latest sheet music.

'Must have cost him a fortune, the silly bugger,' Ted grumbled as he looked down lovingly at his present.

And Becky smiled to herself and thought that sometimes – just occasionally – Philip did manage to do something right.

Becky glanced at her watch. There was a task she had to perform before the afternoon was over, a task she wanted to keep secret from Mary for fear of reviving unhappy memories. The only problem was, she couldn't remember *ever* being able to keep anything secret from her mam. Still, maybe all that goose had dulled Mary's wits, she thought. You never knew your luck!

'Would you mind looking after our Michelle for an hour or so, Mam?' she asked.

There must have been something in the tone of her voice – or perhaps the expression – which tipped her mother off, because instead of saying, 'Course I wouldn't mind, love,' as she usually did, Mary narrowed her eyes and said, 'Why? Where are you goin'?'

'Michael an' me thought we'd just nip down to the bakery for a while,' Becky said, doing her best to cling on to her secret.

'On Christmas Day!' Mary exclaimed. The eyes narrowed

even further. 'There won't be anyone else there, will there?' she asked.

'Well, I did ask Monsieur Henri if he wouldn't mind popping in for a couple of hours,' Becky admitted.

'So they've been bakin', have they?' Mary said.

'Yes,' Becky said, feeling like the mouse must when it realizes the cat has just been playing with it so far, but is now ready to move in for the kill.

'And who do you hope to sell the stuff to on Christmas Day?' Mary demanded, pouncing.

Becky sighed and gave into the inevitable. 'It's not for selling,' she confessed. 'I'm going to take it down to the workhouse.'

Mary put her hands firmly on her hips – a sure sign that she'd been offended.

'And why haven't you asked me to come with you?' she asked.

'When I was little, you used to tell me about what it was like when you and your mam were in the workhouse,' Becky replied. 'You always said you were very unhappy there.'

'And so I was,' Mary agreed. 'Who wouldn't be?'

'Well then, that's why I didn't ask you to come with me,' Becky said, rather lamely.

'Because of them bad memories?' Mary demanded.

'Well, yes,' Becky admitted.

'It's them memories that make me *want* to go with you,' Mary said, reaching for her bonnet. 'I haven't forgotten how much a little bit of kindness can mean when the rest of your life is full of misery.'

It was snowing heavily and the Worrell's Bakery waggon made slow progress on its journey to the workhouse at Leftwich. It was cold, too – the sort of cold which makes your teeth rattle and your nose run – but Mary, perched next to Cedric Rathbone, did not mind.

It's always as well to remind yourself, every now and again, how lucky you are, she thought.

And she *was* lucky. She had a good husband and fine children – even Philip seemed to be turning out right at last. She had a solid business and lovely grandchildren. She wished that just for this special day everyone in the world – kings and paupers, young and old – could be as happy as she was. She wished it, but she didn't think it likely.

It's Christmas Day, Hortense thought bitterly. Christmas Day! The time when families all got together and let each other know – even if they didn't put it into words – just how much they loved each other.

She tried to get up from the narrow bed on which she was lying, and found she couldn't. They'd doped her that morning, and while she was unconscious, they must have strapped her left leg to the bottom edge of the bed, and her right wrist to the top corner.

'It's for your own good,' she remembered her keeper saying as he'd held the chlorine-soaked rag to her face. 'You've been very unsettled today.'

Of course she'd been unsettled! Who wouldn't be unsettled by knowing that she would be kept away from her children on a day like this?

She thought of Gerald. There had been times when she hated him as his father's son, but now, after months of separation, she realized how much she missed him.

She thought of William – poor, helpless baby William – and felt as though her heart would break.

'I'm not having your bastard brat under my roof,' Richard had told her just before they'd brought her to this terrible place.

'Then let me take him with me!' she'd pleaded. 'At least allow me that comfort.'

'The authorities at the asylum would never permit it,' Richard told her.

'So what will become of him?' Hortense sobbed.

'I shall foster him out,' Richard said coldly. 'To someone of the same class as the scum who sired him.'

Where was he now, the poor little thing? Was he happy?

'Let him be happy!' she prayed. 'Let him have good foster parents. They don't have to be rich. I don't mind if they're the poorest people Richard could find – as long as they care for him.'

Yet even as she tried to assure herself that her baby would be fine, every ounce of her mother's instinct screamed out that he was as miserable as she was.

From the room next door to hers, she heard the sound of moaning. Further down the hall, a woman was crying. Hortense strained against the bonds which confined her to her bed. But it was no use, her keeper had done too good a job on them.

She wondered if she would ever be released from this horrible place, or if she would spend the rest of her life behind its grim walls.

She would write to Richard, she thought. She'd beg him to have her set free, would promise him anything if only he would let her see her children again. But that wouldn't do any good. The warden would probably refuse to send the letter. And even if he did, Richard would take no notice of it, because he knew that as long as she was imprisoned, the secret of her love affair with Jack Wright would be locked away, too.

I'll die in here, she told herself.

The moaning in the next room had grown louder. Soon one of the keepers would come and administer more chloroform to the poor tormented soul who had dared to make such a racket.

'Yes, I'll die in here,' Hortense repeated.

A tear ran down her cheek, and then another, and another. She made no effort to wipe them away. She wished she was dead already.

Part Three

1895–6

Chapter Fifteen

Barnaby Smith entered Colleen O'Leary's life through the front door of the New Inn one blustery day in March 1895. He was a tall man with deep grey eyes and a laughing mouth. He was wearing a top hat and an overcoat with a velvet collar, and the moment she saw him standing in the doorway, Colleen found herself wishing that she'd put on her smartest dress when her father had asked her to take over the bar.

Smith looked around the homely pub, evidently found it to his taste, and walked up to the counter.

'Good morning, young lady,' he said in a tone which made Colleen feel very special indeed. 'Could I trouble you for a pint of porter?'

'It's no trouble at all, sir,' Colleen said a little shakily.

She pulled the pint, and Smith slipped a gold sovereign across the bar to her.

'I'm afraid we don't have change for that, sir,' Colleen confessed.

'No matter,' Smith said casually, reaching into his pocket and bringing out some coppers.

Gentlemen – if they came into the pub at all – usually took their drinks to one of the tables, but this particular customer seemed quite happy to remain at the bar, and as she went about her duties, Colleen was conscious that his eyes were constantly on her.

For several minutes, he seemed content just to watch, but finally he broke the silence by saying, 'I see that like myself you are a member of the One True Faith, Miss . . .'

'O'Leary,' Colleen said, feeling flustered. 'How did you know I was a Catholic?'

'Now how *did* I know?' Smith asked, as if genuinely

puzzled himself. 'Perhaps it was the look of serenity in your eyes. Or perhaps it was the aura of purity and goodness which seems to surround you. Then again, I might simply have noticed the crucifix around your neck.'

Colleen hesitated uncertainly for a second, then, seeing that Smith was laughing, she readily joined in with his amusement.

'Do you come from round here, Mr . . .?' she asked.

'Smith,' the customer told. 'Barnaby Smith. And no, I am not native to the area. I come originally from Lancashire, where my family owns a little land, but my business takes me here, there and everywhere.'

'What business are you in, Mr Smith?' Colleen asked boldly.

'I am essentially a merchant,' Smith said, 'though I do have a share in a few small estates in the West Indies.'

'And what are you doing here?' Colleen enquired.

'Looking for investors in a new property I am thinking of developing in Trinidad,' Smith replied.

'And do you expect to be here long?' Colleen asked.

'If the businessmen of the Northwich area are as shrewd as I take them to be, then it should take me but a little while to raise the capital I require,' Smith said.

He finished his drink, placed his hat back on his head, and walked to the door.

'But however short my time here, Miss O'Leary,' he said, turning on threshold, 'you can rest assured that you and I will see each other again.'

Barnaby Smith became a regular customer in the New Inn, though anyone who checked on such things could not have failed to notice that he was much more likely to be there when Colleen was on duty than when she wasn't.

On his third visit, he brought flowers – roses – which he presented to Colleen with something of a flourish.

'Are those for me?' Colleen gasped.

Barnaby frowned. 'Certainly not,' he said. 'It would be

quite improper of me to bring flowers for an unattached young lady.'

'Would it?' asked Colleen, not knowing whether it would or it wouldn't, but wishing he *had* brought them for her.

'I brought the flowers to brighten up the hostelry,' Smith said. 'But if you were to put them in a vase in the window,' he continued, and now she could see the twinkle in his eye, 'I dare say you could look at them and *pretend* they were for you.'

'Spudder, my boy, your golden opportunity has arrived at last,' the Great Marvello announced when he returned to the boarding house from what he described as 'a dazzlingly successful tour of some of the more celebrated Yorkshire music-halls'.

'Me golden opportunity?' Spudder repeated. 'Me golden opportunity to do what?'

'To tread the boards,' the Great Marvello told him.

'Tread the boards?' Spudder said.

'Must you repeat everything I say?' the Great Marvello asked.

'Well, I've not understood a bloomin' word you've said so far,' Spudder confessed.

The Great Marvello sighed heavily. 'Against considerable competition, I have secured a booking at the Warrington Apollo,' he said.

'But that's only nine miles from here,' Spudder said.

'Correct,' the Great Marvello agreed.

And suddenly Spudder understood. 'You're goin' to let me to be part of your act like you promised,' he said excitedly.

'A once in a lifetime performance!' the Great Marvello said grandly. 'A debut which will also be a swan-song!'

'You've lost me again,' Spudder confessed. 'Does all that mean you don't want me after all?'

'It means,' said the Grand Marvello, 'that for just one night you will be privileged to be part of the act which will some day certainly play before royalty.'

'So you do want me?' Spudder said, looking confused.

'Yes, I want you,' the Grand Marvello said. 'Though I'm not sure I won't live to regret it.'

'You won't,' Spudder promised. 'I'll do everythin' you tell me to. Honest, I will!'

'Very well,' the Great Marvello agreed. 'But before your own appearance, I think it might be wise if you attended a performance as a paying member of the general public. In that way, you will be able to see how the professionals do it.'

'All right,' Spudder readily agreed. 'An' I'll come an' see the show, as well.'

'Yes,' said the Great Marvello, mopping his brow with one of his trick handkerchiefs. 'I think that might be a good idea.'

Spudder had never been in a theatre before, but he was having a grand time. There'd been singers and dancers and a man who juggled balls and beer bottles. Spudder hoped he could remember it all, so he could tell Mary about it tomorrow.

'And now, my lords, ladies and gentlemen,' said the man who came on between the acts, 'may I present to you the Great Marvello!'

Marvello walked on to the stage. He looked much bigger and more impressive than he did when he was sitting at the kitchen table in the boarding house, eating shepherd's pie.

'My charming assistant, Esmeralda,' Marvello said, pointing to the edge of the stage.

A girl appeared in the spotlight and Spudder first gaped at her, and then hid his head in his hands. She was wearing less clothes than he'd ever seen a woman wear before. The skirt part of her dress was so short that she might almost not have bothered with it at all, and both her arms were completely bare. Spudder peeped through his fingers just to make sure he'd not made a mistake – and discovered that he hadn't.

'For my first trick, ladies and gentlemen, I would like you to watch my hat very carefully,' Spudder heard the Great

Marvello say.

Spudder kept his hands tightly over his eyes for the first couple of minutes, but then the sound of gasps and applause became too much for him, and he lowered them again just in time to see Marvello produce one of his doves from a cloth bag.

For the rest of the performance, Spudder watched spellbound, though still doing his best to avoid seeing too much of the half-naked lady. How wonderful Marvello was, he thought. He could bring doves and coloured hand-kerchiefs out of thin air. He could make things disappear right before your eyes.

'My final trick is one that has astounded audiences up and down the length of this great country of ours,' the Great Marvello announced. 'Esmeralda, if you please.'

There was a long thin box lying on a set of trestles. The girl walked up to it and stepped inside. Marvello closed the box so that all the audience could see of his assistant was her head, feet and arms, all of which were sticking out through holes.

'And now, ladies and gentlemen, I will saw my lovely assistant in half,' Marvello said.

To Spudder's horror, Marvello actually did produce a saw and began to cut into the box. Spudder covered his eyes again – but this time he had his fingers in his ears, too.

'It was wonderful,' Spudder told Mary early the next morning. 'He cut right through the box with the woman inside it, pulled the two pieces apart, then put 'em back together again.'

'And you saw all this with your own eyes?' Mary asked, a smile playing on her lips.

'Well, no,' Spudder admitted. 'I had me eyes closed. But when I heard everybody clappin' I knew she must be all right, so then I looked.'

'Did you now,' Mary said.

'But only for a second,' Spudder added hastily, blushing

as he remembered how scantily dressed the girl had been.

Mary glanced up at the clock. 'It's half past six,' she said. 'Hadn't you better be settin' off for work? You're already an hour later than you usually are.'

'I'm not goin' in to work today,' Spudder said.

Mary raised an eyebrow in surprise. 'Not goin' in to work!' she said. 'But you never miss a day. What's come over you?'

'I've got to rehear . . . rehear . . .'

'Rehearse?' Mary suggested.

'That's right,' Spudder agreed. 'Rehearse with the Great Marvello. He's sawin' me in two tonight.'

The kitchen table in Number 49 had been moved back against the wall, and a large, coffin-shaped box lay in the space it had previously occupied. Spudder looked down at the box dubiously.

'Shouldn't we have it restin' on two chairs?' he asked. 'I mean, it's going to be hard for you to saw where it is now. An' there's always a chance you'll cut through the oilcloth.'

'I have no intention of sawing it in two here, my dear Spudder,' the Great Marvello said. 'Why, I didn't even bring my saw back from the theatre with me.'

Spudder looked puzzled.

'But I thought we were goin' to practise,' he said.

'And indeed we are,' the Grand Marvello told him. 'But I and my saw are merely a diversion, an effect to bring forth gasps from the audience. It is the box itself which will be doing the real work. And you, of course, my athletic friend.'

'I don't follow you,' Spudder said.

'The trick is not the sawing in half,' the Grand Marvello explained patiently. 'It's what goes on before and after the sawing which really matters.'

'I'm still not sure I'm with you,' Spudder said worriedly.

The Grand Marvello lifted the lid of the box. 'Look in there, Spudder,' he said. 'Now, does that look like an ordinary empty box to you?'

'No,' Spudder admitted. 'No, it doesn't.'

'Climb into the box and I'll show you just how it works,' the Great Marvello said.

There were only a few customers in the pub that afternoon when Barnaby Smith leaned over the bar and said, 'Could I have a word with you in private, Mr O'Leary?'

Paddy was not used to talking to the gentry without the security of a bar counter between them, and the question threw him quite off-balance.

'A word in private, sir?' Paddy asked. 'Now what would it be about, exactly?'

Barnaby smiled. 'If I could tell you that in a public place, then I would scarcely need a private word at all,' he said.

'Just a minute, sir,' Paddy said, and made his way to the other end of the bar where his wife was wiping down the spirit bottles.

'Somethin' the matter?' Cathy asked, noticing that Paddy looked a little flustered.

'That Mr Smith says he wants a word with me – in private,' Paddy told her.

A sparkle came to Cathy's eye. 'Well then, you'd better give him one, hadn't you, Patrick?' she said.

'But what could he want to talk to *me* about?' Paddy asked his wife.

'No doubt he'll tell you that himself,' Cathy replied, openly smiling now.

'And where should we go?' Paddy said.

'You'd better take him into the parlour,' Cathy said.

'I can't take a gentleman like him into our little parlour, can I?' Paddy protested.

'I don't see why not,' Cathy said. 'We've nothin' to be ashamed of. And you might have to get used to seein' Mr Smith in your home.'

'I'm not followin' you,' Paddy said.

'You men can be right thick sometimes,' Cathy told him. 'You just take Mr Smith into the parlour, an' I'm sure he'll spell it out for you much better than I could.'

'If you say so,' Paddy replied doubtfully.

Paddy led Barnaby Smith into the parlour.

'It's not much,' he said apologetically.

'On the contrary,' Smith replied. 'It is a room which positively emanates a feeling of warmth and togetherness.'

'Thank you, sir,' Paddy said, though he still felt uncomfortable.

'Yes, there is definitely a family feeling here,' Smith continued. 'And what greater blessing can a man hope for than a wife and a family?'

'That's true enough,' Paddy agreed. He became aware that they were both still standing, himself rather awkwardly and Smith perfectly at ease. 'Would you care for a seat, sir?' he asked.

'Thank you,' his guest replied, lowering himself gracefully into one of the large, over-stuffed armchairs. 'But I would prefer it, given the difference in our ages, if you would drop the "sir" and address me as either Barnaby or Smith.'

'Oh, I'm not sure I could do that, sir,' Paddy said. 'Not with you bein' a customer and one of the gentry an' all.'

'It really would make me feel more at ease,' Barnaby said. 'Couldn't you try it – as a favour to me?'

'All right,' Paddy said, taking the seat opposite his visitor. 'Now what exactly can I do for you, s . . . Barnaby?'

'I would like to tell you a little about myself,' Smith said. 'I am thirty-two years old and a bachelor. I was educated at Eton School, of which you may have heard, and Balliol College, Oxford, which may also be familiar to you. I have several business interests around the world, and whilst I do not think of myself as a wealthy man, I believe it would be fair to describe myself as moderately prosperous.'

'Where's all this leadin'?' Paddy asked.

Smith smiled. 'You mean, you really don't know?' he asked.

'No, I don't,' Paddy admitted.

Smith's smile broadened. 'In that case, you are a long way

behind your charming wife,' he said. '*She* knew what I was going to ask almost before I opened my mouth.'

'Did she?' Paddy said.

'She did indeed,' Smith told him. 'And now, in order to avoid further suspense, I will put all my cards on the table. Would you, sir, have any objection if I were to approach your daughter Colleen with a view to courtship?'

'I beg your pardon!' said the astonished landlord.

'I would like to – what are the words they use in this area? – I would like to "walk out" with your daughter Colleen, and before speaking to her, it was only right and proper that I should come to you to seek your formal consent. Is that consent forthcoming?'

Paddy looked closely at the other man, at his handsome confident face, at his wide tie and heavy cotton jacket, at his striped linen trousers and elegant boots. That outfit alone would cost the average working man in Marston a couple of months' pay, the landlord thought.

'Well, Mr O'Leary?' Smith said, with not a hint of impatience in his voice. 'Do I have your permission?'

'I don't know,' Paddy confessed.

'I think I understand your problem,' Smith said. 'You see before you a man who many would describe as "a good catch" and you are wondering to yourself why such a man should be bothered to pay court to the daughter of a country innkeeper. In other words, though you would scarcely admit this even to yourself, you think I could do better.'

'Now just a minute . . .' said Paddy, suddenly angry.

Smith held up his hands.

'Please let me finish, Mr O'Leary,' he said. 'There *is* no one better than Colleen. True, she is not what one may describe as conventionally pretty, but such matters have never greatly concerned me. Your daughter has a beautiful soul which shines out like a beacon. She is a charming companion and will, one day, make a wonderful wife and mother. And I am forward enough to hope that when she does enter the matrimonial state, it will be with me as her partner. Would you deny me – deny both of us – the chance to find happiness?'

Paddy scratched his head.

'Put like that, there doesn't seem to be any harm in you callin' on her,' he said. 'But I warn you, if you try takin' advantage of her . . .'

'If that was my intention, don't you think I would choose someone a little less . . . er . . . moral than Colleen?' Smith asked. He smiled again. 'And someone with a less protective father?'

Paddy grinned, despite himself. 'I suppose you have a point there, s . . . Barnaby,' he admitted.

'And now, since my next trick is far too dangerous for me to put the life of my lovely assistant at risk by asking her to be a part of it, I shall call for a brave volunteer from the audience,' the Great Marvello said. He peered into the front stalls. 'How about you, sir?' he asked, pointing.

Spudder stood up as Marvello had told him to, and found himself suddenly blinded by the spotlight.

'You're a great sport, sir!' Marvello said. 'Give him a big hand, ladies and gentlemen.'

The audience clapped enthusiastically and – just as he'd practised – Spudder bowed first in one direction and then the other.

'Now would you please come up on to the stage, sir,' the Great Marvello asked.

Spudder began to grope his way down the row, still blinded by the bright light which was following his progress. It wasn't easy. Other people's knees, which had seemed no obstacle to him when he was taking his seat, now reared up and collided with his own.

'Ouch!' someone called out comically – and most of the audience laughed.

Spudder reached out and found he was touching something hairy.

'Get yer hand off of my head!' said an indignant voice, and

the audience thought that was funny, too.

It was not until Spudder was nearly at the end of the row, however, that real disaster occurred. He tripped over a leg which had been – carelessly – left sticking out in front of him, and fell sprawling across the laps of two well-padded gentlemen.

'I'm . . . I'm dead sorry,' he mumbled as he pulled himself back on to his feet.

The audience had started to clap, and though Spudder didn't know why they were doing it, he thought it only polite to bow, which brought on new waves of applause.

He reached the end of the row without further mishap, and only tripped twice on his way on the steps up to the stage. The Great Marvello did not look pleased, but had obviously decided to make the best of a bad job.

'Now, sir, you and I have never met before, have we?' he asked.

'No,' said Spudder. 'We've . . . never . . . met . . . before.'

The audience roared with laughter, and Spudder wondered if he'd somehow managed to get the words wrong.

'Good,' Marvello said unconvincingly. 'Now if you would just climb into this box, sir, we can finally begin the trick.'

Spudder climbed into the box just as he'd done in the kitchen in the boarding house. Marvello closed the lid, fastened it down, and reached across to the prop table for his saw.

The saw was huge. Spudder gaped at it – especially at the big jagged teeth which glinted evilly in the bright lights.

'I will now cut this gentleman completely in two,' the Great Marvello announced.

He walked over to the box, laid the saw across the top, and began to cut.

Bits of sawdust flew in all directions and the sound of metal tearing into wood filled Spudder's ears.

'I don't want to do it!' he shouted.

The Great Marvello stopped sawing.

'There's nothing at all to be afraid of, sir!' he said in a loud voice, and then in a whisper he added, 'It's only a trick, Spudder. I showed you how it works.'

'You didn't show me how it worked when you had the bloody big saw in your hand!' Spudder screamed back.

Some members of the audience were slapping each other on the back. A couple were even rolling helplessly in the aisles.

'Pull yourself together, Spudder!' the Great Marvello hissed.

'I'm gettin' out of here!' Spudder yelled at the top of his voice.

He pulled his arms back into the box and pushed at the lid. The bloody thing wouldn't budge. His eyes still firmly fixed on the terrifying saw, Spudder pushed harder and the box began to wobble dangerously. Spudder made one last, stupendous effort. The box flew off its trestles and hit the stage with a resounding crash. Then it broke open, and Spudder rolled out and landed at the Great Marvello's feet.

'I'm sorry,' Spudder said, looking up at the glowering magician. 'Honestly I am.'

It was the funniest thing the audience had ever seen. From the stalls to the gallery, the crowd went wild.

'Wasn't Mr Marvello angry with you for messin' up his trick for him?' Mary asked Spudder as they sat together at the kitchen table in Number 47 the following evening.

'He was at first,' Spudder said, 'but then he saw how all the people had enjoyed it, an' he started to pretend we'd planned it all along.'

'Well, all's well that ends well,' Mary said.

'He wants me to do it again,' Spudder said. 'He wants me to do it every night.'

'Well, isn't that marvellous?' Mary said.

'He said he'd pay me what I was earnin' at the farm plus five bob a week an' the cost of me digs when we're on tour,' Spudder continued.

'Marvellous,' Mary said again.

Spudder looked down at the tablecloth.

'I told him no,' he said.

'But whatever for?' Mary asked. 'It's a wonderful opportunity to travel round and see different places.'

'I don't want to see different places,' Spudder said. 'I like bein' here. I like bein' . . . like bein' close to you.'

Mary reached across the table and stroked his hand.

'You're a lovely lad, Spudder,' she said.

Becky and her brother Philip walked slowly along the canal towards Burns' Bridge. In the grass by the towpath, crickets chirped and tiny shrews rustled their way from clump to clump. It was two weeks after Spudder's one and only theatrical appearance, one of those perfect May evenings when the air is so mild and soothing you could almost drink it.

'It was nice of you to find the time to come and visit us,' Becky said, with only a touch of sarcasm. 'How's the comic going?'

'Very well,' Philip told her. 'I'm thinking of putting a completely new character into it.'

'Oh yes,' Becky replied. 'What kind of character?'

'A young woman who can't keep her nose out of other people's business and is always trying to put the world to rights,' Philip told her. 'I'm thinking of calling her Becky Busybody.'

Becky hit her brother lightly on the arm.

'Well, it's lucky for you I *am* a busybody,' she said. 'Goodness knows what sort of mess you'd be in now without my interference.'

'You're right,' Philip admitted. 'If it hadn't been for you, Caspar Leech would have fed me to the sticklebacks in the canal long ago. And don't think I'm not grateful for what you did, Becky, because I am.'

'I don't want gratitude,' Becky told him. 'All I want is for you to keep your nose clean.'

'I will,' Philip promised. 'I've finally learned my lesson.'

Becky glanced at her brother's face and wondered whether what he'd said was true. He looked like he believed it, and he probably did – for the moment. But she knew Philip well, and was sure that the day would come when he either got bored with the comic or decided it was not a quick enough way to make money.

And then he'll come up with some other mad scheme which will land him in hot water, she thought, and I'll have to rescue him *again*.

She didn't mind – there was no point in minding. She was resigned to being Becky Busybody for the rest of her life, at least as far as Philip was concerned.

'Tell me all the gossip, then,' Philip said.

'What! And have you use it your comic next week?' Becky said. 'Besides, now you live in smart London society, I wouldn't have thought you'd be interested in what's going on in little Marston.'

'But I am!' Philip assured her. 'I do miss the village, you know. So go on, tell me all the local dirt.'

'Well, it's not exactly dirt,' Becky said, 'but Colleen's walking out with a young man.'

'Who!' Philip said disbelievingly. 'Big-nosed Coll . . .' He caught the look in his sister's eye. 'I mean . . . Colleen O'Leary.'

'That's right,' Becky replied.

'What's he like?'

'He's very good-looking,' Becky said. 'Well off, as well. I will admit there was something about the way he talks which made me a bit suspicious of him at first . . .'

'How do you mean?' Philip asked.

'It sounded – I don't know – put on,' Becky confessed. 'As if he was only acting the part of a gentleman. But now I think it's just the way he is, being educated and that. And I'm ever so glad for Colleen. It broke her heart when George wrote her that terribly cold letter –'

'Why *did* he do that?' Philip interrupted.

'It beats me,' Becky said. 'If you could have seen his face as his train steamed out of Northwich station, you'd have sworn he was as mad about her as she was about him. But he's a deep one, our George, and I never have been able to get to the bottom of him.'

'And Colleen seems to be really happy with this Smith chap, does she?' Philip said.

'Head over heels in love,' Becky replied. 'You should see them together – she can't take her eyes off him. So I suppose, in a way, George's letter turned out to be for the best.'

'But you would have liked to see him and Colleen married, wouldn't you, Becky Busybody?' Philip said.

'Well, yes,' Becky admitted. 'I mean, why not? He's my brother, she's my best friend, and they would have made a perfect pair.'

A couple appeared from under the bridge, walking arm-in-arm towards them. The man was broad-shouldered and the woman had a trim figure with a narrow waist and firm bosom. The woman waved to them.

'Now *they* make a perfect couple,' Philip said. 'Look at that girl. She's stunning.'

Becky laughed. 'That's Colleen,' she told her brother.

'Colleen!' Philip exclaimed. 'But it can't be! I mean, she used to be such a dowdy little thing.'

'Maybe love changes people,' Becky said.

'Well, I never,' Philip said, shaking his head in amazement.

As the two couples drew closer and it became possible for them to make out each other's faces, Becky noticed a change come over Barnaby. He had been walking with the easy grace of a natural sportsman, but now he seemed to be dragging his feet.

It's almost as if really he doesn't want to get any closer to us, Becky thought.

She turned to make the same observation to Philip, and noticed that her brother was frowning. And then he shivered.

'Is anything the matter?' Becky asked.

'It's nothing,' Philip told her.

'It must be *something*,' Becky persisted. 'You're looking very shaken up.'

'Oh, it's probably just somebody walking over my grave,' Philip said.

'Now there's a cheerful thought,' Becky replied.

Barnaby and Colleen drew level with them.

'Mr Smith, may I present Mr Philip Taylor, Becky's brother,' Colleen said. 'Mr Taylor, Mr Barnaby Smith, my . . . my . . .'

She blushed, and Becky waited for Barnaby to make one of the quips which fell so readily from his tongue. But no quip came. Instead, Barnaby merely stretched out his hand and stiffly shook Philip's.

What's wrong with him today? Becky wondered. He looks really rattled.

Philip was still frowning.

'Don't I know you from somewhere?' he asked Barnaby.

'That's perfectly possible,' Barnaby said, rather brusquely. 'I travel a great deal and meet any number of people.' He took out his pocket watch, flipped it open, looked at it himself and then showed it to Colleen. 'Do you see what time it is?' he asked.

'Oh dear! Nearly five to eight. Me dad's expecting me to take over from him in the bar at eight on the dot. We'll have to get crackin', Barnaby.'

'Indeed we will,' Barnaby agreed. 'Indeed we will.'

For most of the walk back to the village, Barnaby seemed very preoccupied, but then, a short distance from Marston Bridge, he suddenly stopped and took Colleen's hands in his own.

'When you were introducing me to Philip Taylor, you said I was your . . . your . . .' he said. 'But you never finished. What had you been going to say?'

'I don't know,' Colleen replied, gazing down into the

canal.

'Your young man?' Barnaby suggested.

'Perhaps,' Colleen agreed, not taking her eyes off the water.

'Colleen,' Barnaby said softly, 'do you love me?'

He'd never asked her that before and she longed to say, 'Yes, of course I love you! Isn't it obvious?'

Yet she was afraid to. What if she'd misunderstood again? What if she bared her heart to him and then, like George, he told her he was going away?

'Do you love me?' Barnaby persisted.

'We have to be gettin' back to the pub,' Colleen said. 'Anyway, I don't go in for any of that daft nonsense.'

'Don't make a joke of it,' Barnaby implored her. 'Please, Colleen, be honest with me.'

She could deny her feelings no longer. She lifted her head and looked into his handsome face.

'Yes,' she confessed. 'I do love you.'

'And I love you,' Barnaby said. 'With all my heart and all my soul.' He released her hand and went down on one knee. 'Colleen, will you marry me?' he said.

Colleen tried to speak, and found she couldn't, so instead she merely nodded her head.

'Let's get married soon,' Barnaby said. 'How long does it take to have the banns read? Three weeks?'

'Y . . . yes, I think so,' Colleen stuttered.

Barnaby stood up again.

'Then let's get married three weeks from this Sunday,' he said.

It was all so sudden, so overwhelming. Only a few weeks ago she'd been a confirmed spinster, and now Barnaby was suggesting that in less than a month she could be his wife.

'Maybe we should wait a bit,' she suggested. 'We don't want to rush into anythin'.'

'Why not?' Barnaby asked. 'We love each other and always will. I can easily afford to keep a wife. What possible reason could there be for waiting any longer?'

He was right, Colleen thought. There was no reason at all for delay.

'We'll have to talk to me mam and dad first,' she said.

'Of course,' Barnaby agreed. 'That's only right and proper.'

'But if they say it's all right, we could see the parish priest tomorrow,' Colleen said.

'What's wrong with seeing him this evening?' Barnaby asked, hugging her to him.

At Burns' Bridge, Becky and Philip stopped for a short rest.

'You can smoke if you like,' Becky said.

'Thanks,' Philip replied absently.

He searched through his pockets as if his mind were somewhere else. Twice, he patted the cigarette tin in his waistcoat, then moved on.

'What *is* wrong with you, Philip?' Becky asked.

'I *do* know that feller Smith from somewhere,' Philip said.

'Maybe you met him in London,' Becky suggested. 'He goes down there on business quite a bit.'

'No, it isn't London,' Philip said decisively.

'How can you be so sure?' Becky asked.

'You remember when I shivered and I said it was probably because somebody had walked over my grave?' Philip asked.

'Oh, we're back to that cheerful topic, are we?' Becky said.

'That wasn't the reason I shivered,' Philip continued, as if he hadn't heard her. 'I think that for one second, when I first saw him, I recognized him for exactly who he was – and it wasn't a very pleasant memory. Then it sort of slipped away, and all I was left with was a feeling that we'd met before.'

'You've always had an active imagination,' Becky told her brother. 'That's why you're so good at writing them comics of yours.'

'You're probably right,' Philip admitted, grinning and finally finding his cigarettes.

Chapter Sixteen

When he wasn't working himself, there was nothing Ted Taylor liked so much as to stroll up the canal to Rudheath and look in at Becky's bakery. He loved all his children, but – perhaps because she was the youngest – he had a special soft spot for Becky, and it did his heart good to see her at work, ordering her carmen around and smoothing the ruffled feathers of Monsieur Henri.

The bakery was normally a busy place, but on this particular morning there seemed to Ted to be more activity than ever. There were the bakers, sweating over the ovens. There was that Monsoor Henri, flappin' his arms and sayin' *sackre blur* – whatever that meant. Everyone was working at full steam. Only his daughter was missing.

Becky came in through the main door, a pencil in her hand and a frown of concentration on her face.

'Hello, Dad,' she said when she saw Ted standing there. 'I've just been checking they've loaded the carts right.'

'Got a bit of a flap on?' Ted asked.

'We have, really,' Becky admitted. 'I'm catering a whole fête at Mobberly Hall.'

'Mobberly Hall,' Ted mused. 'But that place is a bloody lunatic asylum, isn't it?'

'Yes,' Becky agreed.

'And they're having a fête?' Ted said incredulously.

Becky laughed. 'Not all lunatics foam at the mouth and tear their hair out, you know,' she said. 'Some of them are very well behaved. I believe there are lunatics who are allowed to go off for walks in the country and some even attend church on Sunday.'

Monsieur Henri walked up to them. 'The baking is

finished,' he said.

'Thank you,' Becky replied.

The pastry chef turned to Ted. 'I 'ave bake for the best tables in Europe,' he said. 'An' what 'appen now? I use my genius to produce food for madmen. Instead of ze *gâteau de marrons du Comte* – it mean chestnut cake of the Count – I now 'ave to make *tarte aux pommes du dément*, ze lunatic's apple pie! Zey will probably take my works of genius and stuff zem up zair noses!'

'But there won't only be lunatics at the fête, Monsieur Henri,' Becky told the Frenchman.

'No?' replied Monsieur Henri, suddenly sounding more interested. ''Oo else will zere be?'

'The Mayor of Mobberly for one,' Becky said. 'And I did hear that the Lord Lieutenant of the County might turn up, too.'

Monsieur Henri seemed to swell with pride.

'Ze Lord Lieutenant, eh?' he said. 'Now I am glad I put my 'eart into zis batch of pastries as I put it into all my creations.'

He strutted away, well pleased with himself.

'Will the Lord Lieutenant really be there?' Ted asked his daughter.

'Anything's possible,' Becky said with a smile.

Ted laughed. 'Well, I have to take my hat off to you,' he said. 'You really know how to handle your workers. But I'm still not sure that I fancy any daughter of mine mixin' with a lot of crazy people.'

'I'll be too busy working to do any mixing,' Becky said. 'This is a big chance for me to expand the business.'

'And are you chargin' them the proper rate for the job?' Ted asked suspiciously.

Becky's eyes blinked, like they'd done when she was a little kid and he'd caught her doing something wrong.

'I'm charging a fair price,' she said.

'Now that's not quite what I asked you, is it?' her father said.

'I won't make much of a profit,' Becky confessed, 'but it's for a good cause and anyway, if word gets around, I'll get more bookings. So it's just good business sense, really.'

'Good business sense!' Ted snorted. 'You're as daft as that husband of yours.'

'Michael's making a nice profit out of the rubber trade,' Becky said loyally, though she suspected that he could have been making *much* more if his rubber business really had been his main concern.

'Well,' Ted said, 'all I can tell you is, I wouldn't trust either of you to run a chip shop.'

Paddy O'Leary was getting used to entertaining Barnaby Smith in his cosy little parlour, though each time the two of them were in there together, he could not help but wish that the place was just a little bigger and just a little smarter.

'So what can I do for you today, Barnaby?' he asked, now *almost* comfortable using his future son-in-law's given name.

'I think it's about time we discussed the arrangements for the wedding,' Barnaby said.

'The church, an' that?' Paddy asked.

'No, not the church,' Barnaby replied. 'The reception.'

'Ah!' Paddy said.

He had not given the matter much thought himself. People around Marston didn't go in for lavish receptions. In fact, the biggest he could remember was when Colleen's friend Becky had got married – and even then it had only been cakes and sandwiches in the chip shop.

'I am an only son,' Barnaby said, 'and my family will, naturally enough, wish to see my marriage celebrated in an appropriate manner.'

'Course they will,' Paddy agreed, wondering to himself exactly what celebrating it in 'an appropriate manner' would entail. 'Would you like to hold your reception here?' he asked.

Barnaby shook his head. 'That would mean a great deal of extra work for you and Mrs O'Leary,' he said, 'and I simply couldn't permit that.'

'Then what about the church hall?' Paddy suggested. 'We could get Becky Taylor – Mrs Worrell – to do the caterin'.'

'Another excellent suggestion,' Barnaby said, 'but unfortunately the church hall would be a little cramped for the number of people I am expecting to attend.'

What you really mean, Paddy thought, is that the church hall would be nowhere near fancy enough for you. Still, he did appreciate Barnaby's tact in phrasing his refusal the way he had.

'No, the church hall would certainly be nothing like big enough,' Barnaby said again.

Just how many people *was* the man planning to invite? Paddy thought worriedly. 'So where *are* you thinkin' of holdin' this reception of yours, Barnaby?' he asked.

'I have booked the Crown Hotel,' Barnaby said.

The most expensive hotel in Northwich! He should have expected it, Paddy told himself. Barnaby was used to the best, so it was obvious, when you thought about it, that only the best would be good enough for him on his wedding day. And what if it did cost a lot of money? How often was it that your daughter got married?

Still – the Crown.

'Have they . . . like . . . given you any kind of estimate, yet?' Paddy asked nervously.

'Good heavens!' Barnaby said, holding up his hands in horror, 'I don't expect you to pay for it.'

'You'll have me daughter to support for the rest of her life,' Paddy said firmly. 'It's only fair that I should be the one to foot the bill for the weddin'.'

Barnaby looked embarrassed.

'I don't wish to be insulting,' he said slowly and carefully, 'but I'm not sure you quite appreciate what an affair of this nature will cost. My people will insist of a certain high standard . . .'

'I wouldn't give 'em anythin' else,' Paddy protested.

'. . . which means fresh salmon from Scotland, Russian

224

caviar and only the finest French champagne,' Barnaby continued.

'Are you sayin' I couldn't afford it?' Paddy demanded.

Barnaby seemed to be searching around for a tactful answer – and failing to find one.

'Yes,' he admitted finally. 'That is what I'm saying.'

Paddy felt his hackles rise.

'I've never been what you might call a spendthrift,' he said. 'I've got a nice little nest-egg, and I can pay me way as well as the next man. So tell me how much it'll cost.'

'I don't have the exact figures yet,' Barnaby said uncomfortably.

'Then just give me a rough idea,' Paddy persisted.

'Somewhere in the region of four hundred pounds,' Barnaby said.

Paddy gulped. Four hundred pounds! It would take most men ten years to earn that amount. You could buy half the village of Marston for four hundred pounds.

Paddy bowed his head. 'You were right,' he said, feeling more humiliated than he ever had in his life. 'I can't afford it.'

Barnaby reached across and put his hand firmly on the older man's shoulder.

'And why should you *have to* afford it?' he asked. 'After all, it's not being done for your benefit. It's not even being done for mine. Left to ourselves, Colleen and I would slip away quietly after the ceremony. No, we are doing it simply to please my people, and it's only right and proper that I should bear the cost. Four hundred pounds really is no great sum of money to me, you know.'

'That's not the point,' Paddy told him. 'If a feller's any kind of man at all, he sees that he lives up to his responsibilities, an' one of 'em's seein' that his daughter is wed properly.'

'It certainly seems to be a dilemma,' Barnaby admitted. 'On the one hand you have limited resources and on the other, my people have their expectations.' He sat there gloomily for a few moments, then suddenly brightened. 'What if you were to bear part of the cost?' he suggested. 'Let us say the amount you would have expected to spend if, instead of marrying me, Colleen had chosen one of the workers from the Adelaide Mine? Would that be fair? Would that make you feel happier?'

'Yes,' Paddy said, after turning the matter over in his mind. 'Yes, I think that would make me a lot happier.'

Becky stood behind the large table she'd set up in the grounds of Mobberly Hall and looked around her. Despite the assurances she'd given her father, she really hadn't known what to expect from a lunatic asylum, and she'd certainly felt a few misgivings as Cedric Rathbone had driven her through the main gate.

But it's rather pleasant, she thought. Look at the hall itself, for a start. If she hadn't known, she would have assumed it was the home of a landed gentleman, rather than a detention centre for the insane. And the grounds were pretty, too. The lawn ran down from the house to the gate, its graceful sweep broken only by the occasional flower-bed. Mature trees lined the main drive.

It was probably a very peaceful place when it wasn't throwing a fête, she decided. So maybe it wasn't so bad being a lunatic after all.

She turned her attention to the inmates and visitors who were chancing their luck at the coconut shy. Her brother George had been a dab hand at hitting coconuts, she remembered. He had once won three of them in one evening, much to the disgust of the barker who was running the shy. She wondered how he would feel when he heard that Colleen was getting married. Well, he'd had *his* chance, and he hadn't taken it.

An old lady walked up to the stall and examined the cakes.

'A truly splendid display,' she said kindly. 'Are you responsible for it, my dear?'

'I set them out,' Becky said, 'but it's my bakers who should take most of the credit.'

The old lady raised an eyebrow. '*Your* bakers!' she said. 'I take that to mean that you are a business lady. Or should one say, a lady of business?'

Becky smiled. 'I don't know which of them is right,' she said. 'But yes, I do own the bakery.'

'Well, jolly good luck to you,' the old lady said enthusiastically. 'We need more young women like you. If my own niece had had a little more energy and determination, she wouldn't have ended up in such a state.'

'Is she a patient here?' Becky asked.

'Regrettably, yes,' the old lady said. 'I come to see her as often as I can. It's a strain on me, but I think it does her good.'

'Would you like to try a cake?' Becky asked.

'I would love one,' the old lady replied. 'But ever since they cut my head off, I've had no mouth, you see.'

She smiled vaguely and walked away. If it hadn't been for her grey institutional dress, Becky thought, she'd never have known the old woman was a lunatic until she made that comment about her head. In fact, looking round it would have been impossible to tell any of the lunatics from the visitors without their uniforms.

She felt suddenly uncomfortable, as if she was being watched. She turned slowly round and discovered that she was. A few yards away stood another female lunatic, staring at her intently.

This woman was much younger than the one who thought she had no head – probably not much older than Becky herself – but her hair was lank, her face drawn and her eyes filled with a haunted look. If anybody belonged in Mobberly Hall, Becky told herself, it was her.

The woman approached the stall slowly and hesitantly, but her eyes did not leave Becky's face for a second.

'Would you like to try one of the sweetmeats, madam?' Becky asked pleasantly when the lunatic was almost close enough to touch her.

The woman opened her mouth as if to speak, but stayed silent.

'Or perhaps some apple tart,' Becky suggested, trying her best not to remember Monsieur Henri's comment about *tarte de pommes du dément*.

The woman tried to speak again, and this time she did manage to get a few words out – words which sent a chill down the caterer's spine.

'Becky?' she croaked. 'Becky Taylor?'

The voice, despite its brokenness, sounded familiar. And now Becky thought about it, so did the face, though it was much changed from the vague memory she had of it. Yet she knew of no one who had been committed to a lunatic asylum, let alone an expensive one like this.

'Don't you recognize me?' the woman asked desperately.

Becky looked again, carefully scanning the lunatic's face. Was it . . .? Could it be . . .?

'Hortense?' Becky asked, hardly able to believe it.

Hortense laughed bitterly. 'I know I've altered,' she said. 'They do that to you in here.'

Becky tried to remember what story she had heard about Hortense's disappearance. Something about her finding the Cheshire climate disagreeable and moving back to her parents' home in Hertfordshire. And all the time, she'd been here – a few miles from Northwich!

Hortense glanced over her shoulder, then turned quickly back to Becky. She looked panic-stricken.

'They're watching me,' she said. 'They're always watching me. Pretend you're explaining what's in the cakes,' she pleaded. 'They mustn't think we're talking about anything else.'

It was simply not in Becky's nature to turn down such an urgent request – even from someone who had once been her worst enemy. She pointed to the display.

'These are apple tarts . . .' she said '. . . keep talking, I can still hear you even when I'm speaking myself . . . and over here we have cream cakes . . .'

'I treated you badly when you were nothing but a little dressmaker,' Hortense said. 'I see that now. If I've learned one thing in here, it's that you should never be unkind. Not to anybody.'

Hortense didn't look mad, Becky decided. She looked defeated, crushed by a great weight of sadness.

'. . . cherry tarts . . .' she continued '. . . and these have blackcurrant jam in them. Why are you in here, Hortense? What did you do to make Richard have you locked up?'

'I fell in love,' Hortense told her. 'With my groom.'

It was hard for Becky to reconcile the proud, vengeful Hortense she had once known with the wreck of a woman who stood before her now. It was hard to believe, too, that she could ever have allowed herself to fall in love with a common servant. Yet there was a deep sincerity in her words which made Becky accept everything she was being told as the absolute truth.

'There's more,' Hortense said.

'Then say it quickly,' Becky told her, because Hortense was right – they were being watched. And the watcher, a middle-aged man with a stocky build and hard eyes, was starting to look very suspicious.

'My second child, William,' Hortense said in a rush. 'Richard wasn't his father. That's why he sent him away.'

'That's awful,' Becky said. 'Where is he?'

'I don't know,' Hortense replied. 'But he's having a miserable time – I can just feel that he is.'

'We must get you out of this place so you can go and look for him,' Becky said.

'That's impossible,' Hortense told her. 'Just look behind you.'

Becky glanced over her shoulder. She'd thought earlier in the day how the house could have been a gentleman's home, but the walls, she saw now, could not have belonged to anything but a prison.

'I'm not talking about you escaping,' Becky said. 'There must be other ways – legal ways – to get you released.'

Hortense shook her head. 'Richard would never allow it,' she said, 'and without his permission they'll never let me go.'

'Couldn't your family help you?' Becky asked.

Hortense shook her head again. The middle-aged man who had been watching them from a distance seemed to find that very significant.

'My family disowned me the moment Richard told them who William's real father was,' Hortense said. 'But that doesn't matter. Forget me. My little baby's the only one who matters. Find him for me, Becky. Find my poor little William. Promise me you'll do it! Promise!'

'I promise,' Becky said.

The watcher suddenly decided that Hortense had spent enough time at the cake stall and began walking rapidly towards her.

'He's coming for you,' Becky whispered to Hortense, who had her back to the keeper.

'I know,' Hortense replied. 'I can sense him.'

The keeper drew level and tapped Hortense on the shoulder. She'd been expecting it, but she still jumped like a frightened rabbit.

'You seem to be havin' difficulties choosin' what to eat, Mrs Worrell,' he said in a voice so cold that it made Becky shiver.

'I . . . I don't think I'm really hungry,' Hortense said.

The keeper, a contemptuous expression on his face, looked her slowly up and down.

'No, I'd say you were tired rather than hungry,' he said. 'I think the best thing for you would be to have some of your medicine and then go to bed. Don't *you* think that would be a good idea?'

Hortense said nothing.

'Don't you?' the keeper repeated, more threateningly this time.

'Yes,' Hortense agreed meekly.

The keeper put one of his large hairy hands on her arm, and she allowed herself to be led away.

Chapter Seventeen

Having talked to other businessmen in Northwich about Barnaby Smith, Richard Worrell was not surprised when his clerk handed him Smith's card and told him that the gentleman in question was outside and would like an appointment whenever it was convenient.

'I'll see him immediately,' Richard said.

He'd been looking forward to this meeting with some anticipation, ever since he'd heard that Smith intended to marry Colleen O'Leary.

Because why would any man of substance choose to marry a working-class pot-girl? he asked himself. Especially a plain one like Colleen? This man Smith must be soft in the head.

Yet from what Richard's friends who'd had dealings with him said, Smith was far from stupid. So just what was he playing at? It was a mystery, all right – and one that Richard would enjoy unravelling.

The clerk ushered Barnaby Smith in. He was wearing a check waistcoat under his jacket and carried a fashionable walking cane with a silver knob. He seemed very much at his ease.

The two men shook hands.

'It's very good of you to find time to see me at such short notice,' Smith said.

'Not at all,' Richard said jovially. 'Do take a seat, Mr Smith.'

Smith sat down, and Richard examined him closely. The man was definitely no fool, he decided. Far from it – Richard knew cunning when he saw it, and looking into Barnaby Smith's eyes was almost like gazing into a mirror.

'Whisky, Mr Smith?' Richard asked, reaching for the

bottle.

Barnaby raised his hands in a gesture of refusal.

'I never drink when I'm working,' he said. 'But please don't let me stop you.'

'You won't,' Richard replied, pouring himself a generous slug. 'Now what exactly can I do for you, Mr Smith?'

'As you may know, I am shortly to be married,' Barnaby said.

'I had heard,' Richard replied.

Just what *was* the man's game?

'And before that happy event, I would like to conclude the business matters which originally brought me to this neighbourhood,' Barnaby continued. 'Hence' my visit to you.'

'You're after money,' Richard said, simply to see how the other man would react.

'Isn't everyone?' Smith replied, taking Richard's remark completely in his stride.

'What's your proposition?' Richard asked.

'I am in the process of purchasing some land in the West Indies,' Barnaby told him. 'It's good land, and should give a handsome return on the initial investment . . .'

'Then if I were you, I'd make damn sure that I kept it to myself,' Richard said.

'That is not the way I work,' Smith said mildly. 'I like to keep my finger in several pies, which means that when an opportunity such as this one comes up, I do not always have sufficient funds of my own to exploit it. Thus I have no choice but to let others benefit from my astuteness.'

'You mean, take on partners?' Richard said.

'Exactly,' Barnaby replied.

'Which is why you've been all over the area touting this estate of yours like a pedlar selling ribbons,' Richard said.

'Indeed,' Barnaby agreed.

What *would* it take to rattle this man? Richard wondered. 'And have you managed to talk anybody into it?' he asked.

'Fortunately, a good number of businessmen in Northwich have been shrewd enough to grasp the opportunity when it was offered to them,' Barnaby told him.

'Well, if there have been "a good number" as you say, why have you bothered to come and see me?' Richard asked.

Barnaby gave the other man one of those winning smiles at which Richard himself was a past master.

'I am still just a little short of the final sum that I will require,' he confessed.

'And you thought I'd probably be foolish enough to provide you with it,' Richard said.

'No,' Barnaby replied. 'I thought you would be *intelligent* enough to provide me with it.'

'And how long would it be before I started getting a decent return on my investment?' Richard asked.

'How long do *you* think it would be?' Barnaby countered.

Richard considered it.

'I'm no planter,' he said finally, 'but I know enough to realize that it will be several years at least – and I simply don't want any of my money tied up that long.'

Barnaby smiled again. 'Within *two* years,' he said, 'you will easily have recovered your initial capital, and from then you, you will be making pure profit.'

Perhaps the man was a fool, after all.

'You're talking rot!' Richard told him.

'Labour costs are very low in the Indies,' Barnaby said. 'It is almost as cheap to employ labourers as it used to be to keep slaves. In fact, it is sometimes cheaper.'

'Cheaper?' Richard said questioningly.

'A slave owner feels some responsibility to maintain his slaves at a certain minimum standard,' Barnaby explained. 'An employer does not. If my workers can't live as well as slaves do on the wages I pay them, that really isn't my fault, is it? And if they start to complain, well, there are always many others willing to take their place.'

'You make it sound like an owner's paradise,' Richard admitted, 'but even under those conditions, it would still be impossible to recoup the capital within two years.' He glanced up at the clock. 'I don't think we have anything more to say to one another, Mr Smith,' he continued, 'and as I am an extremely busy man . . .'

Richard rose to his feet and held out his hand to Barnaby. But Smith did not stand up in turn. Instead, he stayed seated and was contemplating the shiny knob of his cane as if he were trying to come to a decision.

'An extremely busy man . . .' Richard repeated impatiently.

Barnaby looked up, and Richard read the uncertainty in his eyes.

'If I were to tell you something in confidence, could I rely on you to keep it to yourself?' he asked.

'Of course,' Richard agreed readily.

And he certainly *would* keep it to himself – as long as it suited him.

'We will be growing some sugar cane on the estate,' Barnaby said, 'but that will be nothing more than a screen behind which we will be hiding our main business.'

'And what will that main business be?' asked Richard, who was still standing but had now lowered his arm.

'Rum,' Barnaby told him.

'Rum is a good commodity,' Richard said, 'but even rum isn't going to make you wealthy in a hurry.'

'You think not?' Smith asked.

'I think not,' Richard agreed.

'It sells for three shillings a bottle,' Barnaby pointed out. 'That's as much as you'll get for Scotch whisky.'

'But how much of that three shillings does the distiller get?' Richard asked. 'The wholesaler wants his profits, as does the retailer. And then there's the shipping costs, not to mention the duty you must pay to the grasping government . . .'

The wide grin on Barnaby's face stopped him in his tracks.

'I count among my circle of acquaintances a senior official in the Customs and Excise Department,' Barnaby said. 'This particular gentleman has a bad habit – he gambles. Worse than that, he is a very poor gambler who loses sums far in excess of his salary. And when he has done that, he comes to me for help.'

So that was it! Richard sank back into his chair.

'You're talking about smuggling, aren't you?' he asked.

Barnaby looked shocked.

'I most certainly am not,' he said. Then the smile crept back onto his face. 'Though you, of course, are at liberty to think whatever you wish,' he continued.

'What I think, Mr Smith,' Richard said, 'is that perhaps we might be able to do business together after all.'

Becky looked out of the window, down at the bustling Manchester street below – at the waggons and carriages, at the old beggar standing outside the pub and the scissor grinder playing on his pipe in an effort to attract customers. Normally, such sights would have fascinated her. But not today. Today her mind was too much on her mission to think of anything else.

She turned and glanced around the office in which she'd been told to wait. In one corner was a desk at which a middle-aged – and obviously genteel – lady was picking away at a typewriting machine with two fingers. In the other corner stood a bookcase, overflowing with dusty cardboard files.

It was the Manchester office of the Lunacy Law Reform Society, previously known as the Alleged Lunatics' Friends' Society! Becky wondered why it should be so often the case that good works were conducted in such dingy surroundings.

The outer door opened and a stocky man with a bushy beard and flowing white hair entered.

'Mrs Worr-rrell?' he asked in a broad Scots accent.

'That's right,' Becky agreed.

'Mackie's the name,' the Scot told her. 'Sorry to ha' kept ye waiting, but I'm sure Miss Dimdale has seen to it that ye've been entertained.'

Miss Dimdale looked up from her typewriting machine and sniffed.

'Tek a pew,' Mackie said, pointing to one of two dilapidated armchairs situated just to the left of the window.

Becky looked at it dubiously, then gingerly sat down. Mackie took the chair opposite her.

'Dinna be put off by yer surroundings, Mrs Worr-rrell,' Mackie told her. 'We spend most of the money we raise on good attorneys. An' by God, we need 'em wi' some o' the cases we handle.'

'I'm sure you do,' Becky said.

'We've been fighting the lunacy laws for years,' Mackie continued, 'and believe me, we know what we're aboot.'

Becky looked into his bright intelligent eyes and felt a sudden surge of hope.

'I do believe you,' she said.

Mackie reached deep into the pocket of his hairy tweed jacket and took out a crumpled piece of paper which Becky recognized as the letter she had written to him.

'It's a vury interesting case you've brought tae me,' Mackie said, as he started to smooth out the letter on his knee. 'Tell me, is this Hortense Sudbury Worrell a relative of yours?'

'She's my sister-in-law,' Becky said, although she'd never really thought of Hortense in quite that way before.

Mackie nodded his large head.

'How much do ye know about the lunacy laws in this fine, free country of ours, Mrs Worr-rrell?' he asked.

'Very little,' Becky confessed. 'Until a few days ago, I'd never met a lunatic – well, not a certified one, anyway.'

'It is precisely the certification that is our first obstacle,' Mr Mackie explained. 'For anyone to be committed to an asylum, it's necessary tae get two doctors to sign certificates saying that person is mad.' He raised a stubby finger. 'But this is the point, Mrs Worr-rrell – any doctor will do.'

'I'm not sure I understand,' Becky said.

'He doesnae have to be an alienist,' Mackie told her. 'Tek your simple country doctor. He may be a quack who learned

236

his trade half a century ago, and has forgotten even what antiquated knowledge he picked up then, but he's considered by the authorities to be an expert on mental health.'

'But that's outrageous!' Becky exclaimed.

'It is indeed,' Mr Mackie agreed. 'Especially when ye understand that he may be making his judgement solely on old-fashioned prejudices.'

'What sort of prejudices?' Becky asked.

'All sorts,' Mackie told her. 'Say, for example that he doesnae approve of dancing but the woman he is examining loves tae dance. What else could that be but a clear case of mental instability, he says to hi'self – and he signs the form immediately.'

'And gets away with it?' Becky said.

'And gets away wi' it,' Mackie repeated. 'A doctor doesnae have to give reasons for his findings, only the findings themselves. But worse is yet to come. So far, we have ainly been talking about doctors who are honest but misguided. Now let us consider the case of medical men who are nae so scrupulous.'

'You mean, doctors who take bribes from the relatives of the person who is supposed to be insane?' Becky asked, thinking she certainly wouldn't put that sort of trick past Richard.

'Either from relatives or from the people who are running the asylum,' Mackie said.

'From the people running the asylum!' Becky said, hardly able to believe her ears. 'What have they got to gain from it?'

'Customers,' Mackie said. 'A private asylum will charge, on average, something between three and four guineas a week for each patient. Now suppose the owner offers tae pay the doctor some of that – say two or three per cent. That's nae a great deal of money – two and sixpence or three shillings a week – but when ye consider that all the doctor has tae do to earn it is sign his name to a wee piece of paper, it's a handsome payment indeed. Consider, too, the possibility that the doctor commits eight different patients. He will then

237

be earning twenty shillings a week extra – which is more than a school teacher earns in total!'

'I don't believe any doctor would stoop to such a disgraceful trick,' Becky said.

Mackie shook his head pityingly. 'Tell her I'm right, Miss Dimdale,' he said to the middle-aged lady, who had now stopped typing and was listening to their conversation.

'Until recently, owners advertised such deals openly in medical journals,' Miss Dimdale said.

'And do ye really think they would have gone to such expense if no doctor had ever taken up their offer?' Mackie asked.

'No, I suppose not,' Becky admitted.

'But enough of this,' Mr Mackie said, suddenly more cheerful. 'Let us get down tae the case of Mrs Hortense Worr-rrell. You said in your letter that the grounds for her certification were unrighteous sex.'

'No, I didn't!' Becky replied, suddenly angry. 'I said that she'd had a love affair.'

Mackie held up his hands to cut off further protest.

'Forgive me, Mrs Worr-rrell,' he said. 'I am only using the term our opponents will use. For my ain part, whilst I consider all adultery reprehensible, I fail to see why committing such an act should make a woman mad while it leaves the man in question perfectly sane. Still, unrighteous sex is a difficult one to fight.'

'Is there *any* chance of getting her released without her husband's permission?' Becky asked gloomily.

'I wouldnae say it was impossible,' Mackie told her. 'Only recently two women previously judged insane were freed from the workhouse asylum in Blackburn. But then, of course, it is always easier wi' paupers, since no one really has a vested interest in keeping them confined.'

As Richard did with Hortense, Becky thought.

'How would we go about getting my sister-in-law released?' she asked.

'The ultimate authority is the Lunacy Commissioners in

London,' Mr Mackie said. 'There are six of them – three doctors and three laymen – and they have the last say on any question of lunacy.'

'We must go to them,' Becky said.

'It is nae that simple,' he explained. 'In the provinces, the responsibility has been devolved to three local justices of the peace, who are always advised by a doctor.'

'Then we must appeal to *them* immediately,' Becky said.

Mackie smiled. 'You seem in a great hurry, dear lady,' he said.

'If you'd seen Hortense, as I have, you'd be a hurry, too,' Becky said hotly. 'You can't imagine what that place has done to her.'

'Yes, I can,' Mackie said. He was still smiling, but now the smile had a sad edge to it. 'I have seen the effects of confinement on many people, including ma ain mother.'

Becky put her hand to her mouth. 'Oh, I am sorry,' Becky said. 'I didn't know.'

'How could ye?' Mackie asked. 'We'll get ye a good attorney, but I shouldnae get too impatient if I were you, Mrs Worr-rrell. The mills of justice grind incredibly slowly at best. And sometimes, ye must realize, they dinna grind at all; for all my efforts on ma mother's behalf, she died in that dreadful place.'

'She's taking the case to the Lunacy Commissioners!' Richard Worrell shouted as he paced furiously up and down his study. 'Becky bloody Taylor has actually had the brass nerve to take Hortense's case to the Lunacy Commissioners!'

'So you've already told me more than half a dozen times,' said Horace Crimp from his chair near the window, where he was indulging in his usual habit of picking his teeth.

'It's all your fault, Crimp,' Richard said, pointing an accusing finger at his lawyer. 'It was your idea to have Hortense committed. And now she hates me more than ever. God knows what she'll do if Becky does succeed in getting her released.'

'Do try to calm down, Mr Worrell,' Crimp said.

'It's all right for you,' Richard complained petulantly. 'But if it becomes public knowledge why I had my wife locked away in the first place, I'll be the laughing stock of the district.'

'But there's no reason why it *should* become public knowledge,' Crimp said confidently.

'How can we stop it coming out?' Richard demanded.

'There will be a hearing –' Crimp began.

'I know there'll be a hearing!' Richard exploded. 'That's what I'm worried about, you bloody fool.'

'The only people who will be present at that hearing will be your wife, her attorney, the doctor, the justices of the peace, and myself,' the lawyer explained.

'God, isn't that enough?' Richard asked. 'It'll only take one of them to open his mouth, and the news'll be all over the county.'

'That won't happen,' Crimp told him. 'The doctor and your wife's attorney will be bound by professional oaths of silence. As for the justices, they, too, are sworn to confidentiality. Besides, they will all be local businessmen, friends – or at least acquaintances – of yours. I am sure they would do nothing to embarrass you.'

'And what about you, Crimp?' Richard asked.

Horace Crimp smiled. It was not a pretty sight.

'As long as you continue to pay me so generously, you can rely on my complete loyalty,' he said.

'But Hortense isn't bound by any oath!' Richard said, coming as close to panic as he ever had. 'What if these fine justices of yours decide to release her?'

'And why should they do that?' Crimp asked.

'Because she's not insane, you idiot!' Richard screamed. 'And that will be obvious to them the moment they see her.'

Crimp scratched his bald head.

'Yes,' he admitted, 'that could be a problem, couldn't it? But not a problem we couldn't devise some way around.'

Chapter Eighteen

'The dresses will never be ready on time,' Colleen O'Leary moaned to Becky Worrell as the two sat side by side in Colleen's bedroom. 'I just *know* they won't be ready.'

'Yes they will,' Becky promised her. 'I was down at Bratt's this morning, and all they've got left to do is to finish off the fine stitching.'

'Fine stitchin' is the hardest part,' Colleen said. 'It's bound to take for ever.'

It was still two days to her wedding, Becky thought, and already her best friend was in a complete panic.

'If needs be, I'll work on them myself,' Becky said. 'I used to be a dressmaker myself, remember. So there's absolutely nothing to worry about, is there?'

Colleen stood up and hugged herself.

'It's not just the dresses,' she admitted. 'It's everythin'. Barnaby's hired the most expensive hotel in Northwich. There'll be hundreds an' hundreds of people there.'

'And why should you mind that on the happiest day of your life?' Becky asked.

'Barnaby's uncle's a baronet an' his father's a *justice of the peace*,' Colleen said.

'And your dad's a pub landlord,' Becky said. 'A very good one, too.'

But mention of justices of the peace had turned her mind to other matters. Hortense's sanity hearing before the Lunacy Commission had been scheduled for the Friday of the following week.

'What can I do to help?' she'd asked Mr Mackie.

'You can hire a lawyer,' he'd told her. 'A guid one.'

Well, she'd done that, but somehow it didn't seem

enough. She wished she could give Hortense more personal support, wished she could be in the room with her when she had to face all those strangers who held her future in their hands.

Colleen had been looking out of the window – at the street down which she'd watched Becky's brother George march out of her life for ever – but now she turned round and walked over to her dressing-table.

'I'll look awful,' she said, glancing at her reflection in the mirror. She turned her head slightly to see if that was any improvement, and then gave a low moan. 'And I won't have the nerve to face all Barnaby's posh relatives,' she told Becky. 'I know I won't.'

'You'll look beautiful,' Becky assured her. 'And with your Barnaby by your side, you could face anything.'

Colleen smiled gratefully. 'Thank you, Becky,' she said. 'I know you're right, really. An' I know that instead of wallowin' in self-pity I should be tellin' meself I'm the happiest girl in the world. It's just that sometimes I get so frightened.'

'Frightened?' Becky said. 'About what?'

Colleen turned to face her.

'What does he see in me?' she asked desperately.

'He sees a wonderful, loving girl who any man would be fortunate to marry,' Becky said.

'That's what he tells me, too,' Colleen said, almost crying. 'But sometimes, when I'm lookin' in the glass, I just can't persuade meself I could ever be this lucky.'

It wasn't going to be a very easy couple of days, Becky thought. Until Barnaby had actually slipped the ring on Colleen's finger, the poor girl was never going to get any peace of mind.

'Barnaby's the lucky one,' she told her best friend. 'Now why don't we both go downstairs and I'll make you a nice cup of tea.'

Colleen sniffed.

'You're very kind,' she said.

'Nonsense,' Becky replied. 'There's not much effort to making a simple cup of tea.'

'You're a very smart feller,' Barnaby Smith congratulated himself as he lay on his hotel bed and slowly smoked an expensive cigar. 'A very smart feller indeed.'

It was just two days before he was due to be married to Colleen O'Leary. Barnaby looked – and felt – perfectly relaxed. His boots lay on the floor, his tie hung loosely around his neck and the waistband of his trousers was comfortably unfastened. And though he could have been thinking of absolutely anything at all, he was in fact making a leisurely assessment of his situation.

Things had gone even better than he'd planned, he thought. It had been so easy to sell the idea of a plantation in Trinidad to the prosperous merchants of Northwich. In most cases, he'd only had to mention the profit they could expect to have them rushing down to their banks to draw out the money.

A few of the town's rich men had needed more working on than that, of course – those people like Richard Worrell, who fondly imagined themselves to be much sharper than they really were.

Barnaby smiled as he remembered how his conversation with the salt works owner had gone, how Worrell had been outright antagonistic at first, but slowly, slowly, had become more and more intrigued.

It was like tickling a trout, Barnaby thought. One false move and you'd have lost him for ever.

But his hand – and his nerve – had remained steady, and he had finally landed Richard. Or rather, several hundred pounds of Richard's money!

In the distance, the clock on Witton Church struck two. Barnaby frowned slightly. Hadn't he asked that pretty little chambermaid to come up to his room at a quarter to two? A quarter to two and not a second later, because he had other matters to attend to that afternoon.

There was a knock on the door. That would be her.

'Come in,' Barnaby called out.

The door opened, but instead of seeing the pretty chambermaid standing simpering for him, there was Paddy O'Leary, holding a large canvas bag under his arm.

In one smooth movement, Barnaby was on his feet and fastening his waistband button.

'I must have been half asleep,' he said quickly, 'or I would never have invited you into my room when I was in such a state of undress. And what if it hadn't been you, my dear prospective father-in-law?' He laughed. 'Why it could have been anybody – even one of the chambermaids, perhaps. And then I'd have had a pretty red face, wouldn't I?'

Paddy laughed too, but in an abstract sort of way, as if he was too worried about the canvas bag he was clutching tightly to him really to share in the joke.

'But what brings you here at this time of day, Mr O'Leary?' Barnaby asked, adjusting his tie.

Paddy thrust the satchel into Barnaby's hands as if he couldn't get rid of it quickly enough.

'The money,' he said. 'My share of the weddin' expenses.'

'You really needn't have bothered to put yourself to the inconvenience of coming all the way to Northwich,' Barnaby said. 'I fully intended to visit you at your home this very afternoon.'

He placed the satchel carelessly on his bedside table.

'Aren't you goin' to count it?' Paddy asked. 'Don't you want to know how much there is?'

'However much there is, I am sure your generous nature will have pushed you into giving more than you could afford,' Barnaby told him.

'One hundred and twenty pounds,' Paddy said.

Barnaby whistled softly.

'That is indeed a large amount for a man of your . . . for any man to pay for his daughter's wedding,' Barnaby said. 'Are you sure you wouldn't like to reconsider and take some of it back?'

Paddy shook his head.

'It's nearly me entire life savings,' he said, 'but it's worth it. Our Colleen hasn't always had an easy time of it, what with the disappointment of George Tay –'

He stopped suddenly, as if he'd just realized he'd made a terrible, terrible mistake.

'It's all right, Mr O'Leary,' Barnaby assured him. 'Colleen has told me all about George Taylor. We have no secrets from each other.'

Paddy swallowed gratefully.

'That's all in the past, anyway,' he said, 'an' there's no point in bringin' it up again now. What I wanted to say, Barnaby, is that I know you'll make me daughter happy, and what's money compared to that?'

'Indeed,' Barnaby agreed.

'And are all the arrangements made?' Paddy asked.

Barnaby turned away so that Paddy could not see the smile which had come to his lips.

'Oh yes,' he said. 'All the arrangements have been made.'

Philip Taylor glanced up at the clock and saw it was a quarter past two. The knowledge did not please him.

'Haven't you got that bloody cartoon strip finished yet?' he shouted across to the artist who was working at a table under the window.

'Not quite!' the man called back.

'Well, get a sodding move on,' Philip said bad-temperedly.

Funny Cuts was due to come out the following morning, and never before had he been as far behind schedule as he was this week. He'd have to get down on his knees and beg the printers if there was even to be the slightest chance of the comic coming out on time.

It was not usually in Philip's nature to admit that anything was his fault, but this time he had to accept that at least part of the blame rested fairly and squarely on his shoulders.

I should never have started buggering about with the comic, he told himself.

But he'd been *so* convinced that dropping some of the established characters and introducing new ones would do wonders for circulation.

He picked up the previous week's edition. '*Gaolbird Joe*', who Philip had thought would be a natural for the front page, grinned up mockingly at him. Philip put the comic aside in disgust. How could he have been so stupid? he wondered.

And so stubborn, he thought.

Week after week he had stuck by Joe and his other new creations, while all the time sales had been falling off. Now, finally, he'd given in, and the artists were having to draw new strips at the last moment, bringing back the old characters.

He looked at the clock again. Less than a minute had passed. He'd promised his sister Becky he'd get up to Cheshire for her best friend's wedding the day after next, but there was no chance of that now.

Over by the window, the artist stood up and reached up to the rack for his coat.

'Where do you think you're going?' Philip demanded.

'Just slippin' out for a cup of tea, guv,' the man said.

'Not until you've finished that bloody strip, you're not,' Philip told him firmly.

Grumbling about slave drivers, the artist hung his coat up again and returned to his desk.

Philip picked up the previous week's edition again.

'Stop laughing at me, Joe, you bastard!' he ordered the character on the front page.

And suddenly – when he was least expecting it – it came to him where he'd seen Barnaby Smith before!

He grabbed the nearest scrap of paper and began scribbling a rapid message on it.

'Fred!' he shouted as he wrote.

The office boy sauntered over to his desk.

'What can I do for yer, guv?' he asked.

Philip handed him the sheet of paper. 'Take this down to the telegraph office – as fast as you can!' he said.

The boy scanned the sheet.

'Blimey, that's a lot of words,' he said. 'It'll cost you a fortune, that will, guv.'

'Don't worry yourself about the cost,' Philip told him. 'Get it down to the telegraph office. And if I find out it's taken you any more than five minutes, I'll give you the thrashing of your life.'

Philip was behaving so unusually that the office boy looked into his face to see if he was joking – and decided he wasn't. It was at least a ten-minute journey and the frightened lad set off at a trot.

Philip leant back in his chair and mopped his brow with a silk handkerchief. He just hoped he'd sent the telegram in time.

'An' Barnaby says that as soon as we've found a house of our own, we must go an' visit his plantations,' Colleen told her best friend. 'Isn't it excitin', Becky? Here's me, hardly ever been out of Marston before, and soon I'll be goin' to tropical islands thousands of miles away.'

'It's wonderful,' Becky agreed, glad that Colleen finally seemed to have got over her attack of panic.

There was a knock on the back door.

'Can you go and answer that, our Colleen?' Cathy O'Leary called from the bar.

Colleen rose to her feet and went to the door. A man in a blue uniform was standing outside.

'Have you got a Mrs Rebecca Worrell with you?' he asked.

Becky joined her friend in the doorway.

'I'm Becky Worrell,' she said.

'Thank heavens for that,' the man told her. 'I've been all over the village lookin' for you.' He held out an envelope to her. 'Telegram from London. Marked urgent.'

Becky took the telegram and signed her name in the messenger's book.

'I hope it's not bad news I've brought you,' he said as he turned to leave.

But who would bother to send an urgent telegram unless it *was* bad news? Becky asked herself.

She slit the envelope open and glanced nervously down at the signature at the bottom of the message.

'Who's it from?' Colleen asked.

'It's from our Philip,' Becky told her, 'and it's quite long.'

She read the telegram through quickly the first time, but the second she was much slower, as if she was hoping to find something there she had missed on her initial reading.

'Is anything the matter with Philip?' Colleen asked.

'No,' said Becky, with tears in her eyes. 'Not with Philip.'

She handed the telegram over to Colleen, and watched, with increasing distress, as her friend read the message for herself.

'Well, I don't believe it,' Colleen said when she'd finished. 'I *won't* believe it.'

But the look on her face said that she did. Becky put her arms around her friend.

'You poor girl,' she said softly. 'You poor, poor girl.'

Barnaby Smith glanced down the railway platform. At the far end stood a sailor, rocking gently on his heels as if he were already back on his ship. A little closer were a clergyman and his wife, deep in conversation. And standing just outside the Ladies Waiting Room were two pretty girls.

Very pretty girls, Barnaby thought.

He gave them a second look. Their dresses and hats were of good quality, if slightly old-fashioned. Their shoes, on the other hand, had the shoddy appearance of footwear purchased from a cheap boot club. And as they chatted to each other, they would occasionally glance over their shoulders, as if fearing that someone would catch them at it.

Servants, Barnaby decided, probably parlour maids who've been spending their day off with Mam and Dad.

He was rarely wrong about such things. He couldn't afford to be. His whole livelihood depended on making a quick assessment of people and then acting accordingly.

He considered approaching the girls and engaging in light conversation. Well, why not? He'd been denied the pleasure of his half-hour with the little chambermaid that afternoon and one of these two might prove an agreeable substitute.

The calculating part of his mind cautioned against such an action – and he had to agree it was right. After all, he'd deliberately chosen this train because he knew there'd be few passengers – few witnesses – and it would be foolish to spoil it now by drawing attention to himself.

The hands on the station clock clicked loudly, recording the passing of another minute. Ten past six. And in the distance, Barnaby could hear the noisy puffing sound of a train which would take him on the first stage of his journey to London.

Right on time!

A thickset man in a bowler hat appeared at the ticket barrier. He had a red face as if he'd been running, and when the clerk held out his hand for the ticket, the man waved his hand dismissively. The clerk was not impressed. He stood directly in the thickset man's path, his outstretched arm forbidding entry.

Barnaby could imagine their conversation.

'Look here, my man, I know I have a ticket somewhere, and if you don't let me through I shall miss my train.'

'I can't help that, sir. I couldn't possibly let you through without seein' your ticket. It'd be more than my job's worth.'

His own father had been like that, Barnaby thought, an officious little time-server, a worm wriggling its way through a life of drudgery. But not him. He was Barnaby Smith. He had climbed to great heights, and now, when he stopped to look down at the miserable people crawling below him, it was only to laugh.

The thickset man had been searching through the pockets of his jacket, and had finally produced something which seemed to satisfy the railway official. Barnaby turned to face the track. He could see the train now. It was slowing down as it approached the station.

Another thirty seconds and he would be on board. Another couple of minutes and the engine would be pulling away, leaving Northwich behind.

The train drew level with the platform. The brakes screeched and bright red sparks flew from its wheels, then it came to a juddering halt. Barnaby reached forward to open the door of the first-class carriage – and felt a tap on his shoulder.

He turned round to find he was looking at the thickset man.

'Mr Smith?' the man asked. 'Mr Barnaby Smith?'

'Yes,' Barnaby replied, not bothering to hide the annoyance he felt. 'And might I ask who you are?'

'I am Inspector Gough of the Cheshire Police,' the man said. 'Might I ask where you're going, sir?'

'To London,' Barnaby said. 'I have a little business to take care of' – he smiled winningly, now he knew it was a policeman he was talking to – 'but I'll be back tomorrow. I'm getting married on Saturday, you see.'

Gough did not smile back.

'I have reason to believe you have no intention at all of returning tomorrow,' Gough said. 'In fact, sir, I don't think you ever intend to return to Northwich.'

From the corner of his eye, Barnaby caught sight of the station master walking up the platform, his flag in his hand.

'This is ridiculous!' he said to the policeman. 'If I was leaving for ever, don't you think I would be taking more luggage with me than this?'

He held up his cloth bag for the inspector to see – and the moment he had done it, he knew he'd made a mistake.

'If I was making a run for it, I'd leave most of my luggage behind, too,' the inspector said, keeping his eyes firmly on the bag. 'Would you mind opening that for me, sir?'

'I certainly would mind!' Barnaby told him. 'You have no right to make such a demand. What did you say your name was? Gough?'

'That's right, sir,' the policeman agreed.

'Well, Inspector Gough, your superiors will be hearing from me,' Barnaby said.

'What name will you be using when you make your complaint, sir?' the inspector said.

Barnaby felt himself break out into a cold sweat.

'I beg your pardon?' he said.

'Will it be Barnaby Smith?' Gough asked. 'Or will you sign yourself Herbert Rose or Godfrey Sutton, as you've sometimes been known to do. Maybe you'll even use your real name – Sidney Crabbit!'

The train, which was on the point of pulling out, was only feet away from him. All he had to do was knock Gough down, Barnaby thought. It wouldn't even have to be a particularly hard blow, just hard enough to ensure that the inspector stayed down while he jumped on the train and was carried away to freedom.

Barnaby felt two strong hands clamp on to each of his arms, and turning his head first to the left and then to the right, he saw that there was a police constable standing on either side of him.

'You took your time getting here,' Inspector Gough said.

'Am I to assume that I'm under arrest?' Barnaby asked.

'That is correct,' Gough told him.

'On what charges?'

'Fraud and bigamy,' Gough said. 'That should do for a start, don't you think?'

Sidney Crabbit, who until that afternoon had been going under the name of Barnaby Smith, was in a cell in the Cross Street lock-up when he heard a door open and saw a police constable enter the corridor.

'You've got a visitor waitin' outside,' the constable said. 'Do you want to see her?'

'Her?' Crabbit asked. 'Who is it?'

'A Miss Colleen O'Leary.'

Crabbit nodded his head sadly. 'Yes, I'll see her,' he said.

At first she was merely a shape in the doorway, but as she

got closer to his cell, he could see how pale and drawn she was.

She reached the cell and stood for a moment, just staring at him through the bars. Then she said, 'You lied to me!'

'Yes,' he agreed. 'I lied to you.'

'Your family never did own any land in Lancashire, did they?' she demanded.

'No,' he said, 'and there was never any property in the West Indies, either. My father was an impoverished railway clerk, and I own little more than the clothes I'm standing up in.'

'How could you do it?' Colleen asked. 'How could you have made me love you so? An' did you have to paint such a lovely picture of the life we'd have together, the house in the country and the holidays in Trinidad? I'd already said I'd marry you, you didn't have to go on promisin' me things you knew I'd never have.'

'Oh yes, I did,' Crabbit told her. 'I needed to make sure you'd go on loving me until your father handed over his money. And sometimes, when I was telling you about the plantation or our estates,' he continued dreamily, 'they seemed so real that I almost believed in them myself.'

'I would have loved you rich or poor,' Colleen said.

'It would have been wonderful, sailing in our private steam yacht on blue tropical seas,' Crabbit said. Then, suddenly he seemed to become aware of his surroundings – of the bars which separated him from Colleen. 'How did they get on to me?' he asked.

'Through Becky's brother, Philip,' Colleen told him. 'He was in Strangeways prison at the same time you were.'

'Ah, yes,' Crabbit said. 'We didn't know each other well, but I thought there was always a chance he might remember who I was.'

'That's why you wanted us to get married in such a rush, isn't it?' Colleen said.

'Yes,' Crabbit admitted. 'I hoped to have the whole thing over before Philip recovered his memory. I almost made it, too.'

'And which wife would I have been?' Colleen asked bitterly.

'My fourth,' Crabbit said. 'Though I never intended to marry you.'

'No, all you wanted was my dad's money, wasn't it?' Colleen said.

'I took money from others, too,' Crabbit said. 'I gave them worthless shares in return for hard cash. But they'll get their money back. I had it about my person, in a cloth bag, at the time I was arrested.'

'I think you're despicable,' Colleen told him.

'You're right,' Crabbit agreed readily. 'But there is one thing you should know. The reason I never intended to marry you as I married all the others was because –'

'Because I'm plain!' Colleen interrupted. 'Don't you think I know that already?'

Crabbit looked shocked.

'Don't ever say that about yourself,' he told her.

'It's true,' Colleen said miserably. 'I only have to look in the mirror to see it's true.'

'You have never been plain to me,' Crabbit said, 'and the reason I decided not to marry you wasn't because I cared less for you than I did for the others. It was because I cared for you more.'

'You've told so many lies before, why should I believe you now?' Colleen asked.

'Because I no longer have anything to gain by lying,' Crabbit said. 'Look at me, Colleen. Look right into my eyes.'

And almost despite herself, Colleen found her eyes being drawn to his.

'As much as a man such as I is capable of love,' he said slowly and deliberately, 'I love you.'

'Thank you,' Colleen said. 'Thank you for that, at least.'

'Do you think you could ever find it in your heart to forgive me?' Crabbit asked.

'In time, perhaps,' Colleen said.

Crabbit hesitated before he spoke again.

'I shall be going to prison,' he said, 'but they'll let me out some day. Will you wait for me?'

'There was someone else I would once have waited for . . .' Colleen said to him.

'George Taylor?' Crabbit said.

'Yes,' Colleen agreed. 'I would have waited for George for ever if he'd just asked me to – but I won't wait for you.'

'Even though you still love me!' Crabbit protested.

Colleen shook her head. 'I don't love you,' she said. 'I never loved you. I loved Barnaby Smith, and you're not half the man he was.'

Crabbit nodded as if acknowledging the truth. The policeman who had showed Colleen to the cell appeared in the corridor again.

'It's time for you to go, miss,' he said.

'Couldn't she stay a little longer?' Crabbit asked, with a hint of desperation in his voice.

'Would there really be any point to it?' Colleen asked him. 'Is there anything we could say to each other that we haven't said already?'

'No,' Crabbit admitted. 'I suppose not.'

Colleen took one last, pitying look at him.

'Goodbye,' she said.

'Goodbye, Colleen,' Crabbit replied, and as she started to walk down the corridor, he called after her, 'I hope you find real happiness one day. God knows, you deserve it more than most.'

Chapter Nineteen

Martin Stanfield, the lawyer retained by Becky Taylor to represent her sister-in-law Hortense, stood gazing around the room in which the Cheshire Lunacy Commission was to hold its session.

It must have been a dining room in the days before this place became an asylum, he thought. Or perhaps a salon, he amended, noting the plaster mouldings that ran around the top of the wall and the imitation Gainsborough which some anonymous artist had painted on the ceiling.

The room had been totally bare when he'd arrived, twenty minutes earlier, but now several of the asylum's servants had arrived and were rushing around filling it with the appropriate furniture for a meeting of the Lunacy Commission.

First they brought in a long heavy table, which they set down close to the far wall. Next, they produced five chairs and placed four of them behind the table and the fifth in front. Finally they returned with two smaller tables and two more chairs and set up one of each in the corners closest to the door.

'Which of these tables is supposed to be mine?' Stanfield asked one of the servants.

'Don't think it really matters, sir,' the man replied. 'Take whichever you fancy.'

Stanfield chose the small table in the left-hand corner, sat down and took his notes out of his leather satchel. This was not a new experience for him – his work for the Lunacy Law Reform Society had caused him to appear before more than a dozen Lunacy Commissions. Nor did he anticipate this being one of his more difficult cases. The grounds for confining Hortense Worrell had been questionable at best.

But the woman herself is my strongest argument, he thought.

When he'd talked to her the previous day, he'd been very encouraged by what he'd found. Hortense not only looked perfectly sane but was also capable of discussing her case in an extremely rational manner. The Commissioners would be impressed, and if they had even an ounce of fairness between them, they would have to order her release.

A small, bald-headed man entered the room and made a beeline for the London attorney's table. As he got closer, Stanfield could see that most of his teeth were rotten.

'Mr Stanfield?' the bald man said, holding out his hand. 'My name is Horace Crimp. I'm representing Mr Worrell.'

Stanfield shook hands and tried not to let it show that Crimp's breath revolted him.

'You're still intending to fight this case right through to the end, are you, Mr Crimp?' he asked.

'Not necessarily,' Crimp replied. 'My client is more than willing to accept a compromise.'

Of course he was! Because he knew that if he fought the case, he would lose.

'Exactly what sort of compromise did you have in mind, Mr Crimp?' Stanfield asked.

'If you're willing to abandon the proceedings now, my client is prepared, at some future date, to drop his objections to his wife being released,' Horace Crimp replied.

'How soon?' Stanfield asked.

'How soon what?' Crimp replied evasively.

'How soon will he agree to her being released?'

'Oh, after a reasonable amount of time,' Crimp replied.

'Which you would define as . . .?'

Crimp shrugged. 'Shall we say – nine or ten years,' he suggested.

Nine or ten years! Stanfield thought. Hortense Worrell would be destroyed by that time. She'd genuinely *need* institutionalizing after another nine or ten years.

'And would your client be prepared to put that promise to

drop his objections in writing?' Stanfield asked, just to get the measure of his opponents.

'Well, no. Not exactly in writing,' Crimp admitted.

'Then I don't think there is anything more for us to talk about,' Stanfield said coldly.

'Please yourself,' Crimp retorted.

Stanfield watched the bald man as he walked over to his own desk in the other corner. He knew Crimp's type of old – the sly provincial attorney who considered himself very smart, but soon became bogged down in the intricacies of the law. And though he was a fair man who rarely went on appearances himself, Stanfield couldn't help but think that Crimp's repulsive features were bound to work in the defence's favour.

The door opened. Four new men entered the room, walked to the long table and sat down. The Lunacy Commissioners and their medical adviser had finally arrived. Both Stanfield and Crimp stood up and bowed to them.

'I will now call this meeting to order,' said one of the Commissioners, a grey-haired man with a self-important expression.

His name was Holdroyd, Stanfield remembered from their meeting the previous day. The other two were Woodward and Bentley. The one on the end, the doctor, was called Jepson.

'We will hear from Mr Horace Crimp first,' Holdroyd said, 'and then from you, Mr . . . er . .'

'Stanfield,' the London lawyer told him.

'Mr *Stanfield*,' Holdroyd repeated, as if it was somehow the lawyer's fault that he had been unable to remember his name.

Horace Crimp stood up, walked into the centre of the room, and surveyed the Commissioners.

'Two highly qualified doctors, one of them an alienist, have certified that this woman, Hortense Worrell, is a lunatic,' he said. 'And we should think carefully before questioning qualified medical opinion,' he continued, raising a cautionary finger, 'because in doing so we do not just discredit one doctor in particular. No! In doing so, we cast doubt on the whole of the medical profession.'

Stanfield rose to his feet.

'Your Worships, I must protest!' he said.

'On what grounds, Mr Stanmore?' the chairman said.

Deciding to ignore the mistake over his name, Stanfield approached the table.

'On the grounds Mr Crimp is trying to suggest that all doctors should agree on what determines insanity,' he said. 'They shouldn't – and they don't. The basis on which my client was committed to this institution is one which more and more medical men all over the country have started to call into question. To wit, she was judged insane purely on the grounds of having committed adultery.'

Holdroyd tut-tutted, as if it were bad form to mention such matters, even at a hearing like this.

'Why she was admitted is not the question now,' he said. 'We are here to decide whether or not she should be released.'

'Exactly,' Horace Crimp agreed. 'And in this particular case, we are fortunate that this fine institution has so closely followed the terms of the 1845 Lunatics' Act.'

'What do you mean by that, Mr Crimp?' the chairman said.

'I mean that in accordance with the law, the staff here have been keeping very comprehensive medical notes on this patient,' Horace Crimp said. He turned to the doctor. 'I believe you have those very notes in front of you, don't you, sir?'

'Indeed I do,' said the doctor. He picked up the notes and began to skim through them.

'I think you'll find that they are a record of consistently unstable and violent behaviour,' Crimp said.

'They certainly do seem to contain a very disturbing story,' the doctor admitted.

'There was no mention of violence in the medical notes I was shown!' Stanfield protested.

'Was there not?' Crimp asked mildly. 'Perhaps you didn't read them carefully enough.'

Stanfield was only just beginning to realize exactly what he was up against, only now getting some kind of picture of the way Horace Crimp worked.

'I believe the records the doctor is examining to be forgeries,' he said to Holdroyd.

The chairman frowned. 'That is a very serious charge to make,' he said.

And a very difficult one to prove once the ink was dry, Crimp thought.

'The charge may be serious,' Stanfield agreed, 'but it is not the first time I have had to make such an accusation, nor, I am afraid, will it be the last. In economic terms, it is worth the while of such institutions as this to hold onto their patients, and many of them will do *anything* to ensure they are not released.'

Holdroyd's face reddened with anger.

'You will gain nothing by insults,' he said. 'Such things as you describe may go on in other parts of the country, but we would never allow them in Cheshire.'

Stanfield looked up at the painted ceiling for inspiration. The faked medical records had cut half his ground from under his feet. He had no choice but to play his trump card.

'Surely the only fair way to pass judgement on the lady's sanity is to talk to her yourselves,' he said.

Crimp must have been dreading this moment, Stanfield thought. Because all the faked records in the world would not stand up against the calm, rational woman who would eventually *have* to be brought into the room and displayed before the Commissioners.

'Have you any objection to calling the lady in now, Mr Crimp?' Holdroyd asked.

The bald lawyer shook his head. 'None at all,' he said. 'I entirely agree with Mr Stanfield. Let her speak for herself.'

Holdroyd rang the bell which lay in front of him. The door opened and Hortense entered with her keeper.

The sight of her made Stanfield almost reel with shock. The day before Hortense had been a hopeful, alert woman with her hair in a neat bun. Now her hair was a bird's-nest, and it was plain to everyone in the room that without the help of her keeper – a large man with cunning, ruthless eyes – she would hardly have been able to stand.

'Could you please take that seat there, Mrs Worrell,' Mr Holdroyd said, pointing to the chair directly in front of the table.

The keeper steered Hortense carefully over to the chair and helped her to sit down.

'You may now leave,' Holdroyd told the keeper.

'With respect, sir, I'm not sure that's really a very good idea,' the keeper replied.

'Why isn't it a good idea?' Holdroyd asked.

The keeper looked down at Hortense. 'This partic'lar patient can turn very violent – all of a sudden-like,' he explained. 'More than once I've had to pull her off one of the other inmates before she could do 'em serious harm. Doesn't matter to her what size they are, either. I've seen her have a go at some really big fellers once she'd got one of her moods on her.'

Holdroyd instinctively pushed his chair a few more inches away from Hortense Worrell.

'Very well,' he said to the keeper. 'You may stay.'

'I must protest yet again, sir!' Stanfield said. 'Mrs Worrell will only be intimidated by having her keeper present during the proceedings. And look at her. Does it seem likely that she's about to become violent?'

Holdroyd *did* look at her, and thought to himself that she seemed more inclined to fall asleep than to go berserk.

'When she's like that, it's often the signal she's got an attack comin' on,' the keeper said. 'One second she's as quiet as a mouse and the next she's as wild as a rabid dog.'

'If her keeper, who knows her better than anyone, feels it is better that he stay in the room,' Holdroyd told the London lawyer, 'then I think we should accept his judgement.'

'Sir, I must . . .' Stanfield began.

'I am the one empowered by Act of Parliament to rule on procedures, not you,' Holdroyd said pompously. 'And if it is my decision that he should stay, then stay he will.'

Stanfield shrugged helplessly and it took Crimp considerable effort to hide his glee.

'Would you care to address any questions to this poor, unfortunate woman, doctor?' the chairman asked the medical man on his right.

'Indeed I would,' Dr Jepson replied. 'Mrs Worrell, would you please tell the Commission . . .'

Hortense's head slumped slowly forward until her chin was resting on her chest.

'Mrs Worrell?' the doctor said. 'Can you hear me, Mrs Worrell?'

Stanfield rushed to his client's chair and knelt down in front of it.

'Do you know who I am, Mrs Worrell?' he asked.

Hortense groaned, and her head shifted slightly. Stanfield took her chin gently in his hand, and lifted her head up again.

'Tell me who I am?' he pleaded.

Hortense mumbled something unintelligible.

'Louder!' Stanfield urged.

'My attorney,' Hortense managed to gasp.

'And do you know why we're all here?' Stanfield prodded. 'Do you know what's going on?'

Hortense opened her mouth as if to speak – then closed it again.

'Try!' Stanfield begged her. 'Please try.'

'Tired . . .' Hortense told him. 'So tired . . .'

'Is there any particular reason you're tired?' Stanfield asked. 'What have they done to you, Mrs Worrell?'

'Wouldn't let me sleep last night . . .' Hortense mumbled. 'Every time . . . I . . . went to sleep, they shook me awake again.'

'Is this true?' Holdroyd asked the keeper.

'Sometimes she can't go to sleep for days at a time,' the

keeper said. 'She always blames it on us. It's one of her symptoms.'

'And how was she last night?' Horace Crimp asked.

'Slept like a baby,' the keeper replied.

'Is there any other reason you're tired, Mrs Worrell?' asked Stanfield, who'd begun to suspect the worst.

'Medicine,' Hortense said. 'Made me take my medicine this morning. Didn't want to, but they forced it down my throat.'

Stanfield lowered Hortense's head on to her chest again, then stood up to face the Commissioners.

'This woman has been drugged,' he declared.

Holdroyd turned to the keeper with a questioning look. 'Is that true?' he asked.

'We did give her some medication,' the keeper admitted. 'Well, we had to, just so she'd stay on somethin' like an even keel. But it wasn't very strong medication, 'cos we were tryin' to keep her awake so she could talk to you gentl'men.'

Holdroyd glanced in turn at his two fellow magistrates. Both of them nodded back at him.

'This woman bears no resemblance to the woman I spoke to yesterday,' Stanfield said.

'Changes from day to day,' the keeper said softly, though not so softly that the Commissioners couldn't hear it.

'I think we've seen enough,' Holdroyd said.

'But I've hardly begun to make my case,' Stanfield protested.

'It was you, I think, who suggested that we let Mrs Worrell make her *own* case,' the chairman said. 'Well, we've given her ample opportunity to do just that. We will confer on the matter, and communicate our decision in writing to all interested parties. You may take your patient back to her room now, Keeper.'

The keeper put his hands under Hortense's armpits and lifted her to her feet. She made no protest, nor did she attempt to resist when he began to lead her away from the meeting which had been her chance of freedom.

The magistrates shook their heads sympathetically. It was terrible, they seemed to be thinking, that a human being could sink to such depths. Horace Crimp, calculating how much he could charge Richard Worrell for this latest piece of villainy, looked on with satisfaction. Only Martin Stanfield seemed displeased with the way things had gone.

Horace Crimp walked along the corridor, knocked on the warden's door, and entered. The warden was sitting behind his desk, totting up figures. He was a tall, thin man with quick, greedy eyes. He claimed to have owned a hotel before he opened the asylum, but rumour had it that it was not so much a hotel as a brothel. It was perfectly possible that the rumour was true, Crimp thought, and as a qualification for running a private madhouse, it was probably as good as the ones most of the other owners had.

The warden looked up.

'Went all right, did it, Mr Crimp?' he asked.

'Most satisfactorily,' Crimp replied.

'In that case, there's no harm in having a little celebratory drink, is there?' the warden asked as he opened his desk drawer and took out a bottle of brandy and two glasses.

'No harm at all,' Crimp agreed, sitting down.

The warden filled the two glasses to the top and handed one to the attorney.

'The medical records I gave you were all right, were they?' he asked.

'Very convincing,' Crimp replied.

'And so they should have been,' the warden said. 'I had one of my medical fellers up most of the night writing them.'

'You mean, reviewing them,' Crimp said sharply.

'That's right,' the warden agreed. 'Reviewing them. And how did Mrs Worrell herself look?'

'Like a lunatic,' Crimp said.

The warden chuckled. 'I'm not surprised after what we put her through yesterday,' he said.

Crimp frowned. Whatever else the warden had learned

during his brothel-keeping days, he hadn't picked up much in the line of subtlety, the laywer thought. Or caution, either!

Crimp looked hastily around the room, searching for any alcove where an eavesdropper might be hiding. Not that it was likely the warden would try to blackmail him at some later date, but Crimp never put past others anything he was capable of doing himself.

It only took the lawyer a few seconds to decide that he and the warden were the only two in the room.

Even so, I'd better leave before the fool says anything else incriminating, he thought.

He knocked back his brandy and rose to his feet. The warden seemed alarmed that he was about to go.

'Always glad to oblige a gentleman like Mr Worrell,' he said hastily, 'but there is still the question of . . .'

'Of the payment for extra treatment Mrs Worrell will require as a result of this disturbance,' Crimp interrupted. 'I think we agreed on forty guineas, didn't we?'

'Fifty,' the warden said firmly.

'Fifty, of course,' Crimp replied. 'I'll have it sent round to you this afternoon.'

She had got it into her mind that the bed on which she was lying was a giant raven, soaring through the air under a bank of menacing grey clouds. She had wanted to escape – to roll off the raven's back and be free of him – even if it meant plunging thousands of feet to her death.

Now, as the effect of the drugs slowly wore off, she began to see things as they really were. The clouds ceased to swirl and became her bedroom ceiling once more. The raven's harsh cry was nothing but the creaking of her bedsprings as she twisted and turned her way through the nightmare.

Looking across at the barred window, Hortense saw that it was daylight. And what a day it was going to be, she told herself. Today she would appear before the Lunacy Commission! Today they would have to set her free!

She began to remember what had happened in the last few hours.

'Get a good night's sleep,' Mr Stanfield had told her. 'It's vital that you appear bright and fresh in the morning.'

And she'd tried to sleep, God knew she had. But *they* wouldn't let her. Every time she had closed her eyes, the keeper had shaken her until she was wide awake again. Once he'd even thrown a pail of water on her face – and laughed out loud as he was doing it.

Then dawn had finally broken and they'd come with the drugs.

'I don't want them!' she'd screamed. 'Please don't make me take them!'

They'd ignored her pleas and the keeper held her down with his big hairy hands while the nurse forced the drugs down her throat.

But that didn't matter now, she told herself. All that was important was the meeting she was going to have with the Lunacy Commissioners.

'Get moving,' she said aloud. 'Got to get moving.'

Gingerly, she swung her feet off the bed and let them rest on the floor. The walls were no longer spinning around, and she was sure that if she took it carefully, she could make it to the door.

She put one foot in front of the other and made her way carefully across the room. It seemed to take an age to reach the other wall, and when she finally did, she found that the door was locked. She tried not to let it upset her. After all, her keeper would *have* to let her out soon, because they would want to talk to her at the meeting.

She turned back towards the window. The sun was in a strange place for this time of day, she thought. It shouldn't be up there until mid afternoon.

And then she remembered!

Her keeper saying, 'This partic'lar patient can turn very violent – all of a sudden-like.'

And she'd wanted to scream, 'No! No! It isn't true!'

Mr Stanfield, the laywer, asking her, 'Why are we here? What's this all about?'

And she'd tried to tell him, but she'd been so exhausted that the words just wouldn't come out.

She made her way back to the bed, slowly and painfully because now that she had no real purpose but to sit down, the journey seemed twice as difficult as the one to the door. Yet she made it finally, and sinking down on to the bed, she buried her head in her hands.

She'd lost her one chance, she told herself, and now they would never set her free.

She thought of all that would mean. She'd never see Gerald again. And what would happen to poor little William? Becky had promised to rescue him, but Richard would never allow that – not as long as she was alive.

Not as long as she was alive!

Hortense looked up at the beam which ran across the ceiling, and then down at her bed. She pulled the sheet free of her blanket and began to twist it into a long thin strip. She worked slowly, because her brain was still befuddled by the drugs, but after half an hour's striving, she had succeeded in making a noose in one end.

Mary Taylor was preparing her lodgers' supper when she heard the latch being lifted. She turned around and saw Becky standing in the doorway. The poor girl was ashen and on the point of tears. Mary flung her arms round her youngest daughter and gave her a comforting hug.

'I'll be all right in a minute,' Becky said. 'Just let me sit down, and I'll be fine.'

Mary helped Becky over to one of the chairs.

'You should never have gone to that asylum by yourself,' she said. 'I'd have been glad to go with you.'

'I know you would, Mam,' Becky said shakily, 'but it was something I had to do on my own.'

'And did they let you see the body in the end?' Mary asked.

Becky shook her head. 'Only Richard and a couple of

people from the asylum have seen it,' she replied. 'It'll not be put on public display.'

'Perhaps that's just as well,' Mary told her daughter. 'Hangin' makes the victim's face go all . . . but we don't want to talk about that now.'

'She should never have done it, Mam,' Becky said, doing her best to contain her tears.

'I know, love,' Mary said sympathetically.

'Mr Mackie said it was only the start,' Becky sobbed. 'After the Cheshire Commissioners turned us down, we could have made an appeal to the ones in London.'

'Maybe she thought with Richard against her, she'd have no chance whoever she appealed to,' Mary said.

'She wasn't like she used to be before she was locked up, Mam,' Becky said. 'She'd changed. She really had. I think . . . I think in time we might have been very good friends.'

'Well, there's nothin' more you can do for the poor woman now,' Mary said.

'Oh, but there is,' Becky said.

'I don't see how . . .' Mary began.

'That day I saw her at the fête, she got me to make her a promise,' Becky said.

'What sort of promise?' Mary asked worriedly.

'She made me swear that I'd find her little boy,' Becky told her, 'and that once I'd found him, I'd look after him.'

'But if even Hortense didn't know where he was, how do you expect to find him?' Mary asked.

Becky clenched her hands in front of her.

'I shall have to go and ask the one person who does know,' she said.

'Richard!' Mary exclaimed.

'Richard,' Becky agreed, clenching her hands even tighter.

'But you can't do that!' Mary said. 'I mean, Richard Worrell's the one who . . . who . . .'

'Seduced me,' Becky said.

'An' when Michael's works was fallin' down . . .'

'He tried to bribe Cedric Rathbone to do nothing,' Becky said. 'I know all that.'

'Then how *can* you go and see him?' Mary demanded. 'How will you be able to stand even bein' in the same room as him?'

Becky's knuckles had turned white.

'I've no choice,' she said. 'I have to do everything I can to find William. I owe it to Hortense.'

Chapter Twenty

Becky stood in the doorway of Richard Worrell's office. She was wearing a long black dress and a black bonnet which completely covered her golden hair. Her eyes were red as if she had been crying, and there was a haunted expression on her face.

So how can she still look so beautiful? Richard wondered.

It had been years since he'd been this close to her – years in which so much had happened – but she still had the power to affect him as no other woman had ever done.

'I never expected to see you in this office again, Becky,' he said, thinking back to the last time she had been there, the night he'd told her he would not marry her but would be happy to keep her as his mistress.

'I never expected to be here myself,' Becky replied, shuddering as she remembered the same dreadful evening herself.

'Would you like to sit down?' Richard asked, pointing to the seat at the other side of his desk.

For a moment he thought she would refuse. Then she nodded. He watched her as she walked across the room towards his desk. What grace she had. How sensual her movements were, even though, he was sure, she never intended them to be.

He found himself falling more and more under her spell with every second that passed. But he couldn't afford that, he told himself angrily. He had to keep his head clear – because at all costs, Becky must never learn what *really* happened in Hortense's room after the meeting of the Lunacy Commission.

Becky sat down, so uncomfortably near to him that it was

almost unbearable.

'This is a rather indelicate time for you to choose to call on me, Becky,' he said. 'I am in mourning for my wife.'

Becky's eyes flashed with anger.

'You hypocrite!' she said. '*I'm* in mourning for Hortense. You didn't give a damn about her!'

'I never wanted Hortense to hang herself,' Richard said. 'I hated the woman, I freely admit that, but it was never my wish to see her dead.'

'No,' Becky agreed. 'But you drove her to it as surely as if you had knotted the sheet yourself. And of all the terrible things you've done, that's the one for which I'll never be able to forgive you.'

'Then why are you here?' Richard asked. 'If you feel like that about me, how can you bear to be in the same room?'

'I want you to do something for me,' Becky said.

Richard shook his head in admiration. How like Becky it was to be so direct, to answer his question without evasion or excuses.

'Go on,' he said.

'I want to know where you've sent William,' Becky continued.

Richard had pushed the boy so far to the back of his mind that for a moment, he had no idea who William was. And then it came to him.

'What I have chosen to do with my own son is no concern of yours,' he said.

'He's not your son!' Becky told him.

She knew! Becky Taylor, who had every reason to hate him, knew the truth about his wife's infidelity!

'How did you find out?' he asked.

'Hortense told me,' Becky said. 'But don't worry, Richard, I'll keep it to myself.'

Why was she being so magnanimous? Richard wondered. If he'd had such power to hurt his enemies, he'd have used it without a second's thought.

'Thank you,' he said.

'I'm not doing it for you,' Becky told him. 'I'm doing it for Hortense. She was in love with her groom. I know that. But to everyone else it would seem like nothing more than a squalid little affair – and I won't sully her memory by making it public knowledge.'

She had a way of making him feel dirty, Richard thought. Whether she really intended to or not, she had a way of making him feel worthless and dirty and . . .

'Where is William?' Becky asked.

'My wife's bastard!' Richard said in disgust.

'Your wife's child,' Becky said as evenly as she could.

'And what is it to you?' Richard demanded.

'I want to adopt him,' Becky said. 'I want to bring him up as if he were my own son.'

'Never!' Richard exploded.

'How could it hurt you?' Becky asked. 'What harm could a small child possibly do to you?'

'He's a constant reminder of the harm his *mother* did to me,' Richard said angrily. 'A constant reminder that she betrayed me.'

'He would be my son,' Becky said. 'You could forget he ever existed.'

'No!' Richard said.

'If you stand in my way, I'll tell the whole world who his father really was,' Becky said.

Richard sneered. 'No, you won't,' he said. 'You wouldn't want to sully Hortense's memory. You told me so yourself.'

'If Hortense were given the choice of saving her reputation or saving her child, I know which one she'd choose,' Becky said. 'If she knew that I had only this one threat I could use against you, she'd want me to use it.'

'Go ahead!' Richard said. 'Dishonour her if you want to. See if I care.'

'Think about it, Richard,' Becky cautioned. 'Think of what it will mean. You'll be nothing but a joke. Your friends will snigger at you behind your back. Children will call names after you as you walk down the street. You'll never be able to hold your head up again.'

'You wouldn't dare do that,' Richard said.

'Wouldn't I?' Becky asked.

Yes, she would, he told himself. There was nothing Becky Taylor wouldn't do when she thought she was in the right.

'And if I allow you to adopt the child, you promise me that no one will ever know who his real parents were?' he asked.

'You have my word on that,' Becky said. 'As far as the rest of the world is concerned, he'll simply be an orphan I felt pity for and have taken into my family.'

Richard reached for a pen. He scribbled down some directions and then slid the piece of paper across the desk to Becky.

'That's where you'll find the brat,' he said.

Becky glanced at what he'd written.

'A barge!' she said. 'He's living on a barge in Liverpool docks! And what's this barge like?'

'I don't know,' Richard told her. 'I've never seen it. The woman I gave him to took him off me at Lime Street station.'

'And what was *she* like?' Becky asked.

'A great ugly sow of a woman,' Richard said in disgust. 'God, how she stank!'

'And you still handed William over to her?' Becky asked incredulously.

'He's not my child,' Richard said viciously. 'He's working-class scum, and she's just the sort of woman who should be bringing him up. And he'll be in good company – the sow told me she'd got at least another dozen little guttersnipes to look after.'

'You're a monster!' Becky told him.

'I look after me and mine,' Richard replied. 'And as far as I'm concerned, the rest of the world can go hang – like Hortense.'

Becky had only just started to tell her mother about little William when Spudder burst into Mary's kitchen.

'We're a bit busy at the moment, Spudder,' Mary told

him. 'What is it you want?'

'Aggie's kicked me out while she does the cleanin',' the young man said. 'An' I was just wonderin' if there was anythin' useful I could do here.'

Mary looked around the room.

'Not really,' she said.

'Them winders could do with a clean,' Spudder pointed out.

'That's true,' Mary agreed, 'but if Aggie finds out you've been doing her jobs again, she'll play merry hell.'

'She won't find out,' Spudder said.

'She's *bound* to notice,' Mary told him.

Spudder grinned. 'She won't if after I've finished cleanin' them, I dirty them all up again,' he said.

Mary shrugged her shoulders. Spudder could sometimes be impossible, but she couldn't help liking him – and once he'd decided he was going to do something, you might just as well give in to the inevitable.

'If I let you clean the windows, will you promise to keep quiet so me and Becky can have our talk?' she asked.

'Yes,' Spudder agreed.

'Well, get on with it then!' Mary said. She turned her attention back to her daughter. 'When are you goin' to Liverpool to pick the little babbie up?' she asked.

'First thing in the morning,' Becky replied.

'Are you expectin' any trouble?' Mary asked.

'No,' Becky said – rather too quickly. 'It should all be pretty straightforward.'

'Then why are you lookin' so worried?' Mary wondered.

'I'm not,' her daughter said.

But you couldn't hide things from your mother – not if your mother was Mary Taylor.

'Becky!' Mary said sternly.

'Yes, Mam?'

'Come clean.'

'I'm a bit worried about what state I'll find him in,' Becky confessed.

'Why's that?' Mary asked.

'The woman who's looking after him takes care of a lot of other children, as well,' Becky explained. 'That's how she makes her living. And from the way Richard talked about her, she sounds a rough type – so I'm afraid she might have neglected him.'

'If he's been neglected, we'll soon make it up to him,' Mary promised. 'But I'll tell you what's got me bothered – you goin' down to them rough docks at all. Still, you'll be taking Cedric Rathbone along with you for protection, won't you?'

'I'd like to,' Becky said, 'but his brother in Lancaster has been taken very poorly, and Cedric's gone to visit him.'

'So who are you takin'?' Mary asked worriedly.

'I don't know,' Becky replied.

'Take me,' Spudder said, lifting his head up – but only for a moment – from his work on the windows.

Becky and Mary looked at each other in astonishment.

'You, Spudder?' Mary said.

'Yes,' the young man replied, rubbing furiously at one of the windowpanes. 'I'd like to help.'

'Do you even know what it is Becky's goin' to do?' Mary wondered, remembering that Spudder was perfectly capable of getting ideas completely back to front.

'Mrs Becky's goin' to go to Liverpool to pick up a little baby who's not bein' looked after properly, and she needs somebody strong to keep her company,' Spudder said.

Mary shook her head in surprise. 'Half the time, you seem to have no idea what's going on around you, Spudder,' she said, 'but you take most of it in, don't you?'

Spudder turned round and grinned. 'Only when I'm interested,' he said. 'Can I come with you? Please, Mrs Becky?'

Becky looked at her mother, and her mother looked back at her.

'Why not?' Becky said.

A dead cat lay rotting in the gutter. A drunk was sprawled in the doorway of a derelict building. The area around the old Liverpool docks would have been depressing enough in bright sunlight, but under the heavy grey sky it felt like the most miserable, God-forsaken place in the world.

Becky tried to look neither to her left nor her right, but she could not help noticing something of what was going on around her. Villainous figures lurked on every street corner and lounged against every lamppost: sailors with razor scars on their cheeks and tattoos on their thick arms; dossers who looked ready to murder their own grandmothers for the price of a drink; burly young men who were watching her with more than casual interest. She remembered the last time she'd been in a situation like this, when she'd gone to try and persuade Caspar Leech to leave Philip alone. She'd had Cedric Rathbone with her then. She wished she had him with her now.

'You're all right, Mrs Becky,' said Spudder, reading her thoughts. 'I'll look after you.'

'Thank you, Spudder,' Becky said, without much confidence.

And then she looked up at him and was surprised at what she saw. She'd always thought of him as a boy, and perhaps he still was – in his mind. But there was nothing boyish about his body. Years of heavy farm work had made it hard and well muscled. It would be a brave man – or foolish one – who thought of taking Spudder on.

They were closer to the actual dock now. Houses and pubs had given way to warehouses, and the only men around were those going about their legitimate business. Becky breathed a sigh of relief.

'Are we nearly there?' Spudder asked. 'Will we get to see the little lad soon?'

'Very soon,' Becky promised.

He was a strange one, Spudder, she thought. He hadn't been in the least bit worried when they'd been surrounded by ruffians, but now they were safe and close to getting what they'd come for, he was as nervy as anything.

It was still a mystery to her why he'd wanted to come with her at all. He'd never shown any interest in children before. Digging the front garden or whitewashing the lavvy had always held much more fascination for him than Michelle or any of Mary's other grandkids. And yet the nearer they got to their destination, the more agitated he seemed to be.

'Is that it?' Spudder asked, excited, pointing to a barge which was moored in a small, dilapidated dock.

'That's it,' Becky said, reading the name on its hull.

God, it was even worse than she'd imagined.

The boat was an ancient coal barge, which looked as if it had not been cleaned up since the days it had plied its trade on the river. A number of ragged children, as filthy as the boat itself, played around the cargo hold or swung from frayed ropes. A couple of the children were very small indeed, and Becky found herself wondering if one of them was the child she had decided to adopt.

A woman appeared on the deck of the boat. She had countless double chins and large, pendulous breasts. Her dress was so soiled that it was impossible to say what colour it had been originally, and her hair cascaded over her flabby shoulders in greasy rat's-tails.

'What the bloody hell do you pair want?' she demanded without ceremony.

'Mrs Black?' Becky asked, thinking as she said it that never had a name more suited a general appearance.

The woman scowled.

'What if I am Mrs Black?' she demanded.

'I'm here to see you on business,' Becky told her.

'Want to dump a brat on me, do yer?' the huge woman asked.

'No, I want to take one away,' Becky said.

Mrs Black was on her guard immediately.

'Nobody who doesn't bring 'em here in the first place gets to take 'em away,' she said belligerently. 'I'm responsible for 'em, I am, an' I love 'em like they was me own.'

One of the children she was responsible for and loved as

her own – a poor half-starved creature of about seven or eight – chose that moment to wander up to Mrs Black and tug at her dress.

'What is it now?' Mrs Black asked irritably.

The child opened his mouth and pointed into it with his finger.

'Bugger off!' Mrs Black told the boy, cuffing him round the ear as if to make sure he'd understood. 'And you bugger off, too!' she said, turning back to Becky. 'I gets money for looking after these young sods.'

'I'm willing to pay,' Becky said.

The big woman's eyes narrowed into a cunning gaze.

'How much?' she asked.

'Ten pounds,' Becky told her.

It was obviously more than Mrs Black had been expecting, and for a moment it seemed as if she would quite faint away with the shock. Then she pulled herself together and her eyes glinted with greed.

'Couldn't yer make it twenty pound?' she asked.

'Fifteen,' Becky replied, her tone stating quite clearly that this was as high as she intended to go.

'Yer've got a deal,' Mrs Black said, smiling in what she probably thought was a winning way. 'Pick any kid yer fancy.' She pointed to the one who had tugged at her skirt. 'Yer can have him if yer like.'

'It's William Worrell I want,' Becky said.

Mrs Black reached up and scratched her matted hair.

'Who?' she asked. 'Oh, yer mean Billy. Well, yer'll have to come inside then. He never comes out.'

Becky stepped gingerly aboard the boat. The deck was thick with grease and so slippery it was almost like walking on ice.

'He'll be down there, somewhere,' Mrs Black said, pointing to a set of rotting steps.

Testing each step carefully as she went, Becky began to descend slowly into the cabin area. The air at the top of the steps had been merely unpleasant, but by the time she reached the bottom the stink of decaying food and urine had become almost unbearable. Becky held her handkerchief to her nose and pressed on.

Only a little light filtered in through the filthy portholes, but it was enough to show Becky that the place looked more like a rubbish tip than living quarters. The smell was getting worse, too, and as it caught her throat she was sure that if she didn't get out of this hell-hole soon, she was going to be sick.

There was a rustling in one dark corner, so light and furtive it could have been made by a rat.

'William?' Becky said. 'Billy? Is that you?'

Behind her, Spudder struck a match, found a lantern and lit it. In the lantern's glow, Becky could see a naked, dirty child of perhaps two or three who was down on all fours and looking up at her with wild, frightened eyes.

'This can't be Hortense's little boy!' she said in horror. 'It just can't be him!'

Yet through the grime which coated his face, she could see something which clearly reminded her of her dead sister-in-law.

'Billy?' she said, advancing slowly towards the little boy.

The child held his hands out as if they were claws and made a threatening, hissing sound.

'Don't be afraid,' Becky said soothingly, but her words only seemed to make the boy fiercer.

'Let me try, Mrs Becky,' Spudder said, and before she had time to object he had eased her aside and was kneeling down on the floor in front of the wild infant.

'Spudder, I don't think . . .' Becky began.

'Come to Spudder,' the young man cooed at the small child. 'Come on. Come to Uncle Spudder.'

Something remarkable was happening. Billy's tiny body relaxed and the fear began to melt away from his eyes.

'Come on,' Spudder said again. 'I'll look after you, Billy. I promise you I will.'

William crawled on his hands and knees across the filthy floor to the kneeling Spudder, and once he had reached him,

278

snuggled up to him as if they were both cats. Spudder stroked the boy for a few seconds, then stripped off his own jacket and wrapped it around the child's naked body.

'Let's get out of here, Mrs Becky,' he said, lifting Billy up into his arms. 'The pong down here's fair makin' me feel sick.'

'Imagine Becky Taylor adopting a kid,' Not-Stopping Bracegirdle said to her cronies who were sitting around their customary table in the best room of the New Inn.

'And why shouldn't she?' Dottie Curzon demanded.

'Well, it's not natural,' Not-Stopping said. 'She's still a young woman, is Becky. If she wants more children, she should have them the natural way, like everybody else does.'

'Then nobody'd ever adopt orphans,' Dottie pointed out.

It was a logical argument, and Not-Stopping, never one to be defeated by logic, decided to change her ground.

'And from what I've heard, he's a real ragamuffin,' she said. 'Nothing better than a guttersnipe.'

'Well, I think it's really kind of her to take a baby nobody else would have,' Ma Fitton said.

'Kind!' Not-Stopping said. 'It's nothing but daft. And a complete waste of money.'

'Not as much of a waste of money as keeping pigeons is,' Dottie Curzon said quietly.

Not-Stopping gave Dottie a sharp look, and for a moment it seemed as if the look would be followed by a cutting comment. Then her face softened somewhat.

'You're quite right, Dot . . . Doris,' she said. 'It's no-where near as much a waste of money as keeping pigeons is.'

The first few days of having Billy at home were the hardest Becky remembered. The cottage, humble as it was, was vast in comparison to his previous home – and it terrified him. And so did the light. If Becky opened the curtains to let in the morning sun, he squealed with fear.

Night and mealtimes were even worse. When she tried to

persuade him to get into the cot she had made up for him next to her bed, he fought her off and huddled up in the corner of the room. When she attempted to get him to eat something, she discovered that he had no idea how to use a spoon. And so she fed him herself, but the food she gave him at first was so rich to his poor shrunken stomach that he vomited it up immediately.

He appeared to understand a few of the words Becky said, but apart from the occasional grunt to show fear or acceptance, he seemed incapable of any speech himself. And he refused to wear clothes in any shape or form, though as the evening chill set in, he was willing to be wrapped in a blanket.

Everyone rallied round.

'I'm your new nana,' Mary told him, and when he simply stared at her blankly she turned to her daughter and said, 'Richard Worrell wants horse-whippin' for what he's done to this poor little mite.'

'I'm your grandpa,' Ted informed him. 'When you're a bit bigger, I'll take you fishin'.'

Mary's boarders pitched in, too. The Great Marvello performed a few simple conjuring tricks.

'Tricks, young sir, which will one day entertain royalty,' he said confidently.

But they did not entertain Billy.

Ned Spratt often appeared at mealtimes.

'Get this food down you,' he said, wincing as he himself tasted the plain gruel Becky had prepared for the boy. 'Lovely grub, this is.'

It did no good at all. There were only two people Billy was willing to get close to – Spudder and Michelle.

The bond between Spudder and Billy which Becky had seen start to form on the coal barge went from strength to strength once they were back in Marston. Spudder rarely spoke and Billy never spoke at all, yet they seemed to understand each other perfectly.

'How do you do it?' Becky asked Spudder in frank

admiration.

'You've just got to know how he feels, Mrs Becky,' Spudder told her. 'Get inside his head, like.'

'And how do you manage that?' Becky wondered.

'It . . . it helps if you've been through somethin' like it yourself,' Spudder said shakily, and though Becky waited for him to tell her more, he had plainly given all explanation he was prepared to.

Michelle, on the other hand, did not try to get into Billy's head, but instead simply contented herself with feeding him when he was willing and cuddling when he was not.

'He won't always let you play with him like that, you know,' Becky warned her daughter, praying that she was right, praying that his time in the barge had not permanently damaged him. 'Some time soon you're going to have to stop treating Billy as if he was nothing more than a sick puppy.'

'Oh, I know that, Mam,' Michelle said scornfully. 'But he's like a sick puppy now, isn't he?'

'Yes, he is,' Becky agreed, and wondered where she'd ever got such a wise daughter from.

If only he'd talk, she told herself during long sleepless nights. Just a few words, so she'd know for sure that he was normal. Just *one* word, so she could stop worrying.

But Billy either wouldn't – or couldn't – do even that.

Chapter Twenty-One

Among the letters which the postman delivered on that frosty morning in early December was one from Michael, and although Becky's first instinct was to tear it open immediately, she forced herself to put it on the mantelpiece instead. Letters from Michael, she told herself firmly, were family business, and should only be opened when all the family was there.

There was a pounding of feet on the stairs, and Michelle burst into the room, rapidly followed by her adoring Billy. It did not take a second for Michelle to read her mother's face and guess that something had happened. And a quick glance at the mantelpiece soon confirmed what that *something* was.

'A letter from Dad!' Michelle said excitedly. 'Read it to us, Mam!'

'Not until you're both washed and dressed,' Becky replied sternly, sticking to her rule that nothing else could be done until the children were completely presentable.

Yet as Becky watched her daughter strip off her nightdress and kneel down at the enamel bowl in front of the fire, she couldn't help wishing that Michelle would hurry up.

'Why did Dad send us a letter anyway?' Michelle asked, rubbing herself with the flannel. 'He's comin' home next week, isn't he?'

'Yes,' Becky agreed, 'but he probably wrote that letter weeks ago. Africa is a long way away.'

'Oh, I know that!' Michelle replied.

But she didn't really, Becky thought. For a little girl – even a very sensible little girl – who had just turned four, even the next village seemed a long way away, and somewhere like the Dark Continent was an unimaginable distance.

Becky turned her attention to Billy, who was waiting patiently for his sister to finish so that he could have his turn. He was making more progress every day, she told herself. He was walking now – tottering steps, it was true, but a great improvement on the crab-like crawling which was all he could do when she had taken him in. And he no longer fought her when she tried to dress him, though he still refused to have anything to do with shoes. But the most encouraging change of all was that his face no longer bore the expression it had worn in the early days – the look of a small, frightened, hunted animal. Now anyone who didn't know would probably think he'd had a perfectly normal, perfectly happy infancy – until, that was, they spoke to him and he only grunted in return.

If only he'd *try* to talk, Becky thought.

Michelle finished her wash and began to dress quickly because, despite the fire, the kitchen was far from warm. Becky changed the water in the bowl, stripped off Billy's nightshirt, and went to work with the flannel.

'Shall I get the letter down, Mam?' Michelle asked, standing on tiptoe to see if she could reach it. 'I mean, it'll make it quicker for you when you want to read it to us.'

'Yes, get the letter down,' Becky said, 'only don't go falling in the fire while you're doing it.'

Michelle reached out and carefully took the letter down. Becky finished washing Billy, rubbed him down and helped him into his clothes. And then, finally, they were ready to hear the letter.

Michelle sat on the rag hearth-rug, and Billy, who never strayed far from her if he could help it, snuggled up by her side. Becky sat in the armchair, and, with fingers which only trembled slightly, opened the letter.

'*My darling wife and children*,' she read.

How like Michael to begin in that way, Becky thought. He'd never met Billy, yet he wrote as if he already loved him. And knowing Michael, he probably did.

'Go on, Mam!' Michelle said impatiently.

'Sorry,' Becky apologized. '*As Christmas draws closer, I have been trying to imagine what it's like to be cold or to feel the tingle of a snowflake falling on my hand, but out here, where the heat clings like a thick overcoat, it's almost impossible to imagine an English winter.*'

'But he won't have to 'magine it,' Michelle pointed out, '"cos he'll soon be home.'

'That's right,' Becky agreed happily. '*In some ways this is a marvellous place,*' she continued reading. '*The jungle teems with wildlife. Leopards, gorillas and elephants are as common a sight here as cows and horses are back home. I even have a pet now, a chimpanzee I've called Fredrick . . .*'

'We saw some chimps in Belle Vue Zoo, didn't we, Billy?' Michelle asked.

And Billy, bless him, nodded his head cheerfully and made a small grunting sound as if he were a little animal himself.

Why couldn't he say 'yes', Becky wondered. Was one little word too much to ask?

'Why don't you finish the letter, Mam?' Michelle demanded.

'I will if you'll just stop interrupting me,' Becky said.

'Yes, Mam. Sorry, Mam,' Michelle replied, although they both knew that Becky didn't really mind the interruptions, because they seemed to make the letter last longer.

'*Fredrick is a lively little creature,*' she read, '*always swinging around in trees or else copying me in such an amusing way that I'm forced to laugh.*'

Becky looked up at Billy.

'Do you understand what your dad's saying?' she asked.

Billy smiled and nodded.

'Are you sure now?' Becky persisted.

Billy's face suddenly lost its happy look and assumed a slightly anxious expression. For a moment, Becky was worried, and then she saw what he was doing.

'He's copyin' *you*, Mam,' Michelle said, confirming her suspicions.

Such a clever little lad, Becky thought to herself. Such a clever, *mute* little lad.

'*Even as I write, the chimp is sitting opposite me,*' Michael continued, '*scratching his head when I scratch mine, and pretending to write when I put pen to paper.*'

Becky pictured the scene in her mind's eye – and didn't like it at all. The idea of Michael scratching his head as he wrote suggested hesitation, and hesitation was not something which was normally a part of Michael's nature. The letter, which had brought her such joy when it first arrived, now began to fill her with dread.

'*The children, I know, would love Fredrick,*' Michael's letter went on. '*I've often thought of bringing my family out to be with me, but for the moment it can be nothing but a dream. Disease is not as rife here as it is along the Oil Rivers, but I could not, in all conscience, subject Michelle and little Billy to such rigours as exist.*'

'I don't understand that bit,' Michelle confessed.

'Dad means he'd like us to live with him, but he's frightened you kids'd get poorly,' Becky explained, thinking to herself that the sudden awkwardness in Michael's style could only mean that he had something difficult to say, and was struggling to find a way to say it.

And there it was. Right at the bottom of the page.

'*I had hoped to be with you all for Christmas,*' Michael had written, '*but unfortunately a few difficulties have arisen, and now that is no longer possible. But be assured that I am thinking of you all and counting the days until I will be able to see you again.*'

'Does that mean Dad's not coming home after all?' Michelle asked.

'Yes,' Becky said heavily. 'That's what it means.'

Becky looked closely at her daughter. Michelle was not crying, she would never cry when Billy was there because she knew it would upset him. But Becky was sure that bitter tears would be shed later, when Michelle was on her own.

'Let's look on the bright side,' she told her daughter. 'He

might miss Christmas with us, but he *will* be home soon after, and it'll give Billy that bit longer to learn how to talk. And won't *that* be a nice surprise for your dad?'

Though she was forcing herself to sound cheerful, she was feeling anything but. 'Give Billy time to learn how to talk,' she'd said. Yet was mere time enough? Or had the hell he had been through on the coal barge robbed him of the power of speech for ever?

And even if he did learn to talk, would Michael be there to hear him? In the letter, he'd spoken of 'a few difficulties', but Becky was sure there was more to it than that. Like 'good business sense', 'a few difficulties' was a code for something else. You had 'difficulties' in safe, homely places like Marston. In the wilds of Africa, you had *trouble*, and where there was trouble, there had to be danger, too.

I don't want to be a widow, Becky thought desperately. I don't want to lose the only man I've ever really loved.

'You're not worried about Dad, are you, Mam?' Michelle asked, her voice thick with concern.

'Of course I'm not,' Becky reassured her. 'Your dad can look after himself.'

But could any man ever really look after himself in a thick jungle full of dangerous animals, poisonous snakes – and God alone knew what other dangers? Africa had already claimed most of her man's time, and however much she fought against it, Becky couldn't help feeling that eventually it would rob her of him for ever.

In his early days as a photographer, Philip had tramped the streets of London with his camera until his feet were little more than a solid mass of blisters.

'Take your picture, sir?' he'd implored swells walking down by the Serpentine.

'How about a snap of you and the kids?' he'd cajoled housewives as they struggled to keep a grip of both their children and their shopping bags. 'Won't cost you much more than a couple of beetroots.'

Once in a while he would have a good run of customers and eat well that night, but more often than not he'd go to bed with a rumbling stomach.

At times, his poverty would make him so desperate that he would almost decide to abandon London and go back home. Almost – but not quite. Rather than flying back to Mam – and a probable beating from Cedric Rathbone – he would force his blistered feet to take him to one of the theatres or music-halls.

Sometimes he'd choose the Alhambra, with its fantastic Moorish façade. On other occasions he selected the majestic Empire or the stately London Hippodrome. He never went inside – he hadn't got the money, even for the cheap seats. Instead, he stood on the pavement, watching the well-dressed ladies and gentlemen enter and telling himself that some day he would be one of them.

He often thought it was this desire to live as they did which had led him to a life of crime. If he hadn't seen the fine gentlemen outside the Empire, would he ever have become a pornographer, taking lewd pictures of young girls fresh up from the country? Of course not! So, in a way, it was not his fault that he'd spent some time in prison – the blame lay squarely with the entertainment palaces of London.

He bore them no grudge for what they'd done to him. In fact, now that he was a moderately prosperous publisher, he made it a habit to visit the theatre at least once a week. It was a habit well known to his acquaintances, too, so it would have come as no surprise to any of them to have found him as he was now, standing outside the Alhambra, apparently waiting for someone.

The 'someone' in question was Harold Hutchins, a young banker who Philip had been cultivating for some months. Harold would be bringing two young ladies with him – his sister and his fiancée.

'Don't mind, do you, old chap?' he'd asked.

And Philip had said that of course he didn't mind, and insisted on paying for their box, even though he himself was to make up only a quarter of the party.

A carriage pulled up, and Harold got out. He turned, and held out his arm to assist his fiancée, Lydia, and once she was safely on the pavement, he did the same for his sister. The sister came as a revelation to Philip. Who would have thought that staid, solid Harold could have been related to such a wispy, graceful creature?

Her name was Emily. She was about twenty, he guessed, a pretty little blonde with an appealing turned-up nose. Philip made sure that he sat next to her in his hired box.

The entertainment was pretty standard fare. There was a comedian dressed in the battered hat and ill-fitting clothes which had almost become the comics' uniform. He was followed by a fine baritone singer, who was replaced, in turn, by a strongman who could bend iron bars with his teeth.

It was quite a good show, as such shows went, but Philip paid it little attention and instead snatched every opportunity he could to speak to Emily. She answered him shyly, averting her eyes from his as she spoke, but Philip had enough experience of young women to be almost sure that she was attracted to him and this would not be their last meeting.

By the time they had been in the box for an hour, he had all but convinced himself that he was in love with the girl. And why not? He was ready to settle down, and Emily undoubtedly came from an eminently suitable background.

Me mam will be pleased, he thought, forgetting for a moment that he was now a sophisticated Londoner.

The next 'turn' to appear on the stage was announced as 'Miss Marie Tomlin'. Philip, who only had eyes for Emily, did not see her walk on, and it was only when she began her first song that he became aware of her presence at all.

'Aw, for the wings, for the wings of ayy doove,' she bawled, as she tried – and failed – to hit the high notes.

'Oh, my God!' Philip groaned.

He turned his head towards the source of the dreadful noise, and caught his first glimpse of Marie Tomlin. She was quite tall and, except for her magnificent bosom, she was very slender. She had flaming red hair and untamed green eyes. She was the most thrilling woman he had ever seen. Next to her, Emily seemed like a little girl, as drab as a maiden aunt, as dull as a winter morning.

'Isn't she terrible?' Emily whispered.

Her lips were so close to Philip's ear that they almost touched it. Only seconds earlier, such intimacy would have overjoyed him. Now it was merely irritating.

'I mean, have you ever heard such an awful screeching sound?' Emily asked – and this time her lips did gently brush against his lobe.

Philip pulled away from her.

'Shut up!' Philip said furiously. 'I'm trying to listen!'

The air was as cold as might be expected for a late evening so close to Christmas, but that was not the reason Philip's hands were trembling. He was standing outside the Alhambra stage door, holding a huge bunch of roses, and at any moment that door might open to reveal the most wonderful woman in the whole world.

Harold Hutchins had been very surprised when he'd announced that he had to leave the theatre.

'But we've got our supper booked in the chop house!' he'd said.

'Can't help that,' Philip had replied. 'I've got an appointment. An urgent one!'

Harold had looked at him strangely, and Philip realized that he had just let months of careful social cultivation go right down the drain. The next time Harold had a party, his name would not be on the guest list. His application to join Harold's club would no longer have the young banker's support. But Philip didn't care – he just didn't care!

The door swung open, and Marie stepped out into the street. She was alone, and he was not sure whether that made it easier – or more difficult – to approach her. He felt his body freeze, suddenly refuse to do what he wanted it to, and realized that if the woman decided to walk away now, he could do nothing to stop her.

She didn't walk away. She stood on the street corner, tapping her foot, as if she was waiting for someone who was late.

Philip, watching her, sent urgent messages to his legs, and after some moments had passed they agreed – reluctantly – to obey him.

Miss Tomlin watched him approach her with indifference, and when Philip held out the flowers, she made no move to take them.

'They're . . . they're fresh today,' he stuttered, thinking, even as he spoke, how young and foolish he must sound.

'Are they now?' Marie said. 'Well, that is nice, ain't it?'

But her hands remained firmly by her sides.

'I want you to have them,' Philip said. 'I think you're wonderful.'

Miss Tomlin put her left hand on her hip.

'I'm waitin' for a gentleman friend,' she told him. 'An' even if I wasn't, yer wouldn't have a chance wiv me.'

'Wouldn't I?' Philip asked miserably.

Miss Tomlin looked him coolly up and down.

'Yer dressed quite stylish for a city clerk,' she pronounced. 'I will give yer that. But yer all the same, you lot. Yer think you can have a girl for the price of a bunch of flowers, then it's off home to the wife and kids.'

'I'm n . . . not married,' Philip stuttered. 'And I'm not a clerk, I'm a publisher.'

'A publisher?' Miss Tomlin said scornfully. 'Ger away with yer!'

'It's true!' Philip protested.

'What do yer publish, then?' Miss Tomlin demanded.

'*Funny Cuts*,' Philip said.

'Do yer!' the girl replied. 'I read that all the time. It's ever such a good laugh.'

'I write some of it as well,' Philip said proudly.

Miss Tomlin looked rapidly up and down the street.

'Yer wouldn't buy me a drink, would yer?' she asked. 'Only, all that singin's made me as dry as a bone.'

'What about the gentleman you were waiting for?' Philip said.

'Oh, sod him,' Miss Tomlin said. 'If he can't turn up on time, he'll have to settle for leftovers, won't he?'

'I suppose so,' Philip said, though he was not really sure what she was talking about.

'Well, are yer goin' to offer me yer arm, or wot?' Miss Tomlin asked.

Almost in a dream, Philip held out his arm – and the girl clamped her hand on to it.

It was three days before Christmas that Spudder arrived at Becky's house unexpectedly, with two parcels in his hands.

'Hello, Mrs Becky,' he said, looking excitedly round the kitchen. 'Where are the kids?'

'Having their nap,' Becky said. 'Why? Is anything the matter?'

'No, nothin's the matter,' Spudder replied. 'It's just that I wanted to give 'em these.' He held up the parcels in front of him.

'And what exactly are they?' Becky asked.

'Their Christmas presents,' Spudder said. 'I've just bought 'em an' I can't wait to see their faces when they open 'em.'

'You're supposed to save them until Christmas Day,' Becky said.

'I know but . . .' Spudder protested.

'If you give them their presents now, you'll have nothing to leave under the tree,' Becky pointed out.

Spudder looked crestfallen, then suddenly smiled as if he'd had a bright idea. 'I'll give them one present now, and another on Christmas Day,' he announced.

'I couldn't possibly let you do that,' Becky said sternly. 'You'd be spoiling them far too much.'

The woeful look returned to Spudder's face, and Becky

couldn't help laughing.

'All right,' she conceded. 'They can open them today. But you'll have to wait until they wake up.'

The waiting seemed like eternity to Spudder. He paced the kitchen until Becky was afraid he would wear out the oilcloth. He straightened the mirror over the fireplace, looked at it again, and then returned it to its original position.

'If they could bottle your energy, they could run a train off it,' Becky told him.

'I've never given anybody a present before,' Spudder said, as if to explain his nervousness.

'Never?' Becky said.

'Never,' Spudder repeated.

At last there were sounds of the children stirring.

'I'll go and fetch them down,' Becky said. 'You stay here – and mind you don't rearrange the furniture while I'm upstairs.'

Spudder looked around him.

'Could I just polish . . .' he began.

'No!' Becky said, hardly able to stop herself laughing again.

When Becky returned to the kitchen with Billy in her arms and Michelle holding on to her hand, she saw that Spudder had laid his gifts on the floor, a few feet apart.

'So they could open 'em easier,' he explained. 'This un's for you, Michelle, and t'other's for you, Billy.'

Michelle looked up worriedly at Becky. 'Is it all right to open now, Mam?' she asked.

'Yes,' Becky said with a heavy sigh.

'But it's not Christmas,' Michelle said, as if she suspected some kind of trick.

'I know, my love,' Becky said. 'But your Uncle Spudder doesn't play the game by the same rules as everybody else. You should have learned that a long time ago.'

Michelle let go of Becky's hand, rushed to her parcel and

began to tear away at the wrapping paper before her mother had a chance to change her mind.

Becky put Billy down on the ground next to his parcel. He looked at it fearfully – as though he thought it might contain a wild animal – and then began to back away.

Spudder picked him up and took him back to the box. Billy made no attempt to struggle. As long as he was in Spudder's arm he felt safe, whatever dangers lurked in the room.

Spudder put him down on the floor again. Billy did not seem to mind that either, as long as he was holding on to his protector.

'This is a present,' Spudder explained gently. 'I'm givin' it to you because I love you.' He took Billy's tiny hands in his own and guided them towards the wrapping paper.

'Pull,' Becky urged Billy. 'Like Michelle's doing.'

Michelle now had her box open, and was excitedly extracting a large toy elephant.

'Look, Mam!' she said.

'It's lovely,' Becky told Spudder. 'But it must have cost you a fortune. You should save your money for yourself.'

'I don't need anythin' besides what I've already got,' Spudder told her.

'Thank you, Uncle Spudder,' Michelle said sweetly.

'Tan koo, Unc' 'pudder,' said a squeaky little voice just beyond Spudder's shoulder, and Becky, turning in amazement, saw that Billy was holding out a lead soldier.

'Did you say something, my darling?' Becky asked, hardly able to speak herself.

'Mam,' said Billy, pointing to her. 'Misha,' he added, indicating his new sister. 'So'jer,' he told them all, proudly holding out his present.

Becky rushed across to the little boy and swept him into her arms. 'You're talking!' she said joyfully. 'You're really talking, Billy!'

It was the most wonderful Christmas present she'd ever had.

Chapter Twenty-Two

It was shortly after the last snows of winter had melted that Jack came home for a brief visit.

'Your hair could do with a good cuttin',' Mary complained almost as soon as he walked through the door – though not before she'd hugged him half to death.

'She treats me as if I was still twelve years old,' Jack told his sister the next day, as they stood watching the bakers turn out the morning's batch of fresh, crusty bread.

'She treats us *all* as if we were twelve years old,' Becky replied. 'That's what mams do.'

'I suppose you're right,' Jack agreed, grinning.

And when he grinned, he almost did look twelve, Becky thought. Though he'd just turned thirty-four and was a respectable merchant, he still had a lot of the wild-haired, wild-eyed boy who had run away to sea in him.

'Is life really hard in Africa?' Becky asked, after she'd checked off the delivery that Tom Jennings was taking to Knutsford.

'I'm not complainin',' Jack replied evasively.

And neither would Michael – that was the trouble. She remembered the letter he had sent her just before Christmas, when he had talked about the 'few difficulties' which would prevent him from being with his family over the holiday, and though she had no idea what those few difficulties could possibly be, she was determined to do her best to find out.

'You've been to see where Michael lives, haven't you?' she asked her brother in that deceptively casual tone which should have alerted him to the danger – but didn't.

'Yes, I've been,' Jack replied.

'What's it like?' Becky asked.

'Well, gettin' there isn't too easy,' Jack told her. 'First you sail down the Oil Rivers, then you've got to travel a long way down the coast. And once you're on dry land, your journey's only just begun, because it's a long march overland to Michael's plantation, and a good deal of it's through jungle.'

'But once you're there, it's pleasant enough, isn't it?' Becky said.

'Oh yes,' Jack agreed readily. 'he's built himself a bungalow and –'

'What's a bungalow?' Becky interrupted.

'It's a house with only one floor,' Jack explained. 'It's got a thatched roof an' a veranda runnin' round it. He's got it really comfortable.'

'And is this bungalow quite big?' Becky asked.

'Yes, I suppose it is,' Jack conceded. 'What made you ask that?'

'Michael thinks it will be all right for me and the kids to go out and live with him in a few months' time,' Becky told her brother, although Michael had said no such thing.

Jack frowned. 'Did he, now?' he said.

'You sound like you don't think it'd be such a good idea, yourself,' Becky prodded.

'Well, I'm sure Michael knows best,' Jack said unconvincingly. 'Of course, you have to be careful of the pygmies . . .'

Becky laughed. 'Pygmies!' she said. 'Aren't they the funny little men Mr Hicks taught us about when we were at school?'

'There's nothing funny about them,' Jack said gravely. 'They're hideous creatures. They never wash, an' then to make matters worse, they smear themselves with dirt an' clay. The stink's somethin' awful. An' they're fierce little buggers, an' all. They're only half the size of most of the natives, yet all the niggers are so scared of 'em you'd think they were giants. They carry these poison blow-pipes, you see, an' every now an' again they raid one of the outlyin' plantations an' kill everybody. Men, women, children – the lot. An' if that wasn't bad enough –' He stopped suddenly, as if he'd just realized that he'd probably said too much. 'Hasn't Michael told you about the pygmies?' he asked suspiciously.

'Yes, he has,' Becky said. 'Only, he called them "a few difficulties".'

Jack began to feel uncomfortably hot. He ran his finger around the inside of his collar. He *had* said too much, he decided, and now he'd have to do his best to talk his way out of an awkward situation.

'You shouldn't go worrying about the pygmies,' he said. 'After all, they can't touch Michael – not now he's got his slave army to help him.'

'His what?' Becky demanded.

Another mistake, Jack realized. Next time he came to England, he really must have a word with Michael first, and find out exactly what Becky was supposed to know.

'Tell me about my husband's slave army,' Becky said in a tone which suggested she wouldn't take no for an answer.

Jack sighed. There was no point in trying to fight Becky once she'd decided she wanted something, he thought. There never had been, even when she was just a tiny kid.

'Well, they're not really slaves,' he said. 'Or they are and they're not, if you see what I mean.'

'No,' Becky said firmly. 'I don't see what you mean.'

'Well, there's quite a lot of slaves in that part of the world . . .' Jack explained.

'Yes?' Becky said.

'And every now and again, your Michael buys a few of them,' Jack added hurriedly.

Could this be her wonderful husband he was talking about? Becky asked herself. Was what little money he sent home the product of *slave* labour? What had Africa done to Michael to change him so?

'What does he do with the slaves once he's bought them?' she asked miserably.

'Well, as I said, he trains some of the best ones up for his army,' Jack told her. 'Oh, I don't want to make it sound too grand or anything. It's just a score of natives with old rifles, but he drills them regularly, and they call him Captain Michael. They worship him – they really do – and they'd follow him anywhere.'

'And what about the rest of the slaves?' Becky asked.

'He has them tapping rubber,' Jack said.

'And doesn't he pay them *anything*?' Becky asked, hardly able to believe that this was her Michael they were talking about.

'Well, no, he doesn't,' Jack admitted. 'At least, not until they've paid for *themselves*.'

'Paid for themselves,' Becky repeated. 'And what in heaven's name do you mean by that?'

'Say he buys a slave for sixty pounds of salt,' Jack said. 'Now, he pays his free workers a pound of salt a week, so what he does with the slaves is, he knocks a pound of salt off what they owe him for every week *they* work for him.'

Now that *did* sound like Michael!

'He buys them for sixty pounds of salt,' Becky said slowly, to make sure she'd got it right, 'which means that they owe him sixty pounds.'

'Yes,' Jack agreed.

'He takes one pound a week off that debt for every week they work for him,' Becky continued, 'so after sixty weeks, they're free men.'

'Well, more like a year,' Jack admitted. 'Or if they've been very willing workers, he sometimes lets 'em go after nine months.'

'In other words,' Becky said, 'he buys them at a higher price than he sells them their freedom for.'

'You could look at it that way,' Jack agreed.

'So every slave Michael buys is costing us money,' Becky said.

Jack grinned awkwardly. 'Well, you know Michael,' he said.

Indeed she did, though that didn't mean he wasn't constantly capable of surprising her.

Monsieur Henri appeared, waving his arms frantically.

'You 'ave employ idiots,' he told her.

'Have I?' Becky said.

'Indeed,' the pastry chef replied. 'I give zees men 'oo call zemselves bakers ze instructions precise on 'ow to mix ze dough. And what 'appen? Zey ignore me *complètement*. Ze new batch of bread, it will be a disaster. My reputation is gone and ze bakery is ruined.'

'Have you actually tried any of the new batch, Monsieur Henri?' Becky asked mildly.

The pastry chef shrugged. 'It only just come from the oven now,' he admitted, 'so I do not yet 'ave the time. But already I know it will be awful.'

One of the apprentices approached with a fresh loaf. Monsieur Henri sniffed it, then cut off a sliver and slowly chewed it.

'Is al' right,' he said, and went rushing off to the other end of the bakery to supervise the production of fancy cakes.

Jack, who had only been able to avoid laughing by holding his breath, gasped for air.

'Is your Frenchman always like that?' he asked.

'No,' Becky said. 'You caught him on a good day. But he's worth the trouble. He's the best baker in Cheshire, and we can sell as much as he can make.'

'Yes, Mam told me you were doin' well,' Jack said. 'And so is our Philip, accordin' to all accounts.'

'Better than well,' Becky said with pride. 'He's talking of starting up two new comics.'

'Has he been home recently?' Jack asked.

'No,' Becky replied. 'But he keeps promising to come, and he says that next time he does, he'll have a big surprise with him.'

'What kind of surprise?' Jack asked.

'He wouldn't tell us any more,' Becky replied. 'He's being very mysterious about the whole thing.'

Jack laughed.

'That's just like him,' he said. 'And what about our George? He's still in Eygpt, isn't he?'

'He is,' Becky said. 'And I hope he stays there.'

'How d'you mean?' Jack asked.

'Well, there's no trouble in Egypt, is there?' Becky said. 'My big worry is that they'll move him somewhere else where there's real fighting, and he'll end up getting his silly head blown off.'

'But that's not very likely, is it?' Jack asked.

'No,' Becky said happily. 'That's not very likely at all.'

The barrack square was baked mud and the sun which beat down on it was so unbearable that even the irritating flies were a welcome distraction. From astride his horse, Sergeant George Taylor of the 21st Hussars cast a critical eye over his men. Their boots and saddles shone from hours of polishing, their swords gleamed brightly in the sunlight. They were immaculate, he decided, not a hair out of place, not a crinkle or a stain to be detected in their uniforms.

'You'll do,' he said, and although the Hussars still stood rigidly to attention by their horses, they somehow managed to breathe a sigh of relief.

'Mount up,' George ordered, and when – in one smooth movement – the men had done so, he wheeled round his own mount and led them to their parade position.

The parade was being held in honour of Sir Herbert Kitchener, who was the new Sirdar – or Commander-in-Chief – of the Egyptian army.

He was a man who brought with him a formidable reputation.

'He's the most rigid, demandin' soldier alive,' one of the other sergeants had said in the mess the night before.

'An' as far as stubbornness goes, well, he could have given old General Gordon a run for his money,' another had added.

'They say he's so ambitious that all his officers hate him,' a third chipped in.

'An' what about the ordinary troopers?' George asked. 'How do they feel about him?'

'They're terrified of him,' the third sergeant said, 'but they'll follow him to hell and back if they have to.'

George hadn't liked the sound of that. Blind obedience was a necessary military virtue, but used wrongly, it could result in disaster.

'Is he a good commander?' he'd asked.

'He's no fool, if that's what you mean,' the second sergeant had said.

No fool, George thought. Well, that was something. His years in the army had taught him that being 'no fool' was a very rare quality in a commanding officer.

A murmur that Kitchener had arrived ran through the ranks – though not through the ranks of George's men, who knew *their* sergeant would tolerate nothing less than complete silence – and inspection had begun.

Eyes front, George did not catch a glimpse of the general until he had ridden down the line once and wheeled round for a second look. The Sirdar was a tall man and he was wearing a fez. He had hard, penetrating eyes, and the largest moustache George had ever seen. He was a force to be reckoned with, the young sergeant decided – a man never to be crossed.

The sun rose higher and the heat became more intense. Several infantrymen fainted, but the Sirdar seemed in no hurry to complete his inspection. Indeed, when he finally did finish, an hour and a half later, there was not a single man of the thousand gathered there who hadn't had Kitchener's eyes on him, if only for a second.

The general manoeuvred his horse into a position where he could be seen by the maximum number of soldiers, and the order came to stand at ease.

'Men,' Kitchener said, 'you are the luckiest soldiers in the British army. Whilst others fester in their barracks, you will see action. I have pledged to re-take the Sudan within two years, to avenge the murder of General Gordon and add yet another land to Her Majesty's glorious empire.'

With many other commanders, there would have been a

spontaneous outbreak of cheering, but you didn't cheer Kitchener – not unless he had made it clear that he wanted you to.

The men were called to attention again, and Kitchener, who showed no signs of discomfort from either the heat or the flies, wheeled his horse once more, and rode away.

So they were going to see some action again, George thought as he led his men away from the parade ground. And this time, it wouldn't be one of the little skirmishes he'd been involved with in the past, but a full-scale, all-out war.

As he ordered his men to dismount, he found himself thinking of Colleen O'Leary. There had been many times when he'd regretted writing her that letter, but now he knew for sure that it had been the right thing to do. There'd be scores of new widows before the war was over – perhaps hundreds or even thousands – but thanks to his letter, Colleen would not be one of them.

It must have hurt her at first, he told himself as he unsaddled his horse, but she'd be over it by now. She probably had a new beau – one who would make her much happier than he could ever have done – and George Taylor would now be nothing more than a dim, unpleasant memory.

Yes, everything had turned out for the best, he decided as he made his way back to the sergeants' mess. He just wished – occasionally – that before he'd said goodbye to Colleen for ever, he'd thought to ask her for a photograph.

When Spudder entered her kitchen, Mary hardly recognized him. Gone was the healthy glow which always seemed to shine from him. Gone, too, was the relentless energy which would never let him rest. This new Spudder – this stranger – was as pale as a ghost and sank into one of the kitchen chairs as if he was so exhausted he could walk no further.

'Whatever's the matter, Spudder?' Mary asked worriedly. 'Is it one of your headaches?'

'I was doin' an errand for Mr Dodge in Northwich and I

saw him,' Spudder said.

'Saw who?' Mary asked.

'That man me father sent,' Spudder said. 'I saw him. I thought I'd lost him this time, but I haven't, have I?'

'Why should you want to lose him?' Mary asked.

'Because if he finds me, he'll take me back,' Spudder said, almost sobbing. 'I don't want to go back. I like it here. This is me home.'

'I know it is,' said Mary soothingly. 'But don't worry, you're over twenty-one now. He can't take you back if you don't want to go.'

'He can!' Spudder said. 'Because I did a very bad thing.'

'What sort of bad thing?' Mary asked.

'I hit me father,' Spudder told her. 'I knocked him down the stairs. I think I hurt him really bad.'

'But from what you've said before, it sounds as if he mistreated you, and if that's true, then you had good reason . . .' Mary began.

'He always told me he'd find some way to get me locked up when I was a bit older,' Spudder continued, as if he hadn't heard her. 'Every time he got drunk he said I'd either end up in a lunatic asylum or prison. An' now he's got a reason, hasn't he? When he tells the judge what I did, they'll lock me up for ever.'

Mary felt tears coming to her own eyes.

'I'll make us both a cup of tea,' she said heavily, 'and then you can tell me the whole story.'

'Me mam died when I was a baby,' Spudder said, 'and me dad brought me up. He was dead strict. He never gave me no presents, an' if I did even the littlest thing wrong, he'd take the strap to me.'

'That's terrible!' Mary clucked sympathetically.

'When I started school, I wasn't very quick at learnin',' Spudder told her, 'but the teachers told me dad I'd probably get better. An' I did try, honest I did.'

'I'm sure you did,' Mary said.

'Anyway, by the time I was nine or ten, everybody could see that I wasn't ever goin' to catch up with all the others. The teacher told me dad that I was back . . . back . . .'

'Backward,' Mary supplied.

'That's right,' Spudder agreed gratefully. 'He said I was backward an' me dad got mad. He's one of them lawyers, you see, and he had said it was a disgrace to the family that his son should be backward.'

'You don't talk like a lawyer's son,' Mary said.

'I know I don't,' Spudder admitted. 'I used to, but when I started workin' on the farms, they laughed at me, an' so I soon learned to talk like what they did.'

Mary shook her head sadly. All Spudder had ever wanted was to fit in and get on with his work, she thought.

'Go on with your story,' she told him.

'Me father took me out of school,' he said. 'He told the teacher he was going to educate me priv . . . privately, but what he really wanted to do was just lock me away where nobody could see me.'

'Lock you away!' Mary said, hardly able to believe her own ears.

'That's right,' Spudder said. 'He used to keep me in this little room at the top of the house. I never saw nobody. I had a bucket when I wanted to go to the lavvy, and he used to bring me food himself, so the servants wouldn't have anythin' to do with me. He told the maids I was dangerous – I heard him through the door. But I didn't dare say anythin' in case he gave me a thrashin'.'

'You poor lad,' Mary said, no longer making any attempt to hold back her tears.

'Sometimes he'd get drunk and give me a beltin' just for being such a disgrace,' Spudder continued. 'An' one day, when I'd grown big enough and I couldn't take it no longer, I hit back. I knocked him down the stairs. He was lyin' there, not movin' at all, when I ran out of the house.'

'And then what did you do?' Mary asked.

'I kept runnin' for a week,' Spudder said. 'And then I got a job on a farm. I've been workin' on farms ever since. But I've never had a real home, not like this one.'

'And you're sure this man you saw in Northwich was looking for you?' Mary said.

Spudder nodded. 'He nearly caught me once in Northampton,' he said, 'but I hid in an old barn for three days, and in the end he went away. You won't let him take me back, will you?'

Mary wished that her daughter was there to advise her, but Becky was in Runcorn on business, and this matter would not wait until her return. Ted wasn't around, either. He'd gone to Northwich, and wouldn't be back until it was time to open the chip shop. So she'd just have to help Spudder as best she could without their assistance. And in a way, she thought, that was how it should be – she was the one who'd taken Spudder under *her* wing – he was her responsibility.

'You won't let them take me away, will you?' Spudder asked again.

'I can't stop them, Spudder, love,' Mary said. 'But you know we'll help you all we can, and if you have to go to trial, I'm sure the judge will take into account the wicked way your father treated you.'

It broke her heart to see the look of utter despair which came to Spudder's face.

'I've . . . I've got to lie down,' he told her. 'I've got one of me headaches again.'

'Spudder . . .' Mary said, reaching out for his arm.

But before she could grab him, Spudder had jumped to his feet and rushed from the room.

Mary gave Spudder an hour to calm down, then slipped round to the boarding house. She knocked on the back door, and when there was no answer she lifted the latch and went inside. The kitchen was deserted as it usually was at that time of day on a Wednesday. Aggie Brock had gone home and Ned Spratt was still at the boat yard.

Mary walked to the foot of the stairs and called out Spudder's name. When he didn't respond, she began to climb the steep steps which led to his bedroom – the room she'd given him because it overlooked the lane, and she'd known he'd like that.

She reached the bedroom door and tapped on it lightly. The only reply was silence. She gently pushed the door open. The room was as tidy as it always was, the bed perfectly made, the rag rug totally straight against the wall. Mary walked over to the wardrobe where Spudder kept his one good suit and three spare shirts. She opened the door and saw that the wardrobe was completely bare – just as she'd thought it would be.

'It's probably for the best,' she told the empty room as the tears streamed down her face, 'but I still wish it didn't have to be this way.'

Mary was preparing Ned Spratt's tea – and crying softly to herself – when she heard the loud, authoritative knock on the back door. She'd been expecting it, and the only surprise was that it hadn't come sooner. She wiped her hands on her pinny and walked over to the door.

The man standing on the step was wearing a frock coat and had hard, expressionless eyes.

'Are you Mrs Taylor?' the man said.

'Yes,' Mary replied.

'And are you the landlady of the boarding house next door?' the man continued.

'I am,' Mary said.

'Then perhaps you can help me,' the man continued. 'My name is Francis Barnes. I'm looking for Clarence Foukes and I believe he might be one of your lodgers.'

Mary shook her head. 'There's nobody here of that name,' she told him.

Barnes took a heavy leather note book out of the pocket of his frock coat and flicked it open.

'He is also known to go by the names of Spudder Jones and

305

Spudder Johnson,' he said, glancing down at the notebook. 'Are either of those names familiar to you?'

'Are you a policeman?' Mary asked.

'I used to be,' Barnes admitted, 'but now I'm working privately.'

'For Spudder's father?' Mary said accusingly.

'Indirectly, yes,' Barnes agreed.

'Well, you can just indirectly take yourself off,' Mary said angrily, 'because Spudder's gone.'

'Damn and blast the man!' Barnes said. I've missed him again. How much longer is he going to lead us on this merry dance? Well, if he should come back . . .'

'He won't come back,' Mary said sadly. 'Not now that he knows you've been here.'

'If he *does* come back, Mrs Taylor,' Barnes insisted, 'then it is your legal duty . . .'

Mary had taken about as much as she could for one day, and instead of listening politely, she slammed the door in Barnes's face and quickly slid the bolt home.

'Mrs Taylor, I think you should know . . .' Barnes shouted.

But Mary didn't want to know. She pressed her fingers tightly into her ears so she could hear nothing of what the frightful man had to say.

She had no idea how long she stood there, blocking off the world – it could have been one minute or it could have been ten – but when she unplugged her ears again, there was silence outside.

She crept over to the window and peeped from behind the curtain. The yard was empty! Barnes had gone!

Mary staggered over to the table and buried her head in her hands. She was crying again and there was nothing she could do to stop it. She'd liked Spudder from the start, but over the years he'd become part of the family, as dear to her as one of her children. And now he was gone and she would never see him again. It was almost as if he had died.

PART FOUR

1897–8

Chapter Twenty-Three

Ted Taylor sat in his favourite armchair with the newspaper in front of him. Once, long ago, he had read bits of it out aloud to his wife and children, he thought. Now, though Mary was still there, ironing away in the corner, it was his *grandchildren*, Michelle and Billy, who were waiting patiently on the floor to hear what he had to say.

He opened the paper and glanced at the headlines. There were only two pieces of news anybody seemed to be bothered about these days – the queen's diamond jubilee and Kitchener's Sudan campaign. He scanned the page, found a paragraph on the horses which would be used in Victoria's parade, and read it to the children.

'Just think of that,' he said when he'd finished. 'Sixty years the queen's been on the throne. That's just a bit longer than your poor old grandad's been alive.'

'Is it, Grandad?' Michelle asked.

She kept her voice as even as she could, because she was a polite little girl and did not want to seem to contradict. But really, she didn't believe a word of what he'd said! *Nobody* could possibly have been doing *anything* before her grandad was born. The world didn't even *exist* before her grandad had been born.

At her ironing board, Mary – who had read her granddaughter's thoughts – laughed rather more loudly than she had intended to.

'Have I said somethin' funny?' Ted asked.

'No, love,' Mary replied. 'Not you. Why don't you see if there's anythin' else in the paper that might interest the kids.'

Ted returned to the paper. The trouble with the reports on the Sudan campaign, he thought, was that they were all so technical.

The journalists had followed the campaign every step of the way and described it in the greatest possible detail. They told of the Sirdar's troops – fourteen thousand men, drawn from a combination of British, Egyptian and Sudanese regiments. They dwelt lovingly on the specifications of his weaponry – twenty-four pieces of artillery and twelve heavy machine-guns. They described the steamers and gun boats he had on the Nile down to the last brass rivet . . .

All of which was fine in its way, Ted supposed, but you couldn't expect to entertain a couple of little kids with it in the same way as you could with the details of a good juicy murder.

'This Kitchener feller's not makin' the same mistakes that General Gordon made,' Ted told his wife. 'But then Chinese Gordon always was a bit of a mad bugg –'

'Ted!' Mary said. 'There's children present.'

'Gordon was always a bit hasty,' Ted amended. 'No, before Kitchener moves on, he's making sure of his communications.'

'What's comm . . . commukikations, Grandad?' Michelle asked.

'Why, love, it means he's making sure his men don't run out of food and bullets.'

'I think that's a good idea,' Michelle said seriously.

'Me, too,' said Billy, who worshipped his big sister, and took any words she cared to utter as the absolute and fundamental truth.

'I worry about our George, though,' Mary said.

'There's nowt to worry about,' her husband assured her. 'It says here Kitchener's havin' this railway built across the Nubian Desert. Imagine that! Havin' a railway built just so your soldiers won't have to walk so far. I tell you, it'll be a picnic.'

The Nubian Desert was his idea of hell, George thought as he stood gazing at the vast expanse of emptiness which lay in front of him. And the railway that Kitchener was forcing across it was the Devil's way of punishing those who had dared to set foot in his territory.

Everything seemed to be against them. The workers would painstakingly put down miles of track and then the skies would suddenly open, drenching the parched land and creating flash floods which washed away both track and sleepers. And if it was not the weather which was attacking them, it was disease. Cholera and typhoid were rife, and even without the railway track itself, it would have been possible to map the army's progress by the neat line of white crosses which ran parallel to it.

The folk in the know reckoned it would take another twelve months to reconquer the whole of the Sudan, George remembered. General Gordon's death – the event which had made him decide to join the army in the first place – would finally be avenged. And at just about the same time, the period he had signed up for would run out, too. He wouldn't take the queen's shilling again, not him. He'd done his bit to serve his country but now he'd had enough of soldiering.

But what will I do instead? he wondered.

Go home. Get a job in the salt works. Be a comfort to Mam and Dad in their declining years. Maybe even get married and . . .

No! He'd had his chance at that once, and he'd thrown it away. Now it was too late.

He looked out at the bleak, silent desert and longed for the lushness of the Cheshire fields and the laughter of English children at play.

Queen Victoria's diamond jubilee was every bit as much the dazzling event it had promised to be. The day started with a huge procession which was centred on soldiers drawn from all four corners of Her Majesty's vast empire. The crowd – which was three times the size of London's normal population – gasped in wonder as they watched the soldiers march past them. There were splendidly uniformed Indian troops and mounted riflemen from Australia. Infantrymen from

Cyprus were followed by native soldiers from Borneo who were so exotic in their costume that it was difficult to think of them as belonging to the army at all.

The parade seemed as if it would never end. For more than three hours the mesmerized spectators stood and watched it march by – rank after rank of fighting men, united only in their absolute loyalty to the little woman who was their queen and had ruled over them for sixty years.

At eleven fifteen exactly, a cannon was fired to announce that Her Majesty herself had joined the parade, and all over London the people cheered and then started to sing 'God Save the Queen'.

Victoria rode in an open landau pulled by eight flawless cream horses. The sky had clouded over earlier, but the second she set off the sun burst through, almost as if it had only been waiting for her to appear. The queen was wearing a black silk dress, trimmed with panels of grey satin veiled in black net and black lace. Her bonnet was trimmed with creamy white flowers and white feathers. Around her neck she wore a diamond chain which had been given her by her younger children.

Her route to St Paul's was lined by adoring subjects. They stood in the streets. They craned their necks out of windows. They balanced precariously on pointed roofs, holding on to chimney stacks with one hand and waving with the other.

After a short service of thanksgiving outside the cathedral, the landau set off once more. First it crossed London Bridge and toured the poorer districts of the East End, then it turned again, re-crossed the river at Westminster and made its way back to the palace through Horse Guards Parade and down the Mall.

Everywhere the public cheered and shouted for their monarch. Victoria was overwhelmed by it all.

'How kind they are,' she kept repeating.

And those who were close enough to see could not fail to notice that tears were streaming down her cheeks.

*

Mary cried, too, when she read the account of the great day in the newspaper.

'Cheer up, love,' said Aggie Brock, who had finished cleaning out the lodgers' rooms and was now attacking their parlour with her customary ferocity.

'What did you say?' asked Mary, almost lost in her own thoughts.

'I said, cheer up,' Aggie repeated. 'It was supposed to be a happy occasion, the jubilee. There's no call for tears.'

'I was thinkin' of the queen's children,' Mary said.

'What about them?' Aggie asked.

'They were all there,' Mary said. 'Imagine that – having all your children there at the same time.'

'You miss your own kids, don't you?' Aggie said.

'I do,' Mary admitted. 'I often think of them – and then I usually end up worryin'. And who could blame me? There's our George for a start, stuck out there in the desert. And our Jack, in all that swelterin' heat with only natives to keep him company. And I haven't even mentioned our Philip, who even as I'm talkin' to you now, is probably workin' out some new way to get himself in mither.'

'Do you ever think about Spudder?' Aggie asked quietly.

'Yes, I do,' Mary confessed. 'Even though he's not one of me own, in some ways I worry about him the most. I mean, if push comes to shove, I know the others can all look after themselves. But our Spudder . . . well, he's just a big kid.'

'He really used to try to make a mess,' Aggie said.

'He did what?' Mary asked.

'After you had a word with him, he really used to try and make a mess so I'd have somethin' to clean up,' Aggie explained. 'But he couldn't do it, bless him. However hard he worked at it, somehow his messes always turned out like other people's tidyin'.'

'He was always a trier,' Mary agreed. She thought for a second, then she continued. 'I don't want this to come as a shock to you, Aggie, but the year after next I'm going to be sixty –'

'You don't look it,' Aggie interrupted.

'I wasn't fishin' for compliments, Aggie,' Mary said. 'What I meant was, I'm goin' to be sixty and when I am, I'm goin' to have to think about slowing down a bit.'

'You mean, you're goin' to close the boarding house when you're sixty,' Aggie guessed.

'That's right,' Mary said. 'It was really Spudder who decided me to open it, and now he's gone . . .'

'Why did you never let his room out again?' Aggie asked.

'I just couldn't bring meself to,' Mary replied. 'Oh, I knew he was never comin' back, but even so, it didn't seem right.'

'You're too soft, that's your trouble,' Aggie told her.

'Would you have let out the room again if you'd been in my place?' Mary asked.

'Course I would,' Aggie said.

'Really?' Mary said.

Aggie shrugged her massive shoulders. 'Well, *maybe* I would,' she amended.

'Maybe?' Mary pressed.

'Oh, I suppose I'd probably have been just as daft as you are,' Aggie admitted embarrassedly.

The Great Marvello strode along the country lane at a brisk pace. He was 'resting', and when he was 'resting' he liked to seize the opportunity to go for long walks.

'It relaxes my mind,' he'd told Mary, 'and a relaxed mind is an inventive one. Some of my greatest illusions have come to me whilst I've been communing with Mother Nature.'

It was true. It had been on such a walk as the one he was taking today that he had invented the disappearing canary trick, and on another that he had solved the problem of the doves and the handkerchiefs.

Moving one leg automatically in front of the other, he let his imagination work on a variation of the levitating lady illusion, and it was only when he finally decided the variation would not work that he realized how far he had come. He was standing in the middle of a small wood, with Lymn Church to his left and the Thelwall Viaduct to his right. Marston, his starting point, was a long way behind.

His stomach rumbled. He patted his pocket and felt the reassuring bulge of the food Mrs Taylor had packed for him. Yes, he decided, it was nearly time to eat. Just ahead of him, he noticed the stump of what must once have been a large oak tree – an ideal picnic table. He sat down on the edge of the stump and pulled out his playing cards. A little practice, and he would be able to convince himself he had earned his grub.

He was halfway through his third trick when he heard a voice from just behind him say, 'By Jove, that's bloody clever.'

He turned round to see a middle-aged gentleman with a large belly and a heavy beard. Was this his land? He certainly looked as if he might be a gentleman farmer.

'I'm not trespassing, am I?' Marvello asked.

'Shouldn't think so,' the gentleman said carelessly. 'I say, have you got any more tricks?'

Marvello showed him several more, and the gentleman was plainly delighted with them.

'Don't get to the music-hall much myself,' he said. 'My mother doesn't approve.'

It seemed to Marvello that a man of his age shouldn't give a hang *what* his mother thought – but he was far too polite to say so.

'That doesn't happen to be food I can see in your pocket, does it?' the gentleman asked.

'Well, yes,' Marvello admitted.

'Couldn't have a little of it, could I?' the gentleman asked. 'I'm absolutely famished.'

'Of course,' said Marvello, who fancied himself as something of a minor gentleman himself.

He opened his package, and the two men rapidly polished off the sandwiches, hard-boiled eggs and apples which Mary had packed for Marvello's lunch.

'Excellent,' the gentleman said when they'd finished. 'Best

meal I've had in a long time.'

He reached into his pocket and rattled some coins.

'No, no!' Marvello protested hotly. 'I couldn't possibly accept any of your money.'

'That's very generous of you,' the gentleman said. 'I hope I can return the favour sometime.' He looked at his watch. 'And now I must go,' he continued. 'I was expected back at the house hours ago. Really, people do make such shocking demands on one's time.'

He held out his hand to Marvello, then walked away whistling.

By the time Marvello returned to the boarding house, Ned Spratt had already polished off his supper and was reading the paper.

'And Mrs Taylor told me I could have your supper, as well, if you weren't back within the half-hour,' he said very disappointedly. 'Where've you been, anyway?'

'As far as Lymn,' the Great Marvello told him.

'See the Prince of Wales while you were there, did you?' Ned asked jocularly.

Marvello felt the hairs on his neck tingle.

'The who?' he asked.

'The Prince of Wales,' Ned repeated. 'It says here in the paper that he's on a private visit to friends in Lymn.'

Marvello snatched the paper out of Ned's hand.

'Here, hang on a minute,' Spratt said.

But Marvello was too intent on gazing at the newspaper to hear him. The Prince of Wales was indeed paying a private visit and the engraving of him which stared up from the page was the exact likeness of the man Marvello had met that very afternoon.

'I have performed before royalty,' he said, re-living in his mind the tricks he had shown to the bearded man.

'You've done what?' asked Mary, who had just entered the room with his supper tray.

'I have conjured before the Prince of Wales,' Marvello said

grandly. 'And you, madam,' he added, remembering the shared sandwiches, 'have catered for him!'

Becky's bread was wonderful stuff, Mary thought as she pounded the dough on her kitchen table one afternoon in early September, but when all was said and done, there was nothing like making your own.

It was probably because she was pounding so hard that she didn't hear the door latch being lifted, and was not even aware that there was anyone else in the kitchen until an amused voice said, 'If there's one thing I like, it's to see other folk workin'.'

Mary looked up and saw Philip standing by the door with a wide grin on his face.

'Why is it that none of my sons ever let me know when they're comin'?' she said, embracing him and leaving flour handprints all over the back of his linen jacket.

'We all know how much you like surprises, Mam,' Philip said. 'And I've got another surprise for you – an even bigger one.'

'What sort of surprise?' Mary asked suspiciously.

Philip broke away from her, walked over to the kitchen door, and opened it with a flourish.

'Please allow me the very great honour of introducing you to Miss Marie Tomlin,' he said.

Miss Tomlin stepped over the threshold as if she was making 'an entrance' rather than simply coming into the room. The first thing Mary noticed was her flaming red hair and wild green eyes. The second was her dress which, with its finely beaded bodice, was far showier than anything she'd have liked to see any of her daughters wear.

'Well, aren't you going to say hello to her?' Philip asked.

Mary wiped her hand on her pinny and held it out to the visitor.

'Pleased to meet you, love,' she said.

'Charmed I'm sure,' Marie replied, in a voice that Mary was sure was a long way from being natural.

'I wasn't expectin' company,' Mary explained, 'otherwise you'd never have caught me in such a mess.'

'Oh, pray don't apologize,' Marie said graciously. 'Your kitchen is just as Philip described it. Quite charming!'

And you, missy, Mary thought, are about as genuine as a tin ha'penny.

Though Mary had taken an instant dislike to Miss Tomlin, it didn't stop her doing what was right – which in this case was to arrange a supper at which the rest of the family could meet Philip's company. So it was that that evening found Philip, Marie, Ted, Mary, Becky and Jessie, all gathered around the table in the Taylors' kitchen.

'What do you do for a livin', lass?' Ted asked the guest of honour.

'Don't you know?' Philip asked, astonished.

'How could I?' Ted wondered. 'I've only met the girl today.'

'But this is *the* Miss Marie Tomlin,' Philip said exasperatedly.

The rest of the family exchanged blank glances.

'I'm a *chanteuse*,' Marie said.

'And what's that when it's at home?' Jessie asked. 'Sounds a bit foreign to me.'

'She's a singer,' Philip explained. 'She's very well known.'

There was an embarrassed silence, and then Mary said, 'Well, we don't know much about the theatre ourselves. We don't have the time, you see, what with havin' to run the chip shop an' the boardin' house an' all.'

'And, of course, this *is* the provinces,' Marie said, as if she were helping out. 'I rarely appear outside London, because I find touring around is just so *passé*.'

The family exchanged more rapid glances, and then Ted said, 'So how's the comic business goin' these days, our Philip?'

'Boring,' Philip replied airily. 'In fact, I'm seriously

thinking about giving it up.'

I knew it! Becky thought. I just knew it was far too good to last. Philip had never been one to stick at anything. Besides, once one of his schemes was going smoothly, it always seemed to lose its appeal.

'So if you give up your comics, what are you goin' to do?' Ted asked. 'Not earned enough to retire on, have you?'

Philip laughed. 'Of course not,' he said. 'But I will come away with a bit of capital, and I intend to invest it.'

'In what?' Becky asked, dreading the answer.

'In moving pictures,' Philip said.

'You mean like that slide show we had for Paddy O'Leary's silver wedding?' Ted asked.

Philip laughed again – and this time there was definitely a patronizing edge to it. 'No, not like that at all,' he said. 'There's a couple of Frenchmen – the Lumière brothers – who've come up with a machine called the Cinématographe. I've seen an exhibition of it myself, at the Empire Theatre on Leicester Square. It's just like watching real people except they're in black and white and move a bit fast.'

'But what's it for?' Ted asked.

'Entertainment,' Philip replied. 'One of the cameramen took a moving picture of part of the queen's jubilee, and she said herself that it was "very wonderful".'

'So you're goin' to be takin' movin' pictures of celebrations and the like?' Ted said.

'No, not celebrations!' Philip said gleefully. 'I've been much cleverer than that.'

Becky's heart sank even further. The cleverer Philip thought he had been, the deeper the trouble he usually ended up in.

'Well, what *are* you goin' to do?' Ted asked.

'I'm going to make moving pictures of stories!' Philip said.

'And I'm going to star in them,' Marie said.

Suddenly, Becky saw it all.

*

319

'We normally go for a stroll after supper,' Philip announced immediately the meal was over. 'For the digestion, you know.'

Mary shot her husband a look as if to ask him how often he thought Philip and Marie had supper together, then said, 'Well, you get off, then. We can clear up here.'

The rest of the family made some show of stacking the plates, but once Philip and Marie were out of the house, all pretence of interest in anything but Marie was rapidly dropped.

'Well, I don't like her,' Jessie said. 'You get the feelin' she's lookin' down her nose at you all the time.'

'And she's no cause to,' Ted said. 'Becky's Michael never did any such thing to us, and if you ask me, this Marie hasn't got half the background that he has.'

'She's got no background at all,' Jessie said with certainty. 'It's nothin' but show. It wouldn't surprise me a bit if this little house of yours isn't like a palace compared to the place where she was brought up.'

'What do *you* think, Becky?' Mary asked, turning to her younger daughter as she always did in times of family crisis.

'I'm not keen on her either,' Becky admitted. 'But I'm more worried about the fact that I think it's her who's talked Philip into this moving picture business.'

'Can't you have a word with him?' Mary pleaded. 'Can't you try and persuade him to stick with comics?'

'First thing in the morning,' Becky promised. 'But if he's as struck on this girl as I think he is, I wouldn't hold out too many hopes about me being able to change his mind.'

Becky and Jessie had already gone home when the young couple returned, and there were only Ted and Mary left to welcome them back.

'There's nothing like a bit of fresh air for making you feel sleepy,' Philip said, yawning exaggeratedly. 'So if you'll excuse us, we think we'll both turn in now.'

He moved towards the staircase.

'Just a minute,' Ted said firmly. 'Where do you think you're going?'

'Upstairs,' Philip said.

'Miss Tomlin may be goin' upstairs,' Ted told him. 'She's sleeping in the back bedroom. But your mother's made up a bed for you in the lodgers' parlour.'

Philip chuckled. 'In the lodgers' parlour!' he scoffed. 'You're being ridiculous, Dad.'

'Ridiculous, am I, young man?' Ted said. 'Well, let me just tell you somethin'. I can't do anything about the way you behave when you're down in London, but while you're here, you'll act like decent folks.'

Marie had joined in Philip's chuckling now.

'I don't see what's so funny.' Ted said.

But Mary did. She had seen the twinkle in her son's eye and had guessed the huge practical joke he had been playing on them all day.

'Miss Marie Tomlin is only Marie's stage name,' Philip said.

'Oh aye, and what's her real one, then?' Ted asked, mystified.

'Since last week it's been Mrs Philip Taylor,' Philip said.

Chapter Twenty-Four

'My name's Walter Spragg,' said the shifty-looking individual with thin lips and greedy eyes who turned up on Becky's doorstep one grey late September afternoon. 'I've got a letter for you, Mrs Worrell. It's from Mrs Hope. I've come fifty miles, just to deliver it to you personal.'

'But I don't know anyone called Hope,' Becky said.

'No, you wouldn't,' Spragg agreed. 'That's because Hope isn't her real name, you see.'

'Then what *is* her real name?' Becky asked.

Spragg pressed the letter against his chest, as if he feared she would try to snatch it.

'Before we come to come to that,' he said, 'Mrs Hope promised you'd give me ten guineas.'

'Ten guineas!' Becky exclaimed. 'Why, if she'd posted the letter, it would only have cost her a penny.'

'But that's the point – she couldn't post it,' Spragg said mysteriously. 'An' you're not seein' it until I get my money.'

The business woman in Becky fought a brief battle with her natural curiosity, and quickly reached a compromise.

'I'll give you a guinea,' she said.

'Ten,' Spragg insisted. 'You might not realize it, but I'm riskin' my job even by comin' here.'

Becky shook her head. 'I'm interested,' she admitted, 'but not *that* interested.'

'Mrs Hope said if you needed any convincin', I was to show you just a bit of it,' Spragg said.

He opened the envelope carefully and took out a single sheet of paper. Keeping his hand over most of it, he held it out so that Becky could see the signature.

'Oh, my God!' Becky gasped.

Of all the names in the world which could have been written there, none could have shocked her as much as this one. It was impossible, she told herself, clutching the doorpost for support. It was totally impossible!

Spragg grinned unpleasantly. 'Mrs Hope said you might be a bit shaken up at first,' he said. 'Want to have another look?'

Becky shook her head. Her logic might scream at her that it was impossible, but she knew in her heart that the signature was genuine – that she had been sent a letter from beyond the grave.

'So do I get my ten guineas?' Spragg asked.

'Yes,' Becky said weakly. 'You get your ten guineas.'

Becky sat at the kitchen table, holding the fateful letter in her trembling hands.

My Dear Becky,

I am sorry for the distress receiving this letter may have caused you, and I thought long and hard about some easier way to break the news. But given my situation, there was no easier way. You think I am dead. And I almost was. After the sanity hearing, I determined to kill myself, and would have done so had not my keeper discovered me hanging there and cut me down.

I don't know what happened next – I think they kept me drugged for several days – but when I became aware of my surroundings again, I discovered I had been moved to this new place. Here, they call me Mrs Hope, and however much I protest against it, they refuse to use my real name. Sometimes I have almost come to believe that I *am* Mrs Hope, and it is only the thought of my children which has kept me from being as insane as they claim I am.

I must get out of here, Becky. It is either that or make another attempt to take my own life, and this time I will not fail. I know you did all you could for me in the past. Will you help me now? The man who brought you this letter – Walter Spragg – is a keeper in the asylum. He will assist you as long as you are willing to pay him, and I swear that once I am free again, I will find a way to make good the money you have spent.

Please don't desert me. You are the only one I can turn to.

Yours desperately,
Hortense

It seemed incredible, and yet, in a way, it all made sense. She understood now why she'd not been allowed to see the body – it was because there was no body to see!

How clever Richard had been, Becky thought. He'd known she would never give up the fight to get Hortense released as long as the poor woman was alive, so he had taken the opportunity of her suicide attempt to make it appear as if she had really killed herself. How he must have been secretly laughing at her that day in his office when she accused him of being responsible for his wife's death – and all the time Hortense was being held captive in a new asylum under an assumed name.

'I hope you burn in hell for what you've done to that poor woman, Richard Worrell!' she said angrily.

His trick had worked for more than two years, but the truth had come out at last. Becky reached for her coat. Walter Spragg had said he would be in the pub if she wanted to see him. Well, she did want to see him – very badly indeed.

Colleen O'Leary stood behind the bar counter of the New Inn and glanced across at the pub's only customer, a man with thin lips and shifty eyes. The man was a stranger to the village, and she didn't like the look of him at all. And from the way he kept glancing out of the window, he seemed to be waiting for someone. Colleen wondered who it could be.

She picked up the *Northwich Guardian*, which was lying on the bar, and flicked through it. Almost all the articles were about the Sudan campaign. Kitchener's troops were making good progress, the paper said, and it was expected that they would reach their goal by the following spring. Then the real fighting would begin.

And George Taylor will be right there in the thick of it all!

Colleen thought.

George, who'd written to her and told her it would be pointless for her to wait for him.

George, who, even when she thought herself in love with Barnaby Smith, had still had a place in her heart.

It had been years since she'd seen him, yet she still couldn't think of him without a feeling of sadness sweeping through her whole body.

The pub door swung open, and Becky stepped into the bar.

'Hello,' Colleen said in surprise. 'What are you . . .?'

But Becky didn't seem to see her at all. Instead, she made straight for the corner table and sat down next to the stranger.

What's goin' on? Colleen asked herself. What possible interest could her best friend have in talking to this unpleasant man? She strained her ears to try and hear what they were saying, but they were speaking in whispers.

'Where is she?' Becky asked.

'Mrs Hope, do you mean?' Spragg asked.

'Of course I mean Mrs Hope,' Becky replied irritably.

'She's in the Hatton Towers Asylum for the Mentally Incurable,' Spragg told her.

'And where's that?'

'Just outside Lancaster.'

'I want to see her,' Becky said.

Spragg shook his head doubtfully. 'Difficult,' he said.

'I could pretend I was her sister,' Becky suggested.

'It wouldn't matter if you were the mother who bore her,' Spragg replied. 'Apart from the doctor and her keeper – that's me – Mrs Hope isn't allowed any visitors.'

Of course she wasn't, Becky thought. Richard had seen for himself what could happen when she had the opportunity to talk to someone from the outside – and he wasn't going to chance it again.

'You said it would be difficult to see her,' Becky pointed

out to Spragg. 'You didn't say it would be impossible.'

The keeper grinned. 'Nothin's impossible when you've got money to pay for it,' he said.

Hatton Towers was no more than a sinister black shape against the dark night sky. Even looking at it was enough to make Becky shiver.

'I can't say I like the idea of you goin' the rest of the way on your own, Mrs Worrell,' Cedric Rathbone whispered.

'Spragg said if I didn't come alone, he wouldn't let me see Hortense at all,' Becky told him.

'Well, I still don't like it,' Cedric said. 'If you're not back in an hour, I'm comin' after you whether you want me to or not.'

Good old Cedric, Becky thought. Always there when she needed him, ready to tackle any dirty job she wanted doing.

'It's time I went,' she said.

She stepped out from her hiding place among the trees and began to make her way slowly and carefully across the pasture which separated the woods from the asylum.

She had chosen a night when there was no moon because that was safer, but it certainly didn't make the going any easier now. The very ground she was walking on seemed to take a malicious pleasure in laying traps for her. She stepped into a ditch and for a moment she thought she'd twisted her ankle. She twice tripped over clumps of grass and fell sprawling forward. And all around her there was nothing but darkness and the hooting of the owls.

It took an age to reach the high wall which surrounded the towers, but once she was there she at least had something to guide her. Keeping her hand in contact with the brickwork, Becky edged her way slowly towards the meeting place.

She had gone a hundred yards when she reached the break in the wall, and the feel of rough brick was replaced by that of the cold, smooth metal bars which made up the main gate. She peered through the bars and could see nothing but darkness.

'Mr Spragg!' she whispered. 'Are you there, Mr Spragg?'

'I'm here,' Spragg replied.

'And have you got Hortense with you?'

'I didn't dare risk it till I knew you were here,' Spragg said. 'I'll go an' get her now.'

Another eternity passed before she heard the soft sound of two people approaching as quietly as they could.

'Got the money?' Spragg said.

His dark clothes made his body almost invisible, and his face was nothing more than a vague white blob.

'Yes, I've got the money,' Becky said, groping for a space between the iron bars.

Spragg took the coins and counted them by feel.

'You've got five minutes,' he said.

The blob which had been his head disappeared, and a new one took its place.

'Becky!' Hortense said hoarsely. 'Is it really you?'

'It's really me,' Becky told her.

'Let me hold your hand,' Hortense said. 'Just for a second.'

Becky slipped her hand thorugh the gap and Hortense grabbed it with the desperation of an injured child.

God, but she feels cold! Becky thought.

'How's William?' Hortense asked urgently. 'How's my poor little William?'

'As I told you in the letter I sent with Spragg, he's fine,' Becky said. 'Now listen, we haven't got much time and this is important. I'm going to see Mr Mackie and ask him to appeal to the Lunacy Commissioners. Is there anything you can tell me which might help your case?'

Hortense was silent for a moment, then she said, 'The doctors.'

'Which doctors?' Becky asked.

'The ones Richard hired to certify me,' Hortense said. 'They'd already decided to put me away before they even saw me. You could tell that by the way they looked at each other.'

Possibly that was true, Becky thought. But how would she

ever go about proving it?

'Anything else?' she asked.

A second white blob appeared on the other side of the gate.

'It's time to go,' Spragg said.

'But five minutes can't be up yet,' Hortense told him, with panic in her voice.

'It's not safe to stay any longer,' Spragg replied. 'You know they check the rooms.'

Hortense squeezed Becky's hand even harder than she had been doing before.

'Just one more minute,' she pleaded.

Becky felt Hortense's hand being wrenched free of hers. There was a sound of a struggle on the other side of the gate.

'If they catch you, they'll punish you,' Spragg hissed.

'I don't care!' Hortense said defiantly.

'And they'll give me the sack,' Spragg said. 'Then who would get your letters out for you?'

'You'd better go,' Becky told her.

'Yes, I'd better go,' Hortense said hollowly. 'Goodbye, Becky.'

'Not goodbye,' Becky said fiercely. 'I'll be back. And if it's the last thing I do, I'll get you out of this dreadful place.'

Becky stood by the gate and listened until the two sets of footsteps had faded away into nothing. She'd come to Hatton Hall to see if she could learn anything she could use in Hortense's favour – and on that mission she had met with complete failure. But she had learned *something*. The moment Hortense had grabbed her hand, she'd known with absolute certainty that the poor woman had not been bluffing when she'd written that if she was in the asylum for much longer, she'd kill herself.

Michelle and Billy were sitting on the hearth-rug, playing with the lead soldiers Spudder had given Billy for Christmas.

'Aren't they lovely together?' Becky said.

'They are,' her mother agreed. 'But how long do you think

they're goin' to stay like that?'

Becky smiled. 'You mean, how long will it be before they start fighting like cats and dogs?' she asked.

'No,' her mother said, stony-faced. 'I don't mean that at all.'

'What then?' asked Becky, alarmed by her mother's tone.

Mary glanced first at the children, and then back at Becky. 'Come into the back yard,' she said.

'The back yard?' Becky repeated. 'Whatever for?'

'We need to go somewhere we can talk privately,' Mary said ominously, looking at the children again. 'Somewhere away from big ears.'

Becky followed her mother into the yard.

'You'd better tell me what's on your mind, Mam,' she said.

'Have you thought about what will happen if your Mr Mackie manages to get Hortense released?' Mary asked.

'How do you mean?' Becky said.

'The first thing Hortense is goin' to want when she's free again is to try an' get little Billy back,' Mary told her.

'But she can't do that,' Becky said. 'He's legally adopted.'

'Is he?' Mary said grimly. 'And who was it who signed them adoption papers?'

'You know who signed them,' Becky said. 'Richard.'

'Richard Worrell isn't Billy's father,' Mary reminded her. 'But Hortense is his mother.'

'I hadn't thought of it like that before!' Becky gasped.

But she did now, and the more she thought about it, the more she was sure her mother was right. The adoption papers were invalid, and if Hortense was free once more, she would have first claim on Billy.

'You've already done a lot more for Hortense than anyone could have expected of you,' Mary pointed out. 'Nobody'd blame you if you dropped it now.'

'I can't, Mam,' Becky said. 'You haven't seen the state she's in, like I have. If I don't get her out of that terrible asylum soon, I know she's going to kill herself.'

'And if you do get her out, then the first thing she'll do is take your son off you,' Mary said.

Becky looked around her helplessly, as if hoping that the water tub or the old mangle would suddenly provide her with a solution to her problems.

'What would you do if you were in my place, Mam?' she asked.

'I don't know,' Mary admitted. 'An' even if I did, I wouldn't tell you. You've got to make the choice, Becky, because it's only you who's really goin' to have to live with the consequences.'

Two scenes began to play themselves out in Becky's mind's eye. In one, Billy was being torn from her arms. In the other, Hortense was swinging by a rope from the rafters. To and fro the pictures went, first the one filling her imagination and then the other pushing it to one side.

'What's it to be?' Mary asked gently.

'If I thought Hortense would be a bad mother to Billy, I'd do anything to stop her getting him,' Becky said, almost in tears. 'I'd even stand back and watch her kill herself. But she wouldn't be a bad mother, you know, and in time Billy would grow to love her just as much as he loves me.'

'So Hortense would get her son back and Billy would get himself a new mother,' Mary said grimly. 'And the only one who'd really be hurt would be you.'

'That's right,' Becky agreed. 'The only one who'd really be hurt would be me.'

Though over two years had passed since Becky's last visit to the offices of the Lunacy Law Reform Society, nothing seemed to have changed. The files were as numerous and dusty as ever and Miss Dimdale still sat in the corner, pecking away with two fingers at her typewriting machine.

Mr Mackie was still there, too, as concerned – and as pessimistic – as he'd been in their previous encounters.

'It's a disgrace what they've done tae your sister-in-law,' he said when Becky had told him the story, 'but I canna quite see how it will be any help in getting her released.'

'They pretended she was dead!' Becky said.

'But that was after the Lunacy Commission had already turned down her appeal,' Mackie pointed out. 'And they could always argue that moving her tae another institution was in her ain best interest. She did try to hang herself, ye know – and that will look bad if we manage to get another hearing from the Commission.'

'*If* we manage to get her another hearing!' Becky exploded.

'We dinna really have any grounds for making the appeal,' Mackie told her. 'And even if they did agree tae reopen her case, from what ye've said she'd probably gi' the appearance of being deranged – and this time wi'out the help of drugs.'

It was true. Her time in Hatton Towers had taken their toll on poor Hortense, and now she would scarcely seem rational to anyone but her closest sympathizers.

'But we can't just let her die,' Becky said. 'There must be *something* we can do.'

'Is there anything else ye can think of which might help her case?' Mr Mackie asked.

'Hortense did tell me that the doctors had decided between them that they were going to sign the committal papers even before they ever saw her,' Becky said.

'And what made her think that?' Mackie asked sharply, as if he thought she might be on to something.

'It was the way they looked at each other while they were examining her,' Becky said.

Mackie was suddenly excited.

'They examined her together?' he said.

'Well, yes,' Becky replied. 'That's what she led me to understand.'

Mackie punched his right palm with his left fist. 'We've got them!' he said.

'How?' Becky asked.

'There's got tae be two *independent* medical examinations,' Mr Mackie told her.

'I'm not sure I understand,' Becky said.

'Each doctor's got tae examine the patient separately,'

Mackie explained. 'If they were both there, the whole procedure's invalid and the committal order is nae worth the paper it's writ on.'

'Does that mean you can get her out?' Becky said.

'Of course!' Mackie replied. 'It might tek some time to go through the formalities, but now we know the truth, Richard Worrell hasna got a legal leg tae stand on.'

She had done the right thing, Becky thought to herself, and if she had to face the same choices again, she would act in exactly the same way. But doing the right thing was going to cost her her son – and she suddenly wished she was dead.

Mr Mackie kept Becky well informed about the developments in Hortense's case. Early in October a formal appeal, which pointed out that Hortense was being detained illegally, was presented to the Lunacy Commission. By the end of November, the appeal had reached the top of the Commissioners' list, and they promised an early ruling. Now there was just one more small step to Hortense being free.

Just one more small step before I lose my darling boy, Becky thought.

She considered preparing Billy for the idea of separation, but she hadn't the heart for it. He was so happy as he was; let him stay happy for a little longer, even if he *was* living in a fool's paradise.

But the weeks of waiting – of dreading – took their toll on her. She couldn't eat. She couldn't sleep. She tried to hide her distress from the children, but without much success.

'Why are you always cryin', Mam?' little Billy asked worriedly.

'Because I love you so much,' Becky told him, sweeping him up and hugging him to her.

'That's a funny reason,' Billy said.

Oh, if only he knew!

It was just three days before Christmas when Hortense, looking pale but determined, appeared at Becky's back door

332

like an angel of doom.

'I was finally released yesterday morning,' she said. 'And I've come to thank you for all you've done for me, Becky. Without your help, I'd have been dead by now.'

'You didn't *just* come to thank me, did you?' Becky asked.

Hortense shook her head. 'No, I didn't' she admitted. 'I'm . . . I'm sorry, Becky, but I've come for William as well.'

How often Becky had imagined this moment in her mind. Yet none of her imaginings had ever come close to the emptiness and despair she felt now.

'You'd better come inside, then,' she said. 'But before you do, we've got to talk over how we're going to handle it.'

'What is there to handle?' Hortense asked belligerently.

'I don't want you rushing in there and throwing your arms round him,' Becky said.

'Why not?' Hortense demanded.

'Because you'll frighten him,' Becky told her.

'He's my son,' Hortense said.

'He doesn't know that yet,' Becky replied. 'And you're going to have to break it to him gently.'

'All right,' Hortense agreed. 'Can I see him now?'

'Yes,' Becky said. 'You can see him now.'

Billy was sitting in front of the fire, playing with his soldiers. He looked up and smiled at the visitor.

'Hello,' Hortense said in a shaky voice.

'Hello, lady,' the boy replied, and then, without giving the newcomer a second thought, he returned to his game.

'I'll pack him a case with enough clothes for him to get by,' Becky said. 'I'll send the rest on when you've given me your address.'

'Thank you,' Hortense said. She walked over to the fireplace and knelt down beside Billy. 'What's the name of the game you're playing?' she asked.

'It's not got a name,' Billy said. He held up one of the figures for her to see. 'This is Uncle George. He's a soldier, an' I've never even seen him.' He held up a second. 'An' this is Uncle Jack. He's very funny.' He presented her with a third, obviously the pride of his collection. 'An' this is my daddy,' he said. 'He's comin' home again soon.'

Yes, he was, Becky thought. She remembered his last, brief visit, earlier in the year. He'd told Billy all about his life in Africa, and the little boy had loved it. He'd described the wild animals in such a way that he'd taken his son's breath away. He'd made the pygmies who lived deep in the jungle seem so comical that Billy had been in fits of laughter. Well, there'd be no Billy to amuse the *next* time he came home.

Suddenly, Becky could stand it no longer.

'I'll go upstairs and get his things,' she said, almost running towards the stairs.

Up in the children's bedroom, she broke down in tears. How could she do this? she asked herself. How could she allow her son to be taken away by this stranger? Yet what choice did she have? If she refused to let him go, Hortense would fight in the courts, and Hortense would win. And Billy, poor little Billy, would only suffer more.

Making an effort to pull herself together, she opened Billy's little case and started to pack his clothes. Each article she placed in it – each tiny piece of clothing – tore at her heart-strings, but finally the job was over and she made her way slowly downstairs.

Hortense and Billy were where she had left them and seemed to be getting on wonderfully.

'. . . an' then me and Mam got some chestnuts an' put 'em in the fire,' Billy was explaining enthusiastically, 'an' just before they got black, we took 'em out again an' peeled off the skins an' ate 'em an' they were lovely.'

'You really love your mam, don't you?' Hortense asked.

'She's the best mam in the whole world,' Billy said with conviction.

'But you never asked me who *I* was, did you?' Hortense asked.

'No,' Billy agreed. 'Who are you?'

Hortense looked up at Becky with tears in her eyes, and

then turned back to Billy.

'I'm your Auntie Hortense,' she said.

They stood together on the doorstep, two women who both so desperately loved the same small child.

'I . . . I don't know what to say,' Becky told Hortense. 'I . . . I just don't know how to thank you.'

'Do you know why I tried to kill myself when I was in Mobberly Hall?' Hortense asked.

'No,' Becky said.

'Because I thought that with me dead, Richard might not make it so difficult for you to adopt William,' Hortense said. 'All that time in the asylums, the only thing that really mattered to me was my children's happiness. Well, William is very happy – I can see that – and I couldn't bear to make him miserable, even for a minute.'

'What about Gerald?' Becky asked.

'I shall try to get him back!' Hortense said passionately. 'I shall do everything I can to rescue him from his father's clutches.'

'If I can help . . .' Becky said.

Hortense shook her head. 'You've helped me so much already,' she said. 'And this is something I have to do alone.'

They hugged for the first time in all the years they had known each other.

'Where will you go?' Becky asked.

'I have a few relations who still might take me in even though I'm a fallen woman,' Hortense replied. 'And if they won't, I'll find somewhere else. Nothing in the future can ever be as bad as what I've already gone through.'

'Good luck,' Becky said.

'Could I . . . could I come and see Will . . . Billy once in a while?' Hortense asked.

'Of course you could,' Becky said with a smile. 'As often as you like. After all, you are his Auntie Hortense.'

Hortense nodded sadly, then turned and walked towards

the hired carriage which was waiting to take her away. And Becky went back into her kitchen to cuddle the child who was now finally – completely – her own.

Chapter Twenty-Five

It was not much of an encampment that George's patrol could see on the other side of the river, just a few shallow trenches and a line of thick thorn hedges. But after nearly two years of sand, heat – and more sand – it was a relief to catch sight of the enemy at last.

'How many of them do you reckon are in there, Sergeant?' the lieutenant in command asked.

George scanned the fortifications thoughtfully.

'It's difficult to say with any accuracy, sir,' he replied after a few moments' study, 'but if you pushed me, I'd have to put it at somewhere between thirteen and fifteen thousand.'

'So we're about evenly matched,' the officer mused.

'Yes, sir,' George agreed.

'Except that we have both technology and God on our side,' the officer said complacently.

Mention of God reminded George that it was Maundy Thursday. At home the catkins would be out. And the weeping willow. The air would be mild and soft as it always was in early spring – so different from the thick, dry, relentless atmosphere which was almost choking him now.

People in Marston would already be preparing for the Good Friday holiday. There would be a football match against one of the neighbouring villages, perhaps Marston's old rival, Great Budworth. Mam would suggest closing the chip shop for the day, but Dad would probably have none of that – not when there was likely to be so much business about. Colleen would be working hard, too, behind the bar of the New Inn – unless, that was, she'd got married and had other responsibilities now.

'Don't you have an opinion on the subject, Sergeant?' the

lieutenant asked sharply.

'Sorry, sir,' George said. 'I missed what you were sayin'.'

'I asked you if you thought the Sirdar would order an attack on the enemy encampment tomorrow.'

Would Kitchener order an attack? Who knew? Who *cared*?

'Yes, I think he probably will, sir,' said George, wishing the only fight which lay ahead of him was with the centre-forward from the Great Budworth football team.

The Battle of Atbara could scarcely have been called a real battle at all. Early on the morning of Good Friday, the British artillery began to pound the enemy positions, and then Kitchener's forces charged. George, whose unit was to be kept in reserve for the mopping-up operations, watched as kilted Highlanders, long-robed Egyptians and wild-looking Sudanese slashed their way through the Dervish defences, shooting or cutting down anyone who stood in their way.

The whole encounter took just a quarter of an hour – fifteen short minutes in which three thousand of the Khalifa's troops met a bloody end and the Sirdar lost a mere twenty-six of his soldiers.

Kitchener was very pleased indeed.

'It has been a *very* Good Friday,' he told his victorious men. 'Now nothing stands between us and Omdurman: nothing stands between us and the murderers of Gordon!'

Then for God's sake, let's get it over with, George thought. Let's get it over so I can feel me feet standin' on good old Cheshire earth again.

On the Tuesday after Easter, Mary woke up feeling slightly off-colour, and by the middle of the afternoon her face was on fire and her head pounded as if there were a herd of horses in there.

'Flu!' Aggie Brock pronounced. 'The best thing you can do is get yourself upstairs and sleep it off.'

'But I can't just go to bed,' Mary protested. 'There's the lodgers' supper to make yet.'

'Don't go worryin' yourself about the lodgers' supper,' Aggie told her. 'I'll take care of all that.'

Now there's a frightenin' thought, Mary said to herself. Aggi was a very good cleaner, but there was no denying she was a bit brutal about it. And if she cooked anything like the way she made beds, she'd be bullying the eggs into frying and scaring the potatoes clean out of their jackets.

'Perhaps the lodgers could make do with fish and chips from the shop for once,' Mary said.

'I've told you, I'll cook for 'em,' Aggie said firmly. 'Now can you make it upstairs yourself or do you want me to carry you?'

'Carry me!' Mary exclaimed.

'You can't weigh much more than a sack of 'taters,' Aggie said, sizing her up. 'An' I can lift two of them, easy.'

Mary looked at Aggie's massive arms.

'I'm sure you can,' she said, 'but if it's all the same to you, I think I'd rather walk.'

When Mary got up the next morning she was feeling much better in herself, but was vaguely worried about what effect Aggie's cooking might have had on her lodgers. If Spudder had still been there – poor Spudder – he wouldn't have cared what was put before him as long as there was plenty of it. But the other two were a very different matter. The Great Marvello had become very particular since he'd eaten with the Prince of Wales, and Ned Spratt's stomach was as finely tuned as a good fiddle. She'd cook a special supper that night, to make it up to them, Mary decided, something they'd normally only get on a Sunday.

Suppertime came, and Mary took the lodgers' tray round to the boarding house. She'd done them roast beef which was so tender you could have cut it with a spoon, and four veg which looked so appetizing that they were almost a meal in themselves.

Though I say so meself as shouldn't, it's more a feast than an ordinary supper, Mary thought as she placed it on the table.

Ned Spratt looked down at his plate and then up again at Mary. He seemed a little disappointed.

'By, but that was lovely grub you gave us last night, Mrs Taylor,' he said wistfully.

'Was it, Mr Spratt?' Mary asked, doing her very best to hide her astonishment.

'Lovely grub,' Spratt repeated, and with a sigh he picked up his knife and fork and began an apathetic attack on his roast beef.

So Aggie couldn't just cook – she could come up to Ned Spratt's exacting standards. Wonders would never cease!

After the Battle of Atbara, Kitchener gave his men three months' rest, and then ordered them to march on Omdurman. It was only two hundred miles, he told his men.

An' so it might be, George thought, but it's the worst two hundred miles *I've* ever seen.

He had never imagined such stifling heat as they experienced on that march. He had never pictured such bleak desolation as the flat, infertile land which stretched out interminably before them.

Kitchener's Sudanese troops took it all in their stride. They were used to the conditions, and besides, the native girls they came across would take pity on them and give them cooling drinks of water from the large goatskin bottles they carried.

But who would spare extra water for the British?

No one!

George was sometimes so thirsty that his tongue seemed to swell and swell until it was four times its normal size, until he almost thought it would choke him.

He worried constantly about his men, and even more about the horses. Riding the animals for any distance was out of the question, but even leading them appeared to put a strain on the poor beasts. Occasionally the company would come across a deep puddle, left over from the last rainstorm, and the horses would lap gratefully at the muddy water – but such puddles were few and far between.

Sunstroke claimed many victims. The officers who were struck down were carried on covered stretchers by native troops. But for the ordinary soldiers there was no such luxury. They were forced to manage as best they could, often clinging to their almost equally exhausted comrades and being virtually dragged across the desert.

There were moments when George was sure that he, too, had been touched by the sun, moments when his eyes changed the desert scrub into the green bushes of home and turned the occasional palm tree they saw into the silver birches he knew so well. For a while, he was convinced that he was a married man, and though he could not see his wife's face, he knew that they were very happy together. The delusion passed – as all such delusions must pass unless they grow deeper – and soon he was Sergeant George Taylor again, concerned more for his men and their horses than he was about his own comfort and well-being.

By the time the army was within sight of Omdurman the soldiers were filthy, sullen and determined to make someone pay for what they had endured. Kitchener was delighted. This was just the sort of spirit he had wanted from his men.

'I heard somethin' in the back yard,' Mary said with sudden alarm as she and Ted were preparing for bed.

'It was probably just a fox,' her husband replied.

'It wasn't,' Mary said firmly.

'There's been a lot of 'em about recently,' Ted pointed out.

'It was louder than a fox,' Mary insisted. 'Keep quiet for a minute, and you might hear it yourself.'

They sat in silence for perhaps twenty seconds before the noise was repeated. And this time, Ted did hear it, too.

'You're right,' he said. 'If that bugger's a fox, then it's the two-legged kind.'

'But we've nothin' worth stealin' in the yard,' Mary said in a whisper. 'I mean, who'd want an old dolly tub an' half a hundredweight of spuds bad enough to go nickin' them?'

'I don't know,' Ted said, 'but I'm not havin' it, whether or not. An Englishman's home is still his castle, and no bugger's goin' to go poking around in my back yard without my say-so.'

He reached for the oil lamp.

'Hadn't we better slip out through the front and call the bobbies?' Mary asked anxiously.

'Sod callin' the bobbies,' Ted told his wife. 'I'll sort this lot out all by meself.'

'Well, for goodness sake be careful,' Mary pleaded. 'And take this with you,' she added, handing him the poker.

Ted opened the back door and stepped into the yard. It was a warm summer evening and it had only just gone dark. And darkness was obviously what whoever was banging around had been waiting for.

Ted swung the lamp around, first casting light on the coal-shed and then on the lavatory. The yard seemed to be deserted. Which meant that the intruder had either gone or was hiding in the wash-house. Ted opened the wash-house door and stepped cautiously inside.

He shone his light on the boiler. Then, moving the lantern in a slow arc, he let his gaze take in the dolly tub and the dolly peg.

Nothing!

He was just about to go out into the yard again when he heard a shuffling sound behind the mangle, and moving his lantern once more, he was able to make out a human shape.

'Come out of there,' he said commandingly. 'And don't try any funny business or I'll have to belt you with this poker.'

The intruder rose slowly and uncertainly to his feet.

'Well, by bloody hell!' Ted said. 'Whatever are you doing here?'

'I missed me home,' Spudder said.

The three of them sat around the kitchen table, drinking a

soothing cup of tea.

'I tried to keep away like I knew I should,' Spudder said, 'but I missed you all too much.'

'We missed you, too,' Mary admitted. 'But why did you hide in the wash-house instead of comin' into the house?'

'I lost me nerve at the last minute,' Spudder said 'I thought you might be mad at me, you see. You're not, are you?'

'Of course we're not mad at you,' Mary said. 'But you can't stay, you know. Now that the feller who's lookin' for you knows you've lived here, he might come back to check up you've not returned.'

'I don't care!' Spudder said. 'If he catches me, he catches me. I'm not goin' to run any more.'

'You could end up in prison,' Mary warned him.

'I know,' Spudder said, 'but it's worth the risk.'

'Gaol'd be rough on a lad like you,' Mary said. 'I think you'd be better off to keep on movin'.'

'Anywhere's like prison when I'm not with you an' Mr Ted and Mrs Becky,' Spudder told her. 'Can I stay? Please?'

Mary looked into his big, soulful eyes, and knew she could not turn him down.

'All right, Spudder,' she said. 'You can stay.'

'Thanks, Mam,' Spudder said. A look of horror crossed his face. 'I'm . . . I'm sorry,' he stuttered. 'I didn't mean to . . . I wasn't . . .'

Mary reached across the table and took his big broad hand in her two small ones.

'That's all right, Spudder, love,' she said softly. 'You can call me Mam if it makes you happy. To tell you the truth, I rather fancy the idea of havin' *four* sons.'

George called his scouting troop to a halt a mile from the Dervish encampment and studied the enemy through his field glasses. There were about eight thousand of them, he guessed, and this was only one of several armies under the Khalifa's command. They had appeared on the plain – quite suddenly – the previous day, while the guns from both Kitchener's encampment and from the steamers on the Nile had been bombarding the city. For a while, it had looked as if they were about to make a full frontal assault on Kitchener's forces. Then, for reasons best known to themselves, they had come to a stop.

In fact, George thought, a direct assault was just what the British were hoping for, because with their superior firepower, they were bound to win. What Kitchener feared – what they all feared – was that instead of attacking, the Khalifa would retreat, and fight a guerrilla war in which the advantage would be his.

The front line of Dervishes had been squatting on the ground, but now they rose to their feet and began to move forward.

'They're going to attack, Sarge,' the trooper next to George said. 'They're bloody well going to attack.'

Could they be that stupid? George wondered. Haven't they heard what had happened at the Battle of Atbara?

Yet there was no doubt that the Dervishes were advancing, and at some considerable speed for men on foot.

'Pull back!' George ordered.

Like the disciplined force he had forged them into, his men calmly turned their horses and galloped back to their own lines in strict formation.

From behind the camel-thorn hedge which marked the boundary of Kitchener's encampment, George and his officer – Second Lieutenant Churchill – raised their field glasses and watched the approach of the Dervish army.

The enemy was advancing from all sides except for the area which backed on to the Nile. George could see thousands of spears and hundreds of flags – but very few rifles.

'A lot of 'em seem to have books in their hands, sir,' he said to Churchill. 'Why's that?'

'It's the Koran,' the officer explained. 'Their holy book.'

344

The artillery began to fire, blowing gaping holes in the Dervish ranks, but as soon as one group of men fell, another took its place.

'This is bloody madness!' George said.

'It is,' Churchill agreed. 'Thank God nothing like it will ever happen to British soldiers.'

At two thousand yards, Kitchener's infantry started volley-firing and then the Maxim machine-guns joined in. The Dervishes were dropping like flies, but still they kept advancing.

'Incredible!' Churchill said.

At eight hundred yards, the Egyptian and Sudanese troops were ordered to fire, and the carnage increased. Only then – finally – did the Dervishes break ranks and retreat, leaving behind them thousands of dead and dying.

Still the shooting continued.

'Cease fire!' Kitchener shouted. 'Cease fire! What a dreadful waste of ammunition!'

As the order passed down the line, the guns felt silent and soon there were only the groans of the enemy wounded to fill the empty air.

'I shall strike while the iron is hot,' said Kitchener, sitting proudly astride his horse in the middle of the carnage. 'We will march on Omdurman immediately.'.

George risked a sideways glance at the commanding officer of the Lancers, Colonel Blake. Though the colonel's face was composed into the military mask appropriate for a man being addressed by the Sirdar, he was seething with anger inside. And because sergeants often hear things they shouldn't, George knew precisely *what* had brought the mood on.

Ever since the retreat of the Dervishes, Blake had been coming under fire himself – from his fellow officers.

'Must say, Blakey, your chaps were a great help.'

'Send off one your lads to post a letter for me, will you – they don't seem to be much use for anything else.'

'Well, at least you can tell the people back home that you actually *saw* the victory.'

It had all been friendly ribbing, and Blake had had no choice but to seem to take it in good part. Yet beneath the surface he was bubbling away like a volcano, ready to erupt when it was least expected.

And that was not good, George thought. An angry officer was a rash one – and a rash officer was a very dangerous man indeed.

'You and your men will reconnoitre the plain ahead of the rest of the army, Colonel Blake,' Kitchener said.

'Sir!' Blake responded crisply.

'Dismissed,' Kitchener told him.

The Lancers saluted and Blake led his three hundred men from the safety of the encampment out on to the empty plain.

They had ridden just over two miles when the dried-up river-bed came into view – and with it the white-turbaned heads of the Dervish warriors who were camping there. Colonel Blake beckoned for Lieutenant Churchill and his sergeant to draw closer.

'How many of the beggars d'you think there are skulking down there, Winston?' he asked.

Lieutenant Churchill screwed up his eyes against the sun and peered into the wadi.

'About a hundred and fifty as far as I can tell, sir,' he replied. 'But that's only a *very* rough guess.'

'A hundred and fifty,' the colonel mused. 'A hundred and fifty of them against three hundred of us – and we're on horseback. What say we go in there and flush the beggars out?'

George felt a prickling at the back of his neck and recognized it as a warning from the instinct which he'd developed during his years in the army. He had great respect for that instinct – it had saved his life countless times – and now it said that something was very wrong.

'Permission to speak, sir,' he said to Blake.

The colonel turned to face him.

346

'Well, Sergeant?' he said.

'We can't be sure how deep that wadi is, sir,' George said.

'Can't be sure?' the colonel echoed. 'Haven't you got eyes? Can't you see for yourself?'

'With respect, sir, your eyes can easily deceive you in the desert,' George replied. 'I'm not sayin' the wadi *is* deeper than it looks, I'm only saying it *could* be. Which might mean that there could be a lot more than a couple of hundred warriors down there.'

'Balderdash!' the colonel retorted.

'But it wouldn't do any harm to send me and a few of my lads to have a closer look before you commit the whole force to an attack, would it, sir?' George suggested.

'If we do that, we'll be giving them extra time to get away, and most of the devils will be long gone by the time the main force reaches the wadi,' the colonel said. 'No, Sergeant, as the Sirdar said himself, we should strike while the iron is hot.'

The back of George's neck was tingling furiously now.

'But, sir . . .' he protested.

'It seems to me that we've had quite enough of sitting around on the sidelines for one day,' the colonel said coldly. 'Instruct the bugler to sound the charge.'

'Yes, sir!' said George Taylor, model soldier and youngest sergeant in the 21st Lancers.

It was obvious the colonel had made a tragic mistake the moment the lead horses started to gallop down the steep slope into the wadi. It wasn't a dried-up river-bed they were entering at all – it was a ravine. And beyond the handful of warriors they'd seen from above lay a small army, perhaps three thousand strong.

To retreat was completely impossible. The lead horses were in a high state of excitement and just maintaining their footing on the slope was a hard enough task. Besides, even if it had been possible to rein these animals in, the horses behind were so close that they would have slammed straight into the leaders.

'We'll have to cut our way through!' Churchill shouted.

As insane as that seemed, they had no other choice, George realized. He swung his arm through the air in an arc, gesturing his men on.

The Dervishes stood in ranks twelve deep on each side of the ravine. Even at a distance, it was possible to see they were grinning. And well they might: though they had done nothing to lure the Lancers into the wadi, they could not have devised a more deadly trap if they'd tried.

George heard his horse snort in a blind panic and felt a pain in his left leg as another Lancer cannoned into him. The Dervishes were not more than fifty yards away now. The front line of warriors threw their spears, and suddenly the air was thick with dangerous black shafts which reached their apex and then came plunging back towards the earth – towards the 21st Lancers.

Keep going! Keep going! George told himself.

There was nothing else he could do!

He heard a grunt and saw the man next to him topple from his horse, a spear sticking obscenely from his chest. They were between the two lines of Dervishes now, and the first row of warriors had knelt down to give the second rank a clear shot.

There was a cacophony of noises – rifles going off, men cursing, horses whinnying and the almost gentle swish of the enemy spears as they glided through the air.

The horse just in front went down, and George urged his own mount over it. Half a dozen Dervishes flung themselves in the path of the advancing force. One grabbed George's horse's bridle and would have had him over if he'd not swung his lance and cut the man down.

The leading riders were almost clear of the ranks of warriors now and could see the exit to the ravine up ahead.

I'm going to live! George thought in surprise. I'm going to get through it in one piece.

The spear hit his shoulder with a dull thud. At first there

was a searing pain and then his shoulder went numb, and he would have been all right but for the fact that his head was swimming and the ground in front of him seemed to be bouncing up and down.

Ahead of him, he saw another lancer sprawling in the dried mud. The man was trying to get to his feet as half a dozen Dervishes descended on him and started to slash him to pieces with their wicked-looking knives.

That's just what'll happen to you if you bloody well fall off, George told himself. Whatever happened, he had to stay on the horse. Yet it was so difficult when your brain was stuffed with cotton wool and there was this sticky liquid clinging to you which you soon realized was your own blood.

They were almost clear of the enemy. He had only to hold on for a little longer and he would be safe.

George lurched forward and toppled out of his saddle.

'Battle of Omdurman!' screamed the headline. 'Sir Herbert Kitchener's Brilliant Victory!'

'They went in for a full frontal attack, these Dervish fellers,' Ted Taylor said, looking up from his newspaper. 'Imagine that – men armed with nothin' but spears going up against machine-guns. It says in the *Graphic* that none of 'em got within three hundred yards of our lads.' He shook his head. 'It doesn't seem right.'

'What doesn't?' his wife asked.

'They lost eleven thousand men with another sixteen thousand wounded,' Ted told her. 'We had forty-eight casualties. I know all's fair in war, but that seems more like a pigeon-shoot than a battle.'

'At least it means our George is safe,' Mary pointed out.

'That's true enough,' Ted agreed. 'From the account in the paper, it looks like they didn't use the cavalry at all.'

There was a frantic knocking on the back door and Ted got up to admit a white-faced Ha-Ha Harry Atherton.

'Whatever's the matter, Harry?' Ted asked.

'W . . . what's the name of that c . . . company your

George is serving in?' he asked.

'21st Lancers,' Ted replied. 'Why do you ask?'

'Th . . . they've just brought out a sp . . . special edition of the paper,' Harry explained. 'There was a b . . . battle . . .'

'The Battle of Omdurman,' Ted said. 'I know, Harry. I've just been readin' about it.'

'N . . . not that,' Harry said. 'This ha . . . happened after the big battle. A c . . . cavalry charge, it was. They're c . . . calling it a second Charge of the Light Brigade.'

'An' were the 21st part of this charge?' Ted demanded anxiously.

'It w . . . was *only* them,' Harry said. 'The r . . . rest of the army was followin' on behind.'

Only the 21st! And they were calling it a second Charge of the Light Brigade – which had been a massacre.

Mary had sunk down into her chair, and Ted himself could hardly find the strength to keep standing.

'Were there many killed?' he asked – though he knew there could only be one answer.

Harry, no longer able to find any words, merely nodded his head.

His left ankle itched unbearably, yet when he tried to scratch it, he found that his arms seemed to be bound tight to his body. And it was hot, so uncomfortably hot.

George opened his eyes and saw that he was lying under canvas. Which meant, his befuddled brain told him, that he wasn't in that hellish valley any more. Though he could remember nothing after he fell off his horse, he must have escaped somehow, and now he was back in base camp.

'You very nearly didn't make it,' said a voice to the side.

George twisted his head. The man who had spoken was blurred at first, and George had to screw up his eyes to bring him into focus.

It was Lieutenant Churchill.

'Hello, sir,' George said. 'I'd salute you, but for some

reason I can't seem to move me arms.'

'That's because your left arm is broken and your right shoulder is badly sprained,' the officer explained.

'What happened to me?' George asked.

'You were hit by a spear, and lost your seat,' Churchill told him.

'I remember that bit, sir,' George said grimly.

'You'd have been a dead man but the fact that one of your feet got twisted up in the stirrup,' Churchill continued. 'It was your horse that dragged you clear.'

'He always was a good mount,' George said with a weak smile. Then he became serious again and asked, 'Did we sustain a lot of casualties in the charge, sir?'

'Seventy men and a hundred and nineteen horses either killed or wounded,' Churchill said. 'And all in a little under two minutes.'

'So I'm one of the lucky ones,' George said.

'It'd be best to look at it that way,' the lieutenant agreed.

'How do you mean, sir?' George asked.

'I'm not the surgeon,' Churchill said evasively. 'He's the one you should be talking to.'

'About what?' George demanded. 'I'm sorry, sir . . . I didn't mean to . . .'

'That's quite all right,' Churchill said kindly. 'Understandable, even, in the circumstances. How are you feeling in general?'

'Not so bad apart from my ankle,' George said.

Churchill narrowed his eyes.

'Which one?' he asked.

'The left,' George said. 'It itches like buggery. I don't suppose you could find an orderly, sir, and ask him to scratch it for me?'

Churchill frowned as if trying to reach a decision, then said, 'I suppose there's no point in waiting for the surgeon to break the news to you. Your ankle doesn't really itch, Sergeant.'

'With respect, sir,' George said hotly. 'I'm in a better

position than you to know whether my ankle itches or not.'

Churchill shook his head.

'No, you're not, Sergeant,' he said. 'You have no left leg below the knee. They amputated it this morning.'

Chapter Twenty-Six

Winter or summer, rain or shine, Monday was washing day at the Taylor house, and always had been. So it came as no surprise at all to Becky when she found her mother in the wash-house one Monday morning in early November.

'Anythin' wrong, love?' Mary asked when she saw her daughter standing in the doorway.

'No,' Becky said. 'It's just that I was missing Michael a bit, so I thought I'd come running home to me mam.'

Mary laughed. 'Well, you're always welcome,' she said.

There was a touch of frost in the air outside, but the fire in the brick boiler was burning brightly and the little wash-house had a lovely warm cosiness about it. Becky thought back to the days before she'd started school, when she would always help Mam with the washing.

'Or hinder her, more like,' she admitted.

Not that Mam had ever minded – she loved having any or all of her children around her.

Life had been so simple back then, Becky thought. Her biggest problem had been getting to the level crossing in time to catch the sweets the engine driver threw her. Still, she wouldn't like to go back to her childhood, she decided. She wouldn't give up what she had now in return for what she'd had then.

Using the big wooden tongs, Mary pulled her sheets out of the boiler and dropped them into the dolly tub. Next, she picked up the dolly peg, placed it in the centre of the tub and began to twist the handle round as hard as she could.

'Do you want me to give you a hand, Mam?' Becky said.

'Do I heck as like!' her mother replied. 'I may be gettin' a bit long in the tooth, but I can still just about manage to do me own washin', thank you very much.'

Becky smiled. She'd always been so independent, had her mam.

'Michael says they'll soon have electric machines to do all this work,' she said.

Mary shook her head, wonderingly.

'That Michael!' she said. 'He's got so much goin' on in that mind of his, it's a wonder his head doesn't explode. Is he plannin' to come home for Christmas this year?'

'Yes,' Becky said happily. 'I think that's why I'm missin' him so much this morning.'

'What d'you mean by that?' Mary asked.

'Well, it's because I know that in just over a month I'll be seeing him again that it's so hard being apart now,' Becky explained. 'Does that make any sense to you?'

'I suppose so,' Mary said. 'But it's hard for me really to know how you feel, because me and your dad never *have* been separated, you see – not even for a day.' She took the white sheets out of the dolly tub and carried them over to the mangle. 'I got another letter from your brother George yesterday,' she continued.

'And what's he got to say for himself this time?' Becky asked.

'He's out of hospital,' Mary told her, 'but the doctor says he's still not fit enough for crossin' the desert.'

'I should think not,' Becky said.

Between them, they spread out one of the sheets and fed the end of it into the mangle. Mary began to turn the cast-iron handle. The sheet was drawn between the rollers and almost immediately water started to drip into the bucket on the floor.

'Anyway, they're givin' our George somethin' he called "light duties around the camp" until he's fit,' Mary continued, 'and then they'll discharge him and send him home.'

'When will that be?' Becky asked.

'He reckons it should be some time next spring,' Mary said.

'That's a long while,' Becky said.

Mary folded the mangled sheet and Becky fed another one in between the rollers.

'If he can just get home safely, I don't care how long it takes him,' Mary told her. 'Anyway, he's had his bit of bad luck. It's the others I'm worried about now.'

'What others?' Becky asked.

'Our Jack, our Philip, your Michael, your Billy, your Michelle, Spudder, our Jessie, our Eunice, our Thelma . . .'

'Hang on,' Becky said, laughing. 'You're about to give me a list of the whole family.'

'Yes, I suppose I am,' Mary admitted.

'But why should you be worried about them?' Becky asked.

'Because disasters always come in threes,' Mary told her. 'Well, we've had George losin' his leg – that was the first – and now I'm waitin' for the other two to happen.'

'Disasters always come in threes!' Becky scoffed. 'That's an old wives' tale, Mam.'

'Well, I'm an old wife,' Mary told her. 'An' clever as you are, Becky, I've seen a lot more of life than you have. So mark my words, we've not finished with bad luck yet – not by a long chalk.'

On her way back down the lane, Becky found that she couldn't get her mother's gloomy prediction out of her mind.

Stop being so daft, she ordered herself. Things always happen in threes! That's just superstition!

Yet sometimes superstition seemed to work, like with the old gypsy who'd told her future when she was a kid.

The gypsy had prophesied that someone close to her would be seriously hurt – and Dad had had his accident down the pit! She'd gone on to say that two men would love Becky as much as they hated each other – Richard and Michael. And hadn't she foretold the collapse of Michael's works – so many years before it had actually happened?

She felt a sudden urge to turn around, run over the bridge and wait outside the school for her children.

Now that really *would* be daft, she thought.

The morning classes wouldn't be over for hours yet. And besides, Billy was getting to be so fiercely independent that he'd really resent being met by his mam as if he was still a little baby, instead of a grown-up boy all of six years old.

As Becky opened the back door and stepped into her kitchen, her eyes went automatically to the photograph of Michael which took pride of place on the mantelpiece. What a confident smile he had, she thought, what fearless eyes.

And yet bravery and confidence were no protection against a poisoned dart. Jack had told her that Michael's army would keep him safe from the fierce pygmies. Yet hadn't he also said that the same army would follow Michael anywhere? Which meant that her husband wouldn't be using his soldiers as his shield, but would be leading them into battle.

'But I'd have known that even if Jack hadn't told me,' she said to her husband's photograph. 'You were never one to let other folk do your dirty jobs for you, were you, Michael?'

There was the sound of footsteps in the alley, and looking through the kitchen window, she saw that Eric Todd, the local postman, had arrived with the second delivery. Becky flung the door open, and Eric grinned at her.

'You always know when you're goin' to get a letter from your Michael, don't you, Becky?' he said, holding out an envelope battered by its long journey.

Yes, Becky thought, she did. Even though she'd never realized it until that moment, her heart was always beating faster and her hand trembling slightly *before* she saw her beloved husband's familiar handwriting.

It was as much as Becky could do to avoid snatching the letter from Eric Todd's hand, and once back inside her kitchen, she broke her own rule and slit open the envelope even though the children were not there.

My dearest wife and children,

Forgive my brevity, but I have a runner leaving for the coast in a few minutes and there is no time for anything but a short note. I have wonderful news. I didn't expect to be home until just before Christmas, but now I am fairly sure that I can clear up what little difficulties stand in my way earlier than that, and I've booked my passage on a ship called the *Star of Africa*. It will be docking in Liverpool on the 15th of December. How I long to see you all!

All my love,
Michael (Dad)

Becky didn't know what to feel. On the one hand, it *was* wonderful news that Michael was coming home earlier than expected. But on the other, there was that reference, 'little difficulties', again – and that could mean a new expedition against the pygmies.

Becky pictured Michael lying in the jungle with a poison dart sticking in his heart, and felt the tears start to trickle down her face. Reaching up to the mantelpiece, she took down Michael's photograph and kissed it.

'Take care, my love,' she said softly. 'Please take care.'

'I won't be wantin' me supper tonight, Mrs Taylor,' Ned Spratt told his landlady.

If he'd told her he'd just been to the moon and brought her back some green cheese, Mary couldn't have been more surprised. Ned Spratt didn't want any supper! The man who lived for his stomach and never missed a meal, was telling her not to bother cooking for him today!

Mary looked him up and down. He'd shaved, something he never bothered to do in the evening – and often enough not in the morning, either, as a matter of fact. He'd put on a clean shirt and was wearing new boots. And he didn't want his supper; however much she tried, she couldn't help coming back to that!

'Has there been a death in the family, Mr Spratt?' she asked sympathetically.

'No,' Spratt said. 'Why did you think that?'

'Well, it's just that . . . I mean . . .' Mary replied, waving her hands about and trying to think of a tactful way of saying it.

'Oh, I see what you mean,' Spratt said. 'It's not like me to miss me three squares a day.'

'Exactly,' Mary said, with some relief.

'Well, to tell you the truth,' Spratt said, in such a way she was convinced that anything he told her would be far from it, 'to tell you the truth, I've developed a bit of an interest in . . . er . . . in whippet racin'.'

'Have you, Mr Spratt?' Mary said, keeping a straight face.

'That's right, whippet racin',' Spratt repeated. 'It'll probably . . . er . . . mean me bein' out of the house two or three evenin's a week from now on. Maybe more.'

'Would you like me to make you some sandwiches to take with you?' Mary asked. 'I've got some of that special ham you like so much.'

Mary had expected him to start licking his lips even at the thought of his favourite ham, but instead her question seemed to throw Spratt into a state of confusion.

'I really don't . . . er . . . want to put you to any trouble, Mrs Taylor,' he said.

'It'll be no trouble,' Mary told him. 'You're payin' for all your meals. You might as well get somethin' out of it.'

Mary moved towards the pantry.

'I haven't got time to wait,' Spratt said desperately. 'Besides, I'm . . . er . . . I'm tryin' to lose a bit of weight. Yes, that's it.'

And when Mary turned round again, he had already disappeared into the yard.

Mary was still puzzling over the mystery of Ned Spratt half an hour later, when she heard a knock at the door.

Now who could that be? she wondered, straightening her pinny and giving her hair a quick pat with her hand.

She opened the door to find a man standing there. He was dressed in a frock coat and had cold eyes.

'Do you remember me, Mrs Taylor?' he asked.

For a moment she didn't – and then it came to her. 'Your name's Barnes,' she said. 'You're the one who was lookin' for Spudder.'

'That's right,' Barnes agreed. 'You won't slam the door on me again, will you, Mrs Taylor?'

Mary shook her head. What would be the point in doing that? Barnes would not have come back alone, and by now Spudder was probably in the Cross Street lock-up.

'I've been waiting for this day for years,' Barnes said. 'For years! Do you know how much time I've spent looking for the man known to you as Spudder Johnson?'

'How much?' Mary asked dully.

'Enough so that when I finally submit my bill to the estate, it'll eat up a fair chunk of his legacy,' Barnes said.

'Eat up a fair chunk of his *what*?' Mary gasped.

Mr Barnes wasn't so bad once you started to get to know him over a cup of tea, Mary thought. You began to realize that his eyes weren't so much cold as businesslike. And if he had a bit of a forbidding manner about him, well that probably came from his training as a policeman.

'Did you know Spudder before, Mr Barnes?' she asked as she offered him a biscuit. 'You know, when he was livin' with his dad.'

Barnes shook his head. 'No,' he said. 'Although I did work for his father on a number of divorce cases.'

'Did his father die?' Mary asked. 'No, that's a silly question. Of course he died, or there'd never have been a legacy.'

'Precisely,' Mr Barnes agreed.

'What I really mean is, did he die after Spudder pushed . . . after he fell down the stairs?'

There was just the trace of a smile on Mr Barnes's lips.

'Well he couldn't have died before it, now could he?' the private detective asked.

'I know that,' Mary said helplessly. 'I just wondered . . .'

She trailed off. Really, there was no way of asking what she wanted to without running the risk of getting Spudder into trouble.

'You were just wondering if his father died as a result of Spudder pushing him down the stairs?' Mr Barnes asked.

'I didn't say that,' Mary told him – although she'd as good as.

'The fall didn't kill him,' Mr Barnes assured her. 'He was certainly badly bruised, and in fact he went to the police to complain. But word of his cruelty to his son was getting around the neighbourhood by that time, and the inspector on duty told him in no uncertain terms that he'd probably got no more than he'd deserved.'

'When did he die, then?' Mary asked.

'A year or so after Spudder ran away,' Barnes told her.

'And was it . . . ?'

'It was a heart attack that killed him – absolutely nothing at all to do with his fall.'

'So the police aren't looking for Spudder?'

'Of course not,' Barnes said. 'If it hadn't been for the fact that he was his father's one and only heir, I doubt if even I would have been still looking for him.'

'What about this money he's due?' Mary asked.

'What about it?' Mr Barnes countered.

'Is it a lot?'

'I couldn't give you the exact figure, even if I was allowed to – which I'm not,' Barnes said.

'But couldn't you give me a rough idea?' Mary pleaded. 'I wouldn't like you to think I've got any interest in it meself – but I have got an interest in lookin' after Spudder.'

Barnes nodded his head understandingly.

'Well, I wouldn't describe it as a fortune,' he told Mary. 'Spudder's father was quite wealthy at one time, but he managed to drink and gamble most of it away. Still, there's enough so you wouldn't be wrong if you described him as a man of substance.'

A man of substance, Mary thought. Spudder!

'Could you put him in touch with somebody who'll advise him on how to look after his money, sir?' Mary said, suddenly anxious. 'He's a lovely lad, is Spudder, but as you've probably noticed yourself, he hasn't got much of a head on his shoulders.'

'He seems to need less guidance than you'd think,' Barnes said. 'When I informed him of his good luck earlier this afternoon, he told me exactly what he was going to do with the money.'

That didn't sound like Spudder at all! He'd never had more than a pound in his pocket in his entire life. He had no more idea of money than he had of what made the sun come up in the morning.

'I still think he needs somebody to help him,' Mary said.

'He's got someone,' Barnes said. 'He asked me if I'd help, and I readily agreed.'

Mary looked at Barnes with new suspicion. He seemed an honest man, but you could never tell.

'Just what *is* he plannin' to do with his legacy, then, Mr Barnes?' she asked.

The private detective's eyes were suddenly as cold as they'd been the first time he appeared on her doorstep.

'My client has arranged to meet me here in about half an hour,' he said. 'If he considers what he's planning to be any of your business, I'm sure he'll tell you after he's talked to me.'

Becky sat at the big table where she usually added up her bills, and gazed down at the blank piece of paper which was lying there in front of her.

It's no good just *looking* at it, she told herself, picking up her pen and dipping it in the inkwell.

She knew quite well why she'd been putting off writing this letter: because as long as she didn't commit her fears to paper, she could convince herself that everything would soon be all right. But now, on the 20th of December, she had finally been forced to admit that whether she wrote it or only thought it, something terrible had happened.

Dear Jack, she wrote, *Michael was due to land in Liverpool on the 15th.*

She'd gone down to the docks to meet him. He hadn't been on the ship.

'Mr Worrell? Mr Michael Worrell?' the purser had said, leafing through his manifest. 'Yes, he did book a passage from Bonny, but then he never turned up.'

'And you don't know why?' Becky had asked anxiously. 'He didn't send you a message?'

'No, he didn't send a message,' the purser replied, 'but I shouldn't worry about it if I was you. Conditions are very unpredictable in the tropics. People are always missing sailings.'

And that was what Becky had kept telling herself all through her miserable journey home.

'Conditions are very unpredictable in the tropics. People are always missing sailings.'

Yet she knew deep inside herself that Michael, *her* Michael, would have found some way to get a message to her. And if he hadn't it could only be because he was . . . he was . . .

She daren't say it – daren't even think it.

He missed the sailing. He's never done that before. Jack, I'm sure that something terrible has happened to him, and there's nothing I can do about it. Will **you** help me, please, dear brother? Will you go and find him for me? You are the only hope I have.

Your loving sister,
Becky

She slipped the letter into an envelope and hurried down to the post office.

But when will Jack get my message? she wondered miserably as she dropped it into the postbox.

He was still working on the Oil Rivers, and could be anywhere between Bonny and the Brasslands – anywhere on

362

a thousand miles of river. It might be weeks before the letter caught up with him! It might even be months!

And by then it will be too late, she thought.

If it wasn't too late already.

The 21st of December came and went, and then the 22nd and the 23rd. Finally, on Christmas Eve, Becky decided that though she'd been saving the job for the whole family to do together, it was time to decorate the tree.

'We'll have such fun doing it, won't we?' she said to her children, though Michelle looked as if nothing in the world would seem like fun to her at that moment.

Becky took out the precious Christmas ornaments which had been carefully packed in cotton wool, and divided them equally between herself, Michelle and little Billy.

'And don't you two race to see who can put their share up first,' she said. 'It's not doing it quickly that counts – doing it prettily is the only thing that matters.'

Billy picked a cardboard model of the Three Wise Men, but Michelle just stood gazing at her ornaments, and after a full minute had passed without her moving, Becky said, 'Is anything the matter, my little love?'

Michelle looked up, and Becky could see that there were tears forming in the corners of her eyes.

'When's Dad coming home?' the girl asked.

What could she tell her daughter? Becky wondered. That he'd be home tomorrow? That he was sure to be back by the New Year? She was almost at the end of her tether, and finding it harder and harder to put on a brave face before the children.

'Mam?' Michelle prompted.

'I don't know when he's coming, my love,' Becky said wearily. 'I really have no idea.'

Billy had been making a determined effort to hang his Three Wise Men from one of the lower branches of the tree, but now he stopped and looked up at his mother.

'Won't Daddy be home for Christmas?' he asked.

'I don't think so,' Becky told him. 'He's been ever so busy with his work, you see.'

'But he promised!' Billy protested, stamping his foot angrily on the parlour floor.

'And he meant it,' Becky said sympathetically, 'but sometimes grown-ups have to break their promises.'

'Well, it's not fair!' Billy said, then he burst into tears and buried his head in his sister's lap.

'He's not really being naughty, Mam,' Michelle said as she gently stroked Billy's hair. 'He's just a bit upset.'

'I know,' Becky said.

'You see, we both miss Dad so much,' her daughter told her.

'And so do I,' Becky admitted.

Michelle looked anxiously down at Billy and then back to Becky.

'Dad *is* coming back, isn't he, Mam?' she mouthed silently.

'Of course he's coming back,' Becky replied, smiling though her heart was breaking.

PART FIVE

1899

Chapter Twenty-Seven

It was a grim February morning and the wind which swept in from across the water chilled to the bone the few poor souls who stood shivering on the quayside, waiting for the arrival of the steamer from West Africa.

Becky hugged herself in an effort to keep warm. Since she'd written to Jack, she'd travelled to Liverpool every time a ship was due in from Africa and met it on the dock. In vain! But this time would be different. Her hands, numb with cold, fumbled with the letter she had already read at least a score of times.

Dear Becky,

I have found Michael as you asked me to. He will be arriving in Liverpool on the *Pride of Glasgow* Thursday next. Please try not to be alarmed when you see him. He *has* been ill, but now is well on the way to recovery.

Your loving brother,
Jack

She folded the letter and put it back in her pocket. Every time she came to read it, she harboured a secret hope that this time the words would be different – Michael had had no more than a slight fever, Michael had never been fitter – but it always read the same.

What exactly did Jack mean? What had been the cause of Michael's illness? And if he really was well on the way to recovery, why hadn't he written the letter himself instead of getting Jack to do it?

The ship's hooter startled her. It was so loud, so penetrating, that for a moment it almost seemed as if the ship had left the sea and crept along the quay until it was right behind her. Becky turned round and saw that a steamer was about to enter the dock. She read the name on its grimy hull: the *Pride of Glasgow*.

'It won't be long before I know,' she said softly to herself. 'However bad it is, it won't be long before I know.'

The *Pride of Glasgow* was dingy and disreputable-looking – the sort of ship they called a tramp steamer.

'They go up and down the coast looking for work. They don't care what they carry, and passengers only travel on them if there's no other choice,' Michael had told her on his last trip home.

Where *is* Michael? Becky asked herself. She could see a few people standing on the deck, but her husband was not among them.

The gangplank was lowered, and the passengers began to disembark. There was a missionary with a small bag and a very big Bible. There was a man in white ducks who carried a shivering monkey in his arms. There were a couple of planters who were met by their families on the quayside. But there was no Michael.

An officer appeared next, a tall man with a great bushy beard.

'I'm expecting my husband,' Becky told him, almost desperate now. 'Michael Worrell.'

'They'll be bringing Mr Worrell ashore in a few minutes,' the officer said, and hurried away.

A group of dockers walked up and began the task of unloading the cargo. One of them, seeing Becky alone and miserable, took pity on her.

'Want one of dese, gerl?' he asked, holding a curiously bent yellow fruit up in front of her.

'What is it?' Becky said.

'It's called a banana,' the man said. 'Dey tastes lovely. My kids can't ger enough of dem.' He waved the fruit to and fro before her eyes, as if he were trying to hypnotize her with it. 'Go on, give it a try, gerl,' he urged her.

Becky shook her head. She had no appetite for food, no appetite for anything but finding out where Michael was.

'Look at dat,' the docker said. 'Some poor bugger must have been taken poorly.'

She turned to see what the docker was pointing at. Two sailors were walking slowly and carefully down the gangplank – and between them, they were carrying a stretcher.

Becky rushed up the gangplank, sank to her knees next to the stretcher and hugged her invalid husband.

'Go easy with him, miss,' one of the sailors cautioned her. 'He *is* a sick man, you know.'

Becky released her grip and stood up so she could get a proper look at Michael. He was thinner than she had ever seen him before, and his skin was the colour of old parchment.

'You look dreadful!' she said before she could help herself.

Michael smiled weakly. 'Flattery will get you nowhere,' he said.

Becky put her hand to her mouth. 'Oh Michael,' she said. 'I'm sorry. I didn't mean . . .'

'Yes, you did,' her husband replied. 'But if you think I look bad now, you should have seen me a couple of months ago.'

'Will you . . . ?' Becky began, on the verge of tears. 'Will you . . . are you going to be . . . ?'

'I'll be fine,' Michael assured her. 'A few weeks' rest and I'll be back to my old self.'

'Can we get movin', miss?' one of the sailors asked. 'I mean, he doesn't weigh *that* much, but even so . . .'

'Yes, yes, let's get moving,' Becky said, suddenly aware of where they were standing and how biting the wind was. 'Let's get him into the carriage before he catches his death of cold.'

It was only when they reached the hired carriage that it became plain just *how* weak Michael was. Without the help of the sailors, he would never have been able to get off the stretcher, and he didn't so much *take* his seat as allow himself to be propped up in it.

'How long have you been like this, Michael?' Becky asked as the coach pulled away. 'What was it you caught?'

'What I caught,' he said, 'was a pygmy poison dart.' He grinned. 'And in the backside, of all places.'

'It's not funny, Michael!' Becky said angrily, although, in a way, she had to admit it was.

'Yes, I'll certainly have an interesting scar to show your family next time we have them round for tea,' he continued.

'Michael!' Becky said, shocked.

'I should imagine old Not-Stopping Bracegirdle would like a look at it, too,' Michael said. 'That'll *really* give her something to talk about in the New Inn, now won't it?'

Becky giggled. She didn't mean to, but when she pictured the village gossip telling Dottie Curzon and Ma Fitton all about Michael's injury, she just couldn't help herself.

'You're impossible,' she chided her husband. 'Completely and utterly impossible.' She grew more serious again. 'Tell me exactly how it happened,' she said.

'We were trailing the pygmies –'

'The ones you told Billy were harmless, funny little things?' Becky interrupted.

Michael grinned shamefacedly. 'I didn't want to worry the little fellow,' he said.

'Or me,' Becky said, determined to let him get away with nothing.

'Or you,' Michael agreed. 'Anyway, they'd raided one of the outlying plantations, killing half a dozen workers, and I knew that if I let them get away with it, none of my people would ever feel safe again.'

'*Your* people,' Becky said, with just a hint of a smile playing on her lips.

'Well, I do feel a certain responsibility for them,' Michael admitted.

'You feel a certain responsibility for nearly everybody,

that's your trouble,' Becky said, though she knew that that was one of the reasons she loved him so much. 'Go on with your story.'

'We trailed them through the jungle for three days,' Michael continued. 'God, but the little devils could move quickly. It was towards the end of the third day that we smelled smoke. I thought that the pygmies must have assumed that they'd lost us, and were having a feast to celebrate. I split my men up and told them all to approach the smoke from different directions.'

'Captain Mike,' Becky said.

'What?' Michael asked.

'That's what Jack said they called you,' Becky said. 'Captain Mike. He said your men would follow you any-where.'

'Your brother talks too much,' Michael said embarrass-edly. 'Anyway, as we got closer to the smoke, we could hear the pygmies chattering away in that barbarous language they have. Then I reached the edge of the clearing where they were camped. I could see a spit in the middle of it, on which they were roasting a wild pig, but there wasn't a single pygmy in sight.'

'It was a trap,' Becky said.

'Indeed it was,' Michael agreed. 'I suppose I should have expected one after I found the doll.'

'What doll?' Becky asked.

'Oh, it was nothing really,' Michael said airily.

'Tell me about it!' Becky insisted.

'It was pinned to a tree by one of their darts,' Michael said. 'It was made out of red clay, but they'd whitened its face.'

'Why did they put it there?' Becky asked.

'For black magic reasons, I imagine,' Michael said. 'It was meant to be me, you see.'

'And it meant that they saw you as their biggest enemy and wanted you dead,' Becky said.

'Yes,' Michael agreed.

'But that didn't make you think of turning back, did it?'

Becky asked. 'Not even for a second?'

'Well, no,' Michael said, as if it had only just occurred to him that such a choice had existed.

And in a way, Becky thought, there *hadn't* really been a choice, because when Michael Worrell was doing what he thought was right, he would let *nothing* stand in his way.

'What happened once you realized you'd been caught in a trap?' she asked.

'I shouted out to my men that we'd been tricked and they'd better be careful,' Michael said.

'Which meant that the pygmies knew exactly where *you* were,' Becky said.

'Yes, I suppose it did,' Michael agreed. 'At any rate, I suddenly saw one of the little devils from the corner of my eye. I swung round and fired at him – I think I winged him – but there must have been another of them behind me, because I felt this sharp prick in my backside, and knew I must have been hit by a dart. The poison took effect almost immediately, and the next thing I remember, my men were carrying me through the jungle on a rough stretcher.'

'And when did all this happen?' Becky asked quietly.

'Some time in late November,' Michael replied.

'But that's three months ago!' Becky exclaimed.

'For the first few weeks, I had a fever. I don't remember much about it at all. I had moments when I was lucid, but for most of the time it was like having one long dream – and a very uncomfortable one at that. Even after I came round, I was still too weak to travel to the coast. I would have let you know – if I'd been able to hold a pen. And then your brother Jack arrived. And that's the whole story.'

'You make it sound so simple,' Becky said. 'You almost died, and you make it sound so simple.'

'Death *is* simple,' Michael told her. 'It's only life which is complicated.'

She wasn't sure whether he was making a joke or being serious. Maybe it was a bit of both.

*

Richard Worrell looked out of the library window at his son, Gerald, who was riding his pony up and down the lawn.

'She's trying to take him away from me,' he said.

'I beg your pardon?' Horace Crimp replied.

'Hortense. She's started legal action. She's trying to take my son away from me.'

'That is unfortunate,' Crimp said.

Richard whirled round angrily.

'It's more than unfortunate,' he told his attorney. 'It's the most terrible thing that's ever happened to me in my entire life.'

'More terrible than when you thought you'd lost your works to Septimus Quinn?' Crimp asked mildly.

'Of course,' Richard said, without a second's hesitation.

'Really!' Crimp said, the surprise evident in his voice. 'Then I take it you will be contesting your wife's action.'

'Yes, I'll be fighting it,' Richard replied. 'What are my chances of winning?'

'Very good, I should think,' Crimp said. 'For a start, you have the child now, which is nine points of the law. Then there's the fact that legal proceedings are not only long and cumbersome but also very expensive – your wife doesn't have much money, I take it?'

'Virtually none,' Richard answered. 'Her family disowned her when they learned about her bastard, and even if she could persuade her father to help her, he's as poor as a church mouse.'

'Excellent,' Crimp said. 'We might also bring in the point that she is a former lunatic.' He frowned. 'Although I don't really see how we would do that without . . .'

'Without what?' Richard asked.

'Without it coming out in open court that the reason she was committed was because she had an affair with a common groom,' Crimp said. 'And then, as you said yourself, you would be the laughing stock of the county.'

Richard turned back to the window. He'd had a number of low hurdles erected on the lawn, and Gerald was trying to

373

urge his pony over one of them. At the last moment, the animal shied away, Gerald swayed dangerously in the saddle for a second, then regained control of his mount. He noticed his father was watching him, and waved. Then he wheeled the pony round and took a longer run at the hurdle. This time, he made it.

'I said, we couldn't bring up her time in the asylum without making you a laughing stock,' Horace Crimp repeated.

'Do you think I care about that?' Richard asked.

'Well, the reason you had your wife committed in the first place *was* to keep her quiet,' Crimp pointed out.

'They can laugh at me until they're blue in the face,' Richard said passionately. 'I can stand their jokes and their sly digs. I'll put up with anything – as long as I can keep my son.'

'I just popped in to tell you I'll not be in for supper tonight, Mrs Taylor,' Ned Spratt said.

'Your whippets again?' Mary asked.

'That's right,' Spratt replied.

'And you don't want any sandwiches, either?' she asked, although he never did.

'Got to watch my weight,' Spratt said, patting a belly which seemed to have actually grown much bigger since he'd started missing his boarding house evening meals.

'Well, have a good time, Mr Spratt,' Mary said.

'I will, don't you worry,' Spratt told her. He walked over to the door, and just before he left he said, 'Lovely weather for June, isn't it? Almost like midsummer.'

June! How quick the time goes! Mary thought.

It only seemed like two minutes since Michael had come home. That had been towards the end of February and here they were, already in June.

Michael had sworn he'd be fighting fit by now, but anybody who knew her incredibly optimistic son-in-law had added a couple of months to that. Still, the lad wasn't doing too badly, she had to admit. He'd been out of his sickbed within three weeks, and now he was walking around without even the aid of a stick.

It wouldn't be like that for George. He'd been given a wooden leg, he'd told her in his last letter. Yes, well, she'd seen wooden legs on ex-servicemen before. Great ugly things, they were, like old-fashioned table legs. The poor boy would never be without a crutch again for as long as he lived. And what chance did he have of getting work, bein' crippled like he was? To think he'd once had the opportunity of being a professional footballer, and now he'd be reduced to hobblin' down the street. It broke her heart even to think about it. It really did.

'And bad things come in threes,' she reminded herself.

First George, then Michael. Who'd be next? It was Spudder she was most worried about. Or rather, she was worried about what was happening to his inheritance. He was still working at the farm as if he'd never come into any money, and every time she tried to ask about the legacy, he became very vague.

'I'm goin' to spend it,' he'd told her.

'Spend it? But what on, Spudder?'

'Somethin' Mr Barnes is goin' to get for me.'

'What sort of somethin'?' Mary asked in exasperation.

'Somethin' I want,' Spudder replied maddeningly.

And press him as she might, he would tell her no more. Now, whenever she even started to approach the question of the money, he would start babbling about the cows on the farm, or the weather, or whatever other nonsense came into his head.

She hoped he wasn't going to do anything foolish and throw away the only chance he'd ever had in his life.

From the moment he'd been fitted with his wooden leg, George had realized the importance of being independent.

Let other folk do one thing for you, and they'll soon be doin' another, he told himself, an' then another an' another, until you let yourself become as helpless as an infant.

That was why he hadn't told anybody he was arriving in Northwich that day. Whatever he said, his mother would drown him in loving care once he was at home, but he could at least make it to Marston under his own steam.

The wooden leg, which joined his real leg just below the knee, was chafing that day, but George ignored the pain and instead thought about the future. When he'd boarded the train in London, he'd noticed a couple more crippled soldiers. They'd been standing on the platform and selling matches – only one step away from begging! The idea that he might soon be doing the same himself had brought him out in a cold sweat.

But what else am I goin' to do? he wondered.

He had a small army disability pension, but that wouldn't be enough to live on. And he wasn't prepared to accept his family's charity – to live off the profits of the chip shop and the bakery – though he was sure it would be offered.

The train pulled into Northwich station and George rose to his feet. A few months earlier such an act would have required a great deal of effort, but now he accomplished it with relative ease.

You're a long way from dead, George, he told himself. There's lots of useful things you can do – if only you can find 'em.

It took some skill to descend from the train with a crutch in one hand and his baggage in other, but George managed it.

A porter appeared at his side. George noticed that his eyes went immediately to the wooden leg.

'Carry your bag, Sergeant?' he asked.

'It's not heavy,' George told him.

'I'm not expectin' any tip,' the porter said. 'I'm just glad to help one of our war heroes.'

One of our *crippled* war heroes! George thought, but aloud he said, 'I can manage – but thanks, anyway.'

There'd been a time when he'd have walked to Marston, arms swinging with military precision, but now he needed a cart. He hobbled to the back of the station where the carmen were waiting for customers, and slung his bag on to the back of the cart which was at the front of the line.

'Do you want me to help you to climb up into the seat, Sarge?' the carman asked helpfully.

'No,' George replied. 'I'll do it meself.'

He was on the point of reaching out for a handhold with which to pull himself up when he felt the back of his neck prickle. His instinct – the sergeant's instinct which had been dormant since he'd woken up in the army cot with part of his leg missing – was suddenly very much alive again. And his instinct was something he ignored at his peril.

If Colonel Blake had followed it instead of his own dreams of glory, there'd never have been that bloody massacre down in the wadi, George thought to himself.

And what did his instinct want him to do now? It wanted him to go into Northwich.

'Are you all right, Sarge?' the carman asked.

George realized he'd been standing there for some seconds, his hand almost touching the cart, yet frozen in mid-air.

'I'm fine,' he said. 'I just don't want to go yet. Look after me bag, can you? I'll be back in an hour. *Then* you can take me home.'

'I'd like to oblige you, Sergeant, what with you bein' . . . what with you being' a soldier an' all,' the carman replied, 'but I have got me livin' to make, the same as everybody else, an' if another customer happens to come along in the meantime . . .'

'I'll pay you to wait,' George said.

After all, what did a few pence matter? How long would they help to ward off the bleak future which lay ahead of him?

'Right ho,' the carman said cheerfully. 'If you're paying me for me time, I'll sit here till Doomsday.'

George walked along Station Road and down Witton Street. He sensed people looking at him, but he ignored them. He'd have to get used to being a curiosity, he thought, because his wooden leg wasn't going to go away.

He reached the corner of Timber Lane and saw a sign hanging outside Moore's Wood Yard.

'Foreman wanted. Apply within,' it said.

George felt another tingle at the back of his neck. So this was where his instinct had been leading him! Bracing himself, he walked across the road and pushed the gate open.

It was a big wood yard and it looked like it was doing good business. In one corner several workers were sorting timber and in another there was a group cutting it down to size.

A dozen men in all, George counted.

He stood there for a minute, studying them, then a man in a bowler hat came up to him and said, 'Can I help you, soldier?'

'Are you the gaffer?' George said.

'Yes, I'm Frank Moore,' the man told him.

'Well, you're advertisin' a job outside, Mr Moore,' George said, 'and I'm applyin' for it.'

Moore glanced involuntarily down at the wooden leg and then looked him in the face again – though he avoided George's eyes.

'I'm . . . er . . . not sure you're quite what we were lookin' for,' he said awkwardly.

'Because of me leg?' George asked. 'Because I can't heft wood? You surely don't expect your foreman to do any of the manual work in a big place like this, do you?'

'Well, no,' Moore admitted. 'But even so . . .'

'I was a sergeant in the army for quite a while,' George said. 'There's not much you can tell me about handlin' men.'

Moore shrugged uncomfortably. 'I'd like to help you out, Sergeant,' he said. 'I really would. But I've got to put the business first, you see.'

'I'm not askin' for charity,' George told him. 'If you took me on, it'd have to be because I was the best man for the job.' He glanced around the yard. 'See that feller over there with the bald head,' he continued, 'he's workin' like the blue blazes now, but the second you've turned your back, you can bet he'll be skivin' off.'

Moore whistled softly. 'How did you work that out?' he asked.

'I told you,' George replied. 'I know about men.'

'Tell me about some of the others,' Moore said, intrigued.

George surveyed the yard, taking his time.

'The big bloke over there's a bloody hard worker,' he said finally, 'but he's got no initiative, which means he's bloody hopeless unless he's constantly supervised. The feller with the saw is all right when he's acutally on the job, but the moment he gets a sniffle, he takes to his bed. What's the reason you haven't fired him?'

'He's the wife's cousin,' Moore admitted. 'Any other observations to make, Sergeant?'

'The feller just loadin' the waggon is the best worker you've got,' George told him. 'You probably considered making him up to foreman.'

'Then why didn't I do it?' Moore asked.

'Maybe you thought it would create too much bad feeling among the other men,' George suggested.

Moore smiled. 'The pay's thirty bob a week, and the hours are absolutely bloody awful,' he said.

'When do I start?' George asked.

The whole family thought it was wonderful that George was back – and nothing short of miraculous that he'd managed to get a job the moment he's stepped off the train.

Michelle had been a baby when he'd gone away, and Billy hadn't even been born, but they'd heard so much from their mam about their famous Uncle George that at first they were overawed.

It didn't last!

'Why have you got a wooden leg, Uncle George?' Billy asked.

'It's hollow,' George explained. 'It's where I keep me brandy.'

'Were you a very brave soldier, Uncle George?' Michelle

asked.

'Of course he was,' Becky told her. 'He's got medals, hasn't he?'

'Huh, that's nothing!' replied Michelle, plainly unimpressed. 'I've got a medal myself – from Sunday School – and I'm only seven!' Then she looked up at her uncle, smiled and said, 'But I'm sure you *were* very brave, anyway.'

'We'll have a real family supper tonight,' Ted declared grandly. 'All of us round one table – the kids included.'

'You shouldn't promise the children that, Dad,' Becky said crossly. 'You know I don't allow them to stay up late.'

'In that case, we'll just have to eat early,' Ted said.

'And who'll run the chip shop while we're having this supper?' Becky asked. 'Not-Stopping Bracegirdle?'

'No, that'd never do,' Ted admitted. 'She'd tell the fried fish all sorts of lies about me.'

'Well then?' Becky asked. 'Who will you leave in charge?'

Ted thought about it for a second.

'We won't open tonight,' he announced.

Becky threw her hands up in mock horror.

'Won't open!' she said. 'Is the world suddenly coming to an end or something?'

'Aye, well, it's not often we get a war hero comin' home,' Ted said uncomfortably.

'With his wooden leg full of brandy,' Billy chipped in.

Colleen O'Leary had volunteered to serve behind the bar even though it was her night off, and now she was sitting in front of her mirror, looking at herself. Her nose was as big as it had ever been, but George hadn't seemed to mind that in the old days. And as for the rest of her face, she didn't really think that had aged much since the last time he'd seen her. So if he'd liked her then, she decided, there was no reason at all why he wouldn't like her now.

She imagined the conversation they would have when he came into the pub later on.

'Do you still go for walks along the canal, Colleen?'

'Now and again.'

'Would you mind if I came with you the next time you went?'

'Not at all.'

'Of course, I can't walk as fast as I used to do.'

'That's quite all right, George. I'm in no hurry when I'm walkin' with you.'

She looked into the mirror and smiled. She had a nice smile, she thought. She wondered why she'd never really noticed before tonight just *how* nice it was.

It was a splendid supper. The pork joint was roasted to perfection, the apple sauce was sweet and tangy. The family tucked in as though it were Christmas Day, until in the end even Spudder – who now took all his meals with them – had had enough.

Mary sat back in her chair and watched with amusement as Ted moved uncomfortably around on his. He wanted to ask her a question, she thought, but he was not sure whether to do it now or leave it a few minutes.

Ted took out his watch and checked the time. 'I'm not bothered for meself,' he said to Mary, 'but as it's our George's first night home, would you mind if him, Michael and me slipped out for a quick drink?'

'If you're not bothered yourself, why don't you let just Michael and George go?' Mary asked mischievously.

'Or why don't you unscrew Uncle George's leg and drink brandy?' a sleepy Billy suggested from the sofa.

Ted looked poleaxed.

'When I said I wasn't bothered, I meant it,' he said, 'but I just thought, since it *is* George's first night . . .'

'He'd need his dad to look after him,' Mary said, smiling. 'Aye, get off, the three of you.'

'What about Spudder?' George asked.

'I don't drink,' Spudder said.

'Besides, he's got the coal-house to whitewash before he goes to bed,' Ted said, reaching for his cap.

Spudder looked puzzled.

'But I did that last week,' he said.

'Where are you goin'?' Mary asked. 'The New Inn?'

'I expect so,' Ted said.

'Does Mr O'Leary still run it?' George asked casually.

'He does that,' Ted replied. 'Mind you, I think he's starting to find it a bit of a strain these days. I don't suppose him and Cathy'd be able to carry on if it wasn't for their Colleen.'

'Colleen still lives with them, does she?' George said.

'Yes, she does,' Ted replied.

'She's not married, then?' George asked.

'Not even courtin', is she, Becky?' Ted asked.

'No,' Becky said. 'She's not even courting.'

As the three men stepped out into the lane, George said, 'Do you mind if we go to the Red Lion instead of the New Inn tonight?'

'The Red Lion's a dump,' Ted said.

'The New Inn's not exactly the Grand Hotel,' George pointed out.

'Oh, I know that,' Ted agreed, 'but most of your old mates will be in Paddy's place.'

Yes, but so would Colleen, George thought, his darling Colleen who could have made him so happy.

He was glad he'd written her that letter. He'd been worried at the time that if she married him, she'd be left a widow. Well, as things had turned out, she'd have been in an even worse state than that – saddled with a cripple for the rest of her life.

He knew he'd have to run into her some time, but he couldn't face it that night, couldn't bear her to see how the strong young man she'd once walked in the woods with could no longer go *anywhere* without the help of a crutch.

'Are you sure you'd rather go to the Lion?' Ted asked.

'Dead sure,' George said firmly.

Chapter Twenty-Eight

September slipped into October. The leaves turned brown, shrivelled and fell from the trees. The hawthorn bushes were weighed down with red berries and people murmured that was a sure sign of a harsh winter to come. Some mornings the ground was covered with a silvery sheen of frost, and children making their way over the bridge to the National School were often seen to be wearing bright woollen mittens.

For Becky, the autumn brought increasing anxiety. Michael had long since abandoned his stick and was now almost back to his old self.

I should be pleased about it, she told herself.

And in many ways she was. But there was at least a small part of her which couldn't help wishing that his recovery had been perhaps a little slower, so that she and her two children could have had him to themselves for a while longer.

Every morning at breakfast she studied him for the signs of restlessness which would tell her that his sense of duty had reawakened and he was itching to be back in Africa. Each night, as they undressed for bed, she held her breath and prayed that he was not about to tell her that he intended to book his passage to Bonny the next day.

Yet to Becky's surprise, Michael made no mention of the tropics. He undoubtedly had something on his mind – she could tell that from his pensive expressions and the sparkle which sometimes came into his eyes – but she did not think it was Africa.

Finally, one evening when they were sitting quietly by the fire together, she decided that she could stand the suspense no longer and would have to tackle him.

'Are you planning to return to the rubber plantations

soon?' she asked him bluntly.

Michael smiled. 'Are you so eager to get rid of me?' he said.

He was teasing, and Becky knew it.

'Well, you are getting a bit under foot, what with being around the house so much,' she told him.

'I suppose I am,' Michael admitted, 'but I'm afraid you'll just have to tolerate me for a little longer, because I have no intention of setting sail again until January.'

'That's marvellous news!' Becky said.

But she couldn't help wondering what exactly lay behind his decision.

Michael read her thoughts, and laughed. 'I've earned some time with my wife and children, don't you think?' he asked.

'Well, yes,' Becky agreed.

Still, it wasn't like Michael just to sit around and let the grass grow under his feet.

'Besides,' her husband continued, 'we're approaching a year's end which won't be like any other.'

'Won't it?' Becky asked.

'Of course not,' Michael replied. 'It'll be the dawning of a new century, and I want to see it in with you by my side.'

'You want to do what?' Becky said.

'To see the new century in with you by my side,' Michael repeated. 'Don't you find it exciting, Becky? Doesn't the idea of it – and all the changes it will bring – fill you with wonder?'

'I don't know,' Becky said. 'Maybe it will, in time. It's just that I've never really thought about it before.'

'Haven't you?' asked Michael, who had apparently given it a *great* deal of thought.

Becky reached across and took her husband's hand.

'I'm not like you, Michael,' she said.

'In what way aren't you like me?' Michael asked, obviously amused.

'I'm very down-to-earth,' Becky said seriously. 'It's enough for me to see that the kids get off to school on time and Monsieur Henri bakes enough bread to meet demand.'

'And what am I like?' Michael said.

'You're a dreamer,' Becky told him. 'A man with a vision. You soar above the ground like . . . I don't know . . . some wild bird, seeing things the rest of us miss out on, and getting excited about events we'd completely overlook if you weren't there to point them out.'

She was suddenly embarrased at using such flowery language, even in front of her husband. Yet wasn't it true? Only a dreamer would ever have believed he could just sail to Africa and rescue Jack, but Michael had done it. Only a visionary would ever have attempted, almost single-handed, to stamp out the slave trade in a vast area of tropical jungle. Yet she was glad that Michael was a dreamer, a visionary. She wouldn't have had him any other way.

'That was quite a little speech,' Michael said admiringly. 'I think there must be something of the dreamer in you, too.'

'Yes, well, when you live with a flanneller for as long as I have, some of it's bound to rub off on you eventually,' Becky said, feeling herself start to redden.

'Quite so,' Michael agreed, a smile playing on his lips.

'So how do you intend to celebrate this new, exciting century that's coming?' Becky asked in an attempt to change the subject. 'With a bottle of real French champagne?'

'With a whole crate of it!' Michael said expansively. 'Maybe even two. But that'll only be the start. My plans involve a great deal more than a bit of bubbly.'

'And are you going to tell me about them?' Becky asked.

'Not for the moment,' Michael said enigmatically. 'No, for the moment I think I'll keep them to myself.'

There'd been trouble brewing in Southern Africa for quite some time, and on the 12th of October, 1899, the Boers from the Transvaal invaded the British colony of Natal and laid siege to the towns of Mafeking, Kimberley and Ladysmith.

'You're well out of that lot, George,' Ted Taylor said to his son.

And George – who would rather have been *in it* with his leg than *out of it* because he didn't have one – replied, 'You're probably right, Dad.'

'I don't understand it meself,' Ted continued. 'As long as I can remember, we've been fighting somewhere. First, it was the Crimean War, and then there was the Indian Mutiny. After that we had the Ashanti Wars, then the Sudan – with them mad buggers Gordon an' Kitchener – and now this. Why can't people just mind their own business?'

'You mean, why can't everybody just run their own little chip shop?' George asked.

'Aye, something like that,' Ted said, not sure whether or not it was his son who was taking the mickey out of *him* for once.

'People are always wantin' more,' said George, who was no longer the simple lad he'd been when he joined the army. 'More land. More precious metals. More power. And however much there is of any of them things, there's never enough to go round.'

'Well, I'll tell you this,' Ted said, 'unless people start being sensible in a hurry, all these wars you read about won't be taking place thousands of miles away – they'll be right here on our own doorstep.'

George remembered the Battle of Omdurman, and could see in his mind's eye the thousands of poor bloody Dervishes being slaughtered like cattle. Most of them had been armed with nothing but knives, but even if they'd had rifles the result would have been the same: men on foot simply had no chance against heavy artillery.

'Thank God nothing like it will ever happen to British soldiers,' Lieutenant Churchill had said to him.

But if his father was right, George thought, then something *exactly* like that would happen.

'Do you really think there'll be a European war?' he asked Ted.

'I do,' his father replied. 'I may not live to see it, but if things go as they are, I don't see any way round it.'

The trouble with his father, George decided, was that though he based his opinions solely on what he saw from his chip shop window – and so should have been wrong every time – the old bugger was very often right. The realization did not do a lot to cheer him up.

'You've still got another half hour until you open the shop,' he said. 'Let's go for a pint.'

'Aye, all right,' Ted agreed, reaching for his coat. 'Do you fancy the New Inn for a change?'

'No,' George said firmly.

After his first night back – when he had refused to go into Paddy's pub – he'd expected to see Colleen in the lane, and somehow find a way to break the ice. And once that had happened, he could have gone back to the New Inn certain that she would treat him as just what he was – a next-door neighbour and her best friend's brother. But he never *had* seen Colleen in the lane. Or rather, he'd seen her, but she hadn't appeared to see him, and had hurried off in the other direction. So now what was he to do – go into the pub and embarrass her? Far, far better to stick to the Red Lion.

'You're sure you don't want a change?' asked Ted, who found the landlord of the Lion a right miserable old sod.

'I'm sure,' George told him.

Mary was just having a cup of tea when there was a knock and Aggie Brock stuck her head around the door.

'Can we have a word with you?' she asked.

'Who's "we"?' Mary said.

'Me an' Ned Spratt,' Aggie said.

Oh dear! What's happened now? Mary thought. She could only hope that Aggie hadn't gone back to her habit of making Ned's bed while he was still in it.

'We can come back later if you're too busy now,' Ned Spratt said hopefully from beyond Aggie's shoulder.

'No,' Mary said resignedly. 'We'd better deal with it now – whatever it is.'

Aggie marched into the kitchen and Ned shuffled in

behind her. Then, by some elaborate twisting and turning, they managed to end up side by side. They made a right comical pair, Mary thought. Ned was not a small feller by any means, but standing next to Aggie he looked like no more than a slip of a lad.

'Will you sit down and have a cup of tea?' Mary asked.

'No, thank you,' Aggie said. 'We've got serious business to discuss, an' it's best said standin' up.'

Oh dear! Mary thought again. She didn't like the sound of this at all. She hoped that Aggie wouldn't lose her temper, because she was really quite fond of her furniture.

'I suppose you'd better tell me what's on your minds, then,' she said, a little worriedly.

'I've just had word today that me husband's gone an' died on me,' Aggie told her.

That would be the one she'd thrown out of the kitchen window when he was dead drunk.

'I am sorry,' Mary said.

Aggie shrugged her vast shoulders. 'He was no use to me when he was alive,' she said. 'I shan't miss him now he's dead.'

But what's all this got to do with Ned Spratt? Mary wondered.

And then she noticed he was holding Aggie's hand.

'We're goin' to get married, him an' me,' Aggie said. 'And since you're his landlady and my boss, we thought it was only right an' proper that you should know about it first.'

Mary looked quizzically at Ned Spratt.

'I love her, Mrs Taylor, I really do,' he said.

'You love my cookin', more like,' Aggie told him.

Ned licked his lips. 'Lancashire hot-pot,' he said dreamily. 'Pipin' hot toad-in-the-hole. Bubble an' –'

'Hadn't you better be goin'?' Aggie said sharply to her future husband. 'There's that slate on my wash-house roof needs fixin' before you have your supper.'

'Oh aye,' Ned agreed. 'So there is. Right then, I'll be seein' you, Mrs Taylor.'

He edged round Aggie and made his way to the door.

'I think I will have that cup of tea now,' Aggie said, lowering her large body on to one of Mary's small chairs.

Mary picked up the teapot.

'I suppose I'd best start lookin' around for a new maid an' a new lodger,' she said.

'You'll have to get yourself a new lodger,' Aggie told her, 'but I shall be stayin' on. I like me bit of independence too much to stop workin' just 'cos I'm gettin' wed.'

'Oh, I am pleased, Aggie,' Mary admitted. 'I'd have been right sorry to lose you. And I hope you an' Mr Spratt will be very happy together.'

Aggie gave Mary a speculative look.

'Ned really does love me – in his way,' she said.

'I'm sure he does,' Mary replied.

'An' he suits me,' Aggie continued. 'Me main complaint about the other bugger I married was that he was always in the boozer. Well, I won't have that trouble with Ned – if it was left up to him, he'd never shift away from me kitchen table.'

'I'd like to hire you,' Michael Worrell told his wife in the middle of November.

'Hire me?' Becky said. 'As what?'

'As a caterer, of course,' Michael replied. 'That's what you do for a living, isn't it?'

'Well, yes,' Becky agreed.

'And I can say completely without prejudice that you're the best one in the area,' Michael said. 'So I'd like to hire you for the party I'm throwing for the village on New Year's Eve.'

'You're going to throw a party for the *whole* village?' Becky asked in amazement.

'That's right,' Michael said. 'I've already booked the school.'

'Whatever for?'

'For the magic show that the Great Marvello will be

putting on. And, of course, for the dance which will follow it. I've made arrangements to hire a gramophone.'

A gramophone! Becky thought. Most people in the village had never even seen a gramophone, let alone danced to one.

'And I expect you'll be having a firework display as well, won't you?' Becky asked sarcastically.

'You must be a mind reader,' Michael said. 'There'll be a bonfire, too, the biggest one Marston's ever seen.'

Becky shook her head in wonder.

'Don't you think it's a good idea?' Michael asked.

'Yes, it probably is,' Becky said. 'It's just that I'd never have thought of it. In fact, I can't think of *anybody* who would have thought of it, apart from you.' She reached up and kissed him. 'Even after all the time we've been married – even after I think I've learned everything there is to learn about you – you can still surprise me,' she said tenderly. 'That's probably why I love you as much as I do.'

'I knew there had to be *some* reason for it,' Michael said, hugging her to him.

Michael's plans for the New Year celebrations did not meet with universal approval.

'Well, you can all please yourselves, but I certainly won't be goin',' Not-Stopping Bracegirdle announced firmly from her customary seat in the best room of the New Inn.

'You said that about the O'Learys' twenty-fifth wedding anniversary,' Dottie Curzon reminded her. 'But when the day came, there you were – right on the front row – watching the magic lantern show.'

'That was different,' Not-Stopping said defensively.

'Why?' Dottie asked.

Not-Stopping groped around for a reason. 'Well, for a start, it wasn't on a Sunday – the Lord's Day – and New Year's Eve is.'

'So instead of goin' to Michael Worrell's dance, you'll be in church, will you?' Dottie asked.

'Probably,' Not-Stopping said vaguely.

'And when was the *last* time you saw the inside of a church?' Dottie wondered aloud.

Not-Stopping looked uncomfortable.

'Well, Sunday's a busy day for me,' she said. She looked down at her empty glass. 'Another round, when you can, Colleen,' she shouted in the general direction of the hatch.

'A nice girl, that Colleen,' Dottie said.

'She might be,' Not-Stopping said, lowering her voice to her conspiratorial whisper, 'but she's not the barmaid she used to be. Haven't you noticed how absent-minded she's got over the last few months?'

'Yes,' Dottie agreed. 'It seemed to start about the time George Taylor came back.'

'So it did,' Not-Stopping said pensively.

Aggie Brock became Mrs Ned Spratt on the 1st of December. It was a quiet wedding.

'Well, we don't want any fuss,' Aggie told Mary. 'I've been through all that sort of palaver before, and Ned can't stand anythin' which interferes with his mealtimes.'

On the morning of the wedding, Ned appeared at the boarding house with a handcart, on to which he loaded up what possessions he'd acquired over his years as a bachelor.

'We're goin' to miss havin' you around, Mr Spratt,' Mary said, handing him an enamel cooking pot which she'd bought as a wedding present for the happy couple.

'I'll miss you, too,' Ned admitted. 'You're the second best cook I've ever met in me life.'

It was only half an hour after Spratt had trundled his belongings away that a caller appeared at Mary's back door with a copy of the *Northwich Guardian* in his hands. He was a tall man of around thirty, with sharp, intelligent eyes and a short, tightly clipped moustache. He was wearing a waisted tailcoat and straight-cut grey trousers.

'My name is Alfred Bingham,' he said, tipping his top hat politely. 'I've come about your advertisement for a lodger.'

His gentlemanly manners and appearance threw Mary

into something of a confusion.

'I . . . I really think you must have come to the wrong place, Mr Bingham,' she said.

Bingham opened the newspaper.

'*Simple, clean accommodation offered to honest working man?*' he asked.

'Yes, well that's it, you see,' Mary said. 'Simple, clean accommodation offered to honest working man. The lodger that's just gone works in a boat yard, an' one of the others is a farm labourer. It's true that Mr Marvello is a bit different, bein' a theatrical gentleman, but even so . . .'

'I like to think of myself as an honest man,' Bingham said. 'And I certainly have to work for my living.'

'But the house you'd be livin' in would be just like this one,' Mary protested. 'In fact, it's right next door.'

Bingham looked over his shoulder into the kitchen.

'Very cosy,' he said. 'If the house next door resembles it at all, it will suit me perfectly.'

Mary realized that they had been standing on the doorstep far longer than was polite.

'Won't you come in, Mr Bingham,' she said.

'That is extremely kind of you,' Bingham said.

He removed his hat and followed her inside. She offered him a seat, and he accepted. She offered him tea.

'I never drink it,' he said. 'I can't quite get used to the ta . . . that is, I've never been able to get used to the taste. How much rent did you say you will be charging?'

She hadn't said, but now she told him.

'That includes food,' she said, in case he thought she was being greedy. 'Breakfast, a packed dinner an' a hot supper.'

'It seems very reasonable, even without food,' he replied. 'But I shall take few meals here. I travel around a great deal, and on occasions you will not see me for weeks at a time. In fact, I am about to embark on a journey today, and do not expect to return until the middle of January.'

'Oh dear,' Mary said, although secretly she was quite relieved. 'I'm afraid I can't hold the room open that long.'

'No one would expect you to,' Bingham told her. He took out his wallet, and Mary could see it was crammed with bank notes. He counted out several, and slid them across the table to Mary. 'This should cover my rent until July,' he said.

'Yes,' Mary admitted, 'it should.'

Bingham stood up.

'Well, then, there is nothing more to say,' he told her. 'Except to wish you and your family a joyous festive season to come.'

'Don't you want a receipt, Mr Bingham?' Mary asked.

'A receipt?' Bingham asked. 'Whatever for?'

'For all that money you've just given me,' Mary said.

Bingham laughed lightly. 'I trust you implicitly, my dear lady,' he said. 'Besides, why would you even bother to try and cheat me over such a trifling sum?'

When he'd gone, Mary sat and thought long and hard about Mr Bingham. In many ways, he seemed the ideal lodger. He was well mannered and had paid well in advance. He'd be cheap to keep since he wouldn't be at home for meals very often. It would have been most unreasonable of her to turn him down.

Anf yet there were some things about Mr Bingham which made Mary feel distinctly uneasy.

He was obviously quite well off, so why did he want to stay in her humble little boarding house?

He had an accent which wasn't local – and didn't seem quite natural, if the truth be told.

And Mary wasn't entirely sure that you could really trust *anybody* who didn't drink tea.

'An artist like me, 'e does not expect to be 'appy,' Monsieur Henri said. 'But now I am desolate.'

'Why don't you tell me what's wrong?' said Becky, who was so used to handling her master baker's crises that she could often do it while her mind was somewhere else entirely.

'Your 'usband, he want a big cake,' Monsieur Henri told.

'A birthday cake for ze year nineteen 'undred.'

'I know,' Becky said. 'Is that a problem?'

'Nothing is a problem if I 'ave ze right equipment,' the Frenchman said. 'But, alas I do not. We do not 'ave a big enough oven to bake the cake your 'usband want.'

'Why don't you just make the biggest cake you can in the ovens we've got?' Becky suggested.

'Because I 'ave done my calculations, and it will not work,' Monsieur Henri said.

'What won't work?'

'On ze biggest cake I can bake 'ere, zere will not be enough space for nineteen 'undred candles,' Monsieur Henri explained.

Becky would have laughed, except that she learned long ago that you did not laugh at a man of Monsieur Henri's sensibilities.

'Perhaps you could use fewer candles?' she suggested.

'Fewer!' replied the baker, clearly outraged.

'You know, one candle standing for five or ten,' Becky said hurriedly. 'So instead of nineteen hundred candles, you'd only need one hundred and ninety.'

Monsieur Henri threw his arms up into the air.

'Zat is to cheat,' he said, 'and I will never cheat. No, I have fail. I am in disgrace – even zough it is not my fault – and I 'ave no choice but to go back to France.'

Becky felt a growing sense of alarm. Without Monsieur Henri, the bakery was nothing.

'Couldn't you bake the cake in several pieces, and then put them all together?' she asked.

Monsieur Henri looked more offended than ever.

'Zat is ze biggest cheat of all,' he exploded. 'Zat is worse zan your idea about the candles.'

'No, it's completely different,' Becky protested.

''ow is it completely different?' Monsieur Henri demanded.

Yes, how *was* it completely different?

'The New Year looks like one big thing, but it isn't,' Becky told him, wondering, even as she spoke, what she was going to say next.

'Yes?' Monsieur Henri said, sounding interested now.

'We . . . we all share in it,' Becky said. 'We're all a part of it. So it looks like one big thing, but it's really made of a lot of little pieces.'

Monsieur Henri beamed.

'So zis cake – it is symbolic?' he said.

'Of course it is,' Becky agreed, making a note to ask Michael to explain to her what symbolic meant.

'Zis I can accept,' Monsieur Henri said happily. 'Zis make sense to an artist like me. It is not a cake, it is a creation.'

Becky smiled secretly to herself as she watched Monsieur Henri return to his work. How many times have I had to make up stories just to keep him happy? she wondered.

And then, to her surprise, she realized that she actually did believe what she'd told him this time. The New Year – the new century – *did* belong to all of them.

Perhaps after being married to Michael for so long, something really has begun to rub off, she thought.

Not-Stopping Bracegirdle was not the only person in the village to disapprove of the coming festivities.

'I can't see what there is to celebrate,' Ted Taylor told his son-in-law. 'It seems to me that as time goes on, things just keep on gettin' worse and worse.'

'In some ways, they are,' Michael agreed. 'But look at the progress that's been made, too. Twenty-five years ago there was no such thing as a telephone and now they're common enough for some quite small businesses to have one. You might even get one in the shop soon.'

'A telephone in a fish an' chip shop!' Ted scoffed. 'That'll be the day.'

'And take automobile carriages,' Michael continued, undeterred. 'Do you know that sixty-six of them took part in the Paris to Bordeaux Race – a distance of three hundred and sixty miles – and that the winner managed to keep up an average speed of fifteen miles an hour!'

'Next thing, you'll be telling me they'll be havin' flyin' machines soon,' Ted grumbled.

'They will!' Michael told him. 'Hiram Maxim actually got his steam-powered machine to fly a few years ago, and once someone's worked out how to power a machine with a lighter petrol engine there'll be no limit to what we can do. We're living in the most exciting time in all history. Change has never come so fast – and it'll get faster yet.'

'I'm not all that sure I'm in favour of change any more,' Ted told him. 'An' I still say that if you're goin' to throw a party for the whole village, you want your bumps feelin'.'

'I'll be needing someone to provide me with fish and chips as part of the supper,' Michael said.

'Oh, well, that's different then,' Ted said, suddenly looking interested. 'How many people were you thinkin' of caterin' for?'

'How would you like to re-enact our famous triumph, Spudder, my boy?' the Great Marvello asked as Spudder stood in Mary's yard re-pointing the wash-house.

'You what?' Spudder asked.

'How would you like to entertain the villagers of Marston with the same trick we performed to such great effect before the worthy burgers of Warrington?'

'You mean, you want to saw me in half again?' Spudder asked.

Marvello sighed. 'Yes, that's what I mean,' he said.

'I don't mind,' Spudder said. 'When would we be doin' it?'

'At the New Year's Eve party, of course,' Marvello said.

'Can't do it then,' Spudder said. 'I won't be here.'

Mary, who was on her way to the wash-house, caught just enough of the conversation to be stopped in her tracks.

'You won't be here?' she said. 'But you'd have a lovely time at Michael's dance, Spudder.'

'I know I would,' the young man agreed. 'But I've got some business to attend to.'

He turned back to his pointing in the hope that Mary would go away. He might as well have spared himself the effort.

'What kind of business?' Mary demanded.

Spudder turned to face her once more.

'Private business,' he said. 'With Mr Barnes.'

A feller like that Mr Barnes, an educated man with police training, could run rings round Spudder if he wanted to, Mary thought. But maybe he's not like that, she told herself. After all, it had been Barnes who'd told Spudder about his legacy in the first place. Didn't that mean he was honest?

Unless the only way he could get his hands on the money was to let Spudder have it first!

'Wouldn't you like to tell me about it?' she asked Spudder coaxingly.

'No, thanks,' the young man replied.

'Or perhaps talk it over with Michael? Michael's a businessman – he understands this sort of thing.'

'I know what I'm doing,' Spudder told her firmly.

Chapter Twenty-Nine

After all the planning and all the anticipation, New Year's Eve finally came. It was obvious from the start that the dance – or 'Michael Worrell's Dance' as it was widely known in the village – was going to be a great success. The gramophone alone would have been enough to guarantee a large attendance, but the addition of Becky's cakes and Ted's fish and chips meant that the school was crammed to bursting.

Before the dance began, the Great Marvello entertained and amazed the villagers with his famous magic.

'The next trick I will show you is one of those that I performed before the Prince of Wales himself,' he told his entranced audience as he shuffled the cards. He spoke as if the performance had taken place at Balmoral or Windsor Castle instead of on a tree stump, and – in a way – he had almost convinced himself that it had.

The climax of his act came when he sawed a member of the audience in half. In the absence of Spudder, Michael had volunteered to be his victim and, despite being so busy with other things, he had found the time to rehearse so well that the trick went perfectly.

The audience went wild when he'd finished, and begged for more, but then Cedric Rathbone put a record on the gramophone and soon almost the whole village – men, women and children – were dancing as they had never danced before.

But little Billy would not dance, not even with the sister he adored, until he had checked up on something.

'Did Mr Marvello really saw you into two pieces, Daddy?' he asked Michael worriedly.

'What do you think?' Michael replied.

Billy reached up and gingerly moved his finger around the waistband of Michael's trousers.

'No, he didn't,' the boy decided, obviously relieved.

'Then go and dance with Michelle,' his father told him, 'because it's never good to stand up a woman, especially after she's spent all week teaching you the steps.'

Michael looked around the room. Everyone seemed to be having a good time – even his grumpy father-in-law – everyone that was, apart from Mary Taylor and Colleen O'Leary. Mary was standing in a corner by herself, trying to look cheerful but occasionally letting her unhappiness slip through. Colleen was wandering around the edge of the dance floor as if she were lost – or as if she were looking for someone. He'd have a word with both of them when he could get a quiet minute, he decided.

Mary was feeling completely miserable. She knew now where the third piece of bad luck which the family was due would fall – it had come through the post that morning. She had the dreadful letter in her pocket, though she had no need to take it out and read it again, because she already knew it by heart.

Dear Mr and Mrs Taylor,

As your landlord, I feel it is only my duty to tell you that I have sold both 47 and 49 Ollershaw Lane. The new owner will be contacting you soon, but as I understand it, he does not wish to keep you on as his tenants and so I am afraid you will have to look for alternative accommodation.

Yours faithfully,
J. Spindle

She'd been looking forward to this evening so much, and now it was ruined, Mary thought. After over thirty years, she and Ted were going to be turned out of their house, the home in which they'd raised all their children.

She hadn't told Ted about it yet. One of them, at least,

might as well enjoy New Year's Eve. But she'd have to tell him soon, because, as the landlord said, they'd have to be thinking about alternative accommodation.

We'll get another house, she told herself.

They'd probably even be able to find one in the lane, built exactly like Number 47. But it still wouldn't *be* Number 47, and you couldn't move your memories with you in the same way as you could move your furniture.

The dance ended at just after eleven, and they all left the warmth of the school and picked their way carefully through the night to the frozen field where the biggest bonfire Marston had ever seen loomed impressively against the sky.

As the villagers stood around, stamping their feet and blowing on their hands to keep warm, Cedric Rathbone lit the paraffin-soaked rag which he'd wrapped around the top of a piece of wood. It started to burn immediately, and now there was one tiny patch of light in the midst of all the darkness.

Cedric walked up to the bonfire, knelt down, and inserted his torch into the base. At first, it seemed to have had no effect, then the torch ignited the paper, the paper ignited the sticks and a rosy glow appeared in the core of the bonfire.

'It's caught!' several excited voices called out – by no means all of them belonging to children. 'It's caught!'

The flames quickly licked their way up the tall stack, and with every foot they climbed, the field became a brighter and brighter place. Halfway up, and each spectator was starting to see beyond his or her immediate neighbours. Three-quarters of the way, and the whole area was covered with a bright red glow.

Michael seemed to be everywhere at once, issuing instructions, shaking hands and slapping people on the back. Becky, for her part, stayed with her two children who, for once, had been allowed to stay up, and were as excited as if this New Year's Eve were Christmas Day and their birthdays all rolled into one.

'When do the fireworks start, Mam?' Billy demanded impatiently. 'When? When?'

'As soon as midnight's rung out,' Becky told him.

'But that's hours away!' Billy protested.

'Oh, is it?' Becky asked. 'In that case, we might as well go home for a cup of tea.'

'We can't!' Billy said. 'It's nearly midnight!'

'Whatever you say, Billy,' Becky laughed, gently ruffling her small son's hair.

Colleen O'Leary appeared from somewhere in the crowd. 'Isn't it a grand do!' she said to Becky. 'Hasn't your Michael done us all proud!'

She seemed cheerful enough, yet Becky thought she could detect a deep sadness beneath the smiling exterior.

'Did you enjoy the dance?' she asked.

'Oh yes,' Colleen said unconvincingly. 'I didn't see your George there, though.'

'He said there was no point since he couldn't dance himself,' Becky told her. 'But he's here now. Look.'

She pointed to her brother who was standing some distance away and gazing into the flames.

'He looks a bit miserable,' Colleen said.

'Well, why don't you go over there and cheer him up then?' Becky suggested.

'Oh, I couldn't!' Colleen said.

'Why not?' Becky asked.

'He hasn't been near the pub since he got back from the war,' Colleen said in a rush. 'I think he must be avoidin' me, Becky.'

'Maybe he is,' Becky agreed. 'But that's no reason for *you* to avoid *him*. After all, it is New Year's Eve.'

Colleen's cheeks had turned a bright red, and though it could have been the heat of the bonfire which had made her blush like that, Becky didn't really think it was.

'Go on!' she urged. 'What harm can it do – a little chat between two people who've known each other all their lives?'

'I think I will just go and have a word,' Colleen replied,

and then, before her resolution failed her, she turned and walked quickly towards where George was standing.

Ted Taylor and Michael Worrell stood watching the blaze in another part of the field.

'That was a fine fish and chip supper you provided us with tonight,' Michael said.

'Aye,' Ted agreed complacently. 'It wasn't bad at all, was it?'

'I've been reading in the paper about the war in Southern Africa,' Michael said.

'Have you, now,' his father-in-law replied guardedly.

'Yes,' Michael said. 'It seems that just before Christmas, the Boers stopped firing live ammunition at the towns under siege, and instead of explosives, they filled their shells with plum puddings.'

Ted scratched his head.

'If I know you,' he said, 'you mean there to be a lesson for me somewhere in the middle of all that.'

'There's a good side to most things,' Michael said. 'All you've got to do is look for it.'

Ted grinned. 'You're a rum bugger, you are, Michael,' he said. 'Still, of me three sons-in-law, at least two of 'em – an' it's Charlie and Sid I'm talkin' about, mind you – have got their feet firmly planted on the ground.'

'They have indeed,' Michael agreed.

'Which leaves only one out of the three that's loopy,' Ted continued. 'Not a bad average, when you think about it. I've no call to complain.'

George was still gazing intently into the blazing bonfire when Colleen reached him.

'What are you thinkin' about?' she asked.

He jumped slightly, but quickly recovered.

'I was thinkin' about all the lads I trained up in the Lancers,' he said, turning towards her. 'Specially the ones that got themselves killed in that bloody mad charge.'

'Are you sorry you ever joined the army now?' Colleen asked.

George shook his head. 'I wouldn't have missed Burma for anythin' in the world,' he said. 'But I am sorry I signed on for a second tour.'

'Because you lost your leg?' Colleen asked, with perhaps a faint tremble in her voice.

'I lost a lot more than just me leg,' George told her.

'How'd you mean?' Colleen asked.

'I lost the chance of ever havin' a wife and kids like any normal feller,' George said.

Colleen looked down at the ground.

'When you were injured . . . ?' she said shyly.

'Yes?'

'It was only your leg you lost, wasn't it?' Colleen continued shakily. 'I mean . . . I don't know how to say this properly . . . you didn't lose anythin' else, did you?'

George laughed, partly at Colleen's embarrassment and partly to cover his own.

'Yes, just the leg,' he said. 'Everythin' else is still in perfect workin' order.'

'Then you could have children if you wanted to,' Colleen told him, her eyes still firmly on her own feet.

'Don't talk daft,' George said brusquely.

'Why not?' Colleen persisted. 'You're still a young man, and you've got a good job in the wood yard.'

'Use your eyes,' George said, getting angry. 'I'm a cripple. How could I ever ask any woman to marry me?'

'There are men who have worse things wrong with them than wooden legs,' Colleen said quietly, thinking of Barnaby Smith. 'Some men are scarred on the inside.'

'That may be,' George agreed. 'But my scars are there for all to see, an' no decent woman would ever consider marryin' me.'

Colleen lifted her head. She looked first at George's wooden leg and then straight into his eyes.

'Don't you think that's rather up to the woman to decide?' she asked.

Mary was looking at the fire and thinking of her absent children. Jack, somewhere in darkest Africa. Philip, married to his *chanteuse*, throwing away his money in what she was sure was a vain attempt to make Marie famous.

'I wish I could have the whole family together just once more in the house they all grew up in,' she said softly to herself.

'Hello!' said a cheerful voice just beside her.

'Spudder!' Mary said.

'I missed the dance in the school, but I have managed to get back in time for the bonfire,' the young man said happily.

Poor Spudder, Mary thought. How could I have been so selfish, so wrapped up in me own worries, that I could allow meself to forget all about you?

Because the problem was, Spudder would have to move, too – out of the only real home *he'd* ever had. And though she thought of him like a son, he wasn't really, and there'd probably be no room for him in the next house they rented.

However was the poor lad going to take the news? Well, he had to be told, and the sooner the better. Mary decided not to put it off a second longer.

'Spudder?' she said.

'I've brought you a present,' Spudder told her.

'That's very kind of you,' Mary replied, 'but there's something we have to talk about.'

Spudder looked totally miserable, as he always did when he'd been disappointed.

'It's a very nice present,' he said dolefully. 'I know you're goin' to like it a lot.'

Mary felt her resolve leaving her. After all, what was the point of breaking the bad news to him that night? Why shouldn't he, like Ted, live in blissful ignorance until the next day?

'I'm sure it's a *very* nice present indeed, Spudder,' she

assured him. 'Where is it?'

'Here,' Spudder replied.

It was only now that Mary noticed the two thick documents he was holding in his hands. Spudder looked down and she could see his lips moving as he read the words to himself. He selected what he had decided was the right one, and handed it over to Mary.

In the flickering light of the bonfire, Mary read the words, *Deeds to 47, Ollershaw Lane, Marston*.

'It's your house now,' Spudder said. 'I bought it for you.'

'But I thought . . .' Mary said. 'I thought . . .'

What had she thought? That she was about to lose her house! That Barnes was going to cheat Spudder out of his money!

She couldn't have been more wrong!

'Aren't you pleased?' Spudder asked her anxiously. 'Don't you like it?'

Mary felt tears pricking her eyes.

'Well, of course I'm pleased, you big daft thing,' she said. 'Of course I like it. It's just you shouldn't have, Spudder. You . . . well, you just shouldn't have, that's all.'

'And look at this,' Spudder said, holding out the other document for her to see.

Mary glanced at it. It was the deeds to Number 49.

'I bought this for meself,' Spudder said.

'So you're goin' to close the boardin' house down, are you?' Mary asked him.

Spudder looked puzzled.

'No, I'm not,' he said. 'Why should I want to do that?'

Good old Spudder, Mary thought. 'That means as far as Number 49 goes, you're my landlord now,' she said aloud, smiling at him.

But Spudder was not smiling back. A worried expression had come to his face as if he had suddenly remembered something unpleasant.

'What's the matter?' Mary asked.

'Goin' down to Stafford to see Mr Barnes was a bit

expensive,' Spudder explained, 'an' I've spent all me wages on trains an' things. So could you wait till next week for the rent?'

'Spudder, you own the house!' Mary said.

'I know,' Spudder said. He looked at her worriedly. 'But I can still be your lodger, can't I?'

'Yes,' Mary agreed. 'But you'll be paying me rent for one room . . .'

'I'll get it to you next week, I promise. I've never been late before.'

'. . . and I'll be paying you rent for the whole of the house. So I'll probably end up payin' you more than you're payin' me.'

Spudder screwed up his eyes as if he was thinking, then seemed to give up the effort.

'Explain it all to me in the mornin', when I'm not so tired,' he said.

Cedric Rathbone had stationed himself close to the bonfire so he could deal with any bits of flaming wood which detached themselves from the main stack, but at the moment there didn't seem to be any danger of that.

Have a fag, lad, he told himself. You've earned it.

He took his cigarettes out of his pocket and lit one up. As he smoked, he looked up and down the field. Everybody was enjoyin' themselves, he thought – there'd be no trouble for him to sort out that night. And he was glad of that, because although he usually enjoyed a good fight, it just didn't seem right to go knockin' people down on New Year's Eve.

He felt a twinge in his right knee. He'd called himself 'lad' earlier, but that was just habit. He was probably still the hardest feller in the area, but he was gettin' old – and soon it would start to show.

His eyes fell on Mrs Worrell, who had one of her kids in her arms and the other holding her free hand. In the light of the fire, her blonde hair seemed to glow and her blue eyes shone like precious stones.

We've been through a lot together, her an' me, Cedric thought. They'd rescued as much of her husband's works as they could, saved her brother Philip from the Manchester underworld and visited a lunatic asylum in the dead of night to see Hortense.

'Aye, we've had some adventures,' he said softly to himself.

She'd always treated him well, had Mrs Worrell, givin' him a job when he was out of work, and never once lordin' it over him like most employers did. An' she probably imagined that she knew him as well as you could know anybody who wasn't family. But she didn't! Because all these years he'd been keeping a secret from her, a secret she'd never even guessed existed. An' what was the secret? That he worshipped an' adored her.

Maggie Cross and Dottie Curzon were handing out baked potatoes when Not-Stopping Bracegirdle sidled up to them.

'I thought you told me you weren't coming,' Dottie said.

'Well, I wasn't,' Not-Stopping admitted. 'But after all, a new century's not somethin' you see very often, is it?'

'About once every hundred years on average,' Dottie said, almost under her breath.

Not-Stopping glanced around her.

'Lot of people here, aren't there?' she said. 'Must have cost Michael Worrell a fortune, and for all his showin' off, I bet he hasn't got much more in the post office than what me an' my Ernie has.' Her eyes roved further. 'And there's Paddy O'Leary. It must be hurtin' his pocket, this do – the amount of trade he must have lost. And by heck – look at that!'

'Look at what?' Dottie asked.

'George Taylor and Colleen O'Leary,' Not-Stopping said.

Dottie did look. George and Colleen were standing very close together and seemed to be having a very earnest conversation.

'There's more to that than meets the eye,' Not-Stopping said. 'He's been keeping away from the New Inn since he got back, but that doesn't mean he's not been seeing *her* on the sly.' Dottie was on the point of saying 'pigeons' when Not-Stopping suddenly smiled and said, 'Still, what's wrong with that when all's said and done? He lost his leg in the service of his country, and she was practically left standing at the altar. Why shouldn't they find a bit of happiness together if they can?'

Dottie's mouth fell open in amazement.

'Are you . . . are you feeling all right, Elsie?' she asked.

'Why shouldn't I be?' Not-Stopping asked.

'I've never heard you so . . . so nice about anybody before,' Dottie spluttered.

'Well, it is New Year's Eve after all,' Not-Stopping said, 'and if you can't be pleasant then, when can you be?' She gave her old friend a stern look. 'You want to try it yourself, sometime,' she told Dottie.

Mary told her daughter about the present that Spudder had just given to her.

'But that's wonderful news, Mam, isn't it?' Becky said.

'Yes, of course it is,' Mary agreed. 'Only . . .'

'Only what?' Becky asked.

'Only, now I don't have to worry about Spudder losin' his inheritance or me losin' the house, I've started worryin' about just who'll get that third piece of bad luck we're still waitin' for.'

Becky laughed.

'Maybe the new century will cancel it out,' she suggested. 'Maybe if we can just get as far as midnight, then God or whoever's behind all this, will let us get away with it for once.'

'You might have a point there,' Mary agreed. 'What time d'you think it is now?'

'About quarter to twelve,' Becky guessed.

'I'll just go an' see if your dad's all right,' Mary said, and hurried away towards her husband.

*

The church bells throughout the area began to chime at midnight, and Michael ordered the fireworks to be set off. It was a magnificent display. The rockets climbed to breathtaking heights before plunging suddenly to earth again. The Roman candles poured out golden rain which suddenly – inexplicably – turned purple. The Catherine wheels spun with such speed that it was enough to turn a body dizzy. The villagers gasped, screamed and applauded. Everyone enjoyed it – with the exception of little Billy who had fallen asleep in his mother's arms.

'Make the best of this,' Michael advised his daughter. 'You'll not see another new century.'

'Why?' Michelle asked. 'Where will I be?'

Michael laughed, kissed his daughter and then put his hand on his wife's shoulder.

'Are you happy?' he asked.

'I'm always happy when I'm with you and the children,' she told him. 'You should know that by now.'

Monsieur Henri appeared, supervising his assistant bakers who were pushing the biggest handcart they had been able to find, and on which sat a huge cake with nineteen hundred blazing candles.

'We all share it,' he said to Becky. 'It look like one big thing, but it is really made up of a lot of little pieces. Brilliant, madame!'

'What was that all about?' Michael asked when they had taken their pieces of cake and the handcart had passed on.

'It was just somethin I told him to keep him happy,' Becky lied, embarrassed to admit that she was growing as fanciful as her husband.

She let her eyes wander from the firework display to the people who were watching it. They were people she had known all her life, people she'd laughed with, cried with, shared the hard times and the good times with. There was Cedric Rathbone, always available when she needed a strong arm and a fearless spirit. There were her mam and dad, who through all their troubles had never taken their worries out on each other – or the kids. And there were Colleen and her brother George, standing so close together that they were almost touching.

She thought of other people, too – people who were not there around the bonfire that night.

Poor Hortense, who was working as a governess now, and saving all she could in the hope that one day she'd get her son back.

Jack, sailing up and down the dangerous Oil Rivers, which had nearly claimed his life at least twice.

Richard, who'd as good as told her that he'd never give up the idea of destroying her husband and winning her back.

Yes, there was always a black side to things, but despite that, Michael was right to be such an optimist. Life could be a struggle, but if you kept going, you usually managed to get through.

'Thank you,' she said to her husband.

'For the firework display?' Michael asked.

'For everything,' Becky told him.

Michael put his arm around Becky's waist and hugged her to him.

'I'm the one who should be thanking you,' he said. 'You've given me more than I could ever hope to pay back.'

The new century was already minutes old and the fireworks were almost over.

In the brilliant light of the very last Catherine wheel, Becky saw her brother George draw Colleen O'Leary to him and kiss her passionately on the lips.